WORST CASE SCENARIO...

Vallon thought she heard a sound above and took the second set of stairs faster. She came up onto the first layer of empty parking stalls. The buzzing was close now, coming from the side of the parking garage closest to the bookstore, but still muffled. The mist diffused the few yellow lights illuminating the expanse of gray concrete, and clung to the darkest corners so she couldn't see what was there.

"Give it up, Simon. The game's old." She was angry now, because dammit, this job wasn't something to play at.

Something moved—low, down next to the concrete wall at the edge of one of the dark spaces. She -reached- and Simon's flame greeted her. He was damned well playing games.

Epithets ready, she headed for him. -reached- not understanding what she saw and, "Oh shit!"

She went to her knees.

"Oh shit, no! Simon! No!"

And the two socked-feet spasmed and jerked, ankles windmilling where they grew out of the concrete wall.

BOOKS BY THE AUTHOR

***The Cartographer Universe* series:**
The Cartographer's Daughter

Afterburn
Aftershock
Aftermath
Afterimage

Terra Incognita
Terra Infirma
Terra Nueva

Mystery by K.L. Abrahamson
Through Dark Water

After Yekaterina
Mareson's Arrow
The Tsarina's Mask
Ivan's Wolf

Romance by Karen L. Abrahamson
Ashes and Light
Shades of Moonlight
Judas Kiss
Second Spring
Surviving Safe Harbor
The Unlocking Saga Books 1-6

AFTERBURN

Karen L. Abrahamson

Dedicated to Barb and Doug.
No matter how many miles separate us on the map.

Acknowledgements:

To Marcelle and Adrian and all the others who have read so many versions of this concept and to the retired USGS staffer who inspired it.

Man is a singular creature. He has a set of gifts which make him unique among the animals; so that, unlike them, he is not a figure in the landscape—he is a shaper of the landscape.
Jacob Bronowski, The Ascent of Man (1973)

Chapter 1-A Laser Diffused By Mist

Vallon Drake climbed out of the black Subaru WRX 265 and slouched against its swept-back side on the rain-slicked street. She chewed her lip as she considered the space at 1525 Broadway where the heritage-blue house used to stand—not the place she had put it. The last of the change tremors still quivered through the soles of her Doc Martins, and mist haloed the streetlights—the kind of mist that made any proper survey reading nigh on impossible.

But then, it wasn't a matter of her having taken a wrong turn and needing to triangulate on an unknown point. She knew the metes and bounds of the Seattle city lot probably better than anyone, given she'd had to replace the damned house a couple of times. She didn't need to refer to the street sign or a map.

Satellite photos said the house was here at 3 p.m. this afternoon. Now it had disappeared, and in its place stood a decrepit, three-story parking garage with a neon sign that pulsed 'vacancy' and 'Parking $10 a day' like a taunt, spelled in vitriolic orange meant to increase her mad. More so with the alarming scent of ozone and ether still thick in the air. All the little hairs rose on the back of her neck.

Not a good sign. She tasted blood and stopped chewing.

"Where the hell are you, Simon?" she growled, her voice too loud and throaty in the night. The silence ached as it must have when the world was new-made.

She'd sent him out to check on the house when she'd had the first inkling something was wrong–again. The darned house seemed to be a focal point for change. A tingle in her hands, a dead zone forming on the city-wide survey map as she used the old fashioned stereoscope she still preferred to do readings.

But the fact he'd broken protocol and hadn't reported in after he'd called in his arrival had forced her out of the strictures of the observation desk and into the damnable rain. Which was worse remained to be seen.

Another tremor underfoot and images of the house burned like an afterimage on the back of her eyes. And behind the blue house image lay others—back to the house she'd lost all those years before.

Old grief and remembrance stabbed her breath away…. That was why she kept the blue house in place. A token of what was lost. Stupid.

She kicked the heel of her Doc Martins with her other foot and crossed the street. No traffic at this time of night, though in the distance she could hear the hiss and whine of traffic on I-5 down the hill. A chill wind sheeted the misty rain and she hiked the collar of her leather jacket up under her hair. Didn't help—much.

No sound. No movement as she stepped up on the curb, but she didn't need to triangulate for every sense to tell her something was wrong. Not even a parking attendant in sight in the evil, orange light.

She -reached- sent her mind out, and turned her gaze inward.

[Dim glimmer of rats creeping into the rear of the newly-made structure.]

No candles of human life.

[The familiar sheeting flame that was Gifted.] Simon, damn him.

She turned her vision outward and found herself turned slightly—toward the side of the parking structure. Simon, checking out the place, probably. The fact that he hadn't checked in or responded to her calls just another example of the irresponsibility that had ended the most recent of her string of relationships.

"How the heck you got to be an agent is beyond me." But then there were those who would say the same about her.

She hauled out her cell again and punched in redial as she followed the flame of Simon's presence around the corner.

The cell buzzed. Buzzed again and a muffled answering ring came from beyond a browning cedar hedge planted to screen a staircase from the used bookstore next door. From down the street came the annoying rattle of an approaching shopping cart, probably the night staff from the local Safeway reclaiming the carts that always walked away with the locals.

What the hell was Simon doing? Rousting derelicts on stairs?

But there shouldn't be any derelicts in a parking lot that shouldn't even exist. The homeless liked the tourist haunts of Pikes Place Market or Pioneer Square.

Unless whoever made this place actually *knew* what he was doing and wanted to add in the bits of realia that gave a new place a sense of history. Like she'd given the blue house cedar hedging last time she remade it.

That sent a chill up her back. She hunched into her jacket and stepped into the ill-lit stairwell. "Simon?"

No answer, but the incessant buzzing of her phone and the matching muffled buzzing that came from somewhere above set all the hairs on her body on end, because no matter what had happened between her and Simon, this wasn't like him.

Not like him at all.

She climbed the stairs, wishing her job as an agent of the American Geological Survey came with a gun instead of a theodolite, sextant, pen, and ink. Sometimes guarding the landscape against illicit change—and undoing those changes—brought its own kinds of danger just because of the part of town it brought you to.

But the area around Broadway wasn't that kind of place. A nice neighborhood stood beyond the stores. Seattle University waited down the block.

The rundown parking garage *so* didn't fit.

The first landing stank of urine, so whoever had made this place had a feel for detail, not like when the bookstore owner had changed the house to another store that held shelf after shelf of a single volume of an idiot's guide to how to run a successful business. That had been the latest change she'd undone.

"Simon?"

She thought she heard a sound above and took the second set of stairs faster. She came up onto the first layer of empty parking stalls. The buzzing was close now, coming from the side of the parking garage closest to the bookstore, but still muffled. The mist diffused the few yellow lights illuminating the expanse of gray concrete, and clung to the darkest corners so she couldn't see what was there.

"Give it up, Simon. The game's old." She was angry now, because dammit, this job wasn't something to play at.

Something moved—low, down next to the concrete wall at the edge of one of the dark spaces. She -reached- and Simon's flame greeted her. He *was* damned well playing games.

Epithets ready, she headed for him. -Reached- not understanding what she saw and, "Oh shit!"

She went to her knees.

"Oh shit, no! Simon! No!"

And the two socked-feet spasmed and jerked, ankles windmilling where they grew out of the concrete wall.

"Oh shit. Oh shit. Oh shit. Oh shit." All the anger washed away. Vallon fumbled in her jacket for the equipment her job required. Black leather case. Mont Blanc fountain pen. A scrap of blank paper no one would remark.

She spread the oily-finished paper—vellum, really—on the concrete and, holding the paper down with both palms, fought to steady her breathing. -Reached-.

Not to Simon this time, but down through the parking lot's smothering concrete. Down through the living soil. Down as deep as she dared go, to the glittering capillaries that spread up from the ley lines that ran through the earth like deep veins.

Carefully now. Gingerly -reached-.

Gold power surged over her skin. Dangerous gold fire merged with her and burned. Her skin singed as she spun a thin tendril of power into her dark core. Light filled her as she snapped back to her body. Holding the heady power inside like potent, destructive cordite.

Focus on the vellum.

Pen and ink. She hung above the blank page.

No time to replace the Broadway house. No time to do this smooth and right. She slammed her awareness into the concrete wall, and to Simon. Still his living flame, but weaker. Much weaker. Sketched lines—the concrete gone in a doorway. Another set of stairs. There. Right there. Held it in her mind.

The acrid scent of anachronistic ink helped her focus. The force of her power turned on the wall. Concrete shimmered.

Shimmered again, like a light bulb surging and dying under too little power. Like a laser diffused by mist. Almost as though something blocked her efforts. The concrete structure shimmied as if someone tried to shake her loose.

"No, damn it."

Simon's bright flame blackened at the edges. She released more power and the wall began to fade, concrete smoking up to join the night mist. This had to work, and work fast.

A flash of power that almost blasted her backwards. Something—some*one*— blocked her, and from the earth came the sound of rumbling.

Surprise almost snapped her link. No one *blocked* change except agents of the AGS. Hell, no one blocked *her.*

She dove deep to the soil and linked more fully to the power than her training ever advised.

Pain stabbed her gut. It raced down her arms like open flame as she poured an invisible golden stream from her hands into the wall. The block shattered like the concrete as her power flooded into the wall.

Concrete softened and flowed. Parted like a sea. Ran down into a deep well that was stairs that went—she didn't care where. Brimstone and ether burned her nose, and then suddenly Simon was there. Released from his prison, he tumbled to the floor, blonde-grey hair caked with concrete, face desperately pale.

The pen fell from her fingers as she released her focus and scrambled to his side. Pulled him to safety as the wall did an old movie fade-in. Pulse? She -reached- for his flame.

None.

She swore and slammed her fists into his chest, praying she could start his heart.

"Jeezus, man." She glanced up to see a kid in a red Safeway vest and she realized she didn't hear the carts anymore. He must have heard her. Come to help. But now he backed away. Backed away and then spun and dove for the stairs.

"Wait!" she called and then couldn't waste time to go after him. "Call the paramedics!"

She bent to help Simon breathe. Come back. Come back. Come back.

A litany of images through her head. Simon in her bed. Simon joking in the staff room. Simon and her grabbing a burger at the Broadway Beef, which he swore was the best place to eat in town.

Chest compressions: one, two, three. Tilt head back to free the airway. Hold nose and breathe for him.

Come on Simon, I'm breathing for you. I'm breathing with you.

But the flame wasn't there. It had to be there. She -reached- stopped the CPR and grabbed the earth power and desperately flooded it into him until his body danced macabre on the cold concrete and the air reeked of brimstone and power.

"What the hell are you doing?"

The voice of authority brought her attention back from her hands, flat on Simon's convulsing chest. Two uniformed Seattle cops stood with their hands on their holstered guns.

"What the hell does it look like I'm doing," she snapped and turned back to Simon to resume CPR. "Trying to save this man's life."

"You a doctor?"

"No, I'm not a doctor." Dammit, the flame still wasn't there. Still wasn't there. Dammit, Simon come back. I know it wasn't good between us, but listen to me on this. Just this once.

"Step away, Miss."

She ignored them. "One. Two. Three." Throwing herself into compressions. Bent to breathe.

Strong hands grabbed her shoulders.

"No, dammit. If I stop, he's dead. He can't die this way. Doesn't deserve to die." She struggled in their grasp. Slammed her heel down on one cop's foot. Twisted and aimed the heel of her hand at the other cop's solar plexus.

The wrong decision. The cop slammed her arm aside, slammed her into the newly-reformed concrete wall and had her hands behind her and cuffed so fast she could barely think.

"Don't move."

The concrete had the uncomfortable feel of newly-healed skin. But when she -reached- for Simon he wasn't there. Gone.

One of them gone and the Gifted were so few, like scattered stars in the sky of humanity.

"You don't understand. I was trying to help."

"Save it, lady."

The other cop checked Simon's pulse and shook his head.

"Dispatch, we're gonna need the meat wagon. Better get someone from homicide down here." He spoke into the mike on his shoulder.

"Homicide!" She tried to turn, but the cop's broad hand slammed her back into the concrete and suddenly the word and the cold, moist air seemed to fill her bones and block her air. No way to triangulate. No wonder they were treating her like this. All the power's heat drained away.

As always, it left her shivering, weak, and, like a junky, in desperate need to be filled. Afterburn.

Her knees gave way.

Chapter 2-A Liquid Silence and Black

Blue Calvin Klein socks on another dead agent.

When Vallon closed her eyes she kept seeing the plaid blue-and-black design that had wrapped Simon's ankles. Even as the blue and red strobes flashed from the street down below. Police. Paramedics. The scent of diesel so heavy in the air she could taste it, though it was better than the ozone stench of change. Or afterburn.

The concrete chill ran up her back as she sat cross-legged next to the metal railing that edged this level of the garage. The wispy rain caught her whenever the wind gusted.

The aches of power use and loss throbbed deep and low down in her body and coupled with the grief. The cuffs' dull pain ran up her arms and the damp air and emotion had her shivering, like a transit in a high wind.

Simon gone and she could do nothing. That broad, teasing smile lost and the feel of his body. All the EMTs in the world couldn't bring him back after the flame was gone. She'd tried to tell them that—not that anyone was listening to her at the moment and that was just, well, typical.

She turned back to the blue-red night, which was better than when she closed her eyes and saw only blue-black plaid. The entire parking lot was surrounded by cop cars, rescue vehicles, and yellow crime scene tape. All for naught.

"So. You feel like being cooperative now?"

The tall detective with the smooth, café au lait skin and the appraising gaze came up beside her. She'd seen him arrive in his long grey trench and the way the uniformed police relinquished control of the scene to him.

"I was cooperative before, if anyone had listened."

Only a tilted brow above espresso eyes in response. He grabbed her arm and half-lifted her to her feet when the cold had almost immobilized her legs. In what must have been a show to gain her confidence, he released her from the cuffs.

The painful surge of blood in her hands made her wince.

"You okay? You found him, right?" Just the right tone to take with a witness or victim. Sympathetic. Friendly. And totally unlikely, given what the uniformed cops had said.

"I'd be a hell of a lot better if I hadn't been manhandled and made to feel like a criminal." She rubbed her raw wrists and glared at him.

"The way I hear it, you threw the first punch." Again, that appraising espresso look had her in its cross hairs and the afterburn throbbed and made the empty place inside her warm again. And seriously interested. A good-looking man, broad shouldered and hard bodied—she closed her eyes to block the thought, because it was entirely inappropriate — and this guy was only looking for a way to pin Simon's death on her. She nodded and fought the trembling in her bones.

"I did. But your guys tore me away from Simon when I was trying to do CPR."

"So you knew the guy?"

"Yeah. I knew him. We worked together."

Another of those long looks and her heart beat faster. She crossed her arms over her chest to contain the unnatural desire to throw herself at him and kiss him right then and there. It was the afterburn talking. Not her. Definitely not her.

A slight smile on his lips and the way his pupils dilated said he knew far too well the attraction she was feeling—which meant, thankfully, nothing more than that he had very good radar for women.

And was probably prepared to use it.

"I'm Detective Jason Bryson. I'd like you to tell me what happened this evening. From the beginning."

She raised a brow at the first name. He was definitely interested. The afterburn flamed a little hotter, a little lower down in her body, and she fought back the need for release.

"I tried to tell those officers." She hauled her wallet from inside her jacket and flipped it open to expose the oval AGS badge with its outline of the continental US and a sextant, and the accompanying officious looking picture ID the AGS's parent agency issued. "I'd like my equipment back, please."

Because she wasn't supposed to have the contraband pen and paper to begin with.

That brought a wall down over his open interest. "Not possible. Evidence stays in our care. Anyone from Homeland Security should know that." He looked more closely. "I didn't realize the American Geological Survey was associated."

"No one does." Just as no one knew of the need to guard the country against change from within. No one beyond the Gifted even noticed a change.

The question in his eyes said he wanted her to explain further, but she'd be damned if she were going to tell him anything, because just about anything she told him was going to be a lie. Instead she fished her phone out. "I need to call in, if you don't mind. They'll have already sent out search parties."

She didn't wait for an answer, simply punched in the numbers that would send the code for assistance and her GPS coordinates. They'd have someone here quickly, she was sure. Until then she could fend off the worst of the questions that still hung in his gaze. She had to say something.

"So I was working the desk tonight. Something—I can't say what—was going down, and so I sent Simon—Agent Lamrey—out to investigate. When he didn't check in as he was supposed to, I came to back him up. I found him as you saw him and was trying to administer CPR when your men arrived and pulled me off."

"That right?"

Doubts placed dark strata in his eyes and she didn't like it, given she'd stuck as close to the truth as possible. But then that was how it always was, wasn't it. Doubts and disbelief when she spoke. But this guy—he almost looked like he wanted to believe. Now she just needed to convince him.

"Damn straight, that's how it went down. There's no reason to hold on to my things. That pen of mine is a keepsake. My father's." As if he'd have purposely left her anything.

Bryson only shook his head. "Not going to happen. Officers Santos and Smythe say you weren't exactly doing any kind of CPR they'd ever seen when they arrived. Care to explain?"

She thought back, and the ache inside began the transition into great hammer-pounding in her head. If they'd seen her try the power surge, what would it have looked like? What would they have thought? Whatever it was, she had to nip this in the bud because Chief Gleason wasn't going to like this death, let alone if the cops pin-pointed on her. Exposing the true nature of the AGS wasn't an option.

"I was doing CPR, like I said. Chest compressions. Artificial respiration. I'm sure you've had *some* training."

"I might have." The dry comeback at her jab only showed his doubt, but his words came out casual-friendly. "So tell me about this unit of yours. What's your area of work?"

"I'm afraid that's classified information, Detective," interrupted a gruff male voice.

Vallon heaved a sigh of relief as AGS Chief Gregor Gleason's gravelly baritone cut through the night. As usual, he'd moved far more silently than a man his size should. He stepped up beside her in an unusual move of solidarity, his cadaverous, six-foot-four frame swathed in an overlarge tan trench coat that almost reached his ankles, his bald head gleaming in the pearlized mist. His presence immediately released some of the pressure she felt from Bryson's regard, and she knew that was Gleason's doing.

"Agent Drake, I'll expect a full report." He nodded down at her over his large roman nose as he produced his badge, and Detective Bryson flashed his own in a clear case of 'mine's bigger than yours'. It looked like Gleason won, but barely. He looked around.

"That my agent?" He nodded at the bagged body as the Coroner's people lifted Simon onto their stretcher.

"I'm afraid so, Sir. I tried…." She left it there, another image of blue-black plaid making her shiver; and suddenly all the emotions and the power loss conspired against her. Tears filled her eyes and she hated the weakness. Hated more that she'd actually grown attached enough to Simon to feel such grief. Simon was only supposed to be convenient, like all the rest. She was getting weak at the ripe old age of 26. "I was too late, Sir. I'm sorry."

Gleason thankfully ignored her weakness. He turned back to the detective, easing himself between Bryson and Vallon.

"I'll expect to be kept abreast of the police investigation, Detective Bryson. As for Agent Drake, I'll forward her statement to you."

"Unacceptable. I need Ms. Drake to come into the office to give her statement."

"And I said I'd forward her statement to you. Agent Drake works in a classified area and I won't have her exposing government secrets."

"And I'd say the secret's already out, Agent Gleason. You've got a dead agent in a parking garage. Don't you want to know what happened to him?"

The two of them stood toe to toe, their breath hot clouds in the chill air. Bryson had to tilt his chin up to meet Gleason's gaze, but both men were clearly accustomed to giving orders and clearly not used to having them set aside.

"Sir, I can give a statement—it just won't be very helpful to the detective. I already told him pretty much everything. I came to back up Lamrey and found him like this. The police arrived as I was trying to revive him."

Gleason's gaze slipped from her face to the ill-made wall beyond the body that showed all the signs of recent, inept change—but what more had she had time for? His face darkened a little with disapproval that twisted her gut, and then he met her gaze. Nodded and turned to Detective Bryson.

"I'm sure you understand that we cannot afford to discuss our work in any detail. If you wish Agent Drake to provide a written statement of what she's told you, then yes, she would be happy to attend your office; but for now I think I must get Agent Drake back to our office while the events of the evening are still fresh."

He caught Vallon's elbow, something she'd normally resist because, in her condition, the close physical contact flared the afterburn like a bolt of need that made her knees go weak, but tonight she knew she didn't dare resist.

"If there is nothing else, detective?" He didn't wait for Bryson's response and started Vallon towards the exit stairs like a gardener with a wheelbarrow.

"A moment, Agent Gleason." Vallon and her boss turned back to Bryson. His café au lait features had gone dark and the muscles along his jaw were bunched tight with anger. "How do I get in touch with you—to keep you informed, of course."

"Aah." Gleason gave his best vulture smile. "Of course."

He fished in his breast pocket and hauled out a crisp white card that Vallon knew held only the Homeland Security seal and an untraceable number that would come through to Gleason's EA. The fact Gleason didn't even ask for the detective's card was the last, decisive blow in the battle of the men's wills.

"I look forward to your report, Detective." Then his fingers dug into her arm and he hurried her down the parking lot to the stairs.

"What the hell are you doing out here, Drake?" His grip only tightened as he dragged her down the last flight of stairs and onto the street. "You were on desk duty for a reason. I had everyone out looking for you."

Vallon shivered at the 'everyone', not liking the thought that he'd have turned Homeland Security loose on her. She pulled loose to face him, keeping her voice as low as his. "I haven't gone rogue. But when Simon didn't check in, I thought he was just playing silly bugger. I didn't want to call out another agent on what could have been a wild goose chase."

"So you disobeyed a direct order that pulls you off field work, and endangered everyone by leaving no one on the desk. I know you don't like inside duty, Drake. No one does, but you've damn well got to learn discipline or I'll have your ass out of the AGS. Hear?"

Vallon tried to face him down, would have faced him down as she had before, because pulling her off field work was just idiotic, but a movement at the parking garage stairs caught her eye. Detective Bryson stepped past the cedar hedging at the bottom of the stairs. She pointedly looked away.

"I said I was sorry. What more do you want?"

Gleason followed her meaning. "Your report. On my desk. Within the hour. Now get back to the office."

He left her then, marching in his lurching skeleton gait to the police line and folding under the tape to his black Grand Marquis. She watched his car pull away before heading for her Subaru, and was too aware of Bryson's gaze on her back and the way her body seemed to sway to lure him on. Dammit, this was the worst case of afterburn she'd had in years. She had to do something to deal with it soon, because this lustiness was just going to cause trouble.

She -reached- into the earth to steady herself in the huge pulsing presence that was the power vortex near Mount Rainier, but flame flashed nearby.

Gifted, by the intensity of light, but not someone she recognized, and after a year in Seattle she pretty much knew the scent and feel of all of the trained Gifted. This presence pulsed so bright, bold and glittering with heat, it was clear whoever it was had to be trained—and powerful.

Definitely powerful enough to turn a house into a parking garage—and to block her rescue attempt.

She yanked back from the earth and found herself facing the shadowed pavement down Denny Street. Outside of the pillars of streetlight, everything was a darkness of trees and lawns and night-bound houses and the liquid silence of Lincoln Reservoir, but the flame was there, like a pulse. Was that a shadowed figure?

She hesitated.

Follow her instincts and see who it was? Or follow orders and head back to the office?

She knew what Gleason would say, but there really wasn't any choice at all. Simon was dead and there was a good chance the darkness had caused it.

She had to know why.

Chapter 3-A First Line of Defense

Detective Jason Bryson admired the sway of the Drake woman's hips as she crossed the street in lithe strides. The sway was for him, he was certain. He'd seen the wolfish look in her dilated eyes and felt the power of her personality as she sparred with him. The dilated eyes weren't from drugs, he was sure of it. As if it would make any difference.

"I'm sure you know CPR, indeed," he murmured, but her taunt made him smile.

"What's that?" Clint Blacklock, his partner who'd been interviewing the Safeway kid, came up beside Jason. Clint was a big man, ham-fisted and rough-voiced. He was a straight-up, by-the-book, high-school football player gone a little too fat and a lot to beer, but he was a good father to his six kids, a good husband to his wife, and as honest a cop as Jason could ever hope to meet.

Jason lifted his chin toward the woman and Clint followed his gaze. "Just something she said. Got a bit of an attitude, that one."

"Not too hard on the eyes—at least from here."

"You should see the front view. And close up."

"That's our suspect you're talking about, I s'pose?" Clint's appraisal was clear.

"Sure. Though her boss says it can't be so. Apparently she works for some secret arm of the American Geological Survey. Part of Homeland Security. You ever hear of something like that? Says she came out to check on an agent and found him." He glanced over his shoulder at where the body had been. There was something seriously 'off' with the scene: no blood, but the body had had a strange, almost deflated look under an odd layer of white dust.

Clint shrugged and looked back at the car. "Not exactly what the kid said. Said she looked wild and was punching the guy."

"Could have been CPR."

"Could've, I s'pose."

"I'm thinking not." Jason watched the woman get to her car, pause. The misty rain made her form shimmer and fade as the light caught her. Her brown gaze had been huge and terribly alone when he'd helped her up. He shivered.

Perfect. She'd been a damsel in distress, before the wolfish look returned. Well he wasn't the rescuing kind. He wasn't a red riding hood either.

"The patrol officers said they found her doing something to the body. Shaking it, one of them said. Or beating it. Vic's body was dancing all over the concrete. Not any kind of CPR I've heard of."

Jason's hand went to the evidence bag in his pocket. It was odd stuff to find at a murder scene. He'd seen her bite back an argument about him not returning it.

It was odder still when the woman didn't climb in her car. Instead she turned and stared down the street into the darkness, glanced back to where her A-with-a-capital-A-hole boss had been parked and then started walking down the street.

Not even a glance in his direction.

"Now that's interesting. Her boss told her to get back to the office and he doesn't look like the kind that takes kindly to disobedience."

"Guess that tells you somethin' 'bout her, don't it."

"Given her boss, you almost got to like her for it." Jason grinned at his partner. "Think I'll see what's got her interested."

He hiked his trench coat collar against the rain and started down the sidewalk behind Vallon Drake. This time she didn't walk as if she were aware of him. This time she strode out in a long, loose-limbed stride straight down the middle of the street that made him think of solitary predators. A leopard, maybe.

Which suggested that the distressed way she acted in the parking garage was just that—an act. Well, Ms. Vallon Drake, let's see what you really are.

He kept well back in the shadows, letting the rain and front yard foliage obscure him. The air stank of wet cedar and sodden earth. Just past the parking garage that had been built in the late 80s to accommodate the many people who came to shop the Broadway strip, the area's shops disappeared and well-kept, heritage houses lined the street. They were all darkened now, so it was only the street lights he needed to avoid.

Just as Vallon Drake was doing.

She eased past the translucent misty columns and stepped ever deeper into the darkness that verged onto the fenced reservoir, but her focus seemed as if she could actually see through the darkness, and some particular thing drew her.

At 11th Avenue she turned south, her form-fitting jeans and black leather jacket fading into the darkness so that he almost lost her, because there were no streetlights. But then would come a shift of the rain, a glimpse of a white hand smoothing rain-darkened hair off of a white cheekbone, and her form grew out of the night.

She'd slowed. Again, like a cat, she trod carefully, pausing as if she were stalking, and what the hell was going on, because suddenly there was a greater stir of the darkness, something dark separated itself from a stand of tree.

She froze. "What the hell's going on? Why are you watching me?"

Her voice rang out crystal clear and over-loud and then a sound like thunder ripped through the street. No flash. No light. But the thunder so close, so loud and powerful he collapsed, clutching his ears. The earth moved, trees swayed, and then everything went still.

He picked himself up, swearing at the mud on his trench coat and trousers. Earthquake? Not like any he'd experienced in the Pacific Northwest before. The air stank of ozone and ether, and there were none of the car and business alarms that were usually set off by an earthquake. And where was Vallon Drake?

There. On the other side of the street, she moved swiftly past the reservoir back the way she'd come, looking back over her shoulder as if someone—something—were on her tail.

He crossed to the place she'd been, half-expecting to find earth torn or charred, but there was nothing. Just trees and the scent of cedar and rain and the salt of Elliot Bay. Clouds overhead held the lights of the city like an old friend guarding something precious.

Not like Vallon Drake. The sight of her sent a shiver down his back.

She walked alone.

§

She was so cold even the afterburn couldn't warm her. Fear could do that.

Vallon keyed her car open before she got there, fighting the need to run. She slammed herself in and locked all the doors. Only then, did she allow herself to breathe. She inhaled the scent of new leather, tried to feel safe. But that was an illusion, wasn't it?

Whoever—whatever—she had followed down that street could probably blast right up through her floorboards if what she suspected were true.

If she hadn't just lost her mind.

Because nobody—nobody—could do what she thought she'd just seen. The figure she'd seen as flame down the street had led her—no, make that lured her—away from the well-lit streets into the darkness that verged the reservoir.

So just *what* had she seen? A flash of dark leather coat over a single, square-shouldered figure. Man then.

Okay. That slowed her pounding heart a little. It was a man. A person.

Just a person with more power than she'd ever seen, felt, or heard of, and something about it brought up an old terror she didn't want to feel again.

Even her instructors at the Acadamy hadn't been able to do what she thought this guy had done. Disappear.

Or else she was losing her mind.

It was as if suddenly, when she'd been about to catch up to him and confront him with his actions, he'd blown apart into a dark vortex that contracted into a single black point that had hung in the air for a moment. It had been suspended long enough to turn golden, and then was sucked into the earth.

The force of energy had almost blown her over, but she'd stood firm. Sometimes feeling the backlash of power could tell you about the user.

But this hadn't told her anything except that there was more cedar and incense-scented power here than she'd ever felt before. Power enough to easily transform a house into a parking garage—or one house into another. Power enough to wipe Vallon Drake—or anyone else—off the face of the earth in an instant.

The fact he hadn't bothered just said she wasn't even worth the effort.

She fumbled the keys into the ignition, turned on the engine, and the smooth, powerful purr helped her settle. Dropping the clutch into gear, she pulled away from the curb and glanced at the cops still working the scene and—what the hell—did a 'U'y to head down Denny to the highway.

The car's rumbling engine, as usual, helped steady her and helped her think, but it was still hard to head for the office instead of just giving into the self-preservation instinct and heading north-south-anywhere on the compass on I-5 and away from what had just happened. She took I-520 across the muffling waters of Lake Washington and took the first Redmond exit, tooling through the tall trees up onto the AGS Campus.

Her car slid into the parking space reserved for the night watchman—as she'd come to call the desk job—behind the low brick bunker that held the AGS and the small apartment complex where the Chief lived. When she stepped out of the car into pine-scented air, the only sounds were the ticking of the Subaru's engine, the light patter of rain, and the soughing of the wind in tall cedar. But the silence belied the shadows on the sound-proof windows. Just about all the building's offices showed occupied, a fact that indicated just how serious the situation was.

Someone had taken out an agent. Again.

She carded her way through the locked door and into the recycled, purified air. It was one of Gregor Gleason's bugaboos—had to be clean air for pure creative thought, he said.

Privately Vallon thought Gleason's need for cleanliness went a tad too far, including the shaved pate he sported because it was easier than trying to make sure nothing got caught in his hair. That was Gleason—smooth and squeaky clean.

The entryway to the bunker was functional, with a reception desk for the daylight hours. A 'T' intersection joined the entry with a long hallway that bisected the long, narrow building from end to end. At the far end, away from the prying eyes of the public, waited the operatives' main, open-concept office, overseen by Gregor Gleason's executive assistant. Gleason's office itself had a panel of one-way glass that allowed him to keep an eye on his 'minions'. Vallon turned towards it, but stopped. Then she spun on her heel and headed the other direction.

If she were going to write her report she needed quiet and not Gregor Gleason breathing down her neck.

The AGS research library was a better place to compose her thoughts. Always had been. She knocked once on the door, didn't wait for an answer, and entered into the nether world of Landon Snow.

As usual the light was dim, a single reading lamp buried in the rear of the large space barely providing enough light to illuminate a path through the maze of glass-fronted bookshelves and tables covered with arcane implements. How and why Landon came to be part of the AGS was something lost from before Vallon's time. He'd been here when Vallon was a child and, given his ageless appearance, she had little doubt he'd be here after she was gone, even though he wasn't an Agent—or at least not Gifted like Vallon or the others.

The air carried the musty scent of old paper and plant matter and the acrid scents of formaldehyde and ether and alcohol. Each table carried the detritus of partially completed experiments—beakers slowly evaporating to salts, others awaiting the liquid condensing in long coils of glass tubing. Vegetation mashed and boiling over small gas flames. Small glass bottles of almost preternaturally clear water—precious, virgin dew. All *not* part of the research library, but the product of Landon's personal passion for Alchemy. The fact the AGS put up with it in order to keep Landon 'in the fold' only increased the man's mystery.

On the walls, in the dim light, glowed what Landon had named the ancient symbols of Thoth, Azoth, Ouroboros, and hermaphrodite.

The latter was particularly appropriate given London Snow himself.

He looked up from reading one of his antique tomes, his albino hair almost shocking in the darkness, his odd, sharp features captured in a startling frieze of black and white shadows that only made his pink eyes that much more surreal.

But not to her. Though what he did for the AGS wasn't clear, she was glad he was here. Had been since the horrible day when her father died. Then Landon had been the one to comfort a distraught twelve-year-old. Now Landon Snow was the closest thing she had to a father—closer even, because her father had never had time for a troublesome daughter. Landon didn't have a lot of time either, but he was as close as she'd allow anyone to get.

"Well, hello, Pigeon." He set the book down. "I've been wondering when you'd show up. Gleason's on the warpath and you're enemy numero uno. Seems you were supposed to be here—oh," he checked the wide face of his analog wrist watch, "I'd say about ten minutes ago, and you know him. Stickler for details."

"He's on the warpath because I left, so he'll just have to wait, won't he?" She shook her head. "He'll get his report soon enough, but him standing over me isn't going to make it come any faster. I was hoping I could hang here 'til I get it done." She cocked her head in question, could see Landon consider, his fine lips almost translucent over his neat row of small teeth.

"So you really have something to do with Lamrey's death?" Genuine interest and that was what she loved about Landon. Good or bad, he was actually interested in *her*.

She settled herself across the table from him and clicked on another reading lamp. Raised a brow at him. "What do you think?"

"Well, I'd say 'no' if it was anyone but you, darling Pigeon, but you've been surprising me since you were this high."

He held his hand as high as the tabletop, and Vallon grinned.

"That long, huh?"

"That long, and through how many desperate calls from the headmaster at the Academy?"

That broadened her grin. "Too many. But to answer your question, I didn't kill him. Might have thought about it a few times, though."

"La la la la la." Landon pressed his graceful hands against his ears. "Too much information, dear heart. What would I do if someone asked me to give evidence against you?"

"Like you would. You know how good I am at my job." She shook her head, because she *was* good—even if Gleason rode her ass all the time. "Nope. Didn't kill him. Weirdest night I ever had, though. And that's going some."

"But you might have killed him, given how well your relationship was going?"

"And I think you're taking just a little too much pleasure out of all this." She held up her hand. "I know. You warned me about Simon. Too old for me, too much a ladies' man, and too set in old-fashioned ways."

"Well, you will do things your way."

He met her gaze and all the fun suddenly went out of his eyes so they were almost the deep red she remembered from the day her father died. Well, disappeared would be a better way to put it.

Landon had picked her up from the Academy on Friday, as usual, because her father never had time to do it himself. Bright sunny day, new leaves unfurling on the poplar and oak, and daffodils and tulips blooming in all the yards. She'd planted some at her house, too, in hopes her father would approve, and she was hoping they'd be there this weekend when Landon brought her home. Except home wasn't there when they arrived.

Nice middle-America neighborhood was the same, but her house—that had been another matter. Landon had pulled up without a second look and Vallon had jumped out, then turned to the house on the corner. Heritage-blue, two-story stood there. She stopped. Looked around the neighborhood. There was Mrs. Krieger's place to the right. Behind it, the overgrown lot that would become a bookstore.

She bolted then, for the front door screaming for her Dad, who was supposed to be working at home that day.

Landon had caught her as she pounded up the hollow-sounding front porch stairs and had dragged her back to the van fighting a screaming, kicking girl until he could get her some place safe. That had ended up being back at the AGS Academy of Geological Science dormitory.

She nodded. "Like that," she said softly, thinking of Landon's eyes. Around her the room hissed and gurgled and the old, cold fear struck her core again and caused a sick reaction with the afterburn. "I hadn't thought of it in years."

Just had nightmares about it that woke her sweating into the night. It was why she volunteered to put the blue house back every time the darned bookstore owner changed it into a store annex. Confront your fears.

"But it was just like that the first time, Landon. The blue house gone. A parking garage, of all things, in its place." Shook her head trying to focus on the case, not ancient history. "Why the hell a parking garage?"

Landon looked back at his book. "Because it's probably one of the most mundane places in the universe, and nothing stays the same inside. It's only a shell." He sighed. "This research is going to be even more important for Gleason, and I better get at it. You better get your report done and make it a good one. I've a feeling it's going to get a lot o' reading."

Vallon knew dismissal when she heard it. Landon was good at it, just like her father had been, and she bit back a smart answer. There were times she felt as if she were only an experiment to Landon. She reached for her black leather case with its pens and selection of paper, and swore.

"You got a pen and paper I can use? Mine's evidence."

An arch of Landon's faint brows and he nodded at the computer humming quietly in the corner. She swung her chair around and brought up a blank page, then stopped.

"Landon?"

"Hmm?" Just like her father, barely attending.

"This couldn't have anything to do with Dad's death could it? I mean, it's the same piece of ground and a house disappeared in both cases. It's got to be more than coincidence, doesn't it? Houses don't just disappear—not often anyway."

"I seriously doubt it, Pigeon. Now get to your report, would you? I've got work to do."

Dismissed and hating it, Vallon closed her eyes and tried to focus through the drumbeat of the afterburn on what needed to be done. The trouble was, telling the whole truth could be even more career-limiting than the simple matter of abandoning her post. Unsanctioned change—using unsanctioned equipment. Heck, revealing what had made her late in returning to the office would be about the stupidest thing she could think of until she had evidence that what she thought she saw was real.

Relegated to her fate, she sketched out the facts of her decision to go after Simon, knowing Gleason wasn't going to be pleased. Simon and she had started their relationship after they'd been on a job together, and dealing with the afterburn of the work had led to a typical agent's tryst in a hotel next to Boeing field. Unfortunately, that tryst had led to other meetings as well—totally against the rules. Although the AGS didn't mind agents dealing with the afterburn together—heck, it was expected, even though the AGS had a nice little arrangement with a local brothel—but for some reason longer-term relationships had to be approved.

When the inevitable breakup came, Simon had been less than adult about the whole thing. He'd refused to take direction from her when she was on the desk—to the point she had been going to confront him.

And that worked so well.

She blew her bangs up over her forehead and considered what she'd written, then hit the print button.

"Bad?" Landon. She'd almost forgotten he was there.

"Bad enough. I figure Gleason could use this to keep me on desk for—oh—the next ten years." She told him what had happened.

"Ten years at least. Well, at least it means we can have coffee together."

"And here I never thought you were a cup half-full kinda guy." She pushed her chair back and tapped together the pages of her report. "Thanks for the hospitality. I figure it's more than I'm going to get inside."

"Don't sweat it, pet. You just need to look deeper: Gleason likes you."

"Like hell."

A small smile from Landon and she wandered back out of the labyrinth of tables to the door and into the hallway's synthetic air. At the door to the offices she sucked up her trepidations and stepped inside the hall she had dubbed the war room.

It was large, filling one entire end of the low-slung building, and the two-level space stank of stale coffee and overworked air filters. The outside edges, the upper level, were crammed with desks pushed back to back, the chairs filled with men and women who should have been out in the city. Now they worked at computer screens showing close-ups of sectors of Seattle topography.

The center of the room held a large pit that contained a map unique in the U.S. A massive, moveable topographic map of the country. Right now it was focused on the Pacific Northwest up to—and rumor had it, beyond—the Canadian border. Suspended over it like a dragonfly head hung a single mechanized chair on a long metal stanchion—the dragonfly body—that connected the chair to the upper level. The chair, or desk, could be shifted to swoop in to closely study features of the map. Right now the map chair was empty—graphic reminder that Vallon had abandoned her post.

And Simon had died.

All the activity in the room ceased at her entrance. The hum of voices went silent.

Then Janet Hunt came pushing out of the gathering of agents. Short and stout, and wearing a flowered dress that gave her a housewife image, Janet had been the one to provide a milk-and-cookies greeting when Vallon first joined the team six years ago.

"My god, Vallon. Are you all right? It must have been horrible." Breathless little voice. Concern on her face that Vallon just might believe was sincere. Janet had always been nice before. Approachable, even, though Vallon had never taken Janet up on her offers of friendship or guidance.

She went to place an arm around Vallon's waist, then stopped herself. "Ouch, girl. You've got afterburn like crazy."

Vallon nodded and tossed her damp, blonde hair over her shoulders. Just being near another Gifted was almost painful.

"Thanks for the concern. I appreciate it." She bit her lip and Janet jerked back——possibly from the ugly pain Vallon felt.

"Well, well, well, nice of you to join us, Drake."

She turned, found herself facing the narrow column of Gleason's chest so close she could smell his faint spiced aftershave and had to step back to see his face. A good thing. The scent sent the afterburn thundering into high gear.

It must have shown, for Gleason grabbed her arm and started to drag her across the room.

"Moore!" His shout for his E.A. cut through whatever conversation had resumed. "We need some inhibitor, pronto." With that he slammed into his office and shoved her into a chair, then scrubbed his hands on the draped, grey flannel trousers that proved he had no ass.

Vallon struggled to her feet and tossed the papers she held onto his desk. "Your report, Sir. I just needed a quiet place to write."

"Landon," he swore. "I told him to let me know if you dragged your sorry ass home."

"If?"

Gleason shook his bullet-shaped head and ran long fingers through non-existent hair. "How the hell do I know what you're going to do anymore, Drake? You're a fuck-up. The worst I've ever had to deal with, and I'm about to give up hope we can make an agent out of you."

She drew herself up. "Sir, I came back as you ordered."

"And didn't report in." Another shake of head. "I need to be kept apprised, Drake. That's what a good agent is supposed to do."

Vallon's jaw clenched. She was a good agent. She'd done as ordered—unlike Simon. She'd topped her class in the Academy. She just wasn't going to do the little dances everyone expected her to. "There's nothing anyone else could have done to save Agent Lamrey, Sir."

Gleason threw his leg over the corner of his desk and sat down as he considered. His pale grey eyes lanced into her as she returned to her chair, and she knew Landon was wrong. Gleason despised her and always had.

"Does that include *not* getting involved with him in the first place?"

Not what she expected. A little shiver ran through her. "You knew?"

A knock came at the door and Moore, a slim woman with sleek black hair coiled on her head and tilted Eurasian eyes, bustled efficiently inside. She carried what looked like a typical eight-ounce bottle of water, but this was anything but. Gleason nodded at Vallon, his lips a tight line.

Vallon accepted it, both resentful and thankful, and sipped as Moore backed out of the room in the silent way that seemed to make Gleason so happy.

She sipped again, thankful for the cool liquid against the heat burning inside her.

"All of it. Now."

"What? You want me to choke?" What he really wanted was for her to be off her game, unguarded as the inhibitor made her.

His scowl said he just might, but Vallon tipped the bottle back and let the cool, minted liquid pour down her throat. Almost immediately the heat that raged diminished. Ice laced through her veins like frost on a window, dampening the afterburn into a dull, duller, dullest glow, but taking with it her Gift as well.

Everything became muffled, and the chill set her shivering—something she fought against. Then the cold transformed to a warm glow that unclenched all the muscles she'd used to hold back the lust brought on by the use of her talent.

She fought against the drowsiness that made her want to close her eyes.

When she looked back at Gleason his face had gone kind, reasonable. Son of a bitch expected her to fall for that in her weakened state. She forced her face still, because she wasn't going to fall for any of his 'I'm your pal' speeches. She'd had enough of those for a lifetime already. Case in point being Simon Lamrey, who'd gotten her into this mess.

"I know everything about my agents, Drake. Everything, and don't you forget it."

Her gaze locked on his and she registered his surprise that she could maintain the focus. "But if you knew…?"

"Why didn't I break it up? There are reasons. Simon and you—there was something there. But the reasons don't concern you—now."

He plucked her report off his desk and anger followed her incredulity, burning at the injustice of it. Here she'd tried to keep things low key to stop Gleason from worrying when all along he'd known. Hell, he'd practically set her up for tonight.

"What if something had happened tonight, Drake? You weren't at your post."

"Something did happen. I responded." She set her jaw.

"You were supposed to be in the chair, monitoring and directing from a distance. In that chair you're the first line of defense against illicit change. What if this had all been a ruse to distract you from some terrorist attack? Or if the Canadians proved to be cannier than our intelligence suggests and shifted the border? You weren't here to warn and respond, were you?"

His voice was quiet, but that was when he was at his most dangerous. The warm drowsiness totally disappeared and she saw Gleason's gaze flicker as she fought off the effects.

"Something happened, didn't it?"

Gleason's face was carved of stone. "Whether something happened doesn't concern you, Drake. It's bad enough you leave your post—I should have your badge for that alone. But then you perform an unsanctioned change with unsanctioned equipment and leave a mess at the scene. What were you planning to do? You know there are people out there with enough gift to notice changes, and yet you purposely perform one without going through the proper procedures."

His voice had increased in volume. He'd leaned forward until he was shouting her back in her chair. Finally the injustice of it made her fight back.

"Enough!" She stood up, leaning on his desk for balance. Stared him down. "I'm sorry I left my post. As I say in my report, when I detected the house's change I immediately called for the nearest agent—as the protocols demand. That was Lamrey. I instructed him to check in within ten minutes of arrival. He didn't. He'd been playing silly bugger with me all shift. So I went after him myself rather than bring in another agent. My mistake. Okay? I'll eat that one. Now why are you focused on me when you should be focused on investigating Simon's death?"

Her chest was heaving. Gleason stared up at her more amazed than he should be, because they'd argued before. Maybe it was that she could do it even when inhibited, because frankly that surprised her, too. But she was *not* going to let him deride her for her decisions. Too many people had done that in her life.

"When I found him, he was in the wall. I had two choices: leave him to die or try to help the poor bastard. So I used *my* instruments. Last time I checked, a pen and ink aren't illegal. And as for the change, hell, there was an entire parking garage to notice—what was my small change going to do?"

Exhaustion made her legs wet noodles under her and she slumped back into her chair clinging to her anger at the injustice. "I would have saved Simon, too—if something hadn't blocked me. If he'd lived, you'd have thanked me."

She rubbed her eyes. The damnable inhibitor headache had started, doubling the pounding already there.

Gleason remained seated like some great Sphinx, but his jaw worked over his anger. Finally he swallowed and his gaze flicked down to her report. Scanned it and came to the end. Brows arched above his hard eyes.

"What's this about another Gifted being nearby?"

What should she say? All she wanted was this over with because Gleason really didn't have much choice but to sanction her in some way. It was just a matter of how. Telling him what she thought she saw would just prolong the interrogation and make her even more suspect in his by-the-book eyes. It had always been like that—even with her Dad.

"It was after you left, Sir. I was headed for my car and you'd already pulled away when I became aware of someone else standing eastward on Denny. I decided to pursue it to see if perhaps it was the perpetrator or a witness. Unfortunately the individual eluded me."

"Eluded you."

Now came the hard part, because she might be trouble in Gleason's eyes, but she sure as hell wasn't crazy.

"Yes, sir. It was dark and rainy and the rain distorted things and made it more difficult to follow. I think perhaps he circled around the reservoir. You know how hard it is to spot one of the Gifted across bodies of water."

She held her breath, feeling the beat of Gleason's regard, and suspected he knew she wasn't giving him the whole truth. When he looked back at her report she dared to breathe again.

"Not a very good job with the wall, Drake."

"The wall?" For a moment she didn't follow the leap in the conversation—the darn inhibitor made it more difficult to track. Then: "As I said, Sir, I had no time to do anything pretty. It was all about trying to get Simon—Agent Lamrey—free in time. Unfortunately, whoever made the garage wasn't about to let it go without a fight. It took a stage-two attack to change the wall and when I had Agent Lamrey free I simply let my control go and got him out."

Gleason's regard had gone deathly cold. "You expect me to believe that this was a conscious change? That whoever did this had the strength to challenge one of my most Gifted agents?"

Vallon held firm before his disbelief, but didn't fail to notice his description. One of his most Gifted. That had to be the only reason he kept her around.

"Sir, that's exactly what I think happened. Now I realize I screwed up leaving the desk, but I've investigated these things before— the accidental changes."

"Drake, don't go off on some tangent just because your lover died."

"Sir, this has nothing to do with Simon—or too much to do with him, as the case may be. Heck, Simon was a fully trained Gifted. A dreamer shouldn't be able to take him out."

"Where do you come up with these ideas?"

She had to stifle her anger even through the inhibitor. And her confusion. Why wasn't he willing to even discuss the possibility someone had purposely taken out Simon? "I know I had a reputation as a wild card at my first posting, but I've investigated enough of the usual cases."

"Reputation? Drake, when I open the manual about problem employees it's your face in print. You don't follow orders. You don't keep your bosses informed, and you are constantly pushing the envelope beyond what's considered safe use of the Gift."

"Sir," she continued. So much for Landon's assessment of Gleason's regard. "I've seen the usual cases. A wish for a bigger house that comes true. A Gifted works at a company and suddenly the company parking lot accommodates a personalized parking spot. All of it's accidental and it's easy to undo because the maker hasn't set it down anywhere and it hasn't been around long enough for everyone else's awareness to make it permanent. But this parking garage wasn't like that."

"Don't be an idiot. No one—I repeat, no one—outside of the AGS knows how to create the changes you've outlined in this report."

Vallon squeezed her eyes shut and then had to jerk herself back from the swift verge of sleep. All the adrenaline had seeped away along with the sex drive. Now she just felt exhausted and hollow. How the heck was she going to get him to understand?

"Sir. You just hypothesized that external forces could have attacked. Maybe they did this."

"Hogwash. Pure speculation and you know it. If it was an external attack, we'd know."

In passing she wondered how, but didn't have the energy to go there.

"Sir, would you please listen? You saw the detail on that place. Did you notice the date on the cornerstone? Nineteen seventy nine—and the garage looked like it could have been that old. And then there was the stink of urine in the stair. Those are details way beyond an accidental or a dream-change. Just like Simon's death. As Gifted as he was, he should have been able to protect himself…and then there's how I had to fight to free him."

She swallowed, because the too-familiar tick of Gleason's left brow—sign of being close to a blow—was vibrating like a kite in a Puget Sound wind. It didn't make sense that he denied her observations.

"Sir, on the way over here I was thinking. We've lost two agents in the past month. Lamrey makes three. Is there any chance the deaths could be connected?"

At that Gleason stood. He circled his desk and sank into the custom built over-stuffed chair that was the only thing that could have comfortably seated his fleshless frame. His gaze, when he finally looked at her was so soullessly calculating that she shivered.

"Agent Drake, you are treading on thin ice here. I know the use of your gift has probably impaired your judgment, so I'm going to cut you some slack. I suggest you go home and sleep it off and tomorrow we'll finish our discussion and decide what to do with you. In the meantime you will not discuss this with anyone. You hear?"

Vallon fought the urge to just tell him what he could do with his job then and there, and wondered for a moment just what was in the inhibitor. But even if she did, Gleason wasn't going to let her off the hook. She knew too much and had too much Gift. They weren't going to just let her walk away.

She shivered, wondering what that would entail, even as she knew she couldn't leave.

Gleason might not admit it, but Agents were dying; and from what she'd seen, someone was hunting them one by one. She shivered again.

And only she knew just what kind of enemy they faced.

Chapter 4-Black and Slick and Glistening

Even with her wipers on, the misty rain made it hard to see. Her headlights seemed to glare blindingly off the rain sheets and any oncoming traffic forced her to slow to a crawl on the drive from the campus to Fremont, the quirky neighborhood across the bridge from Seattle proper. Gleason had kept her under the microscope for so long that all she wanted was to curl up and leave the world for, preferably, a very long time. She hadn't even bothered to let Landon know how wrong he was.

She managed to find street parking only half a block from the small house she rented and trudged uphill, letting herself in through the picket garden gate set in its barren arbor. The rain-drenched lawn glistened blackly in the streetlight. The garden itself was filled with dead plants and fallen leaves from the Japanese maple because she'd just plain been too busy to get to it.

She would.

Maybe this weekend. Get things cleaned up for the spring that seemed so inordinately distant these days.

"Vallon?" The raspy voice out of the darkness set the adrenaline pumping again. Someone stood next to the rhododendron bush under the eaves at the side of the house, and all Vallon could think was 'Simon was number three'. Was she next?

But it wasn't black leather that materialized out of the night. Instead the figure wore a heavy camo jacket, darkened with rain. Long blonde hair hung in rain-formed dreadlocks around the figure's thin face.

Vallon looked. Looked again and spotted an impossibly familiar form under the swathes of clothes.

"Fiona? Fi Murdoch?"

"Thank god thank god thank god." The figure lunged at Vallon, but streetlight showed a terror-filled face that Vallon knew from her distant past in the Academy. Arms came around her and the stink of cigarettes and unwashed body filled her nose.

"Thank god thank god thank god." It came out in a whisper, a chant, a prayer.

But it *was* a voice Vallon knew, even if it was ravaged by—what? What had done this to the young woman Vallon had known so long ago in the Academy? They'd arrived on the same day, but unlike Vallon's situation after her father was gone, Fiona had a mother—and that mother had pulled Fi out of the school when they were thirteen.

Vallon held the matted head away. "It really is you. It's been what?—twelve—thirteen years?" Far longer for Fiona, judging by the state of her white-blue eyes and hollow cheeks. A lifetime, maybe. The wide vacant gaze met Vallon's but it was still difficult to pinpoint Fi's presence.

"It's you it's you it's you." A croon as she tentatively stroked Vallon's cheek and hair with a long rough palm. "It's really you." A slow smile as Fi's gaze locked on. "Long time, bud."

Her gaze jerked to something beyond Vallon and terror shattered the smile. She yanked away, tore back into the darkness at the side of the house, crashing through the foliage to the backyard and the narrow lane.

"Fi! Fiona, wait!" Vallon peered into the street for whatever had scared her old friend, but it was only a rain-drenched residential street, cars crowding the narrow sidewalks, trees filling the yards.

Inking shadows.

She fought back the sense of being watched and went after Fi. In the backyard Fiona was fighting with the rear gate. The previous owner had put a child-proof latch on it. Fiona-proof, too, apparently.

Vallon caught her shoulder and Fiona whirled, her face spasmed with terror. Her fist slammed into Vallon's cheekbone and stars filled her head. She staggered back, but Fiona registered what she'd done.

"Oh no! Oh no! Oh no! Vallon. Vallon. Vallon." It was as if she tried to bring Vallon into being by naming her. Fiona crumpled to her knees on the sodden grass. She wrapped her arms around Vallon's legs. "Forgive me, please. Please. Please."

Shivers wracked her as she pulled back to paw at Vallon's hands as if seeking absolution, and for a moment, with the cold running down her neck, Vallon wanted nothing to do with this creature of the night. Then she shook herself.

Helped Fi up. "Come on. Let's get out of this rain."

She led them across the sodden grass and up onto the small, screened, rear porch, then in out of the pine and saltwater-scented night.

The house smelled warm, yeasty from the cinnamon buns she'd indulged in yesterday, but something else was there, too. A faint hint of cigarette smoke? Probably Fi. She pushed the woman towards a kitchen chair.

"Stay here."

She ignored the wet footprints she laid across the oak floor in the dining room, and went to the living room window that looked out onto the street. Stood hidden beside the curtains and peered out.

All the color had been drained to shades of grey and black. Nothing moved except the rain on bare branches and cedar and spruce. The rain had grown heavier and bounced on the glistening pavement and car hoods. Uphill, the street crested the hill and headed on toward the new Peak Park and the Woodland Zoo. Nothing moved.

Downhill, the houses gave way to the small trendy shops and restaurants that now made up Fremont and gave it the feel of a holdover from the sixties and seventies and the Latin motto '*De Libertas Quirkas,*' or 'free to be peculiar.' She fit right in.

An occasional car followed the leash of its headlights past the intersection with Leary Way. But the Sandhu house three doors down had too many trees in their yard and the hedge on the far side of their property made it impossible to see the sidewalk on her side of the street.

She should just close the drapes and go make Fiona some tea. Hell, she was dripping all over the hardwood. But something wouldn't let her turn away. Something—someone—was out there.

Clutching the gauzy curtain she'd made in a moment of uncharacteristic domesticity, she -reached-. Downhill the night filled with the glimmer of sleeping residents, the faint candle of a raccoon busily raiding someone's trash. Squirrels and birds slumbered in the trees. A great horned owl swooping through the dregs of the night.

As she turned uphill, the flash of a Gifted's presence was so bright she dropped back into herself a moment and had to force herself to —reach— again.

Flame seared the shadows in the lee of the huge rhododendron bush in the yard of the house two doors up. Where the streetlight found the leaves they shivered like tongues held out to the rain, but shadow filled their undersides and the side away from the street. And inside that darkness was a greater darkness.

—Reach —

And the darkness flared and was aware of her.

A hand grabbed her wrist and Vallon nearly screamed. She snapped back into her head and half staggered against the wall, the flame that was Fiona searing into her awareness. Strangely familiar. Vallon yanked away, fighting for control.

"They know," Fiona said. "They watch."

"Who knows? Who watches?" Vallon asked as she peered back into the street.

It was like whoever it was heard her question. Suddenly a piece of the darkness broke off from the bush and stepped into the streetlight.

Still dark. Black and slick and glistening and clearly male. Dark pits of eyes in hawkish, swarthy features seemed to look right at her and Vallon fell back, shoving Fiona behind her. Somehow their legs got tangled and they both came crashing down on a small side table, breaking off one leg.

When Vallon scrambled back to the window the watcher was gone. Hurriedly she yanked the heavier, brocade drapes closed and ran to the door. Checked the deadbolt and wished she had a chain as well. Ran back to the kitchen and locked that door, too. Pulled the bright gingham curtains closed and then flicked on the lights, feeling foolish as she did so. As if four walls were any protection.

As if she were really afraid. Just spooked, that was all—the afterburn to blame.

But color brought life back into the room. The yellow walls, the turquoise cabinets she'd painted to create a bright friendly space—not that anyone was ever invited to visit. All immaculate. This was her safe place. Her home. Her hiding place.

She closed her eyes and inhaled. Everything was fine, even if the man had looked and felt seriously like the person at the parking garage. He was probably just someone Gleason had sent to check on her. Make sure she really did spend the night at home.

The old lino floor creaked, and when Vallon opened her eyes Fiona stood in the room, her eyes fever bright. "You saw. You saw."

Like a crow cawing against danger.

"What did I see, Fi? What?" Vallon crossed to her friend and dragged her back to the white kitchen table. She tried to take Fi's sopping camo-colored coat, but Fi panicked at the suggestion. Vallon left her to drip on the floor and put the kettle on to boil, then grabbed a thick blue towel for Fi from the bathroom. When she returned, Fiona was just sitting and looking at her hands, her face gone slack. Not like the girl Vallon remembered, at all.

Vallon swore and began gently tamping the rain from Fi's sopping hair and face. Demanding answers obviously wasn't going to work any better than taking readings in a snowstorm. Cajoling probably wasn't going to, either. She crouched down in front of her old friend and gave her the towel in case she wanted to continue what Vallon had started. Fi's hands barely twitched to show she'd accepted the towel.

"It's so good to see you, Fi. Has it really been thirteen years?"

Slowly, ever so slowly, Fiona lifted her gaze to Vallon, the action so stiff it reminded her of an antique automaton fortuneteller she'd seen years ago at the Pike Street Market. A small frown placed lines between Fiona's eyes.

"Thirteen." A beat. "Yes." It came out in a triumphant burst as if finding the words had taken great effort.

Vallon sat back on her heels. There was so much she wanted to ask. She decided to use a surveyor approach—take readings, get estimates, before pinpointing her site. On the stove the kettle began to bounce and boil; water slopped onto the burner and hissed.

Fi looked up, alarmed, as Vallon went to the stove and filled a teapot with water and Earl Grey tea bags. "You're still an Earl Grey fan, right?"

Hesitation and then: "Yes." And then: "You remember."

Vallon cast a smile in her friend's direction. Fiona now sat at the table with her hands crossed in front of her like a schoolgirl. "I remember all right. You and I were like this." She held up two twined fingers.

"Best buds forever." Fi's fever-bright smile settled on her face.

"That's right. I didn't know what I was going to do when your mom took you out of the Academy."

The bright smile dimmed. Just like Fi, emotions ready to read.

"But it was good when we were together."

Vallon set the pot on the table as the cat door rattled. Maggie sauntered into the room, black tail high, fur poofed against the rain like a woman's frizzed hair. She barely gave the two women a look as she went to her food dish—empty—and then glared up at Vallon. Then she sat down and pawed at her plate. Always up-front about her wants, that was Maggie. Fi was like that, too.

"Is she yours?" Fi asked, a childlike shimmer of excitement in her voice.

"It's more like I'm hers. Her servant, that is." Vallon sighed and scooped up the food dish, filled it with canned food from the fridge.

"How did you get her? She's beautiful." Fi made coaxing noises and Maggie did her usual flirting act of flicking her tail and staying just out of reach.

"Look at her, acts like she's saying 'I'd love to have you pat me, but I just couldn't possibly.'" Maggie flopped down on the floor and rolled onto her back. "'Unless of course, you come to me.'" She set the cat food down and Maggie scooted to it, all her overtures to Fi forgotten. "I tell you, cats have very clear opinions of people. We're meant to be servants to cats. Only servants."

She shook her head, grabbed two cups, spoons, and some cream and sugar before seating herself. "Do you remember that soccer game against Clover Park? The State Championship?"

The frown again, but followed by a thousand-watt smile that almost broke Vallon's heart. "I do! You were the star—two goals!"

"Not the way I remember it. You passed me the ball so I could take that last shot. If you hadn't set me up, we'd have ended up in a tie. You could have taken the shot yourself."

"Yeah, but you were the better shooter."

And that was the gracious, straight-up honesty Vallon remembered. Always there to be an honest, open friend, more so than anyone in Vallon's life. Even Landon was more of a troubleshooter to dig her out of the messes she created.

Vallon poured the tea, the fragrant perfume reminding her of all the times they'd sat together in their shared room at the Academy so long ago. "We were a great team. God, we made those teachers work."

Another frown. "I think the dorm monitors really hated us."

"Only because we didn't take well to being virtual prisoners. We had our own minds. We found ways to beat them at their own game." Vallon sipped the tea and felt the exhaustion return like a heavy cape across her shoulders. Too much had happened this day and the inhibitor was wearing off, leaving her with the usual sensation of being stretched thin as glass that could shatter in the slightest wind.

When the afterburn had progressed this far, the only thing that helped was lots of time and rest—and preferably a good roll in the hay. One helped her start to refuel; the other brought her body back more quickly into balance. She closed her hands around the teacup for warmth and saw Fi do the same.

"I'll always remember that night we met those guys for a party down by the creek and there we were, a tad *flagrante delecto,* and the monitors found us and we took off through the woods half-naked. We had to circle back for our clothes and the damn guys had taken our panties as trophies."

"We lost our virginity that night." The light dimmed in Fi's eyes.

Vallon grinned across at her friend's solemn face. "Damn straight. And it was fun. Here's to the guys. Bastards." She clinked her cup against Fi's. "I wrote you letters after you left. I really wanted to keep in touch."

Fi's slow smile dropped totally away, and Vallon was instantly sorry she'd said it, but darn it, she had written, and it had hurt worse than anything when Fiona never replied. For years she'd been angry at Fi's betrayal, but now -

"I—tried."

Fi was gripping the cup so hard her fingers had gone white and suddenly Vallon's fatigue was too much. She didn't have the energy to ease around Fiona's loss, Fiona's fears, Fiona's change.

"So why'd you come tonight, Fi? You haven't tried to contact me. Ever."

The fear was back, writ large in Fiona's dilated pupils that almost erased the grey-blue. She glanced at the ginghammed window as if black figures were going to crash through the pane. "Because. I had to warn you."

"Warn me?" That sent the cold deeper into Vallon's veins, so there was no way the tea was going to help anymore. The last shreds of the inhibitor wore away and she swayed where she sat. Had to grab the table to stop from tumbling to the floor.

"Vallon?" Fear clear in Fi's voice.

Eyes closed, Vallon waited for the world to stop its slow, sickening turn around her. She held up her hand.

"It's all right. I'm just really beat." She opened her eyes and managed to stop from wincing, even though the light was like a blade direct to her brain and her nerves were jittery as a flower pot during an earthquake. "Listen. Could we talk in the morning? I'll get you set up in the spare room. You can use the shower, anything. Eat anything in the fridge, but I have to sleep. I'm sorry." She heaved herself up because if she didn't get to her bed soon she wouldn't be moving at all. This was the worst case of afterburn overload she'd ever had. "Come on. I'll show you your room."

Vallon fell onto her bed still clothed after showing Fi her room and shoving a stack of clean towels at her. The white duvet cover raced to meet Vallon and then she was gone.

A cell phone ring drilled into her head, buzzing, insistent. Vallon searched her pockets but the phone wasn't there. Had she dropped it? She looked back the way she'd come. Black pavement. White-slashed lines marking parking stalls turned piss-yellow-grey in the flickering fluorescent light. They ran away in a long row, diminishing in the distance, and the phone rang again, again. Buzzing and buzzing and buzzing so she wanted to cover her ears.

Then another phone answered it. And another. And another, and it drilled into her head, her heart, filling her with dread because there was something important here. An important message and she had to find her phone. Ran searching back along the wall, but the ringing only increased. She had to find the phone and stop the sound. Either that or get out.

Stairs. There were stairs ahead. But the walls shimmered around her and change licked the air. Ozone and ether. Brimstone and heat. She dove for the stairs. Had to escape before the change got her.

Tumbled down one flight. Two flights. How many flights? But then the stairwell seemed to telescope back towards her like a horrible, constricting throat. The terror she'd been fighting slammed into her chest. No breath.

But if she stayed here, the change would catch her as it had Simon. She wouldn't disappear like unGifted. She'd die a horrible death.

She turned, ran back up the stairs, but a dark figure waited, holding Fi in his arms—hostage—and she was trapped as the stair-throat contracted, as she felt it close, as the walls flowed over her legs, her hands. Flowed up her body until there was only her face. Only the vision of the dark figure and Fi.

"Death and destruction. You shouldn't have done it," the figure said in a voice that rolled like thunder as the wall flowed over her head.

Vallon bolted upright, gasping into half-light, and fought to pinpoint her location. Stop the sense of impending disaster.

Grey March light came through white curtains, which meant that it was at least seven a.m. Her bed under her and from the bedside table her cell phone drilled on and on and on. She grabbed it and keyed it on.

"Drake." Her damn heart pounded so loud it was hard to hear, harder to understand with the fear ricocheting around in her head. What was it she shouldn't have done?

"Good morning, Agent Drake. Chief Gleason asked me to phone you." E.A. Moore's smooth, caramel voice.

Vallon ran her fingers back through her matted hair and tried to find a normal response through the thick, sour fur on her tongue and— seemingly—in her head. The afterburn still throbbed, low down and unrelentingly sexy. God, she wanted a man.

But Moore seemed to take Vallon's hesitation as permission to move on. "He wishes you to know that the Seattle PD expect you at their Virginia Street station for an eight a.m. interview."

Vallon rubbed her eyes and grabbed her wristwatch off the table. Seven ten. "Shit." Typical Moore, leaving it so late to call—her own little punishment for upsetting Gleason. Vallon scrambled off the bed and almost fell. Slumped back on the bed, because her legs felt like rubber; and that wasn't a normal response to afterburn, but she had to get moving.

"I'll be there. Tell the Chief I'll be in to work afterwards."

"He expects it. There is the matter of discipline." Smooth voice with not a hint of disapproval, and that made the comment sting even more.

"That's a bit of an assumption, isn't it?" It took everything she had to keep her voice steady and strong.

"Given your past indiscretions, it seems logical. You were flagged as a potential security risk after that incident at the border."

Vallon bit her lip against her frustration. They'd never forgive her 'correction' of the work of a senior Agent who had shoved the Canadian border back a bit too far. She'd only returned it to the correct latitude, but the agent had been pissed big time and so had his boss. It led to her being transferred here and the biggest black mark against her name. So much for doing what was right.

The phone went dead in her hands and Vallon let it drop. Stood again and staggered into the connecting white and blue bathroom, shedding her clothes as she went. A quick shower and she dragged a brush through her hair, then grabbed a clean pair of jeans and a soft, grey cashmere sweater that didn't hurt her afterburn-sensitive skin. She topped it off with her favorite cropped black leather jacket, still damp from the rain last night. Donned them and inspected herself in the mirror. Not a pretty sight. Wide mouth, down-turned. She mustered a smile, but her skin was pretty much the color of her sweater, and her lank blonde hair just accentuated the dark circles under her eyes. She looked serious and intense.

Just the look she was going for, for a police interview and then facing down Gleason. She flipped her hair over her shoulders, pinched her cheeks, and slapped on some pale pink lip gloss, then headed for the stairs.

The open guestroom door stopped her. The bed looked untouched. She went to the bathroom and the stack of thick towels stood unused on the edge of the sink. The blue towel she'd handed Fi in the kitchen coiled like a discarded skin on the floor.

"Fi?" Vallon called as she scooped up the towel for the laundry and headed down stairs. The house echoed around her more empty than usual, so she knew Fi was gone. An open back door confirmed Vallon's suspicion even as she -reached- through the house and found only Maggie's small flame curled in her bed beside the couch.

She shivered, knowing she'd slept with the rear door unlocked. Anyone could have come in. But Fi had to do whatever she had to do. Whatever she'd come to say or do obviously wasn't that important.

Or else she was truly as terrified as Vallon had glimpsed. Clearly life hadn't been kind to Fi Murdoch since she left the Academy.

A warning.

But a warning of what? *Death and destruction, and she was somehow involved.*

Fi had seemed to know about the man in black, but there was something else about her, now that Vallon thought about it. Something she couldn't quite put her finger on, but had noticed last night even in her state.

She checked her watch. It was something she'd have to figure out later, because if she didn't leave now she was going to keep the illustrious Detective Bryson waiting.

She wanted his involvement over with, and her name cleared. She needed her precious pens and paper back. She'd worked too hard making the vellum and ink, using notes she'd found scribbled in the one notebook of her father's she'd found in his office effects.

As she locked up the house and went out to her car, she fought down the ever-present grief and the anger. Not that her father had been the last to abandon her, or even the first. Her mother had disappeared when she was young enough all Vallon recalled of her was a scent of roses and milk tea.

After her father, had come the men—boys, to start, and then lovers that all had left for some reason or another.

It had taught her resiliency and self-reliance until it was her doing the leaving. She had to make her own way in the world.

She climbed into the Subaru and went around the block and down Fremont and over what would always be to her, a troll-guarded Fremont Bridge to Westlake and followed the string of yacht dealerships and expensive restaurants along the shore of Lake Union, then threaded her way to Virginia Street.

The blocky, modern concrete-and-glass structure sat back from the sidewalk, with concrete seating and low hedges and a misleading welcome-garden by the door. Two sodden flags hung limp in the air that felt pregnant with the ubiquitous March Seattle rain.

Vallon pushed through the glass doors and into the typical circulated air of an office building but this carried the slight, unpleasant tinge of unwashed bodies and coppery blood. After registering her name with reception she paced, waiting for the Detective to grace her with his presence. She should have made herself coffee before leaving home, or have picked some up on the way in.

Another track across the foyer. She turned and found herself confronting Detective Bryson. Realized—again—how tall he was compared to her five foot seven. His espresso-colored gaze was a little disconcerting, because, dammit, he was just as good looking as he'd been last night.

Even the scent of his aftershave—something smelling lightly of mornings and sea-air—was good enough to eat. She'd hoped it had been just the afterburn talking, but now the afterburn flared.

"Detective." She stuck out her hand in an effort to control herself. "I received word you wished to interview me this morning."

"Agent Drake."

His palm was long and hard and warm against hers and just shaking it was far too intimate. She could lap him up like a cat with cream.

"I appreciate you coming in."

She flicked her hair behind her shoulders. Dammit, she was preening like some stupid schoolgirl. "So, should we get this over with? I have to get to work."

A half nod of his head and a bit of a smile. "I hope the officer's cuffs didn't leave any marks or bruises."

"Nothing I haven't dealt with before, if that's what you're worried about. I understand they were doing their job, though if they'd taken the time to listen, the whole thing could have been avoided. A misunderstanding."

"Aah." But there was amusement in his gaze as if her comment sounded like made she played with cuffs for fun.

The little hairs on the back her neck stood on end, and she almost wished she'd worn her one-and-only business suit because its structure would hide some of the physical reactions she felt towards this man.

He led her to an elevator and up to the second floor, then along the hallway to a small, windowless interview room. Well, windowless except for the one-way glass on the wall.

The room held only a square meeting table and two chairs. Two files and a pad of writing paper sat in the middle of the table. He motioned her to one chair and she sat, then wished she hadn't because he stayed standing. A blast of cold ceiling air chilled her still-damp hair and made her keep her jacket on.

She looked expectantly up at Bryson and knew this was his power play.

"If you have a pen I'll write out my report."

Again that flicker of amusement as he splayed his fingers over the back of his chair.

"I thought we might have a little conversation, first, Agent Drake. You seemed mighty upset last night and not quite clear. I thought things might go better today."

There was not-quite condescension in his voice that made her jaw clench. "Fine. Ask your questions."

"Would you like a cup of coffee?"

She seriously would have liked to say yes, but sitting where she was, and Agent Bryson's gaze, made her just want out of here. She made a point of checking her watch.

"No thanks, I'd like to keep this as short and to the point as possible so I can get back to the office."

"Such devotion to duty." Sarcasm now.

"What can I say, I love my job." At least it was true. Working with the AGS was the only thing she wanted, or knew how, to do. The use of her Gift was, well, why she got up every morning - and where else could she be paid to use it?

"And just what is it you do, Agent Drake? As I mentioned last night, I wasn't aware that the American Geological Survey was linked to Homeland Security. I did a little research. The AGS isn't the same thing as the US Geological Survey."

Cold pimpled her skin. She met his gaze and stood.

"You were told last night, that information is classified. If that's the direction of these questions, then I suggest you speak to Chief Gleason."

"Sit down, Ms. Drake." He faced her across the table, still loose, still handsome, but his face had gone harder than she wanted to see.

She remained standing and watched the hard edge smoothed away with effort. She needed to make sure this went quickly, and that meant allowing him to get what he needed but not so much she was violating national security.

"Detective Bryson, I can explain, in very general terms, my agency's affiliation with Homeland Security, but anything further you will have to go to my chief. Do you understand?"

"I understand that you're standing when I asked you to sit and I understand that the more you avoid answering my questions the more my partner and I are going to consider you a suspect in Simon Lamrey's murder. Now sit down."

He said it with a cold precision that she was sure he reserved only for those he was seriously going after, and for a moment she couldn't decide what to do or how to answer.

So she did the only thing she could think of.

She sat.

Chapter 5-Afterburn and Arctic Cold

Damnation, it wasn't supposed to come down like that, but this woman just seemed to push every button he had. Blacklock was probably busting a gut over how 'The Slick Man' had managed to fuck this one up so far.

The trouble was, Agent Vallon Drake was way too much his type, even though she didn't look the least bit like Cheryl. It wasn't her physical type—lean, athletic, maybe even a little rangy like one of those lone feline predators, which meant not as many curves as he usually preferred—no, it was more something about her presence. As if she were a bright flame in this room.

Like Cheryl had been.

He eased himself down into his chair, trying to ignore the faint scent of herbal shampoo that somehow seemed sexy as hell coming from her long blonde hair. He was a cop with a suspect. He would be more careful here on out. The safeguards of her face were writ large in unfriendly hazel-green eyes.

"So. Tell me about the AGS, Agent Drake. Use layman's terms that I might understand."

Everything around her was still, taut as if ready to spring. Yup, a solitary jungle cat, all right. Strong and confident: even the way she unconsciously shook out her sleek mane of hair.

"My agency focuses on ensuring the sanctity of American soil from predatory actions that come from either outside or inside our borders. Primarily, we identify risk and take preventative action."

It was a recruitment brochure quote which told him exactly nothing. "Tell me more about that. What's the AGS's background?"

Her brow cocked as if she considered her words.

"The AGS can be traced back to the explorations of Lewis and Clark and other explorers of their time period. They mapped their journeys across the continent. Others around the same time period as well. Mason-Dixon, Zebulon Pike, David Thompson, and so on explored and mapped America. When the AGS, then part of the USGS, first came into being it was at the behest of the American government to survey the continental US. Teams of surveyors covered every inch of this country on foot and the result was the topographical maps we were taught about in school.

"But features change. As technology advanced we got our information from aircraft photogrammetry and stereoscopic analysis of the data. Today satellite photos try to serve the same purpose."

She leaned back in her chair, and though she was dressed primly in her high-necked sweater, she arched her back a little, as if she were *trying* to tempt him with the full curve of her breasts. He looked away.

"Does that provide you and your tape recorders with enough information, Detective?"

He looked down at the few chicken scratches he'd made on the pad of paper before him. Not exactly complete notes.

"So let me see if I've got this right—you're really a bunch of glorified map makers."

Strangely, she went completely still, and that set his antennae into overdrive trying to assess what had caused her alarm. The increased scent of her herbal shampoos said something had aroused her.

"We don't make maps, Detective Bryson. We—correct them."

"Aah. Let me see. You use your high altitude surveillance to keep track of things like vigilante groups, unsanctioned fortifications and incursions onto American soil."

A small smile as enigmatic as the friggin' Mona Lisa. "You could say that, I suppose."

But he'd clearly missed the mark—and, damn it, he'd given her an out. She relaxed back into her chair.

She was cool, this Vallon Drake. Infuriatingly cool, but he'd seen cooler.

"So how did you come to that kind of work? It's a little unusual, isn't it?"

"Is this relevant to what happened last night, Detective?"

The way she stiffened said this wasn't something safe to ask about.

"Relevant in terms of what you were doing there—yes."

Finally she nodded and he felt her thaw a little.

"Fine. I entered the AGS because my father worked there. It's sort of a family tradition."

"And how long have you worked there?"

"In the AGS or in the Seattle Office?"

"Both." If she wanted to answer his questions with questions, he could play that game.

"Five years and nine months, respectively. And the nine months is probably nine months too long according to Chief Gleason." She met his gaze with a dare.

"He's not pleased with your work."

"Let's just say last night didn't exactly put me at the top of the list for employee of the year. I left my post to try to help Simon—Agent Lamrey—and it ended up with you involved."

The accusation was clear. If he'd just back off, things would be better, but the heat was back in her eyes and oh, mama, it was enough to sear his skin right here and now. He could practically smell lust rolling off her.

"Aah." He kept his cool. The fact she clearly admitted leaving her post said she was honest or stupid—or else she was calculating enough to think it might disarm him into letting her go. "So tell me about it."

She didn't even raise her gaze.

"It's really like I said last night. I was—monitoring things and discovered a situation. I sent Agent Lamrey to investigate, but he didn't check in, so I responded. That's how I found him, and that's how your officers found me."

Period. End of story by the way she leaned back in her chair and dug her hands deep into her jacket pockets.

"So what time did you leave your office?"

She told him.

"And that's near Redmond."

She looked at him, a trifle startled, until he produced Chief Gleason's card. "Criss-cross. We happen to have those phone books here, including the unlisted numbers. Tools of the trade." The special phone books allowed you to look up addresses associated to phone numbers quickly. "So how long did it take you to get to Broadway?"

Her face was flushed, like she was uncertain, but uncertain witnesses let their tells come through.

"About twenty minutes, given the time of night."

"So you drove directly to Denny Road."

"I did."

"And what did you do when you arrived?"

"I climbed out of my car and tried to contact Agent Lamrey again by phone. I'd been trying to reach him during the drive, too, but he wasn't picking up. It was what took me out after him to begin with."

He'd have bet she was speaking the truth except—.

He'd already done his homework. He'd surreptitiously taken a photo of Agent Drake last night with his cell, and today he'd shown the picture around the building where Lamrey lived.

"Tell me more about that."

She rolled her eyes and again he was struck by her hot and cold. In this case, cool backbone. She sat in her chair, shoulders straight, figure trim in the same leather jacket she'd worn last night. It suited her curves, but so did the choice of the soft sweater underneath.

"I'd reached him to tell him to attend the site."

"The garage."

"I didn't say that."

"But that's where you went to find him."

The hot daggers in her eyes were enough to tell him what he wanted to know. "So tell me what happened when you got there."

"I told you. I tried calling him. I heard his cell ring and went to find him. I found him there and tried to administer CPR. That's when your men arrived."

He stayed silent and let her stew for a minute because she had tripped herself in her lies and omissions. It was a shame, really. He could have liked her under other circumstances.

Finally he shook his head and smiled because this was when things were going to get interesting.

"I'm sorry Agent Drake, but there are a few inconsistencies with your story. When our men collected the evidence at the scene there was no sign of a cell phone belonging to Agent Lamrey. How do you explain that?"

§

Explain it?

Vallon sat too stunned to speak. She had a pretty good idea where the phone was, but there was no way the good detective was going to believe it. She felt beads of sweat form on her forehead. Not a good thing, but she held it together.

"I have no idea where it is—was. I heard it. That's all I know. I dialed his number and heard it—or something. I followed the sound into the garage. Simple as that. Maybe you should go search the garage again." At least her voice was steady. His face said they both registered it.

"We have."

The circulating air on her scalp went arctic. He must know he was getting to her. Coupled with the afterburn's flare at his masculine presence, the fear and arousal sent weird flashes of hot and cold running through her.

"Well, I heard it."

"Aah." Another doodle and she leaned over to look at what he ostensibly wrote. He pulled his papers away and it pissed her off.

"You say that as if you don't believe me. How about we just put our cards on the table, Detective. I'm due at work and I don't have time for mind games. I've told you what I know." She stood again, hoping he wouldn't call her bluff about work. It was only a little lie. "If you've got enough evidence to make a case against me tell me now, or else I'm out of here."

The thought crossed her mind to just walk out the door, but chances were he'd move fast enough to block her way. He looked athletic enough—like a well-ripped basketball player.

"How long had you been Simon Lamrey's lover, Agent Drake?"

The quiet way he said it stole all the energy out of her anger.

"Oh fuck. Is that what this is all about?" She sank down on her chair. "We dated for a month—six weeks—something like that. A casual thing, nothing serious. It ended two weeks ago."

"And one week ago you were seen at his apartment building in a major argument."

Vallon stiffened. "I won't deny it. I did go to his place and we argued. I went to see him about the idiot things he was doing at work—like not responding to my calls. I was trying to get him to act like an adult. Which is why I didn't send another Agent to check on him. I needed to deal with him myself."

"And because office romances are not exactly encouraged at the AGS?"

"How did you—you interviewed Gleason." Damn him. Damn them both.

"Over the phone. He wouldn't come in. Seemed a mite disappointed in you, though, Agent Drake."

She managed to shrug off her bitterness. Gleason was only the latest in a long line of men she'd disappointed. But that didn't matter. They all went away anyway.

"So you should know I'm telling the truth. I was trying to cover up a stupid office 'romance' as you put it. It ended up blowing up in my face." She shook her head. "I suppose I should have just sent someone else and let the chips fall where they may."

"So tell me again what happened at the garage."

"I told you."

But his espresso gaze had gone hard, brittle, and black. She sighed.

"What specifically is it you want to know?"

"What you were doing when Officers Smith and Cain arrived at the scene."

"Again, I told you, Detective. Chest compressions." But it had been so much more. The power flooding through her. Simon's flailing body. Bryson's gaze said they'd seen it, even though they didn't know what *it* was. All the certainty she'd felt when she walked into the police station had changed to the emptiness she hadn't felt since her father's death. Why had Gleason left her to face this alone? Could they pin Simon's death on her?

Bryson shook his head so slightly it must have been involuntary. It almost looked like regret.

"Perhaps it would interest you if I told you the preliminary results of the coroner's examination."

He flipped open a file in front of him. Gruesome photos of Simon's dead body filled the open file, but a scratchy hand-written report filled the other side. He flipped the file towards her, and she tried to focus on the words, but her gaze kept sliding to the photos. Simon like a slab of meat on a metal table. Photos of his hands, nails ripped as if he'd tried to claw at something. Deep bruises over his bare torso, his limbs. Had she done that?

Suddenly she was choking back emotion, because this man had been her lover. And he was dead. He didn't deserve it and it was her fault. She should have called for backup as soon as he didn't respond. There might have been an agent closer. Might have been.

And there might have been two agents caught by whoever worked the change.

She looked at Bryson. "Did the CPR cause the bruising? I didn't intend it to. I *was* trying to save his life."

"His ribcage was crushed, Agent Drake. So were his legs and arms. I wonder what could do that?"

She shook her head.

"Come now, you weren't doing CPR, now were you? You were angry at Agent Lamrey. He made you risk your job, come out on a cold, rainy night to confront him. You were furious and your temper got the better of you. You beat him to death. And then—and this is the part I really don't like—you took your time. Maybe he was still alive, maybe not, but you took the time to do this."

He reached into his jacket pocket and pulled out a familiar slim, black leather wallet. Her pen holder. He slammed it down on the table so hard she winced. Then he flipped open the other folder on his desk. In it was a plastic document holder that held the hurried drawing she'd made to free Simon. An archway in the wall. Simon sketched on the floor.

The emptiness in her belly swelled as she met his gaze.

"Maybe you'd like to explain: why'd you take the time to fucking sketch his picture."

Chapter 6-Fractalization

The cold air through the Subaru window wasn't enough to wake her up from the evil, waking dream. She was alone as always, and there was danger as always, but this time the whole world had rejected her. Or would.

A murder suspect.

The chill March wind carried spray off the road that chilled her skin, the scent of car fumes, and the ubiquitous sodden-earth scent that came off Lake Washington as she sped towards Redmond were almost cloying. The Gift became a static hum as she sped across the bridge. The clouds hung low and pregnant above the hills, the green forests sullen and forbidding.

The spray on her leather steering wheel got to be too much and she rolled the window up.

What could she have done other than protest her innocence? Telling Detective Bryson the truth wasn't an option. She could just see it: *Yes I work for a secret organization that was formed when a few USGS staffers realized they had the ability to rewrite the landscape with their maps. Last night I simply unmade the wall and pulled Simon loose.* Right. He'd have her in the loony bin so fast her head would swim more than it already did.

So she'd tried, "Recording the crime scene", but that didn't fly because there was no arch left in the concrete wall behind Simon.

Shaken, she'd been released with the news that the only reason she was allowed to go was because they hadn't been able to figure out exactly how she'd killed him and because Gleason's spiriting her out of the parking garage had meant they hadn't gathered evidence off her person. Bryson confiscated her jacket, though. She wasn't sure what information they'd get from it.

She took the exit off I-520 and rolled up into the trees to the AGS, pulled into a parking spot as far from the door as possible, because she needed to pull herself together before Gleason.

Then again, how much worse could the day get?

The wind soughed through the tall fir and cedar that perfumed the hilltop, and stray strands of cloud filtered down through the trees. The sound of highway traffic still hissed through the forest, the lonely sound of leaving. She shivered. A sudden gust of rain pushed her toward the door with the daunting realization that yes, the day could go downhill, even from here.

The cool recycled air didn't help as she shook the raindrops off her hair and brushed them from her sweater. Gleason might be waiting, but she needed to see Landon, so she turned the other way down the hall and pushed inside to the comforting moist warmth of his workroom.

"Landon?"

"Here, Pigeon."

Her eyes adjusted to the dim light as she followed his voice and the sounds of his movements through the labyrinth of tables and found him seated cross-legged on the floor before the confusing antique painting he'd said was called the Azoth.

"You just caught me finishing my meditations." He stood up and barely reached Vallon's chin, his slight form swathed in a researcher's white coat. "You look like you've seen a ghost. Want some tea? I left a pot steeping. You seen Gleason yet?"

"No. I haven't seen Gleason and I can't afford to take tea, but I needed your opinion on something." She looked around, trying to find something to focus on, because pinpointing on one thing, one reading, helped the rest of the world go away. "I just came from my interview with the police."

"Uh huh." Landon seated himself on a stool, primly smoothing his lab coat over his knobby knees. "How was it?"

"I don't know. Not good, I guess. That damned detective is going to try to pin this on me."

"Sit and tell me."

She perched on the edge of a chair, the shivers from the hallway still running through her. Afterburn, she supposed. It left the adrenaline surging. She clenched fists to stop her hands from shaking.

"Dammit, I feel so damned vulnerable I could scream. The afterburn…."

Landon caught her wrist to feel her pulse. Eyes widened. "You've got a good case. Good thing they didn't ask for a polygraph. So what have they got?"

"A witness who saw me over the body. Police officers who saw me doing something they've interpreted as beating Simon."

A look of interest. "What did they see, Vallon?"

The fact he used her name registered on her, but she just looked at her hands. "Something—I don't know where I got the idea except maybe from the flame in all of us—in everything. Like little mini examples of the power we use from the earth. It was—well I'd just made the change to free Simon and I still had all this connection to power so when his flame wasn't there I… I tried to replace it." She raised her gaze to his, saw the shock there.

"Try that again, Pigeon? You did what?"

"I tried to restart Simon—bring him back by replacing his flame. Sort of like—I don't know -."

"Like doctors use paddles to shock a heart into beating? Interesting." He shook his head, considering and stood. "So what happened?"

"Exactly nothing. His body convulsed all over the place, but I was stopped before it did any good if it would ever have done any good." She shook her head against the guilt. "If I'd been faster. Stronger. If I'd called a closer agent."

"There's not too many agents who'd have done what you did, Pigeon." Landon looked like he might try to comfort her, but was discreet enough not to touch her with the afterburn still raging. "So the cops saw."

"They saw. And they think I was in a rage and beating him because his body was crushed. They think they've really got the goods because they confiscated the drawing I did to get Simon out of the wall." She managed a determined smile because being weak wasn't how she wanted anyone to think of her. "Apparently I'm a cold-blooded bitch who took the time to sketch my victim. So—you think they have enough to charge me?"

"And they have motive, too." Landon drummed his fingertips over his lips. "Your ill-chosen relationship. And with each passing day more people become aware of the parking garage and the murder, so it becomes more a part of the world." He shook his head. "Gleason should have done what I suggested last night and just got rid of the whole situation. It's probably too late, now."

He looked at his watch. "Pigeon, Gleason's been pacing his office waiting for you since he got in this morning. I dare say making him wait much longer is just going to make things worse."

"I thought you said he liked me."

"He does. If he didn't he'd have seen you locked up last night. But this isn't the time to push your luck. Better go. Maybe I can come up with some way out of this."

She stood to go. "Or I can."

"Don't you be doing anything rash, now, Pigeon. This is going to take a lot of care."

"And when have I ever done anything rash?" She started through the collection of tables and shelves, not waiting for an answer, because, really, what could Landon do anyway? Everything was messed up and it was going to be a miracle if she came out this one at all, let alone still as an Agent. But she knew he'd try. Landon did that.

At the door she stopped and turned back to him. "Landon?"

He'd already turned back to his table. "Yes?"

"Thanks. Your help means a lot."

That turned him around, a startled look in his pale gaze. "Vallon, what's gotten into you? What's the matter?"

She shook her head because she was too strong to want to cry on his shoulder. She'd last done that when her father died.

"I just wanted you to know. I guess Simon's death brought it home to me—how we live and die alone, scurrying around on this earth all busy in our day-to-day, and never really get the chance to touch someone deeper."

"Vallon, you're not alone. I'm here. We're all here. Tell you what: come talk to me after you see Gleason."

She didn't voice her doubt because she knew he was trying to help. Instead she nodded thanks and went out the door to face her boss.

The war room was quieter today, the buzz of activity confined to a few desks as most of the operatives were out in the field or sleeping off afterburn, either with another agent, a spouse, or in the agency brothel. Otherwise Agents were encouraged to sleep it off, something that could take a few days of complete rest. Or Agents were free to deal with the afterburn through extracurricular activities. And given what had happened with Simon, that was going to be Vallon's choice.

Above the war room's map pit 'the desk' swung across the American topography in a graceful swoop. Elsewhere across the country smaller, regional, installations would be doing the same over their assigned territory.

Red-headed Matt Harper, who'd been one year ahead of her in the Academy, filled the day shift chair and looked up at her briefly. He didn't even nod, but Janet Hunt gave a brief, encouraging smile from across the room. Always the mother - not.

Fighting back her qualms, Vallon hunched through the desks and across the room towards Gleason's closed door. As usual, Moore appeared out of nowhere and eased Vallon aside so Moore could announce her. How the E.A. materialized at the right times was something Vallon had yet to be able to fathom. It was as though she just folded into existence when needed.

Moore waved Vallon into the office with barely a shift of her perfectly arched brows and closed the door behind her. The office was eerily silent. Chief Gleason sat behind his desk reading papers and ignoring her presence.

Vallon's uncharacteristic nervousness turned quickly to indignation when he left her standing by the door.

"Agent Drake reporting as requested, Sir." She stepped forward smartly until her shadow fell across his pages.

Slow enough ice could melt, he raised his gaze to her. Then he checked his watch.

"A bit late in the day to report, isn't it, Agent?"

"I finished my interview with Seattle PD and came directly here, Sir. The interview went long."

He motioned toward the chair and then opened a thick file on his desk. Vallon caught a glimpse of her agency ID photo and her stomach contracted into a small, tight knot. If he were reviewing her personnel file, this couldn't be good.

"I had a discussion with Detective Bryson this morning."

Vallon nodded.

"It seems there's considerable evidence against you in the case of Agent Lamrey's death."

"Evidence we both know he misread because he doesn't know all the facts."

"Has he? I've been reviewing your work file, Agent. Difficulty following orders. Unsanctioned changes. Failure to report another student's behavior. Quite an illustrious history right back to your time in the Academy."

"Now wait a minute. I thought Academy files were closed."

He just held her with a pair of radar eyes and her indignation grew.

"You said work file," she continued. "Yes, I'll admit to using common sense to determine my actions instead of blindly following orders. I'll also admit to making slight changes to undo the consequences of wild changes. I mean, should I have left bare fields after we got rid of a suburb? No, I put the lake that used to exist back in place, and the creeks and gullies that fed it. But going back to school days is a bit much, don't you think?"

Gleason's glare hardened. "You left out the border, Drake. Care to comment on that little debacle?"

Vallon bit back her epithet.

"I think I've explained it enough times, but yes. After Agent Comfry erroneously shifted the border two miles farther north than it should have been, I corrected it. Unfortunately a few American Gifted noticed and claimed the Canadians were attacking."

"And led to militia attacks by Americans onto Canadian soil. There was nearly a war, for god's sake."

Her gaze locked on his. "Sir, I'm sorry that happened, but it wasn't our land."

Gleason glanced at her file. "Your school records show a consistent pattern of insubordination. Who can say whether you'd step even further over the line to use your gifts for murder?"

"But you know that's not true."

"Do I? Such an escalation is not atypical of antisocial personality types."

"I'm not antisocial. It happened as I said." And if he wanted to see antisocial he should hear what she would have preferred to say.

"Perhaps your pattern of behavior should have been picked up on before you were recruited."

"Is that my problem?" It came out even though she was treading on shaky ground.

"It is now. The only reason I haven't fired your ass is because of your father."

"My father." The last thing she needed was a reminder of him. Which was probably why Gleason brought him up. Real professional, poking her with that stick.

"He was an exemplary Agent right through his career. I know. I worked with him. The fact he met his unfortunate demise is an example of the wild chance that rules all our lives. Those chances can't be made worse by unthinking action on the part of our Agents."

"My father has nothing to do with me. I'm not him. In any way, shape, or form." She managed to keep her voice clear, cold and professional. Typical Dad: even from the grave he was screwing her over.

"That's eminently clear. What's also eminently clear is that though your father was a good Agent, he seriously lacked in parenting skills."

Her mouth fell open in surprise, but she still had to defend him. "You don't know what you're talking about."

"Don't I? You haven't read your file." A thin smile that might have carried a hint of kindness, but still soured her stomach. "Now given you don't seem to want to set your own boundaries of behavior, and given there is a risk Detective Bryson might be right in his suspicions even if he is wrong in the methods you've used, I see it as my duty to provide you your first lesson on personal limits.

"You are hereby suspended from all field work. You will be on the night desk for the next thirty shifts at least, and at that time I will reevaluate your performance and determine whether other lessons are required."

"I frigging have boundaries." She kept her voice low, fighting anger at the unfairness of his evaluation.

"Obviously not anything appropriate to your job."

"But no one does thirty night shifts…." The strain of the job was known to send Agents to the psych ward after one shift.

"You will."

Arguing with him was like arguing with Mount Rainier. He'd do what he was going to——as bad as Detective Bryson——and suddenly his attitude made sense.

"This isn't just about the police case, is it? You want to fire me, but someone's not letting you do that. You've been saddled with me and you're trying to use this bullshit case even though you know it's not true. You're fucking screwing with me because you want me to quit!" She stood up, fierce with indignation.

Gleason looked up at her. "Agent, I suggest you sit down until I'm finished."

"You know what? We *are* finished. I'll take your thirty days on the desk, as unreasonable as that is. You can't get rid of me and you're going to have to look at me for thirty days straight. Get used to it."

She spun on her heel and marched out of his office, for once confronting Moore so she looked surprised. Around the war room everyone had turned in her direction so she and Gleason must have been louder than she thought.

She ignored them and stalked across the room to the door, spine straight and chin up. She strode down the hall to Landon's room and slammed inside. Empty.

She left again and stalked out into pouring rain and circled around the building to the small apartment block that stood amongst trees behind the main AGS building. Gleason lived in one side of the duplex. The other side had a small apartment downstairs for Agent-partners dealing with afterburn, while the upstairs held Landon Snow's residence.

The rain soaked her as she clattered up the stairs swearing at Gleason, and at Landon Snow's ignorance of their boss.

"You have absolutely no concept!" She blurted when he answered her pounding on his door.

"Pigeon?" He glanced beyond her, before ushering her in.

"Gleason hates me. I don't care what you say. He just put me on thirty days' desk duty as if he's actually hoping I'll have a breakdown and quit." She stormed into Landon's living room with its spare Swedish furniture of chrome and glass and leather. Plopped down on the couch. "How the hell am I going to do that and stay sane?"

Landon followed her into the room and looked out into the grove of trees beyond the large plate-glass window. A small smile. "Some would say your status is already at issue."

"Thanks a lot."

"You can fault me for a lot, Pigeon, but not dishonesty."

Elbows on knees, she kneaded the ache in her forehead. "What am I going to do, Landon? Thirty days. Heck, one shift and I'm ready to run screaming at the confinement and afterburn." The thing was, when working the chair you were using the Gift constantly to monitor all the shifts and changes occurring across the map. It took far more Gift than simply dealing with an accidental change.

With his cowlicked hair Landon looked like an albino rook. "You're going to have lunch with me. Come on."

He led her into the back of the apartment that gave onto the parking lot, the rain sheeting across the pavement like a pool of uneasy water.

"Terrific. The cops have my jacket."

Landon went to the fridge and pulled out a crisper of fresh vegetables and a package of tofu and began chopping.

"So you get wet. Could be worse. They could have held you. And the jacket isn't going to prove anything given you admit to working on Lamrey when you found him."

That was one little ray of hope. She took the knife from him while he rummaged through the cupboard for a small, well-used wok that he placed on the natural gas stove. Soon oil started to sizzle and pop and he threw in chopped onion and garlic and stirred down the sizzle. The room filled with the scent.

The act of chopping carrots and broccoli without chopping off a finger helped her channel her mad and steady the afterburn. "Sometimes I swear I don't want this job."

Landon glanced at her. Smiled as he used the metal paddle to stir the carrots she added. "Bullshit. You were made for this job and you know it."

"I'm not so sure anymore. Gleason was just reminding me of all the shit I've caused. The AGS doesn't need that. I'm not so sure I need the AGS, either."

"And where would you go?"

"No idea." Then she thought a moment. It was true. Since her father's death the AGS and its Academy were as much like a family as she had.

"Okay," she sighed. "So I'm staying in the AGS—if I'm not in jail. I just…." She wasn't going to reveal how she really felt.

"Pigeon, right now you strike me as adrift." Landon glanced up at her as she dumped the chopped broccoli and celery and mushrooms into the pan. "You're being pulled along and there's all these islands around you and you don't know how to reach out to any of them. Me, for example. I'm here for you. Really."

It was so unusual for Landon to make personal observations about her she considered what he'd said—and rejected it. "I have friends, Landon. I do. Just last night Fi Murdoch came to see me."

There was a pause in Landon's stirring. "Fi Murdoch? Your friend from the Academy?"

She nodded.

"Well, powers-that-be. How is she? How long has it been?"

Vallon suddenly didn't want to tell him all about the events of last evening.

"A while. Good to see her again, though." She cleaned up the remains of the vegetables and scooped them into the garbage disposal and tried to think of a way to open the subject she really wanted to talk about.

"Landon, last night I told Gleason that I thought someone had purposely caused that change. He didn't believe me, but I really think I'm right."

Landon's face remained impassive, but she caught the light of interest in his eyes. "What? You think Fi was responsible?"

"No. No way. I was always better than Fi when it came to the Gift. No, it has more to do with when I tried to free Simon." She told him the details of the parking garage and of the sense of something intentionally fighting her change. "What do you think? Could there be something to it. I mean, there are three dead agents."

He busied himself pouring vegetables onto plates and then setting the table, before neatly folding himself into a chair.

"An interesting theory, Vallon. Very interesting. The possibility of there being other Gifted out there is something I've wondered about for years." He picked up his chopsticks—beautiful blue and gold enamel ones she thought were probably antique. "I wonder why we don't see more people spontaneously recognizing their capacity for change? Seems strange to me, when change is around us all the time."

"What are you saying?" Vallon brought a piece of broccoli to her mouth. Chewed. "Good." She nodded.

"It just seems odd to me. Why did the Gift suddenly manifest itself in the 60s, and not just here, but all over the world? We know the Russians have it and have been experimenting with it for a while. The changes in the Aral Sea are the direct result of poor use of the Gift—overnight setting diversion channels in place for irrigation destroyed an entire ecosystem and economy. The Chinese have been playing with it, too—changes in the Yangtze River gorge to facilitate the building of the Three Gorges Dam, the other major projects in western China where suddenly an oasis that has only ever been able to support a few thousand people can suddenly support a million. Even the Indians have shown signs of it. The suddenly fertile Rajasthan wheat basket where desert produces food for millions. The only problem with it is they've brought the aquifers to the surface to do it and the aquifers aren't going to last forever. And those are just the projects we know of." He shook his head. "Fools, all of them."

Vallon wasn't quite sure what he was getting at. "Are you saying more people cause changes, but they hide it from us?"

"I'm saying those governments who are aware of the Gift have been fostering its development. Most have been short-sighted in its use and it's going to bring about ecological crises at some point. At least here the AGS has maintained a proper focus on preservation—not change. But who knows how many people know they can change and have hidden their talent. Not every country has a voluntary agency like the AGS."

Vallon silently picked at the meal, her mind whirling at what Landon had said. She'd known other countries were probably aware of the Gift, but not that they used it so openly—or that people with the Gift might be conscripted—no, forced—into service.

"So I should be counting my blessings."

"Exactly."

"So the Gift is everywhere, then. Like it is here."

"That's the million dollar question, now isn't it, Pigeon? In my opinion—and it is not shared by everyone—the Gift didn't just suddenly spring into being across the globe. I think the Gift's appearance is more like the spread of a religion like Buddhism—it has its stronghold in some places, and from there it bleeds out into the rest of the world. I keep hoping we'll eventually stumble upon ground zero and be able to find teachers like the Buddhists do in Tibet and Japan and so on."

Vallon opened her mouth to tell him about the person she'd seen last night, but Landon carried on.

"Sometimes I wonder if we even recognize the changes around us. We know a lot and see a lot, but if we had more power would we recognize more changes?"

He must have mistaken her expression for confusion, because he set down his chopsticks and leaned forward and his voice dropped to a dramatic whisper. "I've been theorizing on this for years, but I've had no one to discuss it with—until now. What if the level of your gift allows you to be more aware of changes? We already see that to some degree. You have a tremendous gift and so Gleason likes to keep you on the desk."

"My luck." She groused, even though if it weren't for the afterburn she'd enjoy it. There was something exhilarating about being responsible for connecting to such a wide swath of land.

"But what if there were people with a whole other level of gifts? If they made changes, would we recognize them?" He grabbed her hand. "Think of it like worms and human beings. We both interact on our world, but do the worms even know we exist? Do they notice when we shift a garden plot or dig a foundation?"

"We aren't exactly worms, Landon."

"No, but unGifted aren't aware of changes Gifted make. Somehow when the change occurs, for most of the human population, the whole world shifts to accommodate that change - including their memories. Only those with a certain level of the Gift notice."

He was getting warmed up to his subject now, excitement making his pink eyes gleam red. "Think about all the theories about intelligent life in the universe, pigeon. In an infinite universe, there're infinite possibilities. There's undoubtedly going to be terrestrial life developing on other planets. Given we already know the Gift runs in a bell curve across the population, there should be others more gifted than us."

"But we noticed this change."

"And maybe they wanted us to. Like people from another planet."

The concept left her grappling for solidity. She didn't like the queasy feeling she got when the image of the dark man and the strangeness of his disappearance filled her head. Surely the world didn't have so many layers. Vallon shivered. "I swear someone just walked over my grave."

At that Landon grinned, exposing his small neat teeth. "I feel that way a lot."

"So you're talking about—what's the term—like fractalization, right? The same pattern continues down and down or up and up, through all existence."

"Layer upon layer," he intoned and she almost shivered at the reverence in his voice.

"So I could be right—there might have been someone blocking me even if Gleason doesn't want to believe me."

Landon placed his hands on his hips. "Silly girl. Haven't I been telling you to believe in yourself for years?"

"You have, and I do. Unfortunately there aren't a lot of other people who believe the same way. Gleason just wants me to be another of his minions." Shook her head.

"And who's been watching too many old grade B movies?"

She grinned and suddenly things felt normal. Landon had done that for her—except for the afterburn still singeing her veins. "I guess things have gotten a little out of control today. I needed your reminder. Thanks."

She pushed back from the table and helped Landon clear the dishes and clean up, then checked her watch. "I guess I should go. I want to see if I can find Fi before I have to start my shift."

"I thought you said she'd come to you?" A quirk of brow.

"She did, but she took off. I'm hoping to link up again. For old time's sake." Why she didn't mention Fi's warning, she didn't understand. Maybe it was the dream, or maybe it was the man she'd seen last night. Maybe she didn't want to destroy Landon's impression of her, or maybe it was that she wanted proof of the dark man's existence; and Fi had seemed to know of him. Or that she had a whole lot of other trouble to deal with in the cops. Whatever it was, she was holding her cards close to her chest and doing things her way just as she'd always done.

At the door she paused, considering the pouring rain.

"I've got an extra Gore-tex jacket I can loan you."

She looked back at Landon. Eagerness in his gaze.

Almost too eager, and for an instant Vallon almost didn't trust. Part of the jumpiness and paranoia that came with leaving afterburn too long unresolved. She was going to have to find a way to relieve herself—and soon.

"Nah. Like you said. It's only water." She tossed him a grin and ducked into the rain, clattering down the stairs and jogging to her car before he could try to coax her.

By the time she was inside the Subaru she was soaked, and all the steel in her spine had disappeared. She slumped against the headrest for a moment. Her heart was knocking on her ribs so hard she thought her chest might explode. She gripped the steering wheel and twisted her fingers against the plastic.

What the heck was going on? Landon hadn't done or said anything—except that what she suspected might be true. That should give her relief that she wasn't crazy—not make her distrust him.

She keyed the car on, and gunned the engine as she backed out. Thirty days of afterburn to look forward to, and she was already falling apart. Terrific. She *really* needed a man when Landon was starting to look good.

In the rearview she saw Gleason exit the AGS building and head towards her and the adrenaline surged again. Had he been waiting for her? He'd probably reconsidered and wanted her to take her things and get the hell out of the AGS.

Like she was going to stick around for that. She'd damn well make him have to work to fire her. "Tit for tat, old man."

The car's engine roared as she headed down the line of cars for the street, and blasted past Gleason drilling him with back wash in the process.

"Take that, for yelling at me so loud every other agent heard," she crowed.

Then, still laughing at the look on his face, she was on the street and down the hill and heading towards the city and the intersection of Broadway and Denny.

If the police and Gleason were certain she'd killed Lamrey it meant there was a good chance no one was working to examine other ways the murder could have gone down. She needed to investigate, because no one else was going to clear her name.

Chapter 7-Secrets in the Rain

"So that didn't exactly go as planned, Slick." Clint Blacklock eyed Jason as he pushed into the dimly lit viewing room. The Drake woman had just left in a rush; headed to her office, she said, but he didn't know if he believed her.

"*She* wasn't exactly what I planned," he growled and slouched into a chair and put his feet up, then stretched, trying to get some relief from the tension knotting his shoulders.

"She's not telling us everything."

"Gee, you think? She works for fuckin' Homeland Security." Jason closed his eyes against the disgust he felt. "Sorry, man. There's something about her. I swear one moment she looked so hot I thought she was going to jump my bones right here and the next minute she was the ice queen. Not exactly an easy subject to read—or interview."

He shook his head, but the image of her blonde hair and sullen—no—make that sultry, green-hazel eyes was burned in his brain.

"Well you had her on the run. She started to really crack when you told her about the cell phone. The cracks were fuckin' canyons when you pulled out her drawing. Did you see her face? The way her eyes stayed on that pencil case of hers."

"She wanted it. Bad. Funny, though. It held more of her attention than the drawing did. As if that evidence was worth nothing in comparison."

Blacklock shook his shaggy head. "I never could get into those egghead girls with their purse version of pocket protectors. Now I know why."

"As if anyone could have stood a chance in Patty's presence."

"Might have, if they didn't have those pencil thingies."

Jason rolled his eyes. "Now that we've explained away your preferences in the female kind, can we focus on the case?"

Blacklock reached across the desk and snagged Jason's files and pad of paper, glanced at the doodles, and then raised an all-too-knowing set of eyes to Jason. "Was that preferences in the female kind, you was talking about, Slick? Cause I think you might be causing me some concerns."

"You're crazy if you think I'm going to do anything to wreck our case. You know me. Work's the thing."

"'Ridiculously dedicated', I think were the words I used. Enough I been worried about you." Blacklock glanced down at the pad again, then shoved it across the desk to Jason. "But seriously—look for yourself."

Jason forced himself to look at what he knew was already there. Too many elegant eyes, as if she was looking at him still with that heated way only Vallon Drake had. He stood and went to the door. "Shit. It's like she's a chemical and I react."

"Where you going, man?"

"To check out that parking garage again. She swore she heard that cell. Maybe our guys missed something."

Clint shook his mighty head. "Listen, Slick. You sure this is a case you should be investigating?"

"You suggesting I should tell the Sergeant to reassign the case because I can't control my dick?"

"Hell, no. I'm suggesting you should make sure she's not a cliff and you're not the lemming throwing hisself off."

§

Landon couldn't quite congratulate himself about the meeting with Vallon. Something in her manner at the end had worsened the psychic bombardment he always felt in Vallon's presence. By the powers that be, if he could ever figure out how to motivate her to really learn the extent of her power, what would she be able to do? But right now all he got from her was secrets. He couldn't be as sure as he usually was. Her afterburn got in the way.

He padded to his bookcase and retrieved the heavy tome he desired. The antique copy of the alchemical text, *Buch der Heiligen Dreifaltigkeit*, published in its original German, had once been his great-grandfather's. It always helped to give him focus and direction when he was in a quandary.

Vallon Drake seemed eminently capable of leaving him with that disquiet.

A heavy fist-fall against his front door spun him around. Only one person beyond Vallon ever pounded as if he were going to break the door down. Landon considered simply not answering, but knew he couldn't get away with it.

Sighing at the second interruption of what he'd planned as a meditative afternoon to recover from his first meeting with Vallon, Landon crossed to the door, his soft-soled moccasins whispering like old friends on the hardwood. He needed the quiet.

"Coming. You don't need to bloody break it down."

When he pulled open the door, Gregor Gleason stood fuming in front of him with fury in his eyes and far more than rainwater sopping his suit.

Landon quelled a smile and held up his hand. The big man did rage so well. "Let me guess: you tried to stop her."

"What the hell did you say to her?" Gleason shoved past him into the living room with a squelching sound, and tracked sodden footprints on the hardwood.

Landon bit back a comment and forced himself to smooth-faced calm because confrontation would only increase Gleason's anger and that was not the way to help Vallon. Still, he planted himself in front of the big man.

"What do you think? I calmed her down, of course, fed her lunch and tried to plant some seeds about the bigger picture. Mostly I offered a shoulder to cry on because someone was threatening to fire her."

Gleason glared in response to the gaze Landon hoped was noncommittal, but Gleason gave way first. "Damn woman pushes every button I have."

"And you should remember she also had the highest scores of any Academy graduate. Surely you can cut her some slack." He kept his voice calm, low, sing-song as he would with a beast.

Gleason rolled his eyes. "What do you think I've been doing since she got here? If that damned Lamrey had only done his job she'd have been a lot easier to…."

"And I told you that was never a good idea. Vallon's full attention should be on her job, not a relationship or anything a relationship might bring. By the powers-that-be, it gets me all hot and bothered just thinking about what she might be capable of if we can just foster those skills along."

"Well your 'powers' just better keep the damned woman out of jail and functioning in her job."

Landon decided to take a chance. "And that job would be thirty days of the desk?"

It evoked another glare.

"Come, Gregor, what were you thinking? Are you trying to kill the girl? Drive her insane? No agent can withstand that number of days on the desk: the demands are too high on the Gift. The afterburn alone could kill her."

Gregor slouched further into the room, tracking water across the floor to the plate glass window that streamed with a steady flow of rain so it was like they stood suspended apart from the world inside a giant piece of crystal. Landon bristled at the mess of his floor. He'd agreed on the Vallon Drake project simply because the girl who'd fascinated him with her brilliance as a child had turned into a woman with a powerful force of will—and the most profound Gift he'd ever seen. Not that she knew it. He wanted to find out what she was capable of.

"I didn't sign on to see her become your whipping boy. If you don't ease up I may have to reconsider my involvement."

That got Gleason's attention because he knew Landon was the closest thing they had to influence over Vallon. His shoulders slumped a little.

"I know. I know. Shit, what don't I know?" Gleason turned back from staring out at the rain-sheeted window. "It's just that—something she said last night. I think she's onto our little problem."

"The fact that something blocked her rescue?"

Gleason stepped over to the leather couch, slumped down and nodded. "Something that's taking out Agents."

The abuse of his furniture kept Landon's enthusiasm in check. He went to a cupboard and came back with a towel. "The least you can do is be kind to my stuff."

Gleason dabbed at his face and neck, but paid no attention to the water marks spreading across the couch. "How the hell do we stop this from getting out? Homeland Security is just looking for an excuse to take over."

And that was what they both feared. When the little 'research project' that had been the AGS had come to light during the formation of Homeland Security, the only thing that had left the AGS autonomous was the uniqueness of its operations and the skill-set required to do the work. But if the AGS was no longer even able to protect its own….

Landon's skin went cold, but he shook his head. "More to the point, we can't afford our Agents knowing. That kind of tension and distrust detracts from the Gift and seriously undercuts our ability to take forward our job. Or had you forgotten that?"

Gleason glared up at him. "Of course I haven't forgotten. I *have* the Gift. You think I want to answer to some blockhead grunt who can't even tell when a change is made?" He shook his head and sent small beads of spray from his shoulders to the couch. "But what the hell do we do?"

The jab at Landon's lack of overt Gift and the damage to his furniture was almost enough to break his control. It had been too much working with Vallon twice in one day. In her state, just being in the room with her left him feeling battered and bruised. But better that he deal with Vallon's issues than leave her to go off half-cocked alone. The poor girl practically oozed isolation and he was not going to let her slip farther into it.

Before anything happened to her he needed to understand what gave Vallon Drake the power he sensed, and then figure out a means to duplicate it if the AGS were truly going to protect America.

"Did you think about talking to her? Maybe asking her not to mention it because it might cause trouble? She's got a brain, Gregor.

And she loves her job. Hell, we're the closest thing she's got to family. She's loyal. She'd protect us and it might bring her more in line with what you expect of an Agent."

Gleason's snort of derision just exacerbated Landon's pique—more so because it was accompanied by another shower of water onto his couch.

Landon took a deep breath, trying to rid himself of negative vibrations, and forced himself to sit down across from Gleason.

"You are being as short-sighted as she is. She would have listened. I know you don't believe me, but she would have." He thought a moment and then looked Gleason in the eye. "But now that it's come to this I think you just might have landed us a way to deal with a couple of issues all in one fell swoop."

Gleason raised one hoary brow and straightened. A wee glimmer of hope came into his eyes. "Do tell, oh lord of the darkness," he growled.

At the taunt Landon released his control a little. "I will. But first get your wet ass off my couch."

§

Beyond the two-story buildings that fronted Broadway, the dark glass towers of Seattle were blades through the hearts of the low clouds over the city. They released rain like a cold, grey curtain over the sullen waves of Elliot Bay and Puget Sound, and sheeted down the shimmering asphalt of Denny Way. Southeastward there were so many clouds Mount Rainier was as invisible as if it didn't exist.

When there were no empty parking spots on the busy street, Vallon abandoned her car in a 'no parking' zone behind the bookstore and circumnavigated the block to come up in front of the garage. The heavy rain pinged off her neck, but sank into her shoulders and plastered her hair onto her head and neck. Cold water trickled down her back and soaked her black boots and jean cuffs.

She shouldn't be here. At least she should have gone home for a jacket. She knew both Bryson and Gleason would be pissed off if they knew, but that was just too damn bad. She wasn't the kind to just lay back and take this. She had to find the evidence to clear her name.

Hiking her turtleneck collar up around her chin, she ducked under the yellow crime-scene tape and hustled down the sidewalk to the stairwell, then paused.

Something about this place. She'd felt it last night, too. A certain almost-familiar tingle that sent the hackles on the back of her neck on end.

The thought of Landon's suggestion about layers of Gifted just made it worse. No way he could be right.

Except she'd felt the stranger's power.

Shivering, she -reached- out and ignored the flow of power beneath her. Blocked out the flickering candles of people all around to focus on the feel of *this* concrete. This building. She'd found that a change actually had the taste of the Gifted who caused it.

Licorice, was her first thought. Dark and twisted and undercut with the drunken, arid taste of well-oaked red wine, pungent as unwashed body.

Fi?

She fell back into her body and staggered against the wall. Even that little power use was too much, too soon, after the battle the night before. The 'overindulged' feel of the garage was like and unlike Fi. Dissolution, but something *was* there. Somehow Fi's attendance at her house the very night of the garage's appearance wasn't a coincidence—not with this evidence.

Evidence that was worth exactly nothing in the face of detective Bryson's scrutiny. She screwed up her face, then hauled out her cell phone and dialed Lamrey's number and held the phone away from her ear.

The distant buzz. Again. Upstairs. So the phone was still here, but who knew how long the battery would hold out. She scrambled up the two flights, tracking the sound.

And ran smack-dab into a trench-coated figure.

Vallon fell back a pace and looked up into the strong, angular features of the last person in the world she wanted to see. A strong hand imprisoned her wrist, but she jerked free, backing against the wall and clicking her cell phone closed. The burring of the answering call cut off. Not a black trench coat—more like rain-sodden grey.

"Agent Drake. Twice in one day. What an incredible pleasure."

His voice was cool and so were those espresso eyes, but the hand on her wrist had been hot. Too hot, and she fought back the afterburn he resurrected too well.

Dammit, she needed a man. That's what she should be doing—cruising a bar—not digging herself deeper into trouble.

She pulled herself straighter. "I didn't expect to see you here."

"And I could say the same, given the yellow police tape blocking entry. But then you don't follow the rules, do you Agent Drake?"

She ignored the flush that was already running up her neck. "I thought—given you seemed so sure that I had killed Agent Lamrey—that I should conduct my own investigation."

"Aah." A grin.

That infuriating little word that was supposedly sufficient as a response. "And what are you doing here? I thought you had the evidence you needed for a conviction."

It came out as more of a snarl than she'd intended and his damned grin only deepened.

"Actually, I suspect I'm here for much the same reason as you. I thought your version of events should be explored. I was looking for the phone in case my men missed it." He looked away down the pavement. "I was just giving up when damned if I didn't think I heard a phone." Another grin. "And then you appeared and nearly bowled me over. Of course."

"Of course?"

"Of course it had to be you. If there's one person I can think of who'd be likely to get themselves into trouble by returning to the scene of the crime, you would be it, Agent Drake. So does the AGS sanction your interference in police business?"

She looked away from his far too knowing gaze. "What do you think?"

And at that he did smile, a full-blown, bowl-you-over smile with a set of white fulsome teeth that made her think of Crest commercials and his lips on hers. Damn him.

"You really are a piece of work, Ms. Drake."

"And I'd say it takes one to know one." That firm, full mouth just might be the answer to her afterburn problems.

A bad idea, but he just happened to be available and clearly interested.

"So." He straightened. "Did I hear a phone? Because there isn't anything on this stretch of concrete. I've checked."

She started down the concrete. Heck, what harm would it do if she dialed Simon's phone and let it ring? Detective Bryson couldn't— wouldn't blame her for that because it made absolutely no sense at all that Simon Lamrey's phone should be *in* a concrete wall. The thought of Gleason's anger almost made her smile.

She held up the cell for him to see, showed him as she hit speed dial for Simon's number.

The answering buzz came from down the row of empty stalls.

"Well I'll be...? I searched there." Detective Bryson jogged down the empty garage, Vallon not letting him lead. When they came to the space where Simon had been when the police arrived, they both stopped. Sure enough the buzzing came from the base of the wall. Vallon closed her eyes. Gleason was going to kill her for this.

Bryson dropped to his knees by the wall and placed his palm against it.

"I'll be damned. I can feel the vibration." He stood up to face her, his brown eyes searching. "How the hell would a phone get into a wall?"

"You're asking me? I just got here, remember?"

The buzzing kept it up and he finally grabbed her cell, studied the number and then snapped the phone shut. "Don't want to run that phone out of juice. Now wait here a moment."

He left her and strode down the concrete, trench coat fanning behind him until he disappeared down the stairs.

"What the hell are you doing, Drake?" She could imagine Gleason's epithets. Irresponsible. Juvenile. Loose cannon.

All the things she'd been dubbed during her stay in the Academy. Still, she should probably have let the phone be—at least until she could remove it herself. Of course then they'd probably say she planted it.

She considered taking her leave over the garage wall, but something held her in place and by then it was too late. Bryson came jogging back with a smile and an ancient screwdriver in his hands.

"Never know when you might need one, my father-in-law used to say."

"Used to…."

"He's dead now. A good man. Handy." He was down on his knees looking pretty darn handy himself as he used the heel of his hand to drive the screwdriver into the concrete and chip away a chunk. "Look! Just as I thought. It's close to the surface."

A smooth chrome surface curved away into the concrete. He grinned that big smile again and looked like a small boy who'd just found a secret treasure. "Looks like we got us a mystery."

His use of 'we' grated because he was the enemy who was trying to put her in jail and she didn't need a partner. Besides, look what it had led to for the last guy.

"I believe it's you who has the mystery, Detective. Clearly I didn't lie to you and so I believe I should be cleared of your suspicions."

The grin smoothed away with—was that a hint of regret? But he saved face with his nod. "Of course this makes things somewhat different, but there are still explanations required."

"Explanations."

"Like why you made that drawing; there wasn't a wall in it. And why the hell the phone's in the damned wall. Care to enlighten me how the phone could be there?"

The man was way too astute and way too willing to go to places she didn't want him to go, and suddenly all Gleason's misgivings were hers.

"Does it matter? You seem to be able to make the facts fit your theory no matter what I might say. Good day, Detective."

She turned on her heel and got three steps back towards the stairs when he stopped her, yanked her around.

The contact sent the afterburn popping like flashbulbs, blinding. Her boundaries flash-burned to ash and suddenly she was too close, too close, and all she could feel was his heat.

She looked up at him, focused on the intensity of his gaze. Licked her lips.

"What? You going to arrest me again, Detective Bryson? You'd enjoy that wouldn't you?" Her voice had gone husky.

He released her and fell back as if burned.

"What? You can't handle what you've created?" Pinpointed on him, she ran her hands down her bared throat and gloated at the way he backed away from her. "I was trying to leave you in peace, Detective. See what you've done? Made me hot."

It came out in a throaty snarl, a part of her knowing she was way too out of control this time, another part not caring. She grabbed his trench coat and leaned in, inhaled his cedar scent.

"Nice." Rubbed her cheek up his chest.

"Damn it, Drake, stop it."

He grabbed her shoulders, and that was about the worst thing he could have done—or the best, because suddenly the afterburn roared into full flame and she was against him, leaned up to him and his lips met hers.

Hot. Searing.

The shove sent her stumbling back, breathing hard from his lips and the pounding afterburn and trying to make sense of what she'd done.

Bryson was staring at her in shock. His hand at his lips. Then he turned and prowled away down the garage shaking his head, and she managed to exert a last shred of control.

She fled. Down the stairs and back to her car and sped out of the laneway so fast she almost sideswiped a black SUV parked at the corner. Then she was zooming down Denny, rain bouncing off the pavement, her windshield, and she turned towards Lake Union and Fremont and home.

"You're an idiot. A frigging oversexed idiot." She scrubbed at her lips, trying to rid herself of the warm sweet-coffee taste of them and the sense of passionate response she'd felt. It wasn't that she was really oversexed—it was the damned gift that set her libido on overdrive.

She needed to get laid. She should just go use the AGS's brothel service, but she didn't want her need to be noted by Gleason or anyone in authority. She was in control, but....

"The last thing you need is an affair with the cop investigating you." Turned onto the Fremont bridge and the car skidded a little. She straightened it out and drove through the traffic.

Maybe Gleason was right. Maybe she was a loose cannon because she'd sure enough screwed this one up big time. She aimed the car for an open parking spot at the curb and climbed out and ran through the rain for the house and safety and a place to sort things through.

Her hands were shaking as she fumbled the key into the front door lock and half-fell, soaked and frozen, into her living room. Slammed the door behind her. Silence and the ticking of the kitchen clock from the next room.

But something was different. The air—someone was there.

Chapter 8-The Scent Intrudes

The chill air off Elliott Bay seemed to run directly down Jason's neck as he watched Vallon Drake's sensual retreat. From the two times he'd met her, he figured retreat wasn't her usual *modus operandi,* so something had her well and truly spooked. He waited, watched the stair, and saw her come out and duck behind the bookstore, then leave in a spray of water and squealing tires. When she was gone he could breathe again.

Almost.

"Christ." His fingers scrubbed his lips again, but it didn't help against the heat she'd evoked. Sure, he'd been with women since Cheryl passed, but this was different because along with the desire had come the knowledge this was happening too fast, even though he *wanted* it to happen. Even though it felt like a train wreck. That was bad.

She was a murder suspect, for god's sake.

He shook his head and inhaled the air ripe with car exhaust and wet cedar, trying to dislodge the scent of her from his nose. The soft scent of roses and moist earth heated in the sun. It evoked a simpler time, his first job helping old Mrs. Liebowitz with her garden, his first love.

A shiver ran up his spine. She's a murder suspect, you idiot.

But maybe not. He dug in his pocket, hoping like hell he wasn't making a fool of himself, and called Blacklock.

"Hey, I found the phone."

No greeting. No joke. Blacklock would pick up in an instant that something was wrong.

There was silence and then. "So bring it in."

Jason had to laugh because if he didn't he'd think he was going a little crazy right now after what had happened. "I'm afraid that's a little impossible."

"What—you give it away or something?"

"Nope. But I need you to get a CSI team up here again with a jackhammer or something that can cut through concrete."

Silence again. "Where'd you find the phone, Slick?"

"I think you better come see for yourself. I'm at the scene."

When Blacklock assented, Jason hung up and turned back to the wall that held the phone. How the hell could a phone get in there except on the day the wall was poured? Answer: it couldn't.

Smooth concrete, except now that he looked at it, it wasn't that smooth. There were two distinctly different areas. One was the main wall that stretched floor to ceiling and the length of the garage. The other was right where the phone had been found. The former looked like it had been built in a single pour. But the smooth lines of the forms weren't present in the space by the phone.

He stepped closer and his sense of difference disappeared. He stepped back, and in the shadowed light of the rainy lunchtime a pattern formed on the wall.

He blinked and shook his head. It couldn't be, because it made no sense. He went back to the wall and knelt down to look at the smooth piece of plastic chrome in the concrete.

Unless recovering the phone was what brought the vic and the suspect here in the first place.

He paced the pavement until Blacklock and the CSI team arrived. Blacklock just shook his head at the bit of exposed plastic.

"How do you know it's a phone?"

"I heard it ringing."

Clint's shaggy brow rose above suspicious eyes. "And how might you have heard that?"

Jason sighed. "She came here—I guess after being at work."

"Your girlfriend?"

It stung, given what had happened and how he could still taste the sun-warmed—strawberries?—from her lips. "Not my girlfriend. But yes, Vallon Drake arrived."

Blacklock checked his watch. "Not a very long shift."

"Apparently." He motioned at the site where the body was found.

"So just how did you come across that little piece of evidence?" Blacklock must have picked up on Jason's discomfort. "Something you're not telling me, Slick?"

"Yeah, this." Jason grabbed his partner's arm and dragged him back from the wall hoping that Blacklock would miss all the tells that something else had happened. Christ, he felt like he had bright red lipstick on his face.

The incident with Vallon wasn't something that would be repeated; another loss to go along with all the big losses in his life. He swung Blacklock back toward the wall.

"Look at the wall and tell me what you see."

Clint gave him a strange look.

"Concrete?"

"Fine, but look at the concrete."

Blacklock rolled his eyes, but made a show of considering. A haze of dust and the whine of a concrete saw filled the garage and obscured some of what Jason thought he'd seen, but now that he'd recognized the pattern, he couldn't *not* see it.

"Sorry, slick. It's just concrete."

"Look there." Jason pointed. "Do you see any marks?"

Clint squinted through the dust. "So just what is it I'm s'pposed to be seeing, 'cause I'm afraid I'm seeing concrete and that's it."

Not the reaction Jason wanted. Maybe it was just his overactive imagination, but there was no help for it. He pointed out the features— the blurred marks that arched the top, the long straight lines that looked hurriedly smoothed away.

"Work with me here. It looks like a door, damn it. A door that someone's tried to hide."

Blacklock turned a doubtful look from Jason to the wall. "Okay. I see what you're talking about, but what does it matter that the owners filled in a door?"

"A door to where? That's what I want to know. Think about it. The phone's in the wall. We know Lamrey and Drake
work for Homeland Security. Maybe—maybe something bigger came down here."

"In an empty parking garage? You're kidding, right?"

"The owner of the garage is an off-shore holding company. Maybe there's something beyond that wall and the reason Lamrey was here was to recover the phone as evidence. Maybe Drake came after him to try to stop him. Or maybe Lamrey wasn't the good guy and Drake was trying to stop him from getting something."

"Yeah, right. Are you listening to yourself? Slick, those thriller books you read have eaten your mind."

"Come on, Clint, think about it. Aren't we paid to look at all the possibilities?"

"Yeah. To eliminate them."

"It would explain a lot and fit the facts pretty well."

"And it's fucking fiction."

"Damn it, you're starting to piss me off. Call it a working theory. That's all I'm asking. I'm trying to keep an open mind and examine all the potential theories."

Blacklock's bulk blocked the garage's meager lights as he confronted Jason. "You're pretty fired up about this. Why?"

"I just want to see us down the right track. Not waste our time pursuing false leads."

Blacklock looked him up and down. "I thought our first theory fit the facts pretty well, too, even if we haven't found the instrument she beat him with." Blacklock's gaze narrowed. "Wouldn't happen to have something to do with the fact that your theory places a certain Agent in a better light?"

"It has nothing to do with Vallon."

Blacklock's brows rose again. "It's Vallon, now, is it?"

Jason felt the flush before it reached his face and wasn't sure if it was embarrassment because it was true, or if it was anger at the fact that he'd let things slip and that Blacklock doubted him. He turned away.

"Great, partner. I do my job and try to look at all the possibilities and you accuse me of going after the girl."

"She's a suspect, Slick. No matter how she makes your heart go pitter-pat. And by the way, it'd be nice under different circumstances to see a woman really interest you again. But not a suspect." He grabbed Jason's shoulder, hauled him around. "You listening to me?"

"How could I not, you old bastard?"

"Ah good. Affection. So now that we got that straight, I can see what you're talking about with that wall. It's gonna take a heap of paperwork to get permission to open it up."

Jason caught the sideways look. Shook his head. "And I'm so much better at putting words on paper than you."

"You got that so right, Slick. But tell you what—I got a contact in Homeland Security. Why don't I give him a friendly call and ask what's up?" A beefy hand landed on Jason's shoulder again. "So let's blow this pop stand. All this dust is killing me."

Blacklock swiped at his eyes and Jason stopped. Something about the dust came swimming out of his subconscious like a huge solitary fish, but it dove back down to the nether regions of his mind before he could grasp it. It'd come to him in time. He knew it would, but whatever it was, it sent a tremor of ill-ease up his back.

"You got a problem, Slick?"

Jason caught the professional doubts in his partner's gaze before Blacklock hid it. So he didn't really believe, and didn't want to, even if Jason was determined to pursue this line of investigation.

It brought back a too-familiar sense of loss. Blacklock had been his partner since Jason became a detective. They'd built a bond of mutual trust and respect.

Losing it would be akin to losing Cheryl.

§

All the little hairs rose on Vallon's neck and the sick feeling in her stomach disappeared in a tight ball. A slight movement in the air that shouldn't be there. A taste to it that reminded her of cedar and incense and she knew she didn't have any of those in her house.

Just leave, a part of her screamed. Leave and call the cops.

But the cops weren't her friends right now.

She stepped further into the dimly lit room, the grey light outside placing a caul over the rich burgundy and blues of the furniture. The air shifted again and she turned her head toward the kitchen, and the door to the basement.

Oh, God, no. All her stuff was there. She -reached- and a blaze of Gifted presence came from the rear of the house.

"What the hell are you doing?" The fear morphed into fury and in two quick steps she was in the kitchen.

A sudden movement. A flash of power. A glimpse of black as someone shoved her kitchen table hard into her gut. The force sent her reeling back onto her butt, her head slammed against the wall.

She scrambled up, staggered, and tried to see through her daze. Whoever it was had disappeared through the open back door. She ran to it and peered into the back yard. Rain-soaked lawn. The rusting, children's swing-set the house's previous owners had left in place, the lone swing gliding in the breeze. The rain on the rhododendron leaves sounded like voices and she shivered, rubbed her head, and stepped back inside.

She grabbed the doorknob and released it in shock as a tingle ran up her arm.

She knew the feel. Gift. Whoever it was had done something to her door to get in, because she knew for sure she'd left it locked after Fi had left the door open.

She knelt to examine the lock. It looked the same, but when she tentatively touched it the tingle made her fingers numb.

Power. A lot of it, like a bit of the earth power she used for change, was still left in the door. And that wasn't a trick known by any Gifted she knew.

Gritting her teeth, she grabbed hold of the doorknob and held on, opened herself.

The remains of the power flooded through her and the taste of cedar and incense flooded her senses.

Powerful. No one she knew, that was certain.

The briefly seen figure had been tall and swathed in black. She closed her eyes and tried to visualize.

Definitely male. Lean. Black hair, shoulder length. Dark, ankle-length coat, damp from the rain, but drying from being in her house. The face—she hadn't seen, but she knew it was dangerous even though the guy had hidden it from her as he plunged out the back door.

She released the door and stood. The tingle was less now, would disappear in a few days, which was one of the reasons why she'd gone back to the scene of Simon's death—to see what she could sense of the maker of the parking garage. The power in her door had a totally different feel than the licorice darkness of the concrete, but it still held a powerful sense of danger. So who was he and what did he want?

She eased the door closed, listened for the click, and turned the lock. Checked that the door was secure. So whatever he'd done hadn't disabled the mechanism.

Aside from the table shoved across the room and the chairs that had fallen over in the process, everything looked pretty much the same. But that didn't mean the place hadn't been searched. What had he been after?

Then Maggie's trilling meow came from beyond the basement door and it all came clear.

"Dammit." She crossed the room, opened the door, ready for the tingle because she always kept this door locked, too. Maggie scooted out and began her dramatic parade of feed-me remonstrations.

"You're going to have to wait, girl." Vallon flicked the light on and plunged down the stairs into treacle-thick air, slowed as she reached the bottom.

Her private space was lit by a single, bare light bulb. This basement was the reason she'd bought the house.

Swathed in the earth, the old, bare-concrete foundation was actually cracked in places so it allowed in the sweet scent of wet soil. In places pale finger-joints of tree roots had shoved through the walls and widened the cracks. All of which would have made most prospective home owners run away.

More so with the rain. Today the back corner of the single room, near her sandbox, held a slight puddle of water, but across the center of the room at the base of the stairs a single, wider crack showed a silver runnel of moisture, and yet the room was warm.

She inhaled and closed her eyes and -reached-. The golden power that ran in the earth sat close to the surface here as if the power pressed up through the earth's lithosphere. Environmentalists spoke of geothermal power as the hope for future clean power. The use of the readily available heat in the earth could provide all the heat the world required—if people would only listen. The use of the other power, accessed by the Gift, could provide so much more if they were brave enough to use it.

But the AGS so far had been cautious, limiting the use of the power to what could be found closest to the earth's surface. So Vallon had bought this house and created this room for her own experiments; here, where beneath the scent of wet earth and mold came an aftertaste of ether and spice so rich it made her think of a fabulous Indian masala.

When she moved, the air friction was enough to make her think she'd spark and catch fire. No change to that. Sometimes the nearness even eased the afterburn, but not today.

Her hands shook as she crossed to the makeshift worktable and cupboards she'd built when she first moved in, and a sinking feeling took her stomach. This was what the intruder had come for. She was sure of it.

She'd left out her latest experiment with controlling her Gift. Along with learning to make her own ink and vellum, she'd been trying to hone her skills to draw more power to make very specific changes. The sheet of vellum she'd left drying had shown a sandcastle of delicate proportions that would be impossible to create in real life. Sky bridges and crenellated towers so fine there was no way sand would have the tensile strength to hold—without the power.

But the sheet of vellum wasn't there anymore. She turned back to the sandbox—her training ground. Only a heap of white sand, still vaguely showing the perimeter of the castle's base. She'd wanted to see how long she could hold something in place with just her will and her drawing. It had been a long time....

"Dammit." She swung back to her table.

Her things moved. Bic pens and ruled notebooks shuffled aside. He'd been searching.

She yanked open the first cupboard. Packets of verdigris and lapis, onyx and the yellow scales of butterfly wings. All painstakingly collected. All carefully preserved. Based on ancient recipes, they were meant to be suspended in the alcohol base that made up her inks. A quick scan showed the raw ingredients were there.

Opened the second cupboard and a cry escaped her. Gone, all gone. She sank down on the old wooden stool she kept for while she worked.

Her father's old journal—well not so much a journal as a formulary that had contained ink recipes and the clues that had led her to other things. It was nothing short of a miracle she had it at all, given that it being left for her to find was probably an oversight.

And now it was gone. Missing along with all her sheets of carefully prepared vellum and her special fountain pens.

She spun around and crossed the room to the small alcove with the half wall she'd filled with stretching and drying racks. Empty. All of the paper-fine ewe's belly leather she'd so carefully cured because it was necessary to the Gift, had been stolen away.

"Damn and damn and triple damn." She wanted to cry.

"Mew." Maggie stood at the top of the stairs, her querulous demand a reminder that there were other things in life besides the Gift and its equipment.

"I'll be there in a minute, sweet cheeks." She felt like all her insides had been scooped clean as an eggshell. It had taken her years to learn the trick of making the vellum and inks, and months to make the supply that she used—very judiciously—off the job, for the AGS had done worse than fire agents who took it upon themselves to use the power outside their employment. Rumors said they simply disappeared.

She scrubbed her face trying to understand just how much trouble she was in. If the man in black was working for Gleason, then the AGS knew and she'd pay the price. If she quit, Homeland Security couldn't have loose cannons with the ability to change things running around the country.

And if the intruder wasn't AGS?

She slumped down on the lowest stair and thought about what Landon had said and the implications. With her paper and pen case held by the police and her supply of vellum gone, she was almost defenseless except for a few scraps of vellum that might be around the house.

For some reason the Vellum was the only thing that worked when writing changes. Some Agents said it was a matter of not believing anything else would work and fulfilling that prophecy, others said it was only a matter of focus and ewe's belly worked better. Landon, who would probably know better than anyone because he studied this sort of weird arcane learning, said vellum probably worked because it was made from ewe's bellies and thus was more closely aligned with living things. All that mattered was that Vellum worked and regular pulp paper didn't.

If she ever had to face off against another Gifted, she was screwed.

Maggie scooted down the stairs, sat facing Vallon, and gave another peevish meow.

"I know girl. I'll feed you. But why didn't you stop whoever it was from getting in here and taking my stuff?" Another impatient meow and Vallon stroked the little black head that filled her palm so perfectly. Vallon absently used her Gift and the sandbox stirred, whispered smooth, the air tanging with a whiff of ozone. Maggie went over to sniff it, glanced over her shoulder and chirruped, so Vallon scooped her up, trudged up the stairs.

Her feet were like lead. The heavy air weighed on her, when usually it revived. All she wanted to do was curl up and sleep, but she knew better than to do that. She'd done that when her father had died. She'd felt this kind of abandonment then.

What had saved her was the academy and taking those first baby steps to learn her Gift. And that had brought her here. So what baby steps was she to take now?

She set Maggie down and went through the motions of feeding her. When she was done, she hauled the table back in place, then sank into one of the chairs. What the hell was going on?

Too much, apparently, and as usual all she saw was the evidence of the secrets, never their heart. Dad hadn't ever shared how he really felt. He was too busy with the AGS, and then he was gone. Or maybe he had shown his heart. Maybe he just didn't have a heart for Vallon.

At the Academy it had always seemed like the instructors whispered about her behind her back. Only Fi had been her friend. And after Fi abandoned her there were only the men.

She shook her head. The men were nothing, meant nothing. She had used them for release from the afterburn. She needed to find one now and then she needed to protect herself from whatever was happening because this was the most frightening case of afterburn of all. Too many things had happened, all at the time of Simon's death.

It couldn't be a coincidence.

She grabbed a tablet of paper out of a drawer, but found a small square of vellum she'd had to doodle on had been removed. That sent her stumbling out of the kitchen. She'd had bits and pieces of it around the house. Had the searcher found them all?

Upstairs to her office in the small back bedroom. Full bookshelves lined the walls, antique bindings looking tattered in the grey light from the lone window. A small desk stood under the window, drawers all closed. The office looked the same, but the scent of incense and cedar still lingered.

Two quick strides to the desk. Lifted the green blotter and swore. All the loose bits of vellum underneath were gone. Yanked open the bottom file drawer to where she'd kept her experimental drawings. Empty hanging file folders yawned up at her.

"Who are you, you bastard?"

She straightened and checked one last place. Her bedroom. Side-table drawer slightly ajar and she knew before she looked that her small supply was gone. She shivered and slumped, hugging herself, down on the edge of the bed.

Whoever it was had made sure she was defenseless. It would take weeks to tan and stretch and dry more vellum. That was if she could get organic ewe bellics to work with. And all the facts suggested whatever was coming down wasn't going to wait a month for her to re-supply.

The worst was that they'd stolen the safe feeling she'd always had in her house. Nothing was safe anymore.

The light through the sheer lace curtains left the yellow room filled with grey shadows, and the scent of the cedar and saffron was thicker here—as if the intruder had lingered awhile — and that just plain creeped her out.

She stood and went to the window, peered out into the rain-washed pavement and at the slicked rhododendron bush up the street. No figure there now, so why did she feel as if she were still being watched?

When she turned back to the bedroom, the glare through the window silhouetted her against the framed miniature landscape drawings above the bed.

"Oh!" The surge of recognition shot through her. She was up on the bed, taking the drawings down, carefully breaking the brown paper seal on the back of the frames to reverently remove the drawings. One she had done herself. The other two were the last things she had of her mother's, found among the belongings of her father.

Or at least she had convinced herself they were her mother's because they had been drawn with a different hand than her father's and tucked into the bottom of a box of Vallon's drawings her father had apparently taken to work.

All three were drawn on vellum.

The precious oily feel of the paper filled her with relief. "So you missed some, you bastard. You're not omnipotent and I'm not disarmed." Which helped a little.

She carefully folded the three small sheets of paper, changed from her damp sweater and into her favorite black t-shirt and jeans, then slid the paper into her pocket. Now she just needed a pen loaded with the right ink. She'd hate to harm the pictures, but if it meant her life, she would.

Feeling a little bit safer, she returned to the kitchen and her blank writing pad. She'd been a pawn in someone else's plans too much. Gleason's, for example.

Now she was going to take control.

Chapter 9-Subterfuge

The knock at the front door jerked Vallon back from her notes and the kitchen table. Her chair screeched on the linoleum floor. Any arrival couldn't be good, because nothing good had happened to her in the last two days.

She looked at her half-formed thoughts filling little balloons on the page. They'd flowed from her through the ticking afternoon. All the possible connections. Fi to the parking garage because her licorice taste lingered in the power. Simon's death and the deaths of the two other agents. The intruder, who clearly had a great deal of power, possibly linked to whoever had changed the garage.

The knock repeated itself and her gaze snapped to the gingham-curtained window. The day was fading. She'd been at her mind-mapping a long time.

A third knock.

"I'm coming! Hold on!"

She stopped just before the door and -reached-. Flame on the far side, but familiar and with the very faintest of scents—like a whiff of almonds—but otherwise almost as if his presence were masked. A part of her twisted with impatience as she yanked open the door.

Landon Snow stood there under the dripping porch-eaves looking vaguely like an unwelcome gnome swathed in his green Gore-tex jacket and sodden knitted skull cap.

"About darn well time. You can't hide, you know. I knew you were in there. Don't you know to keep your phone turned on?"

She must have accidentally turned it off at the garage. She lifted her chin. "Why would I? No one I know would call."

"Well Gleason tried."

"What? He still trying to fire me? Well he can't. I won't leave."

A large drop of rain splatted Landon's forehead and he stepped in closer, trying for the miniscule cover of the porch. "I heard that. Listen, can I come in? We need to talk."

She hesitated and didn't know why, except the afterburn was like pepper in her veins. But Landon so rarely left the AGS compound this had to be important. She let him step inside onto the small welcome mat that belied her feelings right now.

Landon pulled off his cap and unzipped his jacket and she, belatedly remembering her manners, took them and hung them on a coat rack by the door.

"Gleason sent you, didn't he?" She deduced because Landon had rarely come to her house since she'd been on her own, even though he'd been like a guardian when she was in the Academy.

She looked back at the little man in time to see him sniffing the air. When he saw her looking, he cocked one of his pale brows and she suddenly realized, though he might not have the Gift, he could smell the presence of power. A quiver of uncertainty ran through her, but she shoved it testily away.

"Well? What the hell's going on, Vallon? You left the Agency like a bat out of hell."

Typical. He was going to take Gleason's side, just as he'd tried to counsel her to go easy with the attitude around Gleason.

"With good reason! Gleason was going to tear me a new one again and I wasn't going to take it. Isn't it enough he put me on desk for a month? But then you knew that, so why are you here?"

She was determined not to let him farther into her house, because she wasn't going to let Gleason's emissary get the better of her — even if it were Landon. Besides, he might scope out what she'd been doing in the basement.

Landon sighed and ran his hands through his hair, leaving it in its typical disarming, cockscomb. "Okay, Gleason did ask me to come, but then I'd have come anyway—to to keep you from hurting yourself."

"You could tear yourself away from your work?"

"Yeah. Surprisingly, I could, Pigeon." He shook his head. "I've got a lot of use for you. Not just because you're your father's daughter. You've got a lot of chutzpa and talent besides. I don't want to see you self-destruct."

"Right." No one said those things unless they wanted something. "Talent enough to get myself in trouble by breaking the rules."

"Rules are meant to be challenged. You just have to know how to do it. What do you think I do in my work?"

"Play with fire and magic potions?" It was an old joke—a line that he'd given her when she asked what he did for a living. Now it hung between then as an almost unfriendly taunt.

He waved away her attitude and looked toward the kitchen. "Look, could we sit down and talk. I could use a cup of tea. It's damn cold out there. The forecasters are talking snow."

"And what do you think?" Grudgingly she led him into the kitchen, flipped on the lights, and sat him down across from where she'd been sitting. She saw his gaze flicker to her notes and rescued the pad, then slid it into a kitchen drawer before filling the kettle.

"Freezing rain, maybe, but no snow." Landon had always been amazingly good at weather predictions.

She set the kettle on the stove and turned back to him, arms crossed and feeling betrayed that he could act like her mentor one moment and then be Gleason's minion the next. "Okay. You're in my house. I'm making tea. Now what do you want?"

A look of forbearance settled like a weight on Landon's face and she realized he was probably a much older man than she'd thought. The bright light overhead placed lines like alluvial fans out from his eyes, and deep canyons ran from his nose to his outer lips and down under his chin.

"You nearly ran Gleason down today."

"That's why you're here? To reprimand me for that?"

"He was trying to stop you, Vallon."

"I sort of figured that."

"Well he wanted to talk to you. To work things out…."

And that had to be a lie. "Why? I said I'd work the desk—that's what he wanted. I'll take my punishment like a good little Agent. So what else is there to talk about?"

"Damn it, Vallon, would you listen a moment?" He stood up to face her, which was actually kind of funny given his stature. It was like having a miniature poodle growling at her and for a second she thought about slapping him down. The power to do it fizzled and frothed and popped inside her.

But then the kettle whistled and she turned away from him. "I'm listening." She busied herself readying the teapot.

"He knows you're a good Agent, Vallon."

Landon came up beside her, watched her movements as if inspecting them. She tensed. Turned to the table and then grabbed two cups from the cupboard. "You said that already. He doesn't show it."

"And you don't exactly show you're a team player." He sat down.

He waited until she'd settled across from him and poured the tea. He picked it up, sniffed.

"Mmm. Red Zinger. Always have had a weakness for rose hips." Landon, always good with his nose, and that was a problem because the basement door and all it hid loomed behind him. She hadn't even locked it.

She sipped her tea, but it couldn't thaw the core of fear that lived even inside the afterburn's heat. "So what? He's going to fire me regardless?"

Landon met her eyes. "He sent me to check on you. He had a message and wanted me to make sure you weren't going to do something stupid."

"So I do stupid things."

"Stop it. Would you stop looking for a fight long enough to listen to reason?"

His skin was even whiter in the glare of the kitchen light. His albinism had fascinated her as a child, and for some reason he'd been prepared to talk about it with her. It had led her to like Landon Snow, though you'd never know it given how she was acting.

She allowed a little of the stiffness to flow out of her neck, but the afterburn still gave her an edge.

"Alright." Sipped again.

Landon shook his head and muttered something incomprehensible, but that seemed to calm him. When he looked back at her the red hue of his eyes had receded into the palest pink-blue.

"Gleason knows you've got the gift. Lots of it. Heck, it was clearly there even when you were a kid. All the precise drawings you used to do. The way you could orient yourself to true north all the time, and find your way around the neighborhood like you had built-in GPS. Your Dad was terrified you'd wander too far too fast."

He stood up to wander the room, scratched Maggie's ears where she dozed under the window, but he paused in front of the basement door. Placed his palm against the wood, and even the afterburn couldn't stop the searing cold.

"Gleason's scared of the same thing as you, Vallon. But this incident at the garage—your efforts to rescue Agent Lamrey—have him rattled. First you say there's someone out there fighting AGS agents. Then you use unsanctioned power with non-AGS tools. He wonders if maybe this whole thing is a cover-up—propagated by you—to hide the fact you really murdered Agent Lamrey."

Fear and incredulity forced her to look away. "That's a lie and you know it. So I had my own pens and vellum. If it hadn't been for whoever created that garage, I'd have saved Simon and you'd all have been celebrating my foresight."

"That might be. But he wasn't saved. And you used unsanctioned power. Maybe it was you who created the garage as a lure. You were on desk."

Landon's familiar, gentle voice made every hair on her neck stand on end. Landon wasn't here as a friend at all. He was here as an Agent. She should have known it when she saw him sniff the air in the house.

She pushed herself to her feet. "How many, Landon? How many Agents are waiting outside?"

"Four." Another sip of the tea. "I thought I could probably do this without them, but you know Gleason. Has to have a backup plan for everything." He set the cup down. "It's like this, Vallon, and I don't like this anymore than you do. You're an Agent trained in the Gift. Inside the AGS we know what you're doing and can forgive a little recreational use of the power, but not like this. What you're doing is too much to be permitted outside AGS bounds."

"I thought you theorized that there are others using power we might not even be aware of?"

"Yes, but you we *are* aware of. Now you have two choices. Relinquish what you have in the house and we get back to business as usual, or else—well—I ask the four agents in." He shook his head. "I'm sorry, Vallon. I really am. I didn't want to have to do this, but I figured there was more chance of you listening to me. I didn't think you'd open the door for anyone else."

She held her hand up to stop him and went to the window trying to sort through her reaction. Through the betrayal. "So the rumors are true."

"Rumors?"

"That you're Gleason's pit bull. I never believed them anymore than I believed the recruitment line that once you were in AGS, you were in for life. I thought it was talking about job security." She turned back to him grabbing hold of the afterburn's searing heat to face down his threat. "So what happens if I choose the four agents?"

"They come in." His palm stroked the wood as it had Maggie, and sent a chill through her. "They take away everything of consequence from the house. Then they get rid of the house. And then Gleason decides what to do with you."

"I suppose quitting isn't an option," she said trying to keep up her bravado when the world seemed to be crashing around her.

Landon shook his head.

It was a drastic enough consequence that she knew whatever they did with her wouldn't be good. Wiped off the map as if she'd never existed. Like her home and the heritage-blue house had been wiped. And here she'd thought the AGS fought to stop changes like that. A little hysteria weaseled up through her gut. Frankly the whole situation was just too damned funny, given everything that had happened today. Her mentor and the one man she trusted doing this to her.

She sure as heck hadn't made the garage, so given what she'd experienced last night, Landon's theory was correct—there were others out there.

"So this is all about paper and pens, is it?" She started to chuckle as she turned back to her old mentor and friend, but managed to catch it. No reason to make him think her unstable. Nope, she wanted him on her side when she was back on the desk, because no matter what he or Gleason said, she wasn't going to walk around unarmed; and the AGS was the best place she could think of to get the pen and ink she needed.

"Of course I'll relinquish what I've got." She stood and went to the basement door. "There isn't much."

§

Xavier watched from the far side of the street as the four men surrounded Vallon Drake's house. They waited as the little man—the dangerous one—went inside. Down the street another man—unGifted— observed the house. If she'd called them, if she told them, Creation, *when* she told them he'd been there, the search would be on.

Not what he wanted. Not what he wanted at all, for secrecy and the ability to be unnoticed were what had kept him safe through all that had come before.

The infernal rain pat-pat-patted his head and the shoulders of his leather trench, and he impatiently brushed away the droplets that ran into his eyes. He reached into the blessed earth for warmth against the near-freezing weather and yearned for the sunshine of his homeland.

A stirring behind the front curtains of the house brought his attention back and he readied himself to leave should they come for him.

The damned fools thought they knew everything when they knew nothing. They groped around like blind men in brilliant sunlight, but he could see. He could see everything, and the pattern sent anger rippling through him.

His coat still smelled of the woman's ashes-of-roses even though he'd dumped her vellum and inks in the back of his SUV. Her house had been warm, but too filled with her scent and the vibrations that came with her secret use of power.

Secret no longer, judging by the four men. If they took her, then regrettably it was over—at least as far as she was concerned.

And if they didn't?

He curled his fingers into a fist and grabbed more earth power against the cold that dwelt within.

If they didn't he would do what he had always done. Deal with the threat.

And perhaps more.

Chapter 10-A Shoal of Flame

Vallon stood in the doorway to watch Landon walk down to the waiting van, lugging the bag filled with her ink supplies and the old tomes from her office. She hid her fury by lifting her hand to him as the driver pulled away from the curb. Hugged herself against the cold that was more than the cold air, and that placed a thin coat of brittle ice on the bushes next to the front door.

She would make this work. She would.

At least they hadn't searched her person, and Landon had barely even seemed to notice the air thick with power in the basement. Perhaps his sensing of it was limited to sensing the Gift's use of power. That was something to remember.

She listened to the sound of the rain on the leaves and the hissing, rush hour traffic from downhill. In the half-light of falling dusk came the heavy scent of lake water, and from a distance the grinding sound of the locks that kept Puget Sound out of the string of lakes that filled Seattle's heart. For a moment she wished she were on one of the boats sequestered in Lake Union. The water would muffle the Gift and she would set sail and head out to the sound and beyond. Maybe go to Canada and beyond the reach of the AGS.

She hoped.

But that was silly. The AGS filled a necessary role; otherwise the rampant changes would cause immeasurable damage to the very fabric of society. It was those sorts of changes that had led to the economic crash of the Great Depression, though history books remembered it differently. But rampant change cut at the very core of things. Change the land and you change the people on that land. Change the people and you change what those people do, what influence they have on society. Change too much of that and there is nothing left but a hollow shell of what had been before. And chaos. They had watched the grand experiment of the USSR

What had happened there could happen here, if the AGS didn't keep a watchful eye.

Like she was being watched? Were there watchers on the watchers?

When she -reached- she knew her Gifted intruder was just down the hill. She stepped inside and quickly shut the door, fighting back the impulse to just march out and confront him. He'd just disappear like before.

Call the cops?

Like that would help.

She went back to the kitchen and pulled out her pad. She'd underlined the connection between Fi and the garage so many times she'd actually worn through the paper in spots. That was where to start. A safe place because Fi had come to her, had tried to warn her about something.

Once she'd learned what Fi knew, then she could circle around the bastard who watched her and come at him from a direction he wouldn't expect—sort of like triangulating a peak from surrounding mountain tops.

She grabbed another jacket—three-quarter length leather — and headed out to her car, purposely ignoring the flare of Gifted that came from the powerful, foreign-built, black SUV parked three cars down from her Subaru. Not AGS, that was for sure, even though the darkened windows of the vehicle masked the presence of her watcher. His unfriendly gaze set the afterburn flaring like sunspots.

She slid behind the wheel. Fi was obviously on the street, so where would she be in this weather? Huddled in an alley somewhere? At one of the shelters? It was doubtful she'd be in Fremont; the area had become too upscale trendy to tolerate many homeless.

Downtown then.

She started the car and headed south towards the towers and Pikes Place Market. Panhandlers frequented the area because of the tourists, even though the City policed it rigorously. The area around Pioneer Square was another possibility. So was the older part of town around Seattle Center and the space needle.

Too many areas to search visually.

She pulled into the curb and watched in her rearview mirror as the big black SUV came up behind her and passed, the driver still invisible. Awareness of his flame seared through her even though she was afraid to -reach-. In the flow of traffic and with the one-way streets, he'd be forced to go a fair distance before doubling back, so she could lose him if she took off quickly.

She watched him turn down the street two blocks away and tucked her Subaru back into traffic. Passed the street and turned away from the direction he'd gone. Turned again and she was heading back the way she'd come, so surely he wouldn't find her.

Zoomed down Broad Street toward the water.

"Take that, Mr. Watchman." Thumped her palm on the steering wheel and turned south again on Alaskan Way by Pier 66 and under the overpass by the glass-fronted World Trade Center.

She dipped her car into one of the few spaces where you could see the open water of Elliott Bay and its huddled masses of container ships. The wind whipped over the promenade that led down towards the numerous tourist shops and restaurants along the water. She had to find Fi, and the only way she was going to do that was to search in her own way. She -reached- struggling through the blockage caused by the nearness of the water—and and the city became a constellation of gleaming beings, flame varying in color from barely a glimmer to the vibrant golden flashes that were the sign of the most Gifted—not that most of them knew that they were.

The flames drifted and flowed like foam on the sea of lesser flame that was the whole of humanity. Strange. She'd never noticed before how the Gifted seemed to form shoals in certain parts of the city. Yes, there was the presence of the AGS like a lighthouse in the fog and yes she could feel the presence of the Academy in its rolling treed setting east of Redmond, but even here in the city there was a shoal of flames around Pioneer Square, another around the Space Needle and the Music Experience museum, and still another located near Pike's Place Market. Even more strange, for those places catered to the more bohemian of Seattle. The artists and lost hippies—and street people.

But it was Fi she needed to find. She sifted through the sensations that accompanied each small flame and focusing on the smooth mint and licorice feel of her friend. There. Brick.

Vallon took a chance and dove into the earth doing something she had only dared once before from the safety of her basement—followed the bright capillaries of power towards her friend's presence. Leapt free of the golden flow and saw through a haze like pitted glass:

Victorian brick.

Arches of glass.

An antique streetcar dinging past.

Cobbled streets and iron benches.

She knew that location. A deep breath and she pulled back and became aware she was still in her car. A black SUV slowed and stopped beside her car, blocking her driver side door.

"Dammit!" Anger cut through her. While she'd played around he'd probably used exactly the same method to find her and now he was here.

She had two choices. Abandon her car or ram her way through and destroy both vehicles' quarter panels. She didn't even know if her car *could* ram its way past the much larger SUV. Well, perhaps three choices. She could act totally unaware of him and simply politely ask him to give her space.

The afterburn part of her voted for the ram, but at least this time she was going to think about consequences. If she were going to stay under everyone's radar while she did her investigation, she had to play it cool.

She beeped her horn lightly and eased the Subaru's nose up the side of the SUV.

It didn't move, and neither did the figure she could dimly make out through the tinted glass. That was possibly more chilling than if he had gotten out. What was the point unless he was trying to creep her out?

A warning?

Then the SUV's side window slowly scrolled down and she got her first good look at her pursuer.

Dark hair as she'd thought, roughly cut chin length so it hung lank in eyes so black she swore they were pinpricks in space. Sharp featured like a hawk, and high, raked cheekbones. A solid, square jaw. A full mouth that, if she wasn't so freaked, she might have thought kissable.

He made her think of North Africans, flowing robes and turbans. Who was that actor in Lawrence of Arabia?

Homeland Security would be *very* interested in this guy.

His hard mouth curved slightly as the force of his gaze slammed into her. Power, so much power that even through the window she caught the feel of him—cedar and incense and desert heat. So much heat the afterburn flared up and torched her skin.

Burned brighter when he lifted a finger, hooked it at her in a clear demand that she approach, and the afterburn-induced terror burned through her because she almost obeyed. Wanted the power he had. Wanted to know and knew if she went, everything would change. And when had any change she sought ever resulted in something good?

She scrambled across the Subaru's central console and half-fell out the passenger-side door. Terror sent her scrambling down the sidewalk, looking over her shoulder.

The dark SUV followed and where could she go? She slammed into the glass doors of the blue Bell Street Cruise Ship terminal and pressed into the fortunate crowd of tourists flooding back after their tours from the docked Norwegian ship.

When she'd lost herself in the crowd she turned back to study the door. -Reached-. Not near. Not here. Her heart pounded like a piston. What did he want of her? Why was he doing this? Her knees shook so badly she needed to sit down, but in this crowded hall of seniors, there were no empty seats.

She grabbed hold of a twist of radiant earth power and let it pour into her. The afterburn flared, seared like an electric shock, and her mouth tasted like ash, but there was nothing she could do about it now—short of taking one of the senior men into the bathroom and giving him the ride of his life.

Wobbling, she made her way back to the door and peered into the street. Why had he done that? What did he want? Judging by his haunted looks, nothing good, that was clear.

Could he be one of those terrorists Homeland Security so feared?

There was no black SUV in sight—at least not that she could see through the glare of headlights on rain-slicked streets in the leaden early evening. Girding herself, she stepped out into the salt-laden wind and headed back to her car. Night was coming. She didn't want to meet him after dark unless she was ready, and that would require ink, pens and vellum she didn't have.

At her car she shakily keyed herself in and then headed down to Pioneer Square.

The city changed from skyscrapers of glass and steel to four and five-story brick buildings that dated back to the birth of the 20th century.

Neon signs advertising ice cream, salt-water taffy, designer clothing, and antiques all bled into the twilight. She found a place to park and climbed out near the heritage building that housed Elliot Bay Books. The rain was falling harder; hard little pellets of sleet that pelted her head and made her hunch into her jacket.

She -reached- for Fi and felt her presence to her left, and followed along uphill from the water into a poorer area. More closed workshops. A few boarded up buildings, grass edging their foundations. No tourists. Just a few dark figures hunched as she was in the assault of salt-stained rain that now sheeted through the streetlights.

When she found herself facing a rain-stained red door in one of the boarded up buildings, she stopped. Fi was somewhere beyond, her licorice scent almost palpable on the air. Vallon hesitated, but she really had no choice. She rapped on the door.

Nothing, and then the rustle of movement. Her skin crawled with the sensation most people described as someone walking over their grave, but which she knew meant the presence of power. But the sound could be rats for all she knew. She huddled deeper into her leather jacket trying to find shelter in the lee of the building.

Then the door opened a crack and a miasma of pot smoke and a slice of ruddy light spilled out and sent her skin tingling. A single, dilated blue eye looked out at her.

"Yes?" The voice and the half a face she could see belonged to a young man with dirty-brown dreadlocks. He eyed her up and down, clearly assessing her clothing and that she wasn't 'from around here'.

Vallon shifted from foot to foot against the cold. Some of the raindrops were coming down white on her jacket. "I'm looking for Fiona—Fi—Murdoch."

"Sorry. No one here by that name."

Dreadlock started to push the door closed, but Vallon stopped him with an arm through the door. Caught his hand and felt the familiar flash of like to like. Gifted. It shouldn't surprise her.

"She is here. She's a friend of mine and came to see me last night, but we didn't get a chance to finish our conversation. I need to find her."

Dreadlock repeated his visual assessment. "You a cop?"

Vallon grinned. "Nope. I got my own beef with them."

Still the door didn't move.

"Listen, either call Fi out to talk to me, or let me in. It's friggin' freezing out here. You know?"

His blue gaze disappeared for a minute like a survey sighting removed, but he didn't try to close the door. Then he stepped back and allowed her step past him, and shut the door behind her.

Cobweb-thick air closed in on her, brimstone-scented; far too similar to the basement of her house. She stopped. A single room, low ceiling lost in coils of smoke, but otherwise filled with a strange golden light. Candles at the edge of the room lit peeling, faded-blue paint on the walls, and on the floor old, occupied carpets and pillows and mattresses.

Flophouse, she categorized. The people here stoned out of their minds judging by the way they all were 'on the nod'.

But not the usual flophouse, what with dreadlock guarding the door. The faces of Gifted—including Fi—looked resentfully up at her from their places like spokes of a wheel around *something*.

Curious, she stepped forward.

Normal logic said it was a simply a rift in the floor filled with shining water, but the intense glow told her it was something more. Heat radiated from it. The flowing substance not gold, not silver, but filled with the streaming of all colors and none, and releasing not brimstone—

though that was the way her mind had interpreted it at first—but perfumes of rose and anise and coriander and clove.

She realized she was on her knees beside it. Had pushed her way through the gifted already there, reached and -reached- out to touch….

"Don't!" One of the reclining street people knocked her hand away. "You'll wreck it."

She pulled her hand back. The speaker was a young Native man clad in a thread-thin grey t-shirt and muddy jeans. Matted black hair was pulled back from his face with a leather thong and decorated with a feather.

"And how would I do that?"

But his black eyes had already returned to the shining pool of what could only be the power she used so carefully.

"Can't take a chance…." His words faded away into a sigh.

Vallon followed his gaze and -reached-. More power than she'd ever allowed herself to contact rammed into her like a sledgehammer direct to her brain. Afterburn roared and she collapsed onto her stomach, managed to claw her way forward, forward, for this was the thing she'd sought all her life. Warmth and welcome and being one with something greater than herself. She rubbed herself against the worn carpet, rubbed her thighs together.

Family and love and fucking forever.

The great golden pool opened perfumed arms. She could throw herself into its sweet embrace and be held safe and warm forever. Never have to care. Never have to worry. All the struggles to find belonging and it was always here. Always in the basement of her house and more than any person could provide. She could lose herself, become something else. Something more.

The afterburn urged her forward until she hung over the edge of the pool. Herself slipping away. Something else filling her.

Heat rippled through her and she reached for the Native youth, pulled him into her breast, wrapped a denim-clad leg around him and ground herself in. Inhaled his musky, unwashed body odor and wet hair and spruce as his mouth found her neck.

One with someone else. Afterburn demanded it. The only way to regain her equilibrium. The only way to be whole.

But Vallon Drake doesn't need anyone.

Like a bolt, that thought cut through her lust and her need to give in to the afterburn's demand. Incense filled her nose.

She shoved the youth away and fought her eyes closed. Then she lurched back, reared up on her knees and tore her gaze from the thing she wanted most in the world to see. Like tearing her heart out.

But the room shimmered and moved. Smoke coiled like snakes. Licorice. The heady perfume was lost. Licorice so potent it clogged her throat and cloyed her nose.

The shimmer increased, gathering the smoke in a twisting wind that guttered the candles and sucked at their flames. Sparks ran in veins across the painted walls and Vallon staggered up, all the room's narcotic effects suddenly burned away, though the afterburn pulsed like a great beast low down in her body.

The glittering skein of lines in the walls increased.

Change. Someone was changing this place, and given the too-familiar licorice scent it had to be whoever had killed Simon. If this building changed, it could do the same to her and all these Gifted.

"Get up! You have to get up!" She grabbed the native kid and heaved him to his knees. He fought her, tried to pull her back down.

She slammed a fist into his gut and he collapsed. She whirled, seeking dreadlock who was seated with his back to the door, his eyes still glazed with the power. She grabbed him and hauled him up. Pointed to the walls.

"Look. Something's happening. We have to get out of here. Get the others out."

He shrugged her off, blinking at the growing eddy in the air, the shimmer in the walls that now cast chips of paint and moldering drywall loose. They joined a small maelstrom near the roof that steadily increased in size and power. The candles wavered.

"This whole place is going to change in a minute. If we don't get these people out, they could all be killed."

He looked at her blankly. "What are you talking about, man?"

He was Gifted, but only enough to see on his own and not trained enough to -reach-.

"Shit." She grabbed the door, yanked it open and shoved him out. Turned back to the room and one of the candles fell over in the wind. The flame caught the edge of one of the carpets and flared in the old wool. New smoke, new light, filled the room and still the young people around the rift didn't move.

"Come on! The place is on fire! You have to get out!" Fi. She had to get Fi out.

They barely stirred. She grabbed the native youth again and yanked him away from the rift in the floor, careful not to look at it herself.

Across the room the flames in the one carpet had spread to two more. They licked at the young people's feet. Fi's feet.

Vallon leapt across the glimmering surface and grabbed Fi, hauled her up, though the girl struggled against it.

"No! No! I have to stay. We have to stay home." Empty eyes. A sharp fist caught Vallon on the temple and put stars in her eyes, but she didn't let go.

"Dammit, Fi. Listen to me. The place is burning down and there's change coming."

Fi's gaze locked on Vallon's face and suddenly awareness flooded in. "Vallon?"

"The one and only, now give me a hand and don't look at that thing in the center of the room."

Fi's gaze flickered to the pool and away to the flames, to the cloud gathering overhead. "What's going on?"

"We don't have time. Grab one of the others and get out. I'll get everyone else."

The smoke from the fire burned Vallon's eyes. She shoved Fi toward the door and the woman slowly picked her way across the room. Grabbed someone and fought their protests, as Vallon did the same. Billowing smoke made it almost impossible to see and sent Vallon coughing.

She got the women closest to the fire moving, but others—the men—were too big. They refused to budge from the glimmering power. The walls shredded further. A fist to her face sent her reeling back. She came down hard against an upright and sank—right into the wall.

Chapter 11-Where There's Smoke

Wolf Amundson, Homeland Security Seattle Station Chief, took the call at 18:20 hours. He knew it because he checked his watch when the cell phone's buzz cut through the clink of crystal and silverware in the *Le Gourmand*. Not exactly très chic, and if there were one thing Wolf disliked it was someone disturbing his appointment with an expensive meal—especially a meal he wasn't paying for.

Too much rode on it.

"Amundson," he growled into the cell phone and glanced an apology at Ray Fitzsimmons who was just tasting his foie gras stuffed homemade pork sausage with demi-glace and compote of winter fruits. The Washington-based Security Czar waved a bird-boned hand 'no matter' and leaned back to sip his lemon water. The long nose, the oddly sloped brow of the man reminded Amundson of one of those flying dinosaurs his daughter's third-grade class seemed to love. Pterodactyl or something.

"Long time no talk to, friend."

The voice at the end of the phone was one Wolf hadn't heard in a while, though he remembered it well. "Clint, old friend. May I call you back? I am in the middle of something important."

He grimaced at the way his speech still carried the too-proper hint of his Danish roots even after all these years growing up in America. He grinned at his boss, whose pasty skin finally had a lifelike color in the muted restaurant lighting.

A pause and then: "Sure. You can call me, but let me tell you what this is about."

Wolf sighed. Clint Blacklock was a good cop and had been a good friend way back in 'the day', but his garrulous nature was not what Wolf needed right now. The escargot were getting cold, damn it. He eased his broad back in the too-small chair.

"Sure. But keep it quick." Wolf followed Fitzsimmons' lead and took a sip of water from the fragile restaurant goblet, though he'd have preferred it be wine. But that was one of Fitzsimmons' quirks: even managers don't drink on the job—at least not in Fitzsimmons' presence. Not if you wanted any hope of promotion, and Wolf did. Too bad, because this restaurant had an amazing wine cellar and could have provided a wonderful accompaniment to the oolong-smoked steelhead sauced with pumpkin and juniper berries that he'd ordered.

"Sure thing, bro. We got a murder a couple of days back. Took place at a parking garage off Broadway and the suspect and vic are employees of an agency in your fold. Before I push any harder on this case, I wanted to know if I'm going to be stepping into a mess of Homeland Security shit. So you have any action going on that might explain the murder of an AGS Agent?"

The water almost choked Wolf. His barrel chest spasmed. "Come again," he asked when the coughing passed. "An AGS Agent murdered?" he repeated softly, aware of the low ambient restaurant noise.

That brought Fitzsimmons upright, the heavy-lidded eyes actually gleaming under the long, sloped brow.

"Yeah. Two nights ago. Found the body in a parking garage with another Agent over him, but my partner's on this thing about maybe there's a walled up stairwell in the garage and maybe it's related to a Homeland Security case. We didn't want to step on your toes, bro."

"Interesting." Wolf made sure not to put too much interest in his voice, but every part of him was at attention. He shoved his fingers through his white-blonde hair. "Tell you what. Let me check and get back to you on this, all right? I'll call you back tomorrow?"

"Sounds good. Call me or my partner, Detective Jason Bryson. And Wolf—we really should get together for dinner one of these days. Say Mexican? I could use a feed."

Wolf's nostrils curled at the thought of the dive Clint's budget would probably limit them to. Their ways had truly diverged over time. "Sounds good. Later, amigo."

Satisfied he'd almost sounded casual at the end, he flipped the phone shut and placed it carefully on the white linen table cloth before meeting Fitzsimmons' hazy-brown gaze. "That was interesting."

"I heard. The AGS. A murdered Agent." The predatory gleam was even brighter. "Do tell."

"It begins."

§

Things had changed a lot since Jason worked patrol in this part of West Precinct.

Jason hitched his trusty trench coat collar up against the pissing down rain and wondered for the umpteenth time what the hell he was doing standing at the edge of the Pioneer district running surveillance on Vallon Drake when no one had asked him to do it.

The dump in the economy had definitely had an impact here. In the square too many of the trendy shops had *For Lease* signs in their empty windows. And here, uphill, the signs of decay were starting to set in. The boarded up windows lined the empty street like so many shuttered eyes.

Pavement gleamed in the amber streetlights that still stood at each corner. The others had been smashed—picked off by stones, he supposed. And he stood in the desolate darkness and old grass and garbage of the alley that bisected the street.

All to watch a woman when he could be warm in his apartment— or at least in the car he'd left parked just back from hers on First Avenue.

Blacklock would shit himself laughing. Right before he referred Jason to the Department shrink.

But the surveillance of Vallon Drake had been illuminating to say the least. Something was clearly going on.

He'd suspected it when he saw the men go into her house. He'd suspected it more when she pulled the quick switch-back near Lake Union and he'd nearly lost her. His suspicions had been confirmed when the big black SUV blocked her car on Alaska Way and she'd bolted down the sidewalk like all the demons in hell were on her tail. He'd been tempted to intervene, but the SUV had left; and when he called in the license number the SUV turned out to be a high-end rental unit. A call to the rental company showed it had been rented to a multinational company out of Portugal and Venice and with a driver listed as Xavier de Varga. Told him nothing.

But Vallon Drake had returned to continue on her way—to here.

The place wasn't exactly what he suspected Vallon Drake was into. He'd called in the address of the empty warehouse and had got back from patrol that it was a known flophouse.

Drugs? Was that what this was all about?

Vallon Drake had walked right up to it like she knew what it was. She'd been allowed entry, but since she'd gone in something niggled at his brain.

Something wasn't right.

It wasn't that she'd been gone too long—only a few minutes by his watch. But his Spidey senses were all a-twitter and he could swear the air carried the scent of ether and electricity like before a storm.

A low rumble like thunder echoed down the street and the streetlights flickered and faded. The earth lurched. Lurched again and the brick wall next to him groaned.

Quake. Small one, but the air was still heavy with that metal scent.

The flophouse's front door flew open and a dreadlocked youth half-fell into the street. Jason thought he caught a glimpse of Vallon and then there was only a strange pulsing light. A second kid—Native this time—staggered out coughing. Thick grey smoke poured out the door, but then eddied, started to suck back into the room like a smoker inhaling. Plainly not right.

All the little hairs on Jason's neck stood on end. The two youths grabbed each other and staggered off down the street. Where was Vallon?

He left the shelter of the alley, and wind off the water slammed into him, driving rain down his neck. Hunched, he strode across the street in time to meet two young women one half-carrying the other. He grabbed them, shoved them against the wall.

"What's happening?"

"Fire," the blonde-haired one croaked, still holding up her friend. A cough wracked through her.

"Jesus." He used his cell to call it in as he entered the building. Old wood beams half hidden in the smoke, and the smell of electrical wiring up in flame. The rear of the room was ripe with fire leaping floor-to-ceiling and eating towards something brilliant on the floor where the kids were laid out as if sleeping. Stoned. On the nod.

Across the room, something caught his eye. One person, Vallon, struggling, but the smoke made everything surreal like she was half-in the wall and fighting to stand.

He grabbed the nearest kid and half-tossed him towards the door. Grabbed another and blocked a punch, then shoved the youth towards the door as well. Smoke thickened the air and a paroxysm of coughing almost sent him to his knees.

More kids still lay on the floor moving sluggishly like half-dead animals. He grabbed another and started dragging when the kid didn't move.

Jason left him by the door and went back for another. He found Vallon struggling with a kid too big for her strength. "Grab the legs."

He grabbed the arms and the two of them fought the comatose figure out the door. They returned for one more and the wind in the room sent hot sparks against his skin. More than singes. A strong sensation his innards were being turned inside out made him almost stagger.

"Get out of here." He shoved Vallon towards the door.

"No way." She looked into the smoke and the sparks overhead as if studying something. "You get out. Now. Or...."

She went stiff and closed her eyes.

"Vallon."

She waved him to silence. "Just get the last one and get out." She stayed where she was.

Jason grabbed the last kid—big, blonde, and unconscious, lugged him up into a fireman's carry and headed for the door just as beams at the rear of the room came crashing down.

"Vallon!"

She didn't move.

He half threw the kid through the doorway. Someone outside dragged him free and Jason dove back into the smoke and ash and falling debris, found Vallon where he'd left her swathed in smoke.

When he touched her she started to collapse. He caught her and dragged her towards the door.

"No! I have to know!" She kicked and clawed at him, but he wasn't having any. He dragged her outside into the red-tinged rain as the fire trucks arrived. None of the kids were still there except for the blonde girl huddled by the wall.

He released Vallon and she rounded on him, slammed a fist toward him that he easily stopped. "Damn you, Bryson, I was trying to stop this."

The rain ran down her angular face and plastered her singed hair to her head and still she was probably one of the most attractive women he'd met in a long time. In her three-quarter leather coat she was sleek as a seal.

"Sure. Like standing in the middle of a fire is going to do anything."

Her fierce gaze said she was going to say something and then thought better of it. His skin tingled as she turned back to the brick-faced building with the yellow door and the blue awning that read 'TOUCH OF BLUE CLOTHING'.

"Looks like a false alarm, Detective." The fire station commander came up to him. "What made you call it in?"

For a moment Jason couldn't recall, but then it came back to him: "I saw something flickering in the shop window. Ms. Drake here, set me straight, but the damage was already done. Sorry about that."

"No harm done. Better safe than sorry."

The commander joined his men in a final inspection of the store and then the huge red behemoth flicked off its lights and lurched into the night.

"So, you want to tell me what you're doing here?" Vallon faced him, anger on her face.

He allowed himself a smile. "Seems we're asking that of each other a lot these days."

"You followed me."

He shrugged. "It's the job. So what were you doing?"

"Window shopping," she snapped.

The way the light lit the anger in her face just made him want to touch her. Maybe he'd wipe away that dark smear on her cheek. Instead he stuck his hands in his pockets.

"You've got something on your face." He motioned to her cheek.

"Too damn bad."

Then she stiffened, nostril's flaring and peered into the shadows. "Cedar," she breathed. "Dammit."

But her voice held a tremor he hadn't heard since the night Agent Lamrey died. She turned back, caught sight of the girl against the wall.

"Fi. Thank god." She tossed a resentful look back at Jason. "Come on, let's get you home."

The blonde woman's eyes flickered open revealing pupils too dilated. When Vallon tried to lead her away, Fi staggered and almost went down.

"Stoned much? What's she on, Vallon? Who is she to you?"

Vallon got her shoulder under Fi's arm and started down the street, but Fi's legs sagged again and almost brought them both down.

"Here, let me help you."

Jason grabbed Fi's other arm, half lifted her to her feet and met Vallon's resentment. Even the rain couldn't wear away her stubbornness.

"You aren't going to be able to manage her like this and you need to get her out of this weather."

He didn't wait for Vallon to give in, but started half-carrying Fi down the way Vallon had headed. "So where're we going?"

"None of your business."

He allowed her silence as he half-carried, half-dragged them down into the Pioneer District. Fi's meager strength finally gave out and she slipped in Vallon's grasp. Jason shouldered her out of the way and scooped the destitute-looking girl up, then headed back toward Elliott Bay Books and their cars. When he started past her sporty Subaru, she grabbed his arm.

"Where the hell do you think you're going?"

"My car. It can hold the three of us comfortably."

She glanced at the unmarked car down the block. The rain had thinned the crowds and the vehicle stood out, blocky and alone.

"If you think I'm climbing in the back of a police car, you've got another think coming."

She was so defiant he thought about calling her bluff and seeing what she'd do about it. Instead he grinned. "What? You got a guilty conscience?"

"I can take her in my car. She needs a bed and to get dried off."

"Dried out, more like. What is she? A relative? Or is this your good deed for the day?"

"Would you just shut up and give me a hand getting her into my car." She glared at him and finally he nodded so she unlocked her car and they settled Fi in the front seat. When they were done she slammed the door closed, faced him like she hated having to do it. "Thank you for your assistance, Detective. I appreciate it."

Cold, formal, and a clear kiss off. Like that would work on him.

"Service. Pride. Dedication. That's our motto." He grinned through her disdain and wondered why he liked to goad her. "I'll follow you."

She jerked up from unlocking the driver side door. "I can take it from here, thanks."

"And if you can't find a parking spot on that street of yours? How are you going to get her home?"

He could see the thoughts racing across her face. Yes, he'd been watching her house. Resentment. Concern. And an instant fear. That was what interested him, because what would a law-abiding citizen fear a police officer might see?

But she finally nodded and slid behind the wheel, turning out from the curb before he even reached the PC. He climbed in and chuckled as he watched her taillights disappear down the road.

She knew she couldn't lose him, but trust Vallon Drake to make a point of not making it easy.

He drove through town and along Lake Union with the city and houseboat reflections fragmented by the black, choppy water. Sleet glowed white in his headlights and slicked the road. If this kept up, in a few hours the Fremont hillsides would be skating rinks.

He crossed the bridge and caught a glimpse uphill of taillights turning in toward her house and gunned the engine to catch up. He slid the car into a spot a block from her house and jogged up to where her car's interior light flashed on.

Vallon was leaned over her friend showing a neat derriere in form-fitting jeans.

"Here. Let me give you a hand," he said.

"I told you, I don't need your help. You've already done enough, thank you very much."

Blacklock would call him a fool, but he did what seemed right at that moment. He grabbed her arm and pulled her out of the car, turned her to face him, even though she resisted.

She glared up at him. "I could charge you with unnecessary use of force."

"And I could charge you with a lot of things, but I'm trying to help, Vallon."

She jerked at his use of her first name. It was a tactical decision, wasn't it? He was just trying to keep her off balance and see what he could learn about what had taken her out tonight and what had her dragging this piece of Seattle's underbelly home. Vallon Drake didn't strike as a do-gooder.

Her sigh, when it came, seemed to come right from her soul. She was lonely, this woman. It was in her eyes and was something he could understand.

"Fine, then. Let's get her into the house."

She left him to lift Fi out of the car and went up to her front door, unlocked it, and peered inside as if checking for intruders, then turned back and scanned the street.

"Looking for a black SUV?" he asked as he climbed the porch stairs.

Her eyes only widened, which was pretty good for hiding her reaction.

"I saw him block you down at the pier. Ran a check. Know anyone named Xavier de Varga?"

She shook her head, but blocked his entrance to her house, which pretty much confirmed his suspicions that she had something she didn't want him to see.

"If we're going to get her out of these clothes and to bed, I need to get her into the house." He said it softly, patiently, and saw her gaze change. Something burned there with a heat he wondered if he could withstand.

"Why do this?"

"I'm one of SPD's finest. Here to serve." His light tone seemed to do the job and she finally stepped away from the door.

The place smelled like her, almost like roses.

He scanned the living room. It was an orderly place, warm-colored, but there were no photos, none of the things he'd come to associate with friends and comrades. Hell, his place still had mementoes of Cheryl and of his days coaching little league, even though he'd sold most of his things and moved into his apartment to try fill himself up with something other than Cheryl's ghost.

"Nice place. Lived here long?"

"Long enough." Her gaze was shuttered again and he missed the human-Vallon he'd seen. "This way."

She led him, dripping across the hardwood floor and to the stairs, then up to a small room that contained a white covered bed and yellow walls. A small silk flower arrangement stood on the lone dresser and the whole place made him think the room had never been used.

"Nice room. I bet your guests appreciate it."

She threw him an annoyed glance as she pulled the duvet back to expose sheets that still had the fold marks of coming straight out of the package. "Set her down here."

He managed to sit Fi on the edge of the bed and started to strip off her sodden camo jacket.

"I can take it from here." She nodded toward the door and this time he obeyed. He stepped out and closed the door and clumped down the stairs. Should he take advantage of the opportunity to look around? She *had* invited him in.

He retreated to the door and toed off his shoes, shrugged his sodden coat off, then padded into the kitchen looking for a mop to wipe up the hardwood. He opened the basement door and flicked on the light, but the sight of bare floor and the scent of moisture and age stopped him from exploring any further. When he was done pawing unsuccessfully through her cupboards he turned around to find her standing, hip-shot and arms crossed in the kitchen door, competing anger and hunger on her face.

"Looking for my deep, dark secrets I suppose?"

Her glance slid to the basement door so maybe he should have looked further.

"A mop actually. I was going to wipe up your floor. Hardwood?"

"Aah." She glanced down at his unshod feet. "Made yourself right at home, I see."

He shrugged.

Something had changed about her. Her pupils were huge and Vallon Drake didn't strike him as the type to do drugs. There was a tension in her neck and a tick in her jaw that made him think of a lightening rod in a storm. Or else she was the storm, which left him....

He shivered and she cocked her brow. Her blonde hair seemed to lift off her shoulders and her hazel-green eyes actually sparked as she came towards him.

"There a problem?"

"Nothing a towel wouldn't fix."

The green increased in her brown eyes like bits of flame. "Is that what would do it?"

It wasn't really a question. She stood toe-to-toe with him, her scent of fading roses flooding his senses as she seemed to sniff his skin.

"I have a towel with your name on it upstairs."

Her sultry voice said she planned more than a towel, and shit, he should just get the hell out of here, because this was such a bad idea.

He managed to step back from her, but it was like stepping through thick mud. When she followed, it reminded him of cats stalking.

"Vallon—Ms. Drake," his gaze skittered around the room and settled on the kettle on the stove. "Why don't you make us a cup of tea. I believe we have matters to discuss. A certain Xavier de Varga, perhaps? Why would he be following you?"

"I've no idea, but it seems there's a lot of following going on tonight."

She bared her teeth and he could have sworn he heard a hiss as she stepped up to him again. This time she placed her palm heart-high on his chest.

Heat slammed into him and sent his pulse into a jagged race that was mirrored in the pulse along her jaw. He shook his head. Shook his head again, at the way she tilted her head back for him, at the weight of her eyelids and the sparks in her gaze that seemed to catch at his soul.

"Damn it, no." But it was a whisper he barely believed as he leaned into her, caught her lips and tasted ashes and burning copper on her skin.

Then her arms were around his neck and his hands were in the sodden mess of her hair, pushing it back from her face so he could taste her mouth, her cheeks, her ears, down to the heated flesh at her jacket collar.

He pushed it off her shoulders and found the softness of skin underneath the t-shirt. The swell of her breast—and what the hell was he doing?

He jerked back so she fell against the table, chest heaving, face flushed, and the green in her gaze was like a laser locked onto him that he couldn't escape no matter how he struggled. He had to look away or—or he'd be caught forever, because there was something about this woman. He thought of ancient Greek gods and how they would prey on people, transform them or fill them with desire.

Well Vallon Drake was in his blood like that: dangerous because he already missed her scent, the feel of her under his hands.

He started past her and saw her shoulders slump. He made it to the kitchen door.

"Don't go."

She spoke so soft it turned him back to her. She stood there, eyes downcast, her throat working as if what she said took all of her strength.

"I'm sorry. I—don't want you to go. I—need you."

He should get his coat and leave. Hell, he should run. Stupidest move he'd ever made, taking off his shoes and coat. Blacklock would bust a gut when he heard.

But he wasn't going to hear, was he, because Jason stopped for a heartbeat too long. He knew it, when she took a hesitant step towards him and he met her. When he buried his face in her tangled hair, her neck, his hands hauling her into him, kneading her tight butt through her jeans, losing himself in the strange smoky taste of her.

She had his tie pulled loose, his shirt ripped loose of his trousers, heated hands running up his chest, ripping the buttons loose so she rained kisses down his chest.

He stripped her t-shirt over her head and thought his heart would stop when their skin met. What the fuck was he doing?

What the fuck.

Madness.

This was absolute, career-ending madness and he was caught in hers.

§

White-hot afterburn. Sheets of it shimmered across her vision, seared through her veins, and the only thing that would heal it—cauterize her wounds — was HIM.

Power poured through her, joining them, just as it was meant to be. Always meant to be. Use the earth's power and you had to give power back. Sex was the only way. Sex she would have.

She bit his lip and tasted copper bruising. Raked her nails down his back and he groaned. Unclasped her bra and shimmied her breasts across his chest. Let go her regrets and slipped her jeans down. He hefted her onto the countertop and she spread herself wide. Shouted together when he slammed into her. Slammed into her and she bucked, ground her heels into his backside, threw her head back.

Joined and bucking, the power surged up from the soil, up through the house, filling her as he filled her. As his long, smooth strokes drove home and home and home and she couldn't get close enough and damn and damn and damn she was sobbing as the top blew off her head, the roof blew off her house, and she screamed.

Heat flooded her as he exploded; as she collapsed limp in his arms. They came around her, his lips at her ear.

"Oh, fuck. What the hell was that?"

His scent of ocean and mornings was overcome with the scent of sweat and sex. His wide palm cupped the back of her head, stroked her hair.

"That shouldn't have happened."

She nodded into him, swallowed, because she didn't know if she could look him in the eyes again. "Sorry about that."

"It's—it was almost like it was inevitable from the moment I met you."

Inevitable. Shit. "More like forced on us."

The last thing she needed.

"Forced?" His warm fingers tipped her face up to his and those dark eyes—the darkest, warmest brown she'd ever seen, seemed to peer into her. Smiled. "I'd say we were two pretty willing participants."

His smile broadened and he leaned in to place a light kiss on her lips and his mouth slid lower to suckle her breast. But it was the wrong thing to say and do.

She pulled away, slid her leg past him and then off the counter and began tugging her clothes on. Damn things were all tangled. She stumbled as she struggled to get her legs into her jeans. Swore softly as, braless, she pulled her t-shirt over her head. Her breasts were tender from his mouth, the nipples too clearly pressing at the soft cotton. She crossed her arms and faced him.

A truly good-looking man, still shirtless as he buckled his belt. Broad shouldered, smooth, café au lait skin, a light ruff of dark fur across his chest and in an arrowed line down to the narrows of his abdomen and groin.

"It was a mistake."

But not truly. For the first time since the events at the garage she could think clearly. The afterburn was gone. The trouble was, the first thing that came to mind when she looked at Detective Bryson, was that she should march him right up to her bed.

"Maybe," he said. "My partner would agree with you."

"You're investigating me as a murder suspect."

"And so now my investigation is compromised. You should be happy about that." He stepped up to her, tugged her, unwilling, into his arms. "I am."

"Cut the crap." She jerked loose. "We had a scare. We fucked because we were alive. That's all there was to it."

He shoved his hands in his pockets, a frown of confusion on his face. "That right?"

That was when she remembered: he wasn't gifted. When the store changed he had been, too. He didn't remember the scare they'd been through.

But the doubt in his voice made her almost swear he was disappointed and that just made it worse. She could not believe she'd allowed this to happen—afterburn or not. If he'd just put his damn clothes on. She looked past him to the door in hopes he'd get the hint.

His face went stiff. "We need to talk. Who the hell is Xavier de Varga?"

The thought of the dark man and his cedar scent made her cringe. "I've no idea."

"Today wasn't the first time you saw him."

Surprised, she looked up at him, but she wasn't going to give him the satisfaction of agreeing or disagreeing. Waited.

"You saw him the night of Lamrey's death, too." By the look on his face it was a stab in the dark, but surprisingly correct. Detective Jason Bryson was no one to underestimate. He had far too sharp a mind.

He stepped up to her so she backed away, but he caught her shoulders roughly, sniffed at her hair and then stepped back.

"Tell me, Agent Drake, why does your hair smell like smoke when there was no fire?"

Her gut tightened and her arms goose-fleshed. There was no way he could remember the fire, but the way he looked at her it was almost as if he did. Or knew something, which wasn't possible given he carried no hint of Gift.

"I've no idea what you're talking about."

"Your hair smells like fire, but there was no fire. At least not that I recall. Strange. A lot of things about you are strange, Agent Drake. A phone in a wall. A dead man. A stranger pursuing you, yet you wander dark streets in the rain. Most women would be running for cover, but not you. Then you turn up, where I report a fire, with soot on your face." He used his thumb to scrub her cheek, hauled it away and showed her. "Soot. I'd swear to it, and yet there was no fire."

"I think you'd better leave." He knew too much even if he didn't know how the pieces connected. But then neither did she.

"You think that's going to make me go away?"

"You'll be out of my house."

He shrugged and buttoned his shirt, then stuffed in the shirttails and shoved his tie in his pocket. He stepped up to her once more and leaned down to kiss her. Tasted her lips with his tongue and damn it, her body reacted with too-pleasant ripples of heat.

"Please go."

But he smiled. "You're going to miss me, Vallon Drake."

She looked away.

"There's something going on and I'm beginning to suspect you're at the heart of it. If you need help, give me a call."

"Help? Is that what you call a booty call?"

But he didn't rise to her bait, just headed out of the kitchen. She stayed where she was, felt the rush of rain-soaked air as the front door opened. Then the damp air and he were gone.

For good, she hoped. Some sunshine would be nice for a change.

Chapter 12-The Truth Underneath

The trouble was, Vallon still felt Detective Bryson on her, in her, and his scent on her skin, —and his observations were just too on the money.

She needed the good Detective looking over her shoulder like she needed Gleason's or Landon's scrutiny while she conducted her investigation.

Because investigate she would, and no one had better get in her way.

She pushed herself away from the counter as a gust of rain rattled against the kitchen windows and snuck through the warped frames to stir the gingham curtains. The clock ticked on the wall. Close to eight o'clock, and she needed to be on the desk at ten. First she needed to talk to Fi.

She left the scene of her and the good Detective's crime and padded up the hardwood stairs, checked Fi, but the woman was still sound asleep, her tangled mat of blonde hair dampening the pristine pillows with a grey stain. The camo coat lay in a heap on the floor, smelling like a wet dog. Vallon scooped it up, emptied the pockets of stones and bottle caps and crumpled bits of paper, then dumped the coat in the washing machine in the upstairs closet and turned it on.

She shed her own clothes in her room, then stepped into the shower and tried to get warm. She stood there, letting the stinging spray pummel her face, and hoped it would knock some sense into her.

All it did was make her sure she'd probably committed the biggest error of her error-laden life. Another man-wreck, only this time he posed a threat not just to her, but to the AGS and Gifted folk everywhere. What would the US populace do if they knew there were people like her around?

With the rise of the religious right, the Salem witch trials came to mind.

She toweled dry and dried her hair, then pulled on fresh clothes— her favorite low-rider jeans that made her feel sexy, and a dark brown, turtleneck sweater. When she returned to Fi's room, the woman had only burrowed further under the covers.

Vallon perched on the edge of the bed and smoothed her old friend's hair off her face. She looked so peaceful, now, without the glitter of fear in her eyes. Almost like the girl Vallon remembered.

"Fi?"

Just slumber's even breath.

"Fi?" She caught Fi's shoulder and shook her gently. "Come on, Fi. We need to talk."

A groan. "I don' wanna get up, Mom."

"You don't have to get up. I just need to ask you a couple of questions, Fi. Then you can go back to sleep for as long as you like."

Fi's breath steadied to sleep again and Vallon shook her head, grabbed Fi's shoulder and shook again. "Fi! We have to talk."

"Wha? Wha?" Wild blue eyes, pale as watered skies. "Vallon? What are you doing here? Did you get away, too?" Then her gaze registered the yellow walls, the smooth sheets under her hands and she bolted upright, threw the covers off, her face a study in fear. "How? Where?"

"Fi. It's all right. Everything's all right." Softly. She used Fi's name to anchor her. Vallon stroked her friend's arms, her frightened face, her hair, and finally caught one of the fluttering hands. "You're in my house, Fi. You're safe."

Fi turned doubtful eyes on Vallon. "Not safe. Never safe. Vallon, we have to get away. Keep moving and she can't find us."

That made no sense. Vallon held Fi's gaze. "Who is she, Fi? What's she doing? Is she the one killing the agents?"

But Fi was shaking her head, pressing her hands to her ears and peering into the ceiling as if it would open up and take her. "Don't talk. Don't talk or she'll know. Move. Move."

She started to scramble off the bed, until Vallon caught her hands again. "I said it's safe here, Fi. It is. I'll protect you."

She hoped. But if what she'd felt at the garage and the fire were correct, she doubted any Gifted she knew was safe from whatever had taken Simon. She had fought to hold the flophouse firm when Detective Bryson had entered, lest he be lost in the change. But then the power had become aware of Vallon's intent as she had tried to follow the power back to whomever caused the change. Fury had licked into her head with a scalding of licorice and brimstone.

Then the place had gone up in smoke while Bryson had dragged her out.

And then the change had been completed.

She caught Fi's shoulders, peered into her dilated eyes. "I need you to tell me what you know, Fi."

Fi closed her eyes and shivered under Vallon's hands. "Don't know anything. Anything."

Vallon fought to keep her voice calm. "Fi, sweetheart, you have to listen. Yesterday you came to me. You said you had to warn me."

That brought Fi's eyes open.

"Warn me about what, Fi? Who is *she*?"

Fi shook her head and wildly searched the room. It was the most pathetic thing Vallon had seen, and once it would have broken her heart. She caught her friend in a hug, inhaled the scent of unwashed body, and underneath, the well-remembered scent of licorice-anise and mint. "It's going to be all right, Fi. It will be. Remember, you came to me for help and I will help you."

"No!" Fi shoved away, her face a map of fear. She captured Vallon's wrists. "I warn. You hear? She—she takes and takes and takes and takes and then she will destroy."

"Who, Fi. Who is it?"

Fi's gaze latched onto hers. A smile, older and filled with more grief than a woman Fi's age should ever know. "You know."

A single tear rolled down her cheek.

"Do I?" Vallon thought frantically back. Who would she know? "Someone from school? One of the staff?"

But she'd lost Fi's focus again. The other woman hunched down as if snakes darted out of the ceiling.

"Fi!" Vallon shook her slightly. "Tell me."

A quiver through Fi's body, then she shook her head. "Don't tell. Don't tell. Don't tell, she tells me — and touches me right here." She touched a ragged-nailed finger to her head. "I got away. I ran." Proud.

"And good thing you did. I've missed you, Fi. Really missed you." And the funny thing was, she had, and hadn't even realized it. Even if this haunted creature wasn't the vivacious Fi she remembered from school. It was Fi's indomitable will that had set Vallon's example way back when. An example she still followed. And under the unwashed clothes, it still smelled like Fi.

"I missed you, too, Vallon." Mists swirled across the moment of lucidity. "But it's a secret." Smiled like a child with a momentous surprise.

"What is, Fi? What were you warning me about?"

Fi's headshake was like a stubborn child's. "I *told* you. She wants. She takes them one by one. You should leave Vallon. Away, away, away, with me. Before it happens."

"Before what happens?"

A look of exasperation. "*She*'s doing it."

Vallon rubbed her forehead to rid herself of the need to shake Fi and force her to answer.

"Doing what." One more time.

Fi scrambled off the bed and went to the window but there was only rain streaming the glass and night backing the room's reflection. Vallon went to her and their two images were almost negatives of each other—Fi almost ethereally fair, Vallon dark and shadow-eyed even with her blonde hair.

"What do you see, Fi?" Because she couldn't see a damn thing except the flare of gifted in the night when she -reached- and one particular Gifted who was too close. She shivered.

"Mountains."

"Pardon me?" Vallon caught Fi's hand and peered out into the night. "Where, Fi. What mountains."

"Mountains in a long line. North to South. Compass points, Vallon. You know compasses. Like at school. Arrows and Rose Lines and North Stars. All along the lines."

Perfectly reasonable judging by Fi's face, but it made no sense at all. She took a stab in the dark.

"What's the matter with the mountains, Fi?"

Fi caught the ends of her damp hair with her fingers and tugged like a little girl. "They're going away," she sang.

"Away?" All the blood seemed to freeze in Vallon's fingers because suddenly Fi's ramblings made a strange kind of sense and yet it was impossible. Someone with the power she'd felt at the flophouse just might be able to smooth the coastal range out of existence. But to do so would exacerbate what was already a ticking time bomb along the coastal faults. The Juan de Fuca plate was already sticking where it submerged under the continental plate. That had held the local earthquakes to a minimum, but when it truly let go, seismologists predicted a quake of a magnitude nine or better.

That was ecological disaster the like of which ancient Indian tales told. Enough to wipe out most of coastal Washington and Oregon and much of the southwestern coast of Canada. The most heavily populated areas.

The question would be why?

She needed to get to the AGS. Not that she wanted to see Gleason or tell anyone about her suspicions. Not until she had something concrete, or Gleason would say she was more than a loose cannon: she was nuts and a fear-monger.

She checked her watch. She should be going, but if she just headed off to work, in all likelihood Fi would just disappear again; and Vallon didn't want to have to go through an evening like this one again anytime soon.

"Fi, honey?"

Fi's watered, wandering gaze finally settled on Vallon.

"I have to go to work. You'll be safe here—at least as safe as anywhere else. Okay?"

Fi scanned the room, nodded.

"I just want you to promise me that you'll stay here. I want my sister back. Okay?"

Fi met her gaze uncertainly. "Family?"

"Didn't we always say we were better than blood?"

Slow smile. "I remember."

"Well you hold onto that thought while I'm away tonight, okay?"

Slow nod as if it took untold concentration. God, what had happened to Fi? She'd always been at the top of the class with Vallon. That was what had made them both a formidable pair.

Fi had been athletic, brilliant, determined. When she'd left the Academy it had been a last, bright light pulled out of Vallon's life.

§

Clint Blacklock's jaded chuckle abraded like concrete on a motorcyclist's back.

"I knew it. You had 'fuckin' idiot' branded on your forehead the moment you met her." He hooked his fingers in parentheses for emphasis.

Jason closed his eyes against the harsh light of the detective office and inhaled the stale scent of damp, cigarette-impregnated clothes.

"You nuts, man?"

"I don't know what the hell happened."

"You want me to spell it out for you? F.U.C.K.U.P. How the hell you expect to make a case against this broad if you're fucking her? You think of that?"

He held up a hand against Jason's retort because those were fighting words. He hadn't 'fucked' her—it was never that crass. Yeah, he'd been a fool to make love to Vallon Drake and even a greater one to tell his partner, but damn it, the investigation was both of their responsibility. If one of them royally screwed up, the other deserved to know.

"Oh, wait a minute. That's right. You're a fucking idiot—emphasis on the fucking part."

Clint scraped his desk chair back and heaved his bulk up. Paced around the desks, cuffed Jason's head, and then sat down again to face Jason.

"You're damn lucky every one's out on that gang shooting right now or I'd march you right into the Captain." He shook his head.

Jason had enough. "You finished? Because I know what a fuckup I've made of the case. That's why I told you. Like I said: there's no excuse, but there's something about her I can't explain. It's like—shit this sounds stupid as hell — but it's like I've got her scent up my nose and I can't get it out. Knew it from the parking garage. Like she's under my skin."

Clint said nothing.

"There's something going on with her, too," Jason ended lamely.

Clint raised brows that looked amazingly like unkempt hamsters, but his lips held a 'prove it' expression. "Like?"

"With that kind of attitude you think I'm going to share hypotheticals with you before I've got evidence?" And with that Jason broke from their usual *modus operandi*. He dug in his jacket pocket pulled out the slim packet of papers he'd kept with him and smoothed them on the desk.

"Whatcha got?" Clint leaned over the desk to snag the photocopies and Jason barely got them away.

"Mind your own business. You want to look at the evidence, look at it, and then we can compare notes." He felt stupid saying it after he'd just shared an even bigger failing with his partner, but spilling the wild ideas that had been running through his head since he left her was just going to make his partner think he was ready for the loony bin.

Hell, he almost thought so, too.

He fanned the copies out in front of him. Photos of the scene.

Close-up: body on the concrete, face frozen in a mute scream, yellow light spilled across the scene emphasizing the lack of blood.

Middle-distance: Side angle of the body, paper and pen on the pavement, the wall beyond, the hazy, arched marking visible in the sidelight. A doorway, it looked like. Or what might have been one.

He pulled out the photocopy of Vallon's sketch and laid it beside the photo.

Match. Like a fingerprint. The drawing showed the same curve of stone, same perspective, same proportions. Seriously the same.

He looked up as Clint slammed a large evidence box down on his desk and dropped the top on the floor. He pulled out the plastic bag with the leather pouch filled with pens and papers confiscated from

Vallon Drake along with the bag that held the original drawing found at the scene. Clint glanced in Jason's direction and he felt like a kid covering his exam from a cheater. He looked down at what he had.

"Police intelligence says to always look for all the possibilities that can explain a series of facts."

"Yeah? Well police training also says eliminate the impossible and the remaining possibility is probably your answer." Clint looked at him. "So what are you trying to say, Slick?"

Slick. At least he was using his favorite nickname, which suggested he missed their partnership as much as Jason did.

"I'm asking how many ways can we interpret this evidence? One, she was at the scene and sketched the death after it occurred. Two, she sketched the wall before anything happened. Three, like she said, she was sketching the scene to preserve evidence."

"Four, a combination of 1 and 2 or 1 and 3. She knew the scene, planned to meet the Vic there, and after she killed him she finished her drawing."

Jason shook his head, sliding into the old groove of police work. "I'm not buying. Yeah, she knew Lamrey and had a relationship with him, but they'd ended it. She had, according to her."

"Well killing the poor bastard is one way to do that."

Jason rolled his eyes. "Clint, would you get over your biases for a minute?"

"If you'll get over yours."

"I haven't got any. Tell me, would a five foot seven woman have the strength to leave a body as crushed as that?"

Clint snorted. "With the right tools, yes—maybe. Besides, uniformed officers reported they saw her doing something strange to the body, so it was leaping and flopping like a beached fish—their words," Clint said looking up from a printed statement and met Jason's gaze. "Seriously, Slick, you really want to argue with that because your boffing some bimbo?"

"She's not a bimbo." Jason could have sworn at himself, because Clint's hamster brows saluted again.

"That right?"

"It might have been CPR applied badly."

"Might have been her applying electro-shock as well—if she'd had paddles in her hands. At least that's what the unis said."

Something nudged Jason's brain, but darted away like a suspect he couldn't catch. Something about electricity.

"Any possibility that might be the case?"

Distracted, Jason shook his head.

"This evening was another weird one. I followed her when she left home, but I wasn't alone. Black rental SUV followed her, too. Rented to a company called CartosNationele on behalf of someone named Xavier de Varga. He stopped her and she took off like a bat outta hell. When he left she headed to Pioneer Square."

"So she went out for dinner."

"Not so much." Jason leaned back in his chair, but kept Vallon's photocopied drawing in his hands. "Went to a—place. A store. I thought I saw flame and I called it in."

The memory proved harder to pull up than he'd expected. But it was—wrong.

He rubbed his forehead.

"You got a problem, Slick?"

He waved a hand in Clint's direction. "Damn it, it doesn't make sense either. I've got this feeling I helped pull a girl out of somewhere, but when the fire brigade arrived the shop was locked up tight." Shop? Then why did the word flophouse come to mind, and the half-formed memory of a dim room and something brilliant through the smoke and flame?

"Has to have been a dream," he muttered.

"What was a dream?"

Jason looked back at his partner. "You ever have one of those times when you…." The look in Clint's eyes wasn't promising. "Nothing. I'm just tired and having trouble keeping track of some things."

Like how sometimes you can't tell whether something is a memory, or a dream, Jase ol' buddy, ol' pal? He'd gone through a lot of that after Cheryl died. He'd thought that problem was over with.

And there was the scent of smoke in Vallon's hair, the taste of it on her skin. He straightened at the thought. That was damned sure a memory, because his pulse quickened just at the thought.

"You seen the coroner's report yet?"

Jason looked up from his ruminations. "What report?"

"Coroner's." Clint waved a sheaf of papers at him.

"What's it say?"

Clint tossed the sheaf of papers. They fluttered down onto the stack of evidence before he could scoop it out of the air. He grabbed them, but in the process brought up Vallon's original drawing. Clint had taken it out of the plastic case.

A burst of light behind Jason's eyes and he fell back into his chair, momentarily blind. He blinked—blinked again — and gradually the room formed around him, Clint's concerned visage across the desk.

"What? What's happening?"

Jason blew out a breath to steady himself and shook his head. "Damned if I know." He considered the papers he'd let go of on his desk. Then he picked up the Coroner's report and gingerly poked a finger at Vallon's drawing. Touching it was like poking your finger in a light socket and sudden recollections filled him. The scent of ozone at the flophouse. The scent of copper on her skin. What the hell?

Rather than make a scene he held his peace and scanned the coroner's report. It confirmed that the ribs were crushed and broken. There were fractures of the occipital bone and skull, extensive bruising over the entire body consistent with crushing. But the blood was normal, the tox screen clear. The eyes, nose, mouth, ears all filled with dried concrete. Now that was weird.

No explanation of what had caused it, but death was attributed to asphyxiation due to a crushed ribcage caused by extreme pressure.

Jason looked at Lamrey's recovered phone in its plastic cover. When pulled from the wall it, too, had been covered in concrete.

He nudged the edge of Vallon's sketch with a finger nail and felt a tremor run up his arm.

Power surge like the one in Pioneer Square. An earthquake and electrical fire. Or no fire at all.

He shoved the original drawing back at Clint. "This should be bagged and kept safe. Have the lab run analysis on it." He watched closely as Clint picked it up and slid it into its plastic holder. No way to know for sure if Clint was experiencing anything, but the chances weren't good, given the calm expression he wore.

It was all Jason could do to stand up casually, but Clint's gaze was on him.

"What is it now, Slick?"

Jason shook his head. "What else? The case? I've got some ideas to check out." He grabbed his trench coat off the hook and headed for the door.

"You want I should come with?" Clint was half out of his chair.

"Nah. Hell-of-a night. I'll do this on my own, but I'll give you a shout if I get into a jam." He patted his pocket for the cell phone, because he didn't need Clint with him when he was trying to put some form to this case.

"One more thing, Slick." Clint stopped him before he could exit. "I made a call to my man in Homeland Security. He's gonna check whether they had something goin' on at the garage. I should hear tomorrow. If there was—well I already talked to the Chief. He says we should bow out graceful-like and let them take the lead. You got that? The bowing out part?"

Jason met his gaze and gave a nod. "Sure thing, partner. But while we're on the case I've got some leads to follow. I'll let you know if it turns out."

He ducked out the door and headed for his car parked at the curb. He had to see Vallon and see her now, because the something weird he'd suspected had just got a whole hell of a lot weirder. The question was whether Vallon Drake would give him an answer.

No, he corrected, the question was whether she'd talk to him at all.

Chapter 13-Sun-heated Clay

"So just how do you plan to handle this?" Fitzsimmons asked, and the rich meal Wolf Amundson had consumed turned leaden. He tried not to show it as he swung to face his boss in the back of the Lincoln town car Fitzsimmons had requisitioned for his visit to Seattle.

The question said it all: Fitzsimmons had passed Wolf the ball and, like Beckham at soccer, he better score.

"Our plan is still in play. It is high time things broke loose. It was one of the matters I asked you out here to talk about."

"Gleason's been left on his own long enough. The AGS must be brought into the fold."

Wolf nodded to hide his impatience at the obvious. "If the killings are finally coming to light it should make all Gleason's Washington backers head for the hills. No one's going to want to defend a bunch of dangerous aberrations running loose in the country. If the AGS can't control their own…." He smiled as he let the last word fade away and glanced out the window.

The limousine had crossed the Ballard Bridge and was hissing along Westlake Boulevard, past Lake Union, the headlights catching in the sleet, and the neon restaurant and yacht club signs melting in the rain tracks on his window. Ahead the gleaming towers of the city looked like the Promised Land.

He wanted a scotch or a glass of well-aged port to finish his meal. It would ease the indigestion he felt coming on with this discussion.

Fitzsimmons bobbed his head like the leathery creature he emulated. "We have to assume control. The weapons potential of these agents is too significant."

"They are supposed to be guardians. That's been Gleason's point. If there are others out there like them—enemies of the country...."

"They can keep watch under careful control just as well as they can do it running loose across the countryside." A shake of that predatory head. "No. It's high time this was acted upon. You've sat on the situation too long."

That brought Wolf upright, his attention back from the towers dripping light ahead.

"It takes time to get the players in place."

"You've had years. I put you here to get a job done before I retire, remember?"

As if Fitzsimmons would ever deign to retire.

"And I have done it—or do you not recall the gifts I sent to Washington?" He glanced at Fitzsimmons and then out the window. Not everything had gone well in those years, but he had managed to pull all their asses out of the fire a time or two. He would continue to do so. He turned back to find Fitzsimmons' cool appraisal on him.

"And fine gifts they were."

"So matters progress?"

"On that front, yes. We are—shall we say—simpatico on how to gild the lily. But that's not why we're here tonight."

The man looked like he'd just swallowed prey, but his baleful gaze turned back to Wolf.

"I repeat. Just what do you plan to do, or must I assume control and give orders here?"

And that was not what Wolf wanted to hear. Fitzsimmons was positioning him as the scapegoat should anything go wrong. There was no more time for small subterfuges. This had to move forward, and quickly. Waiting until tomorrow was no longer an option.

"Let me phone my Seattle PD contact and get the names involved. Then I suggest we have a conversation with Gleason. Rattle him, and it will make your conversations in Washington that much easier." He felt Fitzsimmons' gaze lock on him, but refused to turn his head to meet the other man's glare. Wolf flipped his phone open and dialed, praying Blacklock was still there.

The phone buzzed and buzzed again. After three rings he was starting to consider another approach, but the fourth ring brought a click and "Blacklock."

"Clint. Good. I hoped to catch you. I finished my meeting and thought I would call to get a bit more intel before I make my enquiries. Can you give me the names of the Agents involved?"

A pause as if the cop considered, so Wolf pushed on.

"So when do you want to get together for that Mexican food? I've got time next Wednesday if that works for you?"

"Hell, man. I can wait that long. Sure. I know this little place down by Elliott Bay Marina. *Rosita's*. Say eleven thirty?"

"Sure." Wolf almost considered having his secretary schedule a meeting during that time, but reconsidered when Clint spoke up again.

"Vic's name was Simon Lamrey. One of yours. Our only suspect is another AGS Agent, Vallon Drake. A young thing - 26. Good looking. My partner's looking for some alternative theories, but when you find her beating on the Vic's body that don't hold a lot of water."

"Simon Lamrey and Vallon Drake. Good. Let me check and I'll get back to you." He clicked the phone closed and turned back to Fitzsimmons' waiting presence. "This is better than we thought. Lamrey is one of the group you told me about. And Drake. We will have to check, but given her age, I suspect she is one of the special cadre. We do this right and they'll be in such a crisis everything will come tumbling down."

He paused to look out his window at the darkness. "How do you say it? Like putty? Right into our hands."

"You're sure?"

He didn't bother looking back. "Of course I am sure." Hadn't Fitzsimmons learned that about him yet?

"And what about your little problem?"

At that Wolf turned back to Fitzsimmons. He loomed in the shadows and Wolf almost loathed the man.

"It is not a problem. It was an opportunity and now it has worked for us. And if not, we know who to blame for it, do we not?"

"I—we we can't afford a lot of collateral damage."

Wolf considered his boss. The man was powerful, but like all Washington politicos, also always concerned for his image. Sometimes collateral damage was necessary. Weren't the lost AGS agents exactly that? The whole point was the end results?

"It will be handled. I'll see to it personally. Besides, from what we know, no one's likely to remember anything anyway." He turned back to the night. And perhaps, if there were collateral damage, he could make it work to his advantage. Fitzsimmons could be part of it, and then Wolf could simply take out Gleason and amalgamate the AGS under his control.

Take out Fitzsimmons and more roads opened for advancement: it just needed to look like an accident.

§

When Vallon walked into the AGS war room at nine p.m. Agent James Dean shifted in the airborne 'desk' and touched a button. The almost silent whir of electric motors came from the floor and the desk swooped across the miniaturized landscape to come to rest on the grey tiled floor near Gleason's office.

Moore was nowhere to be seen and neither, thank god, was Gleason, so Vallon slipped through the concentric circles of desks and into Dean's fire.

The man was pale as a ghost, but the afterburn poured off him in waves.

"'Bout bloody well time you got here." He checked his diver's watch, hands shaking, and turned on her with a scowl he couldn't quite pull off. Agent James Dean couldn't have been further from his namesake—all straight-edged crew cut, tie and razor pleated suit trousers—along with a lack of imagination that made him, as far as Vallon was concerned, one of the most difficult of people to deal with.

"It's nine and my shift starts then."

"Agents generally relieve at least fifteen minutes ahead of time to ensure there's time for a status update." Checked his watch again and Vallon rolled her eyes.

"So I had something come up. Brief me while I take off my coat." She slipped off her long leather jacket and tossed it at the coat rack, then slid into the seat he'd vacated, still unfortunately warm, and the seat seemed to hold on to his heavy floral aftershave.

"It will take longer than that."

She looked down at the digital console of assignments—five agents out—and up at him. Touched the screen so it shifted to research mode. Good. Nothing barring her way. Even the side pocket was still full of vellum and fountain pens, but then Dean was never one to do things what he considered 'the old-fashioned' way.

She flipped back to the agent list. "So cut to the chase. What do I need to know?"

"We've got four events under investigation. One's left over from earlier this evening." Dean grabbed a bottle of inhibitor and knocked some back. A deep flush ran up his face.

Vallon nodded, waited as the tremor in his hands quieted.

"Hunt is checking out a couple of light tremors I picked up near Mount Rainier."

"Could just be seismic activity," she assessed. "Who else is out?"

"Chavez and Ingersoll."

"The M and M twins ride again," she murmured and checked their *twenty:* out beyond University of Washington in the Laurelhurst area. "That makes three?"

"The holdover from this evening. Flophouse/storefront change near Pioneer Square."

Vallon stiffened and looked more closely at the Agent assignments. "Moore and Gleason?" She shot the question at Dean.

"The boss said there was something about it he didn't like and that is was high time he got his hands dirty again. So he took the call. Been out since about seven thirty."

Vallon fought back a little surge of concern and nodded. She'd barely left the vicinity by then. "Must be a lot to keep him tied up so long."

"You might say that. Says he's trying to get a handle on who had a hand in the change."

The panic surged a little harder, because it was just too possible that in her attempt to assess who was responsible for the change, some sense of her presence would remain.

"Thanks for the update." She managed to keep her voice steady. "Anything nationally I should know about?"

"Everything's quiet and the other chairs report only the usual activity."

She strapped into the harness, settled her headset in place, and punched the button that would lift her off the floor. A low hum and vibration ran up her back as she rose into the warmer air closer to the ceiling and left Dean behind to immerse herself in the world.

The chair hung above the map pit like a hawk in flight, which was how Vallon always felt when she was up here. At times the impulse to hold her arms out as if she were flying was almost too much to contain, because contrary to what she told Gleason, she loved the view of what was going on in the world.

Especially on active nights.

If it hadn't been for the price of afterburn she would have even requested desk duty. At least occasionally.

She punched her code and the map beneath her reset to the broad expanse of North America. She hovered there and watched the rolling contours of the U.S. All as it should be. When she touched the computer screen, the map shifted beneath her, becoming the night-swathed shapes and contours of the Pacific Northwest.

The dipper shape of Puget Sound. Washington, Oregon, Idaho, and Montana spread out before her in all their glory of folds and peaks and gorges and dry plains and river valleys.

Through the divided screen, light strings followed the thin chains of civilization along river valleys and into the mountains, only to spread into bright basins of light where cities flooded the landscape. She touched a button on the console and the landscape shifted into an overwhelming profusion of green-lit stereoscopic contours. She -reached-, farther afield than the watcher at the desk was intended to, and the deep pulsing boil of Yellowstone filled her with the almost narcotic glow of the earth's power seeping up through the lithosphere. Pulled back a little because it would do her no good to be caught doing something wrong before she even had a chance to do what she intended.

At the touch of a button the chair whirred across the mesmerizing landscape toward Puget Sound and the long chain of peaks and valleys that ran the coast, and the glittering string of well-lit human habitation that clung there. When the chair hung over the dark bulk of Mount Rainier she stopped her motion, keyed in another set of map coordinates, and the scene below her shifted, swooped in on her hawk wings so that the Seattle-Tacoma-Olympia corridor sprang into detailed relief.

Rain-slicked streets and the dark waters of Lake Union, Lake Washington, and Lake Sammamish laid black ink on the glittering table of the cityscape. Vallon spread her hands flat across the console. -Reached-.

The cityscape shifted before her. Still the steep hillsides and treed neighborhoods of the city, but now she saw beyond what she'd come to think of as the thin veil of normal sight and the earth's crust of flickering creatures, to the reality of the bright glow just beneath the boiling surface. This was where the Gifted lived, and the power source for all change.

Faintly, a web of capillary lines flowed under the city like veins under a person's skin. Across the city, change bubbled, flared, and subsided again harmlessly as people dreamed.

Near the harbor at Pioneer Square, a more brilliant flare in the darkness showed where the flophouse/clothing shop vied for existence. Licorice flooded Vallon and her first instinct was to recoil. She stopped herself. Had to know. Let the licorice scent in and found….

"Dammit," she pulled back to the war room and its recycled air, the delicate powder taste of roses on her tongue. Her taste. "Dammit, dammit, dammit, dammit."

All she could hope was that Gleason and Moore wouldn't notice it in the miasma of licorice. Fat chance.

A fountaining flare of power rose from the site like fourth of July fireworks and Vallon sighed in relief. She -reached- and the scent of Gleason's old spice and wet earth power filled her head. Moore's green-tea scent was a faint acrid aftertaste on Vallon's tongue. Then the flare subsided into the green-tinged darkness of the city, and the fine web of the earth's veins underneath.

No sign that the Gifted who had evoked the change even noticed the site had been changed back to the old brick flophouse, and that was a good thing. It supported Gleason's contention that the changes were unplanned.

But the malevolence of the presence she'd battled at the flophouse didn't support that. There'd been purpose there. And anger. And gloating superiority. She tapped her finger on the digital pad and the chair lifted higher. She needed to dig deeper, but first she needed to check on the other agents. Gleason and Moore were on the move—probably returning to the AGS—or hopefully dealing with their afterburn. If she were lucky, it would mean it would be a while before they arrived.

She set her 'wings' at her side and swooped across the city, seeking the glow of more permanent change. Out beyond the weight of the concrete that formed the University, Laurelhurst was an area of tall cedar and oak and spruce and spacious homes that housed many of the well-heeled of Seattle. The docks and boat moorings around the affluent point reminded her of a paramecium's legs.

She honed in on the bright candles that were petite, dark Margarita Chavez and tall, Aryan Mark Ingersall near a lakeside household, the gold veins flickering in and out of her vision as the M and M twins addressed a brightness that, best as she could tell, reflected a swimming pool newly created between a glass-and-steel house and the yacht moored at the shore. As if these people didn't have enough with their expensive view.

So the M and M twins were fine. Dealing with small potatoes given what Vallon had seen in the past few days. She pulled back and scanned the landscape, filtering through the tastes and scents that marked the presence of the Gifted in the population. Fi still rested at Vallon's house. Good. Vallon turned to her last agent.

Janet Hunt and her mom's-apple-pie-attitude and her basket of cookies. The leftover from another era who had always maintained her show of kindness even if Vallon didn't believe it and didn't respond.

Janet had worked with the company long before matters of homeland security brought the AGS to the attention of national security agencies. Then its major function was still confirming the accuracy of existing maps and ensuring borders were maintained. Before anyone noticed the rampant change percolating through the population. Or before it started.

Only Gleason and Janet were left from that era, and Gleason had shifted from Field Agent to Management when Roger Decker, the original head of the unit, had retired. But Janet and her old-fashioned, matronly ways still kept chugging along.

Vallon sighed and followed the flow of the landscape southward.

Janet Hunt. Her Gifted flare and scent of patchouli traveled southeast of Tacoma, past Puyallup and Buckley and along the edges of Mount Rainier National Park toward Wilkeson. Tracking earth tremors, Dean had said.

Occasionally the AGS did get involved in keeping surface seismic or natural disaster damage to a minimum. They'd done it with Mount St. Helens. They could have done it with Hurricane Katrina—if Homeland Security had taken up Gleason's offer.

Mount Rainier was one of the most active volcanoes in the Pacific Northwest, so Hunt's attention was no surprise, but her direction was.

There wasn't any need to go to the mountain. An agent of Hunt's ilk could track along the skein of earth capillaries as easily as Vallon did to find the source of the tremors. That was the purpose of the various computer consoles on the war room desks. Some of the agents even kept computers at home for the same purpose.

So something had forced Hunt out of her house and onto the road.

Vallon sank as deeply as she dared into her map, allowing the sensation of wet soil and tree roots to cover her skin, but there was no hint of issue there.

She turned her attention in the direction Hunt drove and hesitantly opened herself to the flow of power.

It hummed through the earth in a deep, subsonic symphony that shook her bones like afterburn until the pain almost jarred her loose from her body. This was why the AGS never went this deep. Too dangerous, they said. Agents had been lost.

Her hold on the power flickered and dimmed and she shook herself, pressed her hands back onto the desktop digital representation of the map below her and fell back into herself and the feel of wet earth—cold—and felt—heat?

Was something going on with the mountain?

Her awareness sought past Hunt's squat presence guiding her Ford Focus through the rain-drenched night. A sense of the mesmerizing hiss of tires and flashing white lines and 'Welcome to Wilkeson' and then Vallon was past.

Was something not normal? Was the heat enough to get Mother Hunt out on such a night? The earth taste changed to salted sandstone and the anise of coal. Veins of it laced through the soil that had led to the creation of the town to begin with. From above came the weight of the small, two-story town, and the few hundred souls who slumbered the night away.

Something.

The soil suddenly warm as sun-heated clay that stuck to your hands. It coated her presence and made it hard to pull away. She came back to herself into the cool, artificial breeze of the war room's circulated air and worked her hands against the sensation of clay hardened into her pores and mind.

The soil in March shouldn't be so warm.

Vallon peered uneasily down into the map in the direction of Mount Rainier. She should really just let Janet Hunt do her job like Gleason would want, and focus on learning what she could of the flophouse change and whether it was connected to the change at the garage.

But Janet Hunt was out there alone and it was Vallon's job to make sure nothing happened. Vallon picked up the phone to call her as she looked back at the map.

The fact Hunt hadn't called in whatever it was she chased down said that she didn't trust her suspicions and wanted more proof before reporting.

So let her do her job. You'd want that chance. Hell. You'd demand it.

Vallon put the phone down and surveyed the map.

The usual pop and flow of change close to the city like a slow-boiling cauldron. It was what had first drawn Gleason to shift the AGS to a landscape conservation role when Vallon's father had pointed it out—or so the Academy text books had said.

City lights faded and bloomed. Landscape changes, little ones, flickered and died like reflections in the rain, each one a pathetic attempt to gain gratification in an ungratifying world. She could understand that. Most of the changes were as transitory—blooming and fading quickly—as her ill-fated relationships.

Something….

She -reached- and refocused her vision on the pale web of lines under the city and sent her awareness out. Where bright spots illuminated in the web, the same build-up of Gifted she'd seen the other night, and wondered how long those gatherings had been going on. Each lay in an area of more intense light where a group of the webbed lines came together.

When Seattle's glass towers gave way to the old district of Pioneer Square, she tried to duck beneath the streets again, but something stopped her. She tensed, cautiously -reached- again and felt the tide water in the soil. A natural barrier. She followed it, touching the tunnels of Seattle's underground, the sawdust and sewage of Seattle's first town center. Drove inland and uphill to the place where power flowed again. Where the flophouse had been. Or was, now that Gleason had completed the restoration.

Vallon opened herself to the flow of power flavored with Gleason's old spice and damp earth scent. Brick structure pressed on the folds of the earth, but here below there was something different. As she remembered.

Licorice in the soil, overripe and insistent as Maggie at her most hungry. Vallon -reached- further.

Heated soil surrounded her like a comforting shroud. She melted down through the soil, deeper than she'd ever gone. Deeper than the AGS had ever dared explore, but the licorice was generalized and almost impossible to trace.

Pulse.

Vallon jerked as the earth twisted around her.

Pulse.

And the web of power thrummed, undulated, and gathered.

Then the web of earth power flashed and shuddered, the power blinding Vallon.

She jerked upright, blinking, in her chair and found herself twisted to face the damned mountain.

"Shit." She stabbed the controls and the chair hummed and soared and fell toward the Wilkeson area, but Vallon already knew. Already felt the change in the map. Already scrambled for vellum and pen.

Power churned and boiled from the earth near the mountain. Stench of licorice burned in her nose, her throat, teared her eyes.

Her palm slammed down on the emergency alert, even as her other hand keyed in Hunt's cell number.

The call-tone drilled through her headset and into her ear. Again. Again.

"Come on, come on, come on." Why wasn't she answering?

AGS staffers flooded the room. Gleason and Moore, slicked with rain, on their heels. Landon soon after, a bathrobe pulled around him, Gore-tex jacket over his shoulders.

Vallon's world filled with double vision. Gleason and the war room. The too-warm earth under Wilkeson.

The cell phone's ringer buzzed and she switched it to the room's intercom. The digital readout showed Hunt's name.

"What's going on, Drake?" Gleason elbowed his way through the crowd of agents, Moore and Landon like elfin children at his giant's heels.

Vallon steadied her breath, juggling the double focus. Be calm. She could deal. "Something's happening at Mount Rainier, Sir."

It came out crisp. Professional.

The war room began to shiver and shake. The tiles undulated under their feet and sent Vallon's chair in a long, wild, sickening swing across the map that almost tore her from her focus. Her fingers automatically raced over the chair controls. The mad swing continued.

"Quake!" Gleason roared.

Perfect. Hunt had been tracking tremors and she'd found one. More than that, too.

Licorice scent rammed into Vallon and almost doubled her over.

She. The scent clearly belonged to a she.

The chair. It was as if something else had taken control. In the war room the stench of burned wire vied with licorice for dominance and became a single stench of electric power.

"Drake, get that damned chair down!" Gleason roared.

She tore herself from Hunt's location, toggled switches, slammed her fist onto buttons, but nothing worked. Nothing responded. Pen and Vellum went flying like missiles across the room.

In desperation she cut power and the chair slowed, slowed, lowered. Vallon heaved a sigh of relief, unbuckled to meet Gleason. Began to stand.

The chair jerked sideways, caught her on the thighs and knocked her back onto the console as the chair leapt up, away from the map, slammed through the crowd of Agents and underlings like a car through a crowd and barely missed Gleason's head as Vallon struggled to regain her seat.

Too late.

The wall came up too fast. Impact drove Vallon headfirst into oblivion.

§

Wall-of-gold-comes-up-to-a-man-and-says-what-do-you-get-when-you-cross-an-Academy-graduate-with-a-golden-calf?

Man-answers-I-don't-know-and-the-wall-smashes-him-into-the-floor-and-says-to-the-barkeep-gild-the-lily,-baby.-Gild-the-lily.

The voice came like a fast coastal wind carrying licorice sand and salt and seawater that drove into Vallon and left her skinned raw and trying to understand as…

Janet Hunt drives her Focus along the rain-drenched two-lane road. Her headlights shimmer on the slick foliage to either side. Clouds obscure the hulking presence of the mountain before her as the shimmer on the wet spruce and pine increases. Light, not headlights, turns golden and she slows the vehicle, aware something is wrong. Sniffs, and suddenly the vehicle windshield disappears.

Rain slaps her face and gets in her recently-permed hair and it pisses her off because something is happening/has happened/is about to happen.

Slows her car and the concrete pavement shivers. Trembles. Undulates like a quake-snake-shake and—is gone.

Hot metal wheel under her hands, hot springs poking through her seat, and the scent of licorice so thick she can't breathe. She -reaches- into the soil, but can't find what is happening. Just heat. Licorice stench. Coming from everywhere. -Reached- into the earth to smooth the landscape back into place, but nothing happens.

The metal sears. The plastic steering wheel melts under her hands.

"Shit," says the mouth that butter wouldn't melt in. Outta the car and springs away. Turns back when she slips into loose soil up to her knees. How did she get here? Mesmerizing white lines on dark pavement. Knows she made a mistake coming. Coming alone. Getting out of her car and trusting she can handle anything thrown her way. The trees have gold halos around them as they wink out of existence.

The wet slop she stands in quivers and dances and her car's headlights shake,rattle,roll, as something hauls the rear of the car down into the earth.

Headlights stab sky and glare off raindrops, and what was hard stone that held her softens and she sinks up to her waist. Afraid she sinks up to her breasts, swimming in the damn stuff and swearing as she hauls out her phone. Get a warning out. Sliding up to her neck, one arm stabbed up to keep the phone free. Static and then ringing, ringing, ringing.

"AGS," a voice answers, but Janet Hunt's mouth fills with mud that runs unbidden down her throat, stoppers her ears, her nose. The headlights stab upward and in fear her final gaze follows. Sees.

Something new under the night sky.

"Vallon! Damn it, Pigeon, come on back, girl."

"I told you, you shouldn't move her. Her neck could be broken. She should be headed for a hospital."

"You want to answer EMT questions?" Deep booming voice.

Wet cloth on her face. Vallon struggled up from the oddest set of dreams and found herself stretched out on a hard surface. Floor, her mind categorized. Gleason wouldn't let her be moved. Soft dabs of a cold cloth on her head and the almost non-existent scent of almonds told her Landon was here. And Moore. That was the other voice.

She opened her eyes and found a circle of faces around her. "What?"

"It's all right, Drake. Damn chair apparently went crazy. You hit the wall." Gleason peered down at her as she tried to sit up, and the floor shook.

The room had strange halos around the lights, the faces, their eyes. *Halos on tree branches and a sense of change.* She shivered, clamped her eyes shut a moment because two scenes juxtaposed across her vision.

The war room, filled with concerned faces.

Mount Rainier with a new mountain spur where the town of Wilkeson used to be.

A pulse of power ran up from the floor and she scrambled to her feet and stood swaying, waiting for the signs, the horrible licorice scent. Was the AGS next?

"I need vellum and pen."

Floor tiles stayed the same. She looked up when she realized her ragged panting was the only sound in the room.

"Drake? You sure you're okay?" Gleason's assessing gaze cut through her, but his voice told her the correct answer.

Nodded even while the top of her head felt like it came off and her brain melted through her ears. Didn't they feel it? No one brought her what she needed. She grabbed the wreckage of the chair, found another pen, more vellum in the console.

"Pigeon, maybe you should lay down for a few minutes."

She held up her hand to stop him, trying to steady her vision, her connection to the landscape around Wilkeson.

"Janet. Have we been able to contact Janet—Agent Hunt?" She searched from face to face to face. "Shit, maybe there's still time."

The wrecked chair was no hope. She ran for the map pit, leapt down even though the delicate map wasn't meant for someone's tread.

"There's been a massive change, or is about to. Hunt went out to check it. She was down by Rainier." She spread the vellum, uncapped her pen, -reached- even though the clarity of the vision was compromised by the halos across her sight.

"Look! Can't you see?" So clear. Bright flashes of earth power.

A huge fissure in the landscape. The map changed. Earth rose. Wilkeson wisped away like sand in the wind. Trees multiplied on a ridge.

Vallon fell to her knees. Started to draw the landscape as it had been.

Gleason must have seen something in her face. "Get Hunt on the line," he yelled.

Vallon plunged into the earth's crust, sped away southeastward. Found the heat, the change. Hunt.

Had to find Hunt. Had to save her. Sketched the road, the town.

There. Flickering flame. Vallon wrenched at the earth surrounding the woman. Tore it away in great sheets of mud. But Hunt only sank. Mud into soil. Hard-packed and firm. She pulled power from the soil and redirected its moisture. Sent the water away like an upwards rain.

Licorice sent groundwater pouring in.

She grabbed earth power and formed dams against the river of water, but an opposing force melted them away with the heat. Heat from deep in the earth.

"Damn it. This isn't gilding the lily!" She didn't even know what it meant.

Her hands shook when she tried to push her hair from her face. Even her fingers had halos around them that seemed to suck at her mind, tug her down into the mud like Janet. She could barely see what she drew.

The room was silent. All she saw were two huge feet at the edge of the pit and then Gleason's knees popped as he stepped down and knelt in front of her.

"What did you say?" His lips had gone white.

She stayed focused on the battle for Janet. Just shook her head and plunged deeper, after the heat. After whoever was doing this.

The mud. The mud. Sucking her down. Janet going under holding her phone. Finger hitting the emergency button as her head went under. Burning. Burning subsonic vibrations in Vallon's flesh, bursting her apart. She had to get free.

Janet? Where was Janet?

Her flame faded out and now the Licorice woman caught Vallon and hauled her down. Or was it the earth itself grabbing hold of its own. Taking her back to its breast and crushing the life out of her.

No breath. No life. Too deep, and she had no control here, no chance of life. She screamed and threw herself back.

Snapped through soil and rock and dropped the fire-hot pen in time to hear Gleason.

"Where the hell's that phone line with Hunt?"

"Gone." The certainty was like a searchlight's glare flavored with licorice that made Vallon gag.

"So, Gleason? You lose another agent now?"

She looked up at the new voice. Tall, smooth-skinned man with golden hair, but the air was dark around him. Not Gifted. Beside him stood a thin, birdlike man with a predatory razor stare pinned on her. She wished she had the strength to move.

She rubbed her eyes against the crushing pain, the afterburn, the overwhelming sense of failure because Janet was dead and gone, and tried to free herself of the sensation that someone had walked over her grave.

Someone other than these strangers was watching. And because she'd gone too deep, someone knew what she was thinking.

That someone was feeding her an afterburn so debilitating Vallon could barely breathe.

Chapter 14-The Unsteady Earth

All the blood left Landon's head when he saw the newcomers. The air stank with their unGifted scent like vinegar and ashes—none of the perfume that allowed him to 'sess out the Gifted from among the broader population, none of the heady rush up his back he got when he considered Vallon.

Gleason stood beside Vallon, then climbed out of the pit. He glanced at Landon and jerked his head in Vallon's direction. She was on her knees, tears running down her face as she retched.

Perfect.

"Amundson." Gleason stiffly nodded greeting. "Director Fitzsimmons. I didn't know you were in Seattle." Gleason kept his voice calm and controlled as he ran his palm over his smooth pate. It was a movement that, if you knew Gleason, showed just how shaken he was by this evening's events and the newcomers' presence.

Landon leapt lightly down onto the map and stepped carefully over the beautifully detailed liquid topography, trying not to damage the delicate membrane that was the map's surface. A slight queasy sense of movement up his legs as if the world were less steady. That was his version of the Gift, though he had no gift to see. He went down on his knees beside her, and the map swayed and undulated.

"Vallon?" She jerked away when he touched her shoulder, but not before he felt the searing heat of her. Her face was flushed with fever, and yet her lips were white.

"She's gone. I couldn't do anything, Landon. Whoever did this was too powerful."

"Shh." He looked up to see if anyone else had noticed her comment. "You're overwrought. It's difficult to see someone die."

At least she nodded and met his gaze. "It's a woman. There's something…."

He shook his head slightly, hoping she'd get the message. This was not the time to be spilling the AGS's secrets.

"She's powerful. Somehow she's using deep earth power."

That news almost froze him, but he managed to turn back to the Agents standing at the map edge. "Would you get back to work? Someone needs to monitor the city. Vallon's in no shape to carry on with the desk."

They muttered, but nodded as they retired to the computers around the room; but they still cast glances in his and Vallon's direction. They'd heard something—too much.

Vallon's breathing was too rapid and shallow. The woman was in shock.

"Come on, Pigeon. Take a deep, slow breath."

A brief nod.

"So what the hell's going on, Gleason?"

Landon glanced back at the AGS Chief. He stood, Moore flanking him, facing down the two interlopers. Fitzsimmons was a deadly man who'd fought his way up from CIA field operative to Director of Homeland Security by having a hunger for power and the unerring ability to assess and use any opponent's weakness. When he took over Homeland Security it was a mishmash of differing agencies duking it out over jurisdiction. He'd dealt with it by swallowing most of them up.

Except for the AGS.

He'd been gunning for it ever since.

Wolf Amundson was the Homeland Security version of a pit bull with aspirations. He'd probably been put in place as Liaison specifically to get to the AGS.

Not a good pair to show up on a night like this.

Gleason glanced in Landon's direction. Nodded.

Landon looked back at Vallon, her pale hair tangled wild around her face. She still panted like someone about to be sick. He had to get her out of here and away from Fitzsimmons' scrutiny. Vallon was strong, but few could stand against Fitzsimmons even on their good days.

"Can you stand?"

She gave a single nod.

"Good. Then we need to get you the heck away from here, understand?" He shifted so she could catch sight of the Homeland Security head.

Another nod and he offered her a hand, but she shook him off. Heat came from her in waves.

Standing looked as if it took everything she had. She staggered a step, the map membrane giving under her like a waterbed. Another step and she pulled herself upright, and this was what he loved about Vallon Drake. She had a strength of will few could match. By the time she hiked herself up out of the map pit she almost looked herself, except for her flushed features, the too-dilated eyes, and the tremor in her hands.

"My office." He led her through the desks towards the door.

"Hold it. Where the hell do you think you're going with that Agent?"

Landon turreted around to Fitzsimmons, who had broken away from Gleason. Vallon continued to the door.

"She's in shock. I'm taking her to my office to recover."

"This is Vallon Drake. Correct?"

Landon cast a question at Gleason, but the man's face was impassive granite.

"Yes." He'd only answer what he had to. "She's in shock— amongst other things—and needs to rest."

He followed Fitzsimmons' piercing gaze to Vallon, who stood proud as a wild thing near the door, and for the first time doubted that anyone would ever get a full read on Vallon Drake. Maybe that was a good thing.

"She needs to be questioned. Held. My information is she's already a suspect in a murder and now she's responsible when another Agent is lost. Who the hell knows what she'll do?"

"Well, I've got a much better chance of assessing that than you do." Landon turned to Fitzsimmons and saw he'd erred.

The man's face had gone dark, his grey flesh ruddy in the folds that led from his nose to his mouth and down to his chin. It looked like he bled.

Or fed on someone else's blood. In this case he'd prefer Landon's.

But he wasn't going to let this creature railroad Vallon into something. Landon looked to Gleason and saw the slight lift of head that was all he dared give as a nod. It was a nod, wasn't it? The sign to continue with their plan?

He had to be sure, because moving their agenda forward while under Fitzsimmons' and Amundson's scrutiny was going to be a tad more difficult.

"I'll take her to my office and then secure her."

"Gleason, you trust this midget to manage her?" Amundson.

Landon wished for the Gift. He'd have seen the floor open up to swallow the Seattle Station Chief—but that would have only exacerbated their problem.

"Landon knows his job, gentlemen. Now what do you say we allow Mr. Snow to do it, and retire to my office so that my staff can do their jobs. It seems we have some repairs to do tonight. Moore, see to it."

He turned on his heel and led Fitzsimmons and Amundson to his office. He ushered them inside and then threw an urgent look in Landon's direction.

§

The sleet slapped the windshield so hard Jason might as well have been screaming down I-5 into a storm at eighty miles an hour. The soggy mixture obscured his vision just as bad, even though he was stationary. Tension ran down his arms to hands white-knuckled on the steering wheel of his little BMW.

Why he was sitting here in the AGS parking lot with the cedars almost bent double in an unnatural wind and the almost-sleet pouring down, was a question he couldn't answer.

"Either get out of the car and do what you said you were going to do, or go the hell home."

He should do the latter. His shift was over. He didn't have to prove anything to Blacklock.

Trouble was, he had something to prove to himself and the only person who could help him with it lay beyond those busy doors.

There'd been a stream of people arriving in the last thirty minutes—a lot like what happened at the police station when something big was in the wind. He looked out at the trees.

"An ill wind." Something was coming down and Vallon Drake was in that building.

Swearing, he launched himself out of his car and hunched across the parking lot, muttering about idiots and asylums. He tried the main door and then swore louder when it rattled on its locks. He spotted an intercom and slammed the button with his fist.

A moment and then, "American Geological Survey. May I help you?" The voice was slightly breathless. And overhead a camera whirred up his body to his face.

Jason hauled out his shield, flashed it.

"S.P.D. Name's Bryson. I need to speak to Vallon Drake."

Silence, and then, "Wait a moment, if you please."

"The hell I will. It's pouring out here."

But the intercom had already gone silent, leaving him standing in a pool of amber light with the rain making sodden work of his knock-off Burberry trench coat and shirt collar, and the trees howling in their branches like wild women.

He should have gone home. He should just admit his mistake, cut his losses, and let Clint take the lead on this one. Step back before he dug himself in so deep he could never get out.

"Thank you for waiting, Detective Bryson. Agent Drake will see you now." He heard the door buzz open and was tempted to just turn around and walk away. Taking this step was going to be one he couldn't take back. As final as Cheryl's.

He closed his eyes and yanked open the door. Cheryl had always told him to be a risk taker. In her last days she'd said she wanted him to have a life—to find someone. Well, Vallon Drake just might be someone if she came out the other end of this investigation.

The bland scent of recycled air met his nose and the exhaust system blew a cold breeze down his neck. And yet there was an electric feel to it that set the hairs on the back of his neck on end. It was a feeling he recognized from a camping trip with Cheryl to Yosemite National Park. An earthquake had shaken the place while they were there. Beforehand everything had stopped—the wind, the bird call in the trees. It had creeped him out then, too.

He searched the ceiling for cameras, spotting nothing, but a cursory look really couldn't ensure his privacy. He took his coat off and shook it out on the floor. They left him outside—they could clean up the mess.

He started down the corridor to a T intersection and almost ran into Vallon, the effeminate, albino man he'd seen leave her house at her elbow, but now strangely dressed in moccasins, pajamas, robe, and a rain jacket.

"Agent Drake. Thank you for seeing me." He kept it formal, hoping she would be the one to break the ice, but her face said there wasn't much hope of that.

She looked exhausted. Dark circles under her eyes—dilated again, as badly as a kid on acid.

"What brings you here on such a bad night," the snow-haired man said in a voice pitched too high. The guy had the look of the perennial target for bullies when in school—more so in his getup. But he seemed to wear his oddity like a triumphant badge as he hovered at Vallon's elbow.

"And you are?"

"Pardon me. Landon Snow, at your service. I'm an associate of Agent Drake."

Such formality, and Vallon still hadn't said anything. Jason made a point of turning to her. "I needed to ask you some follow-up questions and I thought I could catch you at work rather than intruding on your free time."

Her dark gaze flickered in her pale face. Bloodless lips almost seemed to curve into a smile. "Such a considerate man."

Landon's gaze snapped to her, and Jason realized this gnome of a man was far more than a business associate. Guard, maybe? Observer, certainly, with his too-sly eyes. Jason wouldn't trust him as far as he could throw him.

"I try. Is there somewhere we can speak in private? An office, perhaps?" He glanced at Landon. "Alone?"

"This really isn't a good time, Detective. There has been some—difficulty—this evening, and I was just taking Agent Drake somewhere to recover."

Which explained the pallor of Vallon's face and the visible tremor in her hands that was so unlike the woman he'd dealt with before.

Her gaze shifted to Landon slower than it should have, and her throat worked as if she were trying to locate the words. "I can deal with this."

Landon seemed to hesitate. He looked over his shoulder back the way they'd come. A long corridor lined with doors, and a door with a window at the end. Jason caught a glimpse of a Eurasian-looking woman's face.

"May we use your office, Landon?"

Hesitation, but then an interested look on his face and, "Of course. Mi casa es su casa." He flourished his arm at a door and Vallon ushered Jason into a darkened room, leaving the little man cooling his heels in the hall. Jason wouldn't put it past him to have his ear pressed against the door.

"This is an office?" He scanned the room. Walls covered with the weirdest shit Jason had seen in a long time. Tables—science lab type—covered with too many glass tubes and bubbling beakers. "What? You build Frankenstein here?"

Jason did his best Igor impression, but it didn't even elicit a smile.

"His work room. A library. Landon does research for the AGS."

He glanced from her to the bubbling concoctions. "And this relates to geological surveys how?"

She closed her eyes and fatigue settled like a mantle over her. It was clear he hadn't come at a good time, and yet he had to do this regardless of her state.

"It's really none of your business. Now what did you need to talk to me about?"

So she was going to play it as if nothing had happened. Probably better for the both of them, though he seriously wanted to put some color back in those cheeks.

"I've got some follow-up questions from the investigation."

She nodded, and motioned him toward the rear of the large room.

Strange shit sat on the tables. The smell of rot and fermentation saturated the air. Bubbling jars. Was that a hamster cut open? And the pictures on the wall between the stacks of books—why would anyone display a drawing of a snake swallowing its tail, a creature that was a half-man-half-woman Chimera, or something that looked suspiciously like the pyramid and eye off the greenback. The strangeness of it left him guarded, and careful he didn't touch *anything* as Vallon led him into what felt like the nether regions of a bad dream.

Then a desk lamp flared on and she motioned him to a chair by a desk covered with papers.

"So?" She didn't sit even though she needed to steady herself.

"We got the Coroner's full report."

Again no comment, and he couldn't figure out whether it was just the fatigue he sensed, or whether she was being purposely reticent.

"It confirms preliminary results that Lamrey died of asphyxiation. Every bone in his body was crushed. All your CPR couldn't have saved him."

"Or caused the injuries, as you suggested during our initial interview."

"My partner might think that, but I'm not so sure." He said it softly and her gaze snapped to his. Exhaustion radiated off her. "Why don't you sit down? We're going to be a while."

"I suppose that should have been my line." She eased herself into a chair as if it hurt, and he wondered what had happened since he left her.

He met her gaze. "The report also says there was concrete in all his orifices. Care to share your explanation of that?"

But she already had. A tightening around her eyes showing how the news disturbed her. The flicker had been real grief unless she was a consummate actress, and from what he'd seen of Vallon Drake she was as up front as it got, if a tad secretive about herself. Honest, but not about to reveal her inner workings to anyone.

She sighed. "I can't say." She went to stand up, but he stopped her with his hand over hers.

She froze, yet the heat in her hand almost burned. And there it was—the surge of—what? Attraction? Electricity, that made him think he was connected to the whole damn world.

"Is that really appropriate, Detective?" She slipped her slim fingers from under his and the sensation was gone, leaving the room dimmer than before.

He quirked a smile. "Perhaps more appropriate than either of us wants to think. But I'm not finished here. Sit."

She did, her dilated eyes locked on him as he hauled his photocopies out of his jacket pocket and flattened them on the table edge then spread her drawing of Lamrey's death-sprawl and the arched wall beyond him.

"I thought we covered this."

"We did, but there are things that don't add up—or do add up to a theory that I think you might be able to help me with."

"I already told you, I didn't kill Simon Lamrey. I was trying to save him."

"Funny, but I almost believe you." He left the sketch in front of her, then slid the photo of the concrete wall with its arch beside it.

Her brows raised and she swallowed, then met his gaze. "I suppose I should thank you for your vote of confidence."

"I'd rather you told me what really happened."

A glance back at the documents before her and then, "I've told you what happened, Detective. All I can."

"Aah. Well then. No explanation for the lines of arch that match your drawing?" He pointed them out. How the hell was he going to do this and not come off sounding like an absolute fool? How the hell had he gotten to the point where he could even consider something like this? He left the papers where they were.

"Creative license?"

Jason sat back in his chair.

"You know, policing really lets you see the weird side of the human condition. The old shopping-cart woman who walks around with foil on her head to protect her thoughts, and when she takes the hat off she suddenly turns up dead. Then there're the psychics who provided information that helped solve the Green River murders, and the person who walked through a burning house and came out totally unscathed. Weird shit that can't be fully explained."

He watched her expression try to conceal how she was trying to make sense of his story so far. She looked guarded but interested. Just where he needed her.

"Shit like that makes a man wonder, but he sure as heck isn't going to discuss that kind of thing with his partner. Nope. Those are thoughts you keep to yourself—or tell someone you really trust. My wife used to say there's always something strange under the sun."

"She doesn't say it now?"

"She's dead." It came out flat and bald and the twisted feeling in his gut was just the same as it always was when he said it. Cheryl, gone. Maybe that was why he was doing this—because he couldn't let go. He watched Vallon realize he wasn't a philanderer—just a pathetic widower.

"I'm sorry. I didn't know." An indication her guards softened, and that was a good thing.

"It doesn't matter. Let me get to my story. Makes me shake my head because who the hell is going to believe it?"

Suddenly she looked as if she wanted to escape, her gaze flickered to the darkness where a red exit sign glowed red over the door.

"So it seems to me maybe an Agent could be going to back up a partner at a parking garage, but she finds something totally weird. Like maybe when she phones her partner she hears a phone and follows the sound, but she finds something really strange. Like maybe her partner is—" He held her gaze now. "Is in the wall—like his phone. She somehow manages to get him free, but when she tries CPR the police show up and all they see is a woman bent over a dead man."

"You couldn't possibly believe that." But the shutters closed on her face suggested something different. Clearly he was onto something.

"Couldn't I? Let me tell you a little story."

"Another? My, aren't I lucky." She sat back, arms folded in a prove-it position across her chest.

"It's a story I haven't told anyone, because when I think about it I feel like I'm losing my mind." And why he was baring himself to this woman when she could easily ruin his career with this information, he didn't know.

"When my wife died I thought my world had ended. Cheryl was everything to me. Even though she'd asked to be cremated, I couldn't do it. I had her buried up at Crown Hill Cemetery thinking how she could enjoy the trees and the view. One particularly bad day when I desperately needed her to be alive I went to visit. Damned if I could find her grave. I even did a standard grid search. It was like—like I'd wished her grave out of existence or something. There were flowers I thought I recognized on the spot I thought the grave had been, but no headstone. Nothing.

"I was furious. Totally furious. I went stomping across the hill and stood there looking at one of the graves feeling like the whole world had done me a bum deal. And then I thought about the gift Cheryl and I had had. She was everything—the light to my darkness. The laughter in my life, and I realized I'd been so lucky to have her even for such a short while. I knew she'd want me to move on. She'd even told me so. And suddenly I just wanted her grave to be there so I could tell her how much I loved her. Funny thing was, when I went back across that hill, I almost tripped over her grave with the flowers I'd put there and I'd swear on a stack of bibles that it was sitting exactly where the empty place had been a while before."

He watched her gaze flicker, a small sense of recognition as if finding a kindred spirit. He wondered why that almost made him happy.

"So you see, sometimes I think it's possible for things to move. Shift. Change."

Alarm rose briefly in her gaze and then she sat up with a small shake of the head. "I'm sorry, Detective. I really don't see what any of this has to do with me. Agent Lamrey was dead on the pavement. That's all I have to say." She stood up and almost staggered before catching herself on the desk. "And now I'm afraid there are urgent matters I really must attend to. If you'll excuse me?"

It took him a moment to remember to stand. He'd hoped—no, he'd been sure—that she would tell him what had really happened.

Instead she ushered him out the weird room to face the white gnome.

"Landon, could you show Detective Bryson out? I really need to get back. Goodbye, Detective. As always, a pleasure."

Politeness, or was she trying to send him a message. He kept his response to a nod, and allowed Landon to lead him to the door. The little man waited as he pulled on his coat.

"Agent Lamrey's death has been very stressful, Detective. For all of us."

"Death always is," he said, his voice rough in his ears. He stepped to the door and shook the little man's hand. "So's change."

Landon's gaze barely flickered, but his pale eyes dilated as if all light disappeared. Jason stepped out into the rain and hunched back to his car. Slid behind the wheel and looked at the door.

Landon stood there, watching back.

Chapter 15-Out of the Past

"Report, man. What the hell's going on here?" Fitzsimmons' snarl lashed out at Gleason, but somehow, to Amundson, Gleason seemed made of granite.

Of course, granite only needed to be chipped away.

Or a stick of dynamite would work as well. Amundson planned to be the one to light the fuse.

Gleason sat behind his desk, palms flat on the gleaming surface, and everything in perfect order around him. One file lay on the side of the desk. Framed photos hung perfectly aligned on the wall showing Gleason with politicians, a triumphant Gleason holding the reins of a large dark horse, a much younger Gleason with a cadre of other young men and women Amundson recognized from files he'd read. The original group of six agents who'd formed the AGS as an offshoot of the US Geological Survey.

IIis research had shown that the six had been a single geological survey team and somehow they'd convinced the powers of the US Geological Survey that they should be a team unto themselves to 'identify and address the gaps in the geological system caused by the meridian system' – whatever the hell that was. Typical of the time—specialization breaking agencies down further and further.

It was time for the splintering to stop.

Gleason sighed—finally. His broad hands whitened as he seemed to press harder into the desktop. So the situation *was* getting to him. Good.

"I'm truly glad you're here," Gleason said. "It has been a most difficult few days. Yes, we lost an Agent the other day. We're still investigating what happened, and that is why I didn't bother you with the news. My report would be sent after the investigation's complete." He met Fitzsimmons' gaze. "I thought you had better things to do than worry about a single Agent's death."

"You thought." Fitzsimmons hunched forward in his chair. "You thought? You didn't think at all—or else you did, and decided to hide things."

Gleason only cocked his head. "You are reading too much into the lack of one phone call, Director."

"Don't you condescend to me, " Fitzsimmons' beak of a nose targeted on the AGS Chief. "You should have reported to me. I made that eminently clear at our last meeting. Now I'll repeat my question one last time. What the hell is going on?"

Gleason, living more dangerously than Amundson ever wanted to, stood up. You had to admire him for his foolhardy bravery. He peered down from his height at the Director.

"What's going on, Director Fitzsimmons, is that someone seems to be taking out my agents, and by spending time with you I'm not focusing on finding whoever it is."

Fitzsimmons was on his feet so fast Amundson knew the explosion was coming. But Gleason getting thrown out of the AGS and having Fitzsimmons arbitrarily shut the agency down was the last thing Amundson wanted. That would quash his plans to consolidate the AGS with Seattle station. After an amalgamation, watch how fast his star would rise.

"Gentlemen. Please." He rose and stepped between the two men. "This is no way to deal with difficulties—fighting amongst ourselves. It is what the enemies of this great nation would wish."

He looked from face to face, forcing himself to make honest eye contact. Finally Gleason nodded and sat. Fitzsimmons gave him a flat, black glare.

"Please, Chief Gleason. Tell us what has happened, and perhaps we can help." Amundson sat and carefully crossed his legs in the European style that so set him apart from his peers. He cultivated the slightly effeminate gesture to encourage others to underestimate him.

"I said we lost an agent two nights ago. We lost another tonight. In both cases the agent on the desk indicated that another Gifted caused the change that killed the agent." His voice was clipped, factual, with barely a hint of resentment. Generally well played, but there was a hint of secrets there, too. Things Gleason did not want uncovered. Too bad for him.

Fitzsimmons glowered in his chair, so Amundson took the lead.

"And how did this Agent Drake become involved in the previous case?"

Gleason chewed his cheek and met his gaze. Clearly he didn't like what he was about to say.

"She was on the desk. She left to backup Agent Lamrey when she couldn't raise him by phone. She apparently found him partially encased in a wall, but was blocked from rescuing him by an unknown subject. When she did get him free, it was too late."

"Unfortunate." Fitzsimmons' comment came out in a hiss and Amundson held up his hand. They were getting somewhere. They didn't need to get into another argument.

"That is what she claims."

Gleason nodded.

"And this evening? What occurred that left Agent Drake in such a state?"

Gleason swung his bald head towards Amundson as if he suddenly realized his danger didn't come just from Fitzsimmons. His chair squeaked at the movement. My god, the man was not as astute as Wolf had thought. He smiled to himself. This was going to be more fun than he had anticipated.

"We don't know. As you saw, we have not exactly had a chance to debrief Agent Drake."

"But what do you know, Chief? There must be something you can say to explain the mess in your office. That machine alone was over a million dollars if I recall, and now it lays smashed on the floor."

"You know my budget, now, do you?" But a hint of fear came in the anger.

"Chief Gleason, Director Fitzsimmons made me your Liaison to Homeland Security. I take my duties seriously. Now if you will explain to Director Fitzsimmons and me…."

"Agent Drake was on desk. She hit the alarm at about 2135 hours. I was out on business but had just arrived in the parking lot when it sounded. Agent Moore and I found the war room in operation when we arrived. Then there was what appeared to be an attack on the AGS itself. A quake. It threw the desk and Agent Drake into the wall, but she still attempted to assist Agent Janet Hunt, the Agent in distress. She was unsuccessful, and Agent Hunt was lost."

The precise, measured words provided an overview, but none of the detail and none of the insider knowledge Gleason would have. Simply the facts. He would have done the same, but would have given anything to have had access to the thin man's brain.

"This is the same Agent Hunt who started with you in the AGS?"

Gleason turned at Fitzsimmons' question and a sigh escaped him. "Yes. It was, and it pains me. Janet Hunt was a valued member of the team and a friend."

"Like Vallon Drake is a valued member?" Amundson took back the conversation.

"Yes." But it was more guarded, as if Gleason were not quite sure where this was going. That was a good thing.

"Tell us about her."

Gleason paused briefly. "She is young. The—daughter of one of our best agents. Talented, if a trifle rough around the edges."

"What does that mean, if you please?"

The hands on the desk slid into fists.

"It means she's sometimes difficult and tries things her own way. But she always admits her mistake and comes back to the fold—the AGS way. She knows the limits."

"Does she? The woman I saw out there looked like she had seriously surpassed her limits."

"You saw her exhausted. She'd just fought for an Agent's life— and lost. How would you look in those circumstances?" The ire in the man's voice was music to Amundson's ears. He was slipping the shivs under Gleason's skin.

"Or perhaps she was exhausted from killing Agent Hunt, too?"

Fitzsimmons' comment left a void in the office except for the quickly masked intake of Gleason's breath. The Director cocked his head like a bird eyeing its prey.

"What? This did not cross your mind? An Agent can go rogue, Chief Gleason. Or have you forgotten this in your zeal to protect your agency? Perhaps that is why you have not reported these incidents to myself or Director Fitzsimmons. If I may ask, just how many deaths have there been, Chief Gleason?"

A barely contained shudder seemed to run through the thin man, and Amundson knew he'd won.

§

The detective sat too long in the parking lot, but finally he left in a spray of taillight-soaked water. Landon turned back to the corridor, pulling his robe around his knobby knees. He really should go home and dress first, but Vallon still stood at the T, her florescent-stained hair shifting slightly in the circulating air, her body pressed, trembling, to the wall. Afterburn radiated off her like a furnace. It would consume her from within if they didn't get it managed. In the early days of the AGS an agent had almost died from untreated afterburn. He needed to help her through this.

"By all creation, you look like you're going to fall over, Pigeon."

A weak smile and, "I just might."

He tried to take her arm, but she shrugged him off. "Not a good idea, Landon. We wouldn't make beautiful music."

He held his hands up, feigning dismay. "You're not my type, Pigeon. You'll have to get inside under your own power."

Somehow she found the strength to return to his door using only the wall to steady her uneven gait. Then she was inside, and made it to the lone desk lamp and the chair illuminated there. She collapsed and buried her face in her hands so he truly wished he knew how to comfort and protect her. The poor kid hadn't had protection like that ever.

"Oh god, Landon. What have I done?"

"Why don't you tell me?"

She glanced up at him and she was steel and velvet at the same time, and more vulnerable than he'd seen her since the day her father was suddenly gone. She closed her eyes and nodded.

"I couldn't save her, Landon. I tried. I truly did—just like I tried to save Simon. Oh, god, I'm such a screw up. I leave my post. I get caught using the Gift—by the cops no less, and then I…." She hunched down in her chair. "Then I use one of those cops to relieve the afterburn and now he's coming to me telling me stories like he actually knows about the Gift."

She raised panicked, grief-stricken, brown-green eyes to him before he could even consider all she'd revealed.

"How can you trust me when I don't trust myself? I didn't save her. I should have saved her. I could have saved her but I was too-fucking afraid."

The uncharacteristic tears showed just how distraught she was. But she fought them back valiantly and sat up to face him.

"So why don't you just do your job and tell Gleason and we'll get this over with?"she asked. You can lock me up or turn me over to the police—whatever it is you do with agents you can't trust anymore."

Landon sat back and crossed his arms over the Gore-tex. He should be feeding her inhibitor, forcing her to drink if she wouldn't on her own. But he couldn't take the chance she wouldn't understand or would just fall asleep.

"So you think anyone else could have done any better than you, Pigeon?" he asked quietly.

The room held only the sound of her ragged breath and the hush of the movement of air. Finally she raised her gaze to his.

"I'm a loose cannon. Gleason said so. I'll never be as good an agent as my Dad."

"He says a lot of things, Pigeon, but I doubt he said that. Gleason says different things to different people. Whatever will work—if you get my meaning."

"He plays people."

Landon nodded.

"Like me."

He nodded again.

"So just what is he playing at now?" she asked, fatigue loud in her voice.

"Trying to save all our lives, Pigeon."

That seemed to wipe some of the exhaustion off her face as she tried to parse out his meaning. Finally she shook her head. "Sorry. I'm not tracking."

"Exhaustion, I'm sure. You're too quick a study most of the time." He leaned on his desk and prayed he could get this right, because at this moment he suspected Vallon might be all that stood between the AGS and its annihilation.

"It's like this, Pigeon. We're aware of the deaths and we suspect a connection, but we've also suspected that it might be someone inside the AGS causing it." He heard her breath catch.

"You thought it was me."

"Actually the thought did cross Gleason's mind, but neither of us truly believed it. It's been going on too long."

A frown as she considered that bit of news, but he couldn't wait for her to figure out all that it meant. "The problem is that there isn't anybody but us with the Gift to do this. We keep track of the population. We recruit anyone with enough potential power. There aren't that many who have the Gift and control of it. That's why there's the Academy. We finally started to think we could enhance our agents by schooling the children of our Agents right from the start."

"So you needed to keep your suspicions quiet. You couldn't very well tell your Agents because that would put your enemy on guard."

"Exactly." He nodded. "And we couldn't very well tell Homeland Security, either. They've been trying to take us over for years. They'd use an inability to contain an Agent as a rationale for our amalgamation."

"Is that a bad thing?"

At that he chuckled. "Now there's a question, Pigeon. Tell me, just how is a unGifted supervisor going to know if you're doing your job? He or she won't remember anything that you did. Difficult to do an employee evaluation. I dare say he or she won't even be able to come up with assignments because he or she won't recognize a problem when he or she sees one."

"But what if it's not someone inside? What if it's someone outside the AGS? Landon, there's this man—Xavier de Varga, his name is. He was following me. The detective got his license number and found out his name. He—he feels like he's got a lot of power."

Landon sat stunned. "That's why you let me ramble on the other day."

He wanted to grab her, shake her for everything she knew, but the buzz of Landon's phone cut him off. He looked at the call display. Gleason.

"A moment," he said, settling himself before he picked up the phone. With her news it was difficult to do so. "Snow."

"Drake still with you?" The clipped voice said Gleason was still under observation.

"Yes, we're sitting here having a most illuminating chat."

"I see. Well, if she's had to be medicated to get some rest, perhaps this isn't the time to interview her. Perhaps sometime tomorrow after the shock has worn off."

So he wasn't on speaker phone. "We're under threat?"

"Yes. I understand. It was the worst we've seen. A direct hit."

"I'll get things in play."

"See that you do. And Snow, see that you take care of Agent Drake. She has things to answer for tomorrow. See she understands she's to be in my office at four p.m."

The phone went silent and Landon slowly dropped the handset into the cradle, considering Vallon as he did. He stood and regretted what he was about to do.

"We've got to get you out of here, Pigeon. Homeland Security has you in its sights and they're going to use you to take down the rest of us."

The afterburn showed in her glazed eyes. He crouched in front of her.

"You with me, Pigeon? Unless you want to be the key to taking down the AGS, you've got to get moving."

Her over-bright gaze locked on his. "What's *gild the lily*, Landon?"

He almost fell back into his chair with surprise. "Damn it, Vallon, where do you get these things? First Xavier de Varga, and now this? It's an archaic phrase about unnecessary adornment."

"So. What would it mean to the AGS?"

Landon checked his watch to cover his shock. He had to get her out of here and set her on course like he and Gleason had planned.

"There's no time, Pigeon, and it has nothing to do with this situation. You need to listen. Focus. Gleason and I need you to carry on with your investigation." He held up his hand. "Yes, I know you were already determined to investigate, we're just going to help you." He bent down and hefted the file box he'd prepared onto the desk. "This is everything we have on the agents who have been killed. Are you willing to carry on?"

"Willing?"

She struggled up, and again he was struck by her strength. There was tenacity there he didn't think he'd seen since her father, no matter what she thought.

"What choice have I got? I want my name cleared."

"Good girl." Landon wanted to hug her, but instead he shoved the box toward her. "The bad news is I estimate you've got a maximum of about sixteen hours before Homeland Security comes looking for you. Gleason's bought you time by saying you're to report at four, but once they're on you I'm afraid you're on your own. You'll be a rogue Agent on the run, and Homeland Security will be looking to bring you down."

A bitter chuckle. "Better and better. Dad would be so proud."

"He would be."

She flipped open the lid of the box and her face went still. She reached in to rifle the files. Looked at him.

"Jeezus. How many?"

"Seventeen."

The afterburn flush had faded from her face, but two highpoints of color formed now. "How far back does this go?"

And he knew she was no longer the little girl he'd rescued from a changed house's front porch. He couldn't protect her anymore.

"All the way back to your father."

Chapter 16-Faces Like Petals

The rain drove against Vallon's windshield, sluicing silver fingerprints down the glass and making it almost impossible to penetrate the blackness caught in her headlights, just as the afterburn made it almost impossible to think.

Only sheets of rain and slick buildings and streets. At three a.m. nobody was on the road except the cops and a few shift workers on their way home to bed. Nobody but her, alone as she was meant to be.

It was why her father had left her. Her mother, too. And all the men since then. She glanced over to the box of files. Maybe it contained some answers about why. She had sixteen hours to find out.

That Landon and Gleason were depending on her seemed strange. That they had trusted her all along even stranger. And Landon's tale of the danger suggested that there was far more to the world than met the eye.

She shivered.

Sixteen hours until she gave Homeland Security the weapon to take over the AGS, and here she was, checking out something she hadn't told Landon about, so she hadn't trusted Landon, either. But then he hadn't answered her question about 'gild the lily'.

Her hand went to her jacket pocket to fondle the last thing she had received from Landon. It was a symbol of how serious the situation truly was. A new Mont Blanc pen loaded with ink and a folded piece of pristine, government-issue vellum.

She drove the car down off I-520 onto I-5 and then navigated toward the old district that was Seattle Center. The bright folds of the Music Experience melted into the night. The Space Needle formed-disappeared-reformed through the windshield as she wormed her way down into the older areas between Denny Way and Broad Street.

She pulled into a space beside the road and parked, then -reached-. The darkened city disappeared into a landscape of flickering flames. The brief sparks that were most of the city dwellers spread around her like the stars or the sea of lights that was Seattle after dark, but nearby lay a brighter shoal of torchlight. Gifted.

She climbed out of the car and hiked her collar against the rain, then shifted the files to her trunk.

It was when she turned to walk down the street that she felt the tremor. She -reached- and the AGS burned like a bright beacon in the night. Something happened, and she found the strength to follow a surge of brandy-flavored power—Margorita Chavez—aimed at Mount Rainier.

In the darkness and the rain Vallon staggered against the light standard, pressing her head against the cool metal. Power ranged through the earth. The ridge of land that had formed where Wilkeson once existed began to wisp into the night. Trees wicked like candles. Stone flowed away.

In the flat expanse of treed parkland the brandy-scent surged, then faded away. A new Gifted worked—bayberry-scented. Ingersoll.

Clapboard buildings shimmered and formed in the rain. A light in a window, and antique neon sign. She felt the newly formed lives asleep in their beds. Chavez and Ingersoll had done good. Better than she had done. But then, whoever had opposed her wasn't there anymore. Or at least they didn't care about the changes the AGS had worked.

Which begged the question: why did they change Mount Rainier at all?

She dropped back into her body, but this wasn't the time to figure out the answer to that question. She hunched against the deluge and jogged down the street, rain soaking her trousers and Doc Martin's and running down her scalp under the collar of her jacket.

The Terry Avenue Shelter was a two-story brick building with barred windows and black steel door that stood under an awning that was edged with overflowing eaves. A river of water ran across the pavement in front of it, but Vallon waded through and knocked on the door.

No answer, which didn't exactly surprise her given most shelters quit accepting people after about eight p.m. Those who wanted to get in out of the rain had to make a decision early.

She tried the door, but the lock held. It rattled on its hinges. She -reached- and the flare of Gifted was beyond the door. Did she dare go in? Chance finding what she'd found at the flophouse in Pioneer Square? Could she get free this time if she did?

She had to try, because she had to understand, no matter the consequences to her afterburn. She was going to be laid up for days as it was. She dug into the jacket breast pocket for the vellum and pen. So smooth, the paper was a balm to her anxious afterburn. She uncapped the pen and unfolded the vellum against the door. -Reached-.

Cold steel, born of molten earth and fire. Brick, fired of clay and shale. She breathed it in, dry ash and heat still lingered for her nose. She sank—into it. Running through the smooth structure of the steel, the crystals of brick. Found.

The place where steel and brick met.

The wooden doorframe, tasted of old leaves and forest mold, and slumbered with the memories of height and sunlight. There.

Steel bored slightly into wood. Vallon hesitated. This was nothing she'd ever done before, but Xavier de Varga had. He had to have gotten into her house this way.

She touched pen to vellum and drew, as her mind told her to. Steel tongue faded away from high relief to low. Smoothed over in contours that ran the length of the door. Wood eased its tight frame, gave up its moisture to allow:

A click, and the door hinges groaned.

Vallon sagged, gasping, and fighting the afterburn against the brick. Who knew how long she could go on like this? Well, she wasn't going to deal with her afterburn here.

She studied what she'd done. Still a steel door, but its wooden frame had shrunk back as if desiccated from heat and age. She eased the door open, feeling the familiar tingle she'd felt from her kitchen door. No steel bolt fed out from the lock. The entire door edge was a smooth expanse of steel. Nothing could be secured against this kind of power. Did the AGS know?

She hauled herself upright. Whether they did or not, didn't matter. This was one skill she wasn't going to share with them—yet.

She held the changed door in her mind as she stepped inside.

The reek of dust, old men, and filthy clothing assaulted her nose upon entry. She pulled the door closed behind her and faced a silent vestibule and another locked door.

Her pulse thumped in her head, the bump from hitting the wall throbbing with each breath. She was taking a huge chance—break and enter the least of her crimes.

But she had to know if her suspicions were true. And this might help track whoever was murdering agents. That was worth the chance she was taking.

She used the vellum and drew the second locked door open; the vellum connecting the smooth metal with what it was to become. She -reached- felt the steel like her skin, and smoothed the lock away with her mind and her ink. A gentle tug and the door opened.

She stepped into almost-darkness and wondered what Landon would say if he saw how she used her Gift now. Not quite what he'd expected.

To one side, a night light illuminated a hallway and a closed doorway marked 'staff—no admittance'. The dim flicker of the unGifted attendant came from beyond the doorway. She crept forward, seeking.

The hallway guarded a series of dormitories, judging by the number of people she sensed beyond each door. But as she trod the corridor the air grew heavy with scent of licorice. She stopped, scanning the rooms with her inner sight.

The door at the end of the hallway guarded a mass of flames so bright it almost blinded her inner sight. Strange none of the other rooms held Gifted. All the little hairs stood up on the back of her neck. An electric pulse too similar to what she'd felt near Pioneer Square seemed to run through the air and send the bump on her head thumping harder.

She touched the dormitory door. Stopped.

Going through the door placed her in danger of being caught again if what she suspected was true. But this time she would be on guard. The latch clicked loudly in the silent hallway and she eased the door open onto a too-familiar tableau.

The row of cots had been dragged away from the walls to form a star around a center-point in the room. Old men—the cast–offs of society—curled on the thin mattresses, their faces turned like petals toward the center.

A shifting, golden glow filled the room's core and placed deformed shadows across the fly-cast ceiling and walls. The stench of licorice and unwashed bodies hung so powerful her stomach threatened to rebel—and yet....

The golden glow pulsed like a siren song, warm and golden and honey-sweet as a yellow-flowered licorice tree. She wanted to step into that glow, remove herself to become part of that many-layered licorice world so vivid she could almost see:

White beaches, and palm tree shadows like trails on the sand.

Blue waves, and the breeze carried the light scent of salt and licorice and crab baking over a fire.

Happy voices from the people gathered around the fire, and she would be one of them.

So simple—she could live her life there, drifting on the beach. Simple and free. None of the concerns of her life. Happiness.

So much happiness.

Her lips pulled into an unaccustomed bow and that shocked her back a step. The damned glow was insidious. She doubted she would ever be that happy, and in that was the falseness of this place.

But the licorice scent said it was also a conduit to whoever was doing these things—including taking out Simon and Janet, and presumably every other agent back seventeen years.

Including her father.

Vallon grabbed hold of the doorframe to stop herself from being drawn into the room. Then she carefully, tentatively, -reached-.

Power blasted her like the room exploding. She dug fingernails into the doorframe. Earth. Pulsing. Her own pulse changed to match, and the earth's heat seared through her, weakened her grip.

Power dragged her forward a step.

Another.

Her mind ripped further from her body than it was meant to—sucked her down. Sucked her out of her flesh like a siphoning straw. Shattered her so she was swept far and wide in the web that spread under the streets and hillsides of Seattle.

Thin, so thin the licorice wind could take her like a sail and she—Vallon—would be no more. It would almost be better. She would be part of something more. Something great.

Would stop *them.*

The satisfying purpose rammed through her. Intent so powerful her body stepped forward again. Again.

Her shins banged against the metal bar at the foot of a cot. The pain broke through her compulsion.

She staggered.

It wasn't *her* purpose.

She scrabbled for the shredded pieces of herself, like trying for laser readings through wind and heat. Nothing solid. Nothing clear. Nothing to hold on to, and wasn't that what Simon had said: that she was too distant, too secretive, too hard to read?

Was that all she was? A being made of half-made dreams and impressions?

No! Vallon Drake. She was Vallon Drake.

A stutter in the brilliant gold, and suddenly it was as if laser light lit on her. Blinding. Precise. And Vallon knew that the person behind the killings was aware of her.

Was aware of who and where and what she was.

Terror tore her loose. She slammed back into her body. Half-fell on top of one of the old men, his stench burning away the licorice scent.

She righted herself. Across the room one of the old man sat up.

"Hey, sweetie, you here for a date?" He made a smooching sound that made her skin crawl.

A hand found her thigh and she yanked away.

A hand found her ass and she punched him in the gut.

The afterburn burned through her veins, stuttered her thoughts, slo-mo'ed everything, and made triangulating her feet, her footsteps, her location almost impossible.

The old men pushed to their feet.

The noise would wake the staff. She had to get out of here. Get safe, because the licorice woman was like a treacle shadow in the corner of the room, the corner of her mind, and the sticky reach of her fingers could take Vallon down.

She turned, ploughed into an earnest-looking young man with rumpled clothing and sleepy eyes.

"Hey! What are you doing?"

He tried for her arm, but she slipped past his touch and dashed down the hallway thanking whoever had set only one night staff in the shelter. She slammed her shoulder into the vestibule door, the outside door, and stopped in the rain soaked street.

She turned to the door and hauled out the vellum and drew. The door was steel, smooth, chill, except for the tongue that had found its way to moist wood. She held the image in her head until it was so. Someone slammed against the door. The doorknob rattled and Vallon managed a grin.

She hadn't quite put back the inner workings of the lock, which should slow them all down.

She jogged to her car and then, almost on autopilot, drove like a madwoman through the hissing streets past the dark expanse of Lake Union, over Fremont's Aurora Bridge with its lurking troll.

If only the licorice woman were so benign.

The slopes of Fremont Hill were cloaked in darkness and trees, streetlights spilling their amber pools of light. She was forced to take a parking spot a block uphill from her house. She claimed the file box from her trunk and limped down the hill, fighting back the afterburn fatigue, the panic that she didn't want to recognize for fear it would immobilize her.

The licorice woman had *known* her. Knew who she was — and Vallon racked her tired brain trying to make mutual the recognition.

A welcome porch-light blazed from the front of her house. So Fi was still there. At least there was that.

She lugged the box up the stairs, fumbled for keys, but the door opened before she could get them in the lock.

Detective Jason Bryson stood framed in her doorway.

Chapter 17-Fadeout in Rain

"He's hiding something, of course." Wolf waited until the Town Car door slammed behind him before turning to Fitzsimmons. To speak in the parking lot would have been unwise, even with the rain acting as a natural barrier to microphone pickup. He trusted Gleason or his white rat, Snow, would have had them trained on Fitzsimmons and himself to glean whatever they could, to try to save themselves.

It was what he would have done.

"You speak the obvious. That call to check on the woman. Likely a signal. We should have demanded it be on speaker phone."

"And that would have shown we did not trust him."

"He already knows we don't trust him, you fool."

Wolf didn't respond. The car cruised down the highway through the gusting rain under the firm guidance of Fitzsimmons' driver.

Fitzsimmons himself stared out the side window. "God, how do you stand it here? This darkness and rain. Weren't you in Florida before?"

Wolf decided responding would be less dangerous to his career. "One becomes accustomed. I have my ultra-violet lights at home. I take my vitamin D. It is the heat I miss, if anything."

The car swayed in a gust of wind as I-520 swept down towards the Evergreen Floating Bridge and the dark waters of Lake Washington. The Seattle towers dripped light in the rain.

Florida had been a lovely interlude of sun and sand, and it had been an active posting dealing with the ongoing flood of Cuban refugees and the drug trade. His experience dealing with the politics of the rich had served him well since arriving in Seattle, as well.

"But Seattle and taking down the AGS has the better potential for promotion."

Fitzsimmons' statement of fact turned Wolf to him. He managed a smile.

"Actually, yes. A chance you gave me."

"I'm glad you recognize that fact."

Fitzsimmons rubbed his chin on his shoulders in a manner reminiscent of birds preening, then he caught Wolf again in an eagle glare.

"So what are you going to do with Gleason?"

A test, and one Wolf planned to pass. He smiled more openly now, because he could almost taste AGS blood and feel the pats on his back as he got news of his promotion.

"Gleason has tried to buy himself time. I suspect he's trying to get stories straight amongst the staff. That's what I'd be doing."

Fitzsimmons nodded.

"So if he's given himself—what?—ten or fifteen hours, we don't let him have it. We do the one thing he clearly doesn't want us to do— we pick up his Agent for questioning."

"When?"

Wolf checked his watch. "How does time enough to get home and change my clothes sound? This is one takedown I want to lead myself."

§

Jason's presence slammed into Vallon's afterburn like a laser beam on point. Triangulation, and she fixed on him.

She swallowed back the moan in her throat, but couldn't stop the rush of heat between her legs as she closed the front door behind her.

"What are you doing here?"

He looked too damned comfortable, in stocking feet and with shirtsleeves rolled up to expose a shadow of dark forearm hair that matched the shadow along his jaw. He shrugged.

"I got the impression you couldn't talk freely where we were, so I thought I'd meet you where we could. Talk that is." His gaze locked on the file box. "Here. Let me give you a hand with that."

He reached for the box, and before Vallon could stop him, his hands touched hers.

Just the glance of fingers burned through her and sent the afterburn surging. Her vision doubled, worse than any bump on the head could do, and she staggered, ripped away from him, but he caught her elbow.

"Vallon? Vallon, are you all right?" He dragged her inside from the door as she tried to turn and run. "Damn it, Vallon, what's the matter? Do I need to take you to a hospital?"

She ripped free and blinked back the haze of unthinking need that threatened to throw her into his arms.

"I need sleep. I need to forget this whole day even happened."

She set the box on the ancient, leather-bound trunk that served as her coffee table and saw his glance lock there.

"Just some work stuff. You want some coffee? Where's Fi? I take it she let you in."

She doffed her coat and sodden shoes and headed for the kitchen, then stopped at a sudden thought.

"She *did* let you in?"

"She did. But then she got a bit strange and said she had to leave. She took off like a bat outta hell."

Vallon sagged against the wall. "Dammit. I wanted to talk to her."

"And I had to talk to you." Even with her eyes closed she could tell he stood too close. Heat came off him in waves, and all her self-control wavered like hot air in a desert.

She didn't want to open her eyes, but couldn't help it when he caught her wrist.

"You look like you might faint."

She pulled herself away, because she would not have another episode like their last meeting in the kitchen.

"I'm fine. Wait in here while I make the coffee."

A hint of a smile said he knew damn well what she was thinking of, and damn it, he was too damn sexy and too available for both their good.

She forced herself into the kitchen, though she ached to deal with the afterburn. Her hands shook as she filled the coffee pot.

"You know, tea might be better."

She whirled around in shock and that wasn't like her. She was solid. He stood framed in the door, arms crossed as he studied her and must have seen her resentment.

"Sorry. I have a habit of sneaking up on people. My wife used to say I was a secret agent in a past life."

She emptied the coffee pot and filled the kettle, considering how his dead wife filled his conversation, as her father filled her head.

"How long has it been since you lost her?"

A pause, and she glanced at him as she set the kettle on the stove, and then put a red rooibos teabag in the pot.

"Three years and two and a half months."

And how many days, hours, minutes, she wanted to ask, because she knew he would know. Just as her internal clock could tell her how long it was since she arrived outside the house that wasn't there anymore for the first time. Since she'd been an agent, she'd volunteered to fix the heritage blue house in place every time the darn bookstore owner changed it. A form of therapy, she supposed. She nodded at him and busied herself with the tea.

"Forget what they tell you; time doesn't make it easier. You just get better at kidding yourself."

The kettle boiled and she poured the water into the pot and turned, hearing a clink. He took a couple of mugs off the open shelves, raised his eyebrows for approval, and her mouth went dry.

She nodded.

He was trying too damn hard to be helpful and put her at her ease when all she wanted—no, needed—was for him to leave. Why hadn't she told him to leave? That should have been the first thing out of her mouth, and instead she'd invited him for tea?

Kicking herself, she followed him into the living room, placed the cups on the table, and shifted the box to the floor. When he settled on her couch and looked up at her innocently, there was nothing she could do but sit down as far as she could from him on the couch and pour the tea.

"So, what were your questions, Detective?"

Another amused smile. "Detective, is it?"

"It's what you are." Keep it business-like because he was not her type. She didn't have a type—only mistakes.

"All right." He sipped his tea, but she couldn't hold her cup. Her hands were shaking so badly he'd see, and the whole room seemed to pulse in and out as if she was trying to get a reading through fog. The connection to whoever was out there still held, and left her as nervous as Maggie in front of a dog.

"So how could Lamrey have gotten concrete in all his orifices if he wasn't in that wall?"

The muddiness of her thoughts made it hard to pinpoint what she should say. She kept looking at him, and away, hoping perhaps if she did it enough times she'd get a reading.

"So you're still suggesting he was *in* the wall?"

A nod. Another sip and she realized she'd made a serious mistake sitting with him in the mood lighting that was all she kept in the living room. She stood up.

"Craziness."

"Is it? Sort of like the fact all the records and my memory say there was only a false alarm in Pioneer Square, but your hair and clothing smelled like smoke. It's like what I see has no relationship with what really happened. Sort of like a veil over my eyes, and I'm only allowed to see certain things."

He'd thought about this too much, and Landon and Chief Gleason would go nuts if they heard this coming from a unGifted.

Or had she been wrong?

She -reached- and his form was replaced by the simmering dark flame that filled most people, but there was something different. Gold sparks rose through the darkness, breathed out a hint of licorice and spice.

Vallon froze, dropped out to ordinary sight and found him, eyes narrowed and studying her. Had he been changed or not? He didn't seem dangerous.

"So where did you go?"

She shivered and stood, turned to the front window where the rain streaked the glazing into rippling, street-lit color.

"It was strange. Like you looked right through me and I…." His face was puzzled. "It was like I felt it."

And that sure as hell shouldn't be.

"Why do I feel it, Vallon?"

His words and his breath warmed her neck and she almost punched him. Whirled, and his hands steadied her when the damned afterburn almost collapsed her legs.

Flares like sunspots at his touch. Her vision changed to one of heat waves and rippling shadow, and all her boundaries fell away.

She existed in no man's land. No place at all. And how could anything matter to the outside world when she was trapped inside one of those unbounded places that everyone else in the world had forgotten existed.

She looked him in the eye, saw he felt it too. She reached up to stroke his face. Hard angles and the grit of new beard thrilled through her palm.

"This is wrong, you know. We're on opposite sides of this thing."

A small shake of his head. "You're wrong. We're on the same side until my theory's shot down."

His palm came up to cup her head and he leaned down to kiss her with a salt-sweet touch.

"Well far be it from me to shoot a man's theory dead." She caught his hand because there was nothing else to be done with the afterburn pounding in her head and turned and led him to the stairs. He hesitated. "I'm not going to do what we did last time. My bedroom's there."

But he knew that. The scent of his spring morning and sea scent hung on the stairs as if he'd checked out the house in her absence. Had he gotten into her locked basement?

No time to think on it now. Up the stairs to the back bedroom with the yellow duvet-covered bed and the empty picture frames at its head. She hadn't known what else to fill them with so she'd hung them as they were: a reminder of danger. She left the lights off and turned to him, stripped off her top and stepped up to him.

"So?"

"Pretty bold, Vallon Drake."

"And you like that. It's what attracted you in the first place."

"Maybe." He leaned down in the grey light from the street to trail a kiss from her lips down the side of her jaw to the arch of her neck and she could have purred, but the afterburn forbade it—demanded so much more. "Or maybe it was the danger you presented. My partner says I'm on self-destruct mode. Destroy my career."

She stopped him with a kiss. Bit his full lower lip and demanded that he answer. He did. Ravenous and powerful, he shoved her toward the bed, followed so they could continue their hungry exploration. She pulled his shirt off and she ran her hands over the rough hair of his chest—down to his trim waist and the buckle of his belt.

Disobedient hands shook as she tried to work it. He brushed them away and freed himself, stepped out of his trousers and impatiently unzipped her jeans as he shoved her onto the bed. He hauled them off her, then lay down beside her.

"Better. Much better." His palm ran light as rain down her side and sent her shivering in delight.

Enough.

She pushed him onto his back, was up and straddling him so that only her silk and his briefs separated them. Ran herself along his body and he groaned.

"So. We going to do this or what?" Her voice was hoarse with afterburn. If they could just get this done she could think clearly again.

In answer he hauled her down, quick fingers flicked her bra free, slid it free of her shoulders, and tossed it aside. Hands down her back, slid into her silk panties to cup her ass, as he sat up to suckle her breasts.

Sparks shocked her. Her breath was harsh in her ears as she grabbed his head, wanted more teeth and pleasure, but also pain. Just enough to remind her she lived and hadn't disappeared with her father.

He rolled her off of him and stripped off her panties, his briefs, and she shoved him back down, straddled him again. She closed her eyes, arched her back as he entered and—she moved. Rocked. Shook.

Like the earth, and she moved with him, bucking as he held her in place, as they strained together, as she demanded and took, as he rose to her.

Air stained with their sweat and moans. The bed quaked and groaned as the tempo increased. Increased and the afterburn built, built, built, steaming behind a dam ready to burst.

She shook. Jason shook. The bed, the room. As she threw her head back and yelled triumph as Jason sat bolt upright and yelled.

"Cheryl!"

And that was just plain wrong. She dropped into herself, suddenly cold.

"Vallon! Vallon! Vallon!"

The screams came with the explosion in her core and Vallon collapsed on top of Jason, slick with sweat, the afterburn flooding out like a golden tide pulled by the moon of the earth. To sleep.

"Vallon!"

Not him. Not Jason, who cradled her against his chest murmuring apologies for calling her Cheryl.

The bed shuddered and her eyes flashed open.

"Vallon!" From outside.

The room shook. Pounding came from the door downstairs, and the walls streaked and faded. Window glass wisped away.

Rain splattered her back, then her upturned face, catching her in the eye. A gossamer ceiling. Roof joists, like ribs, misted and were gone. She began to drop through the bedding. Through the man in her bed, and her nose filled with licorice.

"No!" She bolted upright and grabbed Jason. Dragged him off the melting bed. "Grab your clothes." She already was. "Come on! Come on!" Her damn pen and vellum were downstairs.

He stood dazed, like a beautiful deer alone in the headlight of power streaming up through the earth. Already his form wavered at the edges, fingers stretched long as if his hands blew away; his black hair broke into a thousand tiny pieces—all dragged away in the wind of the change. Terror filled his eyes, when they finally met hers.

"Whhhhaaaatttssss hhhaaaappppeeennnniinnnggg…?"

She grabbed his hand and -reached- for the earth but a power was there before her—golden—licorice-scented and pulling more power from somewhere than Vallon had ever seen before. She tried to find power, but licorice was in the air, the earth—black tar on earth breath. Nothing for her there.

She grappled with the power, used everything she had to spread herself into a wide veil to protect her home, but without pen and ink it couldn't be done. Licorice rent her efforts like knives.

Jason moaned. His shoulders blew away even as she dragged him, stumbling, down the diaphanous stairs. They came to a gap where they were totally gone.

"Hold on. Dammit, hold on." Even if the bastard called her Cheryl he didn't deserve this. No one did.

They had to get out or they'd end up like Simon. She grabbed Jason's arm, pulled him close. Wrapped the arm holding their clothes around his waist. "Jump. We have to jump."

She did, and he stumbled with her, barely catching on stairs that gave under her feet like swampy soil. She sank in to her knees and she scrambled up, helped Jason right himself and dammit, dammit, dammit they had to move. Run, jump, or they weren't going to make it.

The ceiling slowly, inexorably folded toward them, assuming a new incline. She kept glancing at Jason, keeping his form solid in her thoughts, her own power draining away as she fought the assault that would take them both.

How could she hope to stand when Simon—a fully-trained, prime-of-his-life, Agent — had been caught in a wall?

Around the corner of the stairs, and the living room flickered below them. The couch shimmered and was gone. The coffee table faded to silver as an old photograph fades.

"No!" She grabbed Jason, leapt for the floor, for the coat rack that held her tools. When she hit, she sank in to her chest. Jason, released, collapsed to his knees. He looked at her.

"Vallo -?" The powerful wind wisped away his face.

"Jason! Jason!" -Reached- and clawed at the golden wind. She felt someone—Chavez?—there with her, feeding her power, but then Chavez was gone, depleted.

Vallon fed the image of Jason's face into him and the wind seemed to part around him. His features returned. His shoulder reformed.

From beyond the door the screaming continued. "Vallon! Vallon! No! Stop!"

Fi. The door rattled in the wooden frame. So there was method in the attacker's means. The door would be locked solid, Vallon was sure. Her house was a trap and the trap was meant for her.

"Vallon!" The way Fi screamed, she'd wake the whole neighborhood and that was the last thing Vallon needed. Ridiculous she'd think it, as she hauled herself up out of the ensnaring floor—only to sink in again.

"I'm here, Fi. I'm coming." She grabbed Jason's hand, but his fingers were gone.

No! She flooded power into him; his hands solidified for a moment, but she sank deeper into the floor. Deeper, and there was no way she could reach the door, or her tools, or safety.

"Run, Fi. Run." She held onto Jason and felt herself fall. Was this how Simon had felt?

Chapter 18-Winked Out

"I swear the man gloated while he turned his pit bull on me." Gleason shook his head as he paced the confines of his office and paused at his desk to stab his finger at the intercom. "Moore, isn't there anything you can do to turn up the air circulation? This place stinks of Amundson."

Landon looked up mildly. "I think he wears that scent to mark his place." He smiled. "Not much more than an animal. A crafty one, but not much more."

He kept himself calm, hoping his demeanor would help Gleason settle. The last thing they all needed was for Gleason to go off half-cocked. The trouble was, Landon still hadn't even had the chance to change into more suitable attire. The best he'd been able to achieve was to replace the Gore-tex with a white lab coat over his bathrobe and pajamas. He didn't like the way his ankles looked so naked.

"You should hold on to the fact we got Vallon out of here and on task as we'd planned. I know it was a shock to her, and that she's dangerously close to afterburn overload, but she was hungry for the task. You should have seen her face."

That brought Gleason around, interest replacing some of the worry about Fitzsimmons' machinations.

"So you think she'll investigate?"

"Wouldn't you? Her father's file is in that box." Landon studied his fingernails, and then looked up. "In case you hadn't noticed, all her problems go back to her dad. The man never spent time with the kid. She was always trying to make him notice her. Unfortunately, the behavior just continued to today."

"So I've finally noticed her."

Landon nodded. "And in the right way—by assigning her a special task that shows you trust her. If this works out, she'll be on track. A top agent in the fold and loyal to you for trusting her."

Gleason's stony gaze met Landon's. "You were the one who gave her the assignment. The loyalty will be to you."

"Give her some credit. She knows the orders came from you."

Gleason turned away. "I just hope you're right." He shook his head. "Damn it. Can't they do something about this air?"

Landon inhaled the scent and set his own irritation aside. "He'll have read the reports about the Gifted and our sensitivity to scent. He'd know just how much this would bother you. Think of that."

At that, Gleason seemed to force himself under control. He went to his desk, sat down, and looked at his research chief. "You really should get changed. Or get some sleep. I can manage from here."

Landon stayed where he was. "We should talk about contingencies. I figure Vallon's got 16 hours—fifteen and a half now — until she's due at your office, before Fitzsimmons sends in the hounds. What do we do if they pick her up before she finishes her investigation?"

Gleason sighed, and suddenly the big man looked diminished and tired. "How about pray. Knowing Vallon she won't go easily. It'll play right into their story about rogue Agents."

"I'm not buying that it'll happen, but I agree we need to prepare for the worst. I'll get the files ready and you should get Moore to prep the computers for purging both the mainframe and the backup. If they are going to take over, then let them start from scratch." He allowed a thin smile to form on his lips. "Who knows, they might even need us."

An increased hum in the ceiling, and papers stirred on Gleason's office. The man relaxed. "You are one bloodless, S.O.B., Landon. It's what I love about you."

Landon shrugged and allowed himself a momentary resentment that Gleason understood him so little. There were things that were necessary in life, and understanding the Gift was like food to his body.

Understanding how the Gift manifested differently in himself—and just what that meant—most of all.

"Not bloodless. I just have confidence in Vallon Drake. She's brilliant, tenacious, and talented." He paused, but he had to get this over with. "While we're on the topic of issues, there is one more thing. Vallon asked me about Gild the Lily."

That straightened Gleason in his chair. "She said it when she was in the pit, but I told myself I'd misheard. There's no way in hell she should know about that old project. It's been locked in my personal folders for years."

"Well she got it from somewhere, and she's asking questions."

Gleason fell back in his chair. "Jeezus. Just what we need—that old specter being resurrected."

"It was a reasonable idea at the time, but thank god cooler heads prevailed."

"Like you and me." Gleason smiled.

"Yes. And we'll be cool now, as well. Besides, it can't harm us—we never acted on it."

"We can be cool, but can Vallon Drake? That's what concerns me, Landon. Normally I think your plan could work, but with H.S. thrown into the mix, I'm not as sure. And if she's asking us about Gild the Lily, she's going to ask other people. Maybe start people prying." Gleason drummed his fingers on the desk, hit the intercom again. "Moore, start emergency dumping procedure Alpha Eight."

A pause, and then, "Yes. Sir."

The intercom went silent and the two of them sat in silence, Landon trying to determine the next steps to take.

"Cat's out of the bag, now," Landon said. "The agents aren't stupid. They'll know something big is up."

A knock at the door, and Moore stuck her head inside. "Chief? Something's happening. An attack on Vallon Drake."

"What?" Both men were on their feet and out the door.

It couldn't be true. Landon's stomach clenched. Vallon was the most Gifted they had. There was no way she'd be caught like the other agents. She couldn't be.

But the war room's scent of burned out machinery was overrun by the scent of fear.

Across the map pit a crowd had formed around one desk; Chavez's, Landon realized. She and the others had been put on duty monitoring smaller areas of the city from their computer consoles.

Now the smaller woman sat hunched over the screen, her hands gripping the edge of her desk and sweat forming on her brow.

"Get back to your posts," Gleason growled, pushing a path through the other officers, Landon in his wake. Then they were crowded around her desk, peering at the screen.

Fremont street pattern. Landon tried to –reach- with his meager Gift, but got nothing but a vague sense of movement and change, an aftertaste of ozone in the back of his mouth that left him weak in the knees and hating his limitations.

"Holy Christ," Gleason muttered and leaned down over Chavez, who was moaning as she peered into the screen.

Gleason's power flared as he leaned over Chavez. He had a powerful gift, to show so much power after all he'd been through this evening. Then suddenly Chavez went limp in her chair. Gleason staggered.

"My God." Gleason turned dilated eyes on Landon, stark fear radiating off him. "She's gone."

Landon shook his head. "No. That can't be. She's too powerful." He rolled Chavez away from her desk and bent down, touched the computer, but the lights flickered in the room. Someone yelled, and the earth shuddered and lurched. Lurched again and he fell against the computer. The lights went out and the screen died.

Darkness filled the room, and the sound of panicked breathing.

"Someone get the emergency power online," Gleason growled. "Everyone stay calm."

Someone nearby was trying unsuccessfully to stifle quiet sobbing as they waited. And waited. Chavez, Landon realized. Seeing what she'd seen was a shock.

He moved towards the sound, found her in the darkness, and caught her hand. "It's going to be all right. Vallon is okay, you'll see."

She shuddered as the room had, and he felt her shake her head. "You did not feel it." Her accent came thickly. "I try to help her, try to block the change, but it was like I was not even there."

She was crying openly as the lights flickered and returned. Gleason stabbed the computer 'on' button and the machine hummed to life.

"It'll be all right. You're safe here."

She looked up at him with terrified eyes and shook her head. "No. I'm not."

"Mother of God. More change is building."

Gleason's strained comment turned Landon back to the computer. Fremont again, though the grid lines on the screen told him nothing more.

"None of us are," Chavez whispered.

Landon looked at her and she must have seen his question.

"Safe."

§

In the disintegrating house, Jason was unGifted sand to be washed away in the sea of change. But Vallon could not — would not — leave him to the whirlwind eddies that stole her breath, even if he were no help getting out the locked front door of her house. If she could even reach the door, her jacket.

Almost up to her waist in the syrup-thick floor, the change trapped her movements. Rain through the roof soaked them both, stinging in the swirling, haloed winds.

If she could focus her power on the floor under her she might be able to do it, but Jason's shoulders and arms thinned when she tried to divide her focus. She couldn't take a chance. He could be totally lost in an instant—or damaged irrevocably.

She half swam, half waded, toward the wall through nimbus light, dragging Jason with her. If she could get there she might pull them both through. But the walls had shifted first, glowed less than everything else, and looked suspiciously solid. A prison. A death trap.

Meant for her.

Almost there. She stretched out her hand through the abrasive change, the whirlwind of particles. Barely touched—gyprock felt solid, but the coat rack wisped away like Jason.

"No!"She sobbed. She didn't want to die like this. She shifted toward the more distant door.

A crash stopped her dead. Around her the house contorted and became something new. The ceiling drew up and up, two stories.

Always wanted a vaulted ceiling. Bitter thought. But the rain stopped pelting her head.

Another crash and the floor thickened. Thickened to solid and it was impossible to move, floorboards squeezed in, and her flesh and pelvis groaned.

The crushing pain made it impossible to think. She could barely breathe. She was up to her waist and Jason was caught so only his face was free, though he no longer faded. The agony of failure filled her. It should not be like this. She was better than this.

Another crash and the front door splintered. Darkness and sheeting rain flooded in. She caught a glimpse of Fi's terrified face and then a dark-cloaked figure rushed in on the wind.

The floor solidified where he strode, tall, dark with soaked, shoulder-length hair that glinted with rainbows in the room's weird light. He reached her, grabbed her hand, and the floor seemed to release her on command. She stepped up, free.

"Focus," he growled. "Focus on what this place is supposed to be and I will feed you power."

"But...." The ferociousness of his black glance bit off her objection. She squeezed Jason's hand and did as she was told. -Reached-and closed her eyes. Incense-and-cedar-scented power rammed in and joined with her own. She would have gone to her knees except for the dark man's grip on her arms.

House: two-story. The curve of the corner staircase. The kitchen with its cupboards and open shelves of dishes. Her bedroom with its yellow quilt, the empty frames above the bed and Jason reclining on the bed. She stopped herself, wondering why she would place him there. But her hand was empty when she opened her eyes.

Basement, thus and so, the glittering silver seam there. Her belongings. The living room where they stood. The coat rack by the door. All as she recalled it, and power flooded in, filled her until she thought she would scream at the immensity of it, burst with its foreign-wine taste on her tongue. She felt faint with its humming in her ears, her bones, her teeth, as it flowed in and then out again to sculpt her house out of the acidic licorice power.

More than she could bear.

"You will hold steady," he hissed into her ear. His hold dug into her arm.

It was all she could do to nod and stand against the licorice power that tore at her, tore at the house, the yard, the huge rhododendron bush outside. Stand against—with—the power he flooded her with. She recognized its taste.

Deep earth.

Then everything stopped. Between one heartbeat and the next the lashing wind ended. The stench of licorice faded in the wet breeze through the open door. Her house—the house she loved—ticked around her and her knees tried to give once more as the damned afterburn washed over her with its debilitating combination of lust and fatigue.

Too-strong hands set her trembling as they guided her to the couch and helped her sit, then handed her clothes that she'd dropped as she fled. Mortification flushed her face as she hurriedly covered herself, and hated his advantage.

She looked up at the owner of those hands. Dark skinned from too many years in the sun. Black eyes that showed too much awareness of her and a full mouth that was, dammit, too dangerously both cruel and kissable. Ink-black hair fell across his brow and in lank strands, but his hawk nose reminded her of mysterious, blue-clad men of North African deserts. Strange, when the rain off his trench-coated shoulders puddled on her hardwood floor. He looked perhaps forty years old.

"Is it over?" she asked feeling small and weak and not liking it. She yanked her shirt down over her head.

He looked around him as if inspecting the house, closed his eyes and—'sniffed '?—and she had the strange feeling that something swathed her like a cloak. He glanced her way and smiled. A good smile. One that didn't look too-often-used.

"It is over for this time, yes. But we must leave this place." He looked down at her and at the coffee table that somehow she'd remembered to imbue with two cups of half-drunk tea and a box of files. His smile—sardonic, now—flickered across his features and a hint of flame burned briefly in his eyes. Devil-man.

"Not badly done, Agent Drake. A good focus on the details."

"I'm trained to spot details." It came out resentful of his help and petulant as a small child. Not exactly how she wanted to represent herself. Not that she wanted to trust him—even if he *had* saved her and Jason's lives. His cedar and incense filled her nose. Just how was she supposed to react to this man? She shook her head.

"Thanks for the help. That was one heck of a change."

A quirk of brow, but he left her, peered into the kitchen, and had the audacity to go to the basement door, flick on the lights and peer down even though she knew the door had been locked. When he was done he returned to glance up the stairs to the second floor.

"Looking for something in particular?" If she weren't so tired, if the afterburn weren't so intense in his presence, she might have been less sarcastic.

"Modern methods leave many details unremarked and empty spaces breed all manner of beasts."

"Like what just attacked my house?"

A hard, considering look this time, but something in the air made her feel safe. Not that she was looking for safety.

"Who am I to say?" His light, not-quite Spanish accent just aggravated his nonchalant words.

"How about the guy who's been following me and trying to frighten me off?" She struggled to sit up, to find balance to face him, but it didn't come.

"Is that what you think?" His small hint of a smile looked almost sad.

"What else am I supposed to think?" She staggered up to face him because he had frightened her before, and just because he'd helped her didn't mean he should be trusted. Especially not when he wouldn't answer her questions straight. Heck, the man held enough power to wipe her off the face of the earth—easily. "Just who are you, Xavier de Varga, and what do you want?"

That she knew his name didn't seem to faze him.

"You would not believe."

"Try me." She crossed her arms and waited, then decided to start with the easy stuff. "For starters what have you done with Fi and Jason?"

"Your friend is still outside, I believe. Too smart to enter in the midst of such a power storm. The unGifted one? Wherever you put him, I suppose. Upstairs?"

That stopped her. She went to the broken door and checked outside. "Fi?"

A huddled figure stirred from the darkness near the rhododendron bush—she really needed to cut the darn thing back from the side of the house—and skittered across the sodden lawn.

"Vallon—Val? Are you all right?" Her eyes were huge, glassy pools in her face.

"Right as rain. Come on. Let's get you in where its dry and warm." And hopefully stable.

Vallon draped her arm around her friend's shoulders and brought her inside. Tremors jerked through Fi, and when she tried to push her hair back from her face her hands shook with palsy. Vallon sat her down on the couch, disregarding the potential damage to her upholstery, and turned back to the stranger in the room.

Too close. He studied her intently, and again his gaze showed a flicker of answering flame that made her afterburn surge. Just her type— someone she should be high-tailing it away from.

His eyes showed no sign of afterburn's dilation, but judging by her pounding heart she was sure hers were. Heck, her heartbeat was so loud she was sure he'd hear it. And he had this damn expression in his eyes that could almost be protectiveness. She didn't need protection.

"You are well? Your foe was—shall we say—difficult?"

And that was an understatement like she'd never heard. "What do you know about her? Who is she? Why is she doing this?"

Again the raised brow met the ragged forelock of his hair as he stepped up to her. He was a tall man, almost as tall as Gleason, so even though she was five foot seven she was forced to step back or feel diminished. After a step Vallon stood her ground. But damn he smelled good.

"Well?"

"*Mea culpa, Menina.* Many pardons. I had not thought you would know it was a she." He shook his head.

And if she weren't so tired, and if he hadn't just looked at her in that way, she would have been pissed off. She stepped closer. "So you didn't think I was skilled enough to get that sense?"

He raised his hands, but carefully avoided touching her. "Desculpe-me, Menina—sorry. I think no such thing. Only I was not prepared for you to know. It seems I underestimate you."

"Damn straight."

He quirked a nice grin. "You are my—how do you say?—favorite? Favorite."

"Well ain't that nice. Here I have a guardian angel who watches over me, but who's prepared for me to be a little slow and a tad behind the times. So is that why you stepped in? You thought I couldn't handle whoever she was—is?"

"Could you?"

The fact she couldn't answer in the affirmative just aggravated the raging heat in her veins. The trouble was, just looking at his rugged features was like smoothing a cat's coat. She wanted his touch and knew she didn't dare. She gave one ragged shake of her head.

"At least you can tell me who you are."

"Would it be enough to say, a friend?" He eyed her. "I suppose not. I am, as you named me—*o Guarda*—a guardian."

"Guardian of what? From where? And why?"

"So many questions. I guard all things. It is a large job. Most tiring." Another rakish grin. "I am sorry, but other than that I cannot say."

She rolled her eyes at his attitude and his deflecting answer, and yet she definitely liked this man. No way was he going to give her what she wanted to know, but no way was she going to let him off so easily.

"Vallon?" Fi's quavering voice broke Vallon's attention. "I'm really sorry about what happened. I—I got scared when he came." She looked nervously at de Varga and then at the door. "Then the other one came and I couldn't stay. Something. I felt it in my toes, Vallon. All the way down in my toes and…." She shook her head. "I tried to stop it, Val. Really I did."

A gust of rain blasted in from the doorway, sending raindrops skittering across the floor. Not rain—hail. Vallon fought the broken door back into the jam, afraid that Fi would cut and run. The door listed in the wall, a huge crack splitting the wood in two.

"I never wanted you to leave, Fi." She turned back to de Varga.

"Fi, this is Mr. Xavier de Varga. He tells me he's our guardian, which means you can call on him for help anytime. Right Mr. de Varga?" She half meant it as a taunt, a test.

"To be sure." He half bowed in a manner so old-school she doubted her estimate of his age. His actions and speech suggested he came from the old courts of Europe, not modern-day Madrid or some such.

She planted her hands on her hips. "Good. Then now that we've got your role down, tell me. Who is *she*?"

"That, Senhorita, is one of the facts I have been trying to ascertain." A shake of head. "It is not so easy. She is well guarded."

Fi looked from one of them to the other, her expression strange. Her gaze returned to Xavier again and again, and she shivered.

"Here, sweetie, let's get you out of those sopping clothes and I'll check on Jason." She looked at Xavier. "You. Don't go anywhere." She stopped herself. "Please?"

Another slight bow. "If I go, it will be at your side."

His smile sent a frisson of goose-flesh across her skin. It was worse than anything she'd felt before. The attraction she'd felt for Jason was a pale thing by comparison. But then Xavier's face went serious.

"You must hurry. We must leave. Already I feel the power build again. It will not be long and she will strike anew. We must get some place safe."

That stopped Vallon on the stairs. She was tempted to -reach- to check his facts, but.... "Is there such a place?"

"I know of one or two." That smile that sent sweet daggers into her chest.

"I'll just bet you do," she said to herself as she dragged Fi up the stairs. Because how the heck had she missed him when she was on the desk. A Gifted as powerful as he was would stand out like a bonfire on a dark night in the Seattle topography, and yet she'd never noticed him before.

But abandon her house and go with him? She knew nothing about him except he had stalked her. He could be an axe murderer for all she knew.

Except he had saved her house, her lover, and her; and his smile, his scent of incense and cedar of Lebanon, all made her weak in the knees. She rubbed her nose, trying to rid herself of the scent. *A vision of dark faces over dark robes and awnings of red and blue shadows under sun-flared blue sky.*

There was no help for it but to try to keep him near. Perhaps she could take advantage of his interest in her to learn all he knew. Landon would expect it, even if it weren't her main job right now.

Come on Vallon, quit kidding yourself. *You* want to know more about him. She shook her head. God help her, it was true.

In the guest bedroom, she helped Fi out of her soaked clothing. In only her grayed bra and panties she was thin—too thin. She'd obviously been on the street a long time.

"I'm going to find you something else to wear. I'll be right back." Surely in her closet there had to be something that Fi might make do with. But Vallon had always been bigger—taller—than Fi, and now the bone-rack of Fi's body said she would swim in Vallon's clothing.

No help for it. She left Fi fussing in the bathroom and went to her room, hesitating before the closed door, still feeling the strange muffling of her senses. She'd assumed she'd find Jason here, but what if he weren't? What if he were just gone, as most unGifted were gone when things changed?

During a change, reality shifted. UnGifted didn't remember the change and also didn't remember the people who were lost—at least that was what the AGS research had shown so far. Unfortunately, or fortunately, the Gifted did remember, the accuracy of their recollections dependent upon the level of their power. And with the number of Gifted in the population, it meant dramatic changes could bring about a national crisis if two segments of the population remembered things differently.

She inhaled and yanked open the door. Light from the hallway streamed in to illuminate the yellow bedspread, tangled sheets, and a patch of smooth skin. Suddenly she found herself holding her breath.

Dead or alive? She stepped inside and touched his shoulder and Jason—truly Jason - sighed and rolled toward her, his café au lait features caught in the light. Eyes gleamed as he caught her hand.

"Vallon," he pulled her down beside him. "Why'd you leave?" A kiss that momentarily stole her breath and sent the afterburn surging, and yet she stiffened because *he* was downstairs.

Yet she opened her mouth to Jason's tongue, allowed him to ease her down next to him, the afterburn flashing and glittering inside her, demanding release.

The memory of Xavier's hands on her sent her upright on the bed. Not Jason's hands.

Broad, spatulate hands on her arms as power poured through her like an intoxicating symphony of music-color-scent. She remembered it now. Intimacy that left her breathless as his power found her deepest core.

He had known it, too. Thus the smile as if he waited for her to realize he knew more than simply the visual curves of her naked skin.

"Vallon? What is it?" Jason's hand stroked down her arm, came around her to cup her breast as he nuzzled her neck and kissed her there.

She leapt up, shivering at the feeling she was trapped here. "Get up. Get dressed. We have to leave."

"You're sure?" He stretched like a jungle cat and sent a heavy-lidded look in her direction. "Wouldn't we have more fun here?"

She shook her head impatient with his bedroom banter. "It's too dangerous. He says we need to find some place safe."

He rolled out of bed, puzzlement on his face, but beautiful in his nakedness. He tried to grab her again. "He?"

She ducked away, leaving him to grab clothing that shouldn't be there.

"Xavier de Varga is downstairs right now. We were—attacked. We need to leave my house."

"Attacked?" He stepped into his boxers, then turned to her. The broad V of his chest sent the afterburn keening. But now was not the time and Jason Bryson was no longer the figure of her desire.

Tucking his shirt into his trousers he came up to her, ran his hands up her arms so she shivered. "This isn't over, Vallon. I intend to do more than have sex with you."

"Really? My name isn't Cheryl, and I'm not about to get involved with someone who's so obviously still grieving."

The café au lait color rouged in the hallway light.

"That was a mistake that shouldn't have happened."

"The whole darn thing was a mistake."

He used his thumb edge on her jaw, her lip. "So say you." He leaned down to plant a kiss, but she was too quick for him.

"Go on downstairs. Xavier's there. I've got to find Fi some dry clothes."

She flicked on the bedroom light and felt his gaze on her as she ransacked her closet for the smallest pair of jeans and t-shirt she could find, as well as an oversized sweatshirt, underwear, and bra. She bundled them together and stood. He was still there, puzzlement on his face.

"I remember."

She almost dropped the clothes. "What do you mean?"

"You said we were attacked. I remember—some of it. The house fading away and I was—stretched, I suppose is the best description I can come up with. And then I don't remember anything until just now when you woke me."

She didn't know what to say, because she was an idiot for letting slip that they were attacked, and it was frigging impossible that he could remember anything.

She pushed past him because she just couldn't have this conversation. Gleason would have a bird. "You're talking crazy."

"It's like Cheryl's grave, isn't it? Like what happened to Agent Lamrey?"

She stiffened and marched into the guest bedroom.

"Fi? You decent?" No answer. "Fi?" She pushed inside and the bedroom lay empty. Went to the bathroom and found Fi crouched on the floor, a white towel half-wrapped around her, her long wing of matted dreads covering her face.

"Fi? What is it honey?"

Terrified eyes looked up at her. "She looked at me." Fi's soft voice echoed off the white tiled walls. "I looked in the mirror and saw her."

Fi's quavering voice died in the room and she rocked against the sink vanity. Vallon knelt beside her and opened herself but there was no stench of licorice.

"It's okay, Fi. She's not here. It's only me and you, just like old times. See?" She pulled Fi into her and smoothed her hair back from her face, motioned around them. "See?"

A nod into her chest, but the shivers still ran through Fi.

"I found some clothes that might fit. You interested?"

A slight nod and Vallon helped Fi to her feet and led her out into the bedroom.

"Here's the stuff. It'll probably be big, but it's the best I can do."

"Still good." Fi held the clothing up to her emaciated figure and a slow smile of old delight flickered a moment. "Good taste, I see."

"I had a good teacher."

There was a fleeting sense of concern on Fi's face.

"You, Fi. I meant you. Remember how you were always showing me what was in style?"

Fi's expression steadied and her gaze grazed over Vallon's rumpled attire of jeans and t-shirt. "You have your own style now."

After dressing and Fi finger-combing her mass of hair back from her face, Vallon led her downstairs to find Jason and Xavier eyeing each other like two roosters across the opened box of files. Her stomach clenched. She flipped the box shut.

"Detective Jason Bryson, Xavier de Varga, the man in black and apparently my guardian angel. Xavier de Varga, Detective Jason Bryson. In case the overload of testosterone stopped you from introducing yourselves."

"Aah, the charm of *Senhorita* Drake. But then, you have noticed."

Vallon frowned in Xavier's direction. His face had gone predatory again, now-dilated eyes tracking Jason as he stood to offer Vallon or Fi his seat. Vallon waved the offer away.

"If we're leaving, now's as good a time as any. I just need to get Maggie."

"Maggie?" Xavier frowned.

"Maggie the Magnificent," Fi offered, smiling.

"More like Her Majesty, Maggie," Vallon said.

"Her cat," Jason explained, a tinge of petty triumph in his voice that he knew and Xavier did not.

Something Vallon needed to nip in the bud right now.

"She's usually inside at night." The horrifying thought crossed her mind that Maggie might have been lost in the change. She felt a stab of guilt that she hadn't thought of her cat when she was trying to save the house.

"But she came outside with me, Vallon," Fi said. "I had to chase her home. We're good buds, Maggie and I."

And that was probably true. "You probably gave her more attention today than I usually do in a week. She'd be your slave for life, for that and an extra meal."

Fi's bright gaze faded. "Wasn't I supposed to feed her?"

All Vallon could do was shake her head. "Of course you could feed her. She's the world's biggest con artist. I'll bet she had you thinking I starve her."

"Well…."

Vallon draped her arm across Fi's shoulders and felt the other woman tense. Either she felt Vallon's afterburn or else she wasn't used to being touched. "So let's find my little manipulator and then blow this pop stand."

"We should not wait. The power builds, Vallon. Look and you will see."

In one stride Xavier was across to her, grabbed her hand. It wrenched her out of her body as he drew her against him. Down, down through the earth's crust, the soil shimmering around her. Down deeper—too deep, and it burned her blood, her flesh. About to ignite, she fought him. Drove a fist into him, but not before he forced her to see.

Something. A fissure in the earth, growing and glowing, a space where three of the lines of the earth web met to become a glowing mass of barely contained power.

She fell back into her body and staggered back from Xavier. "What the hell was that?" she panted. Jason came up beside her, bristling with an apparent need to protect.

"Your fate, *Senhorita*. Unless you leave here quickly."

Jason tried to put an arm around her and she jerked away.

"Would you both just stop? I don't need anyone's protection." Even if it might not be true.

Both men raised their brows and suddenly this place was just too crowded.

"Listen, pick a place and you two head out. Fi and I'll get Maggie. We'll meet you there. Okay?" She motioned to the file box.

"But we need to talk," Jason said.

"We'll talk there. Please. I just need some space for a moment. Now where?"

Xavier and Jason eyed her, neither of them looking particularly happy.

"There is the danger," Xavier began.

"I'll be fast. Just catch Maggie and be gone."

"How about Denny's on Broadway," Jason offered. "*You* know where that is."

"Denny's. Fine. I'll see you there. Now scat." She herded the two men to the door. She needing space to get the raging afterburn under control or there was going to be a threesome on the floor pretty darn quick. She shoved them both outside, and then turned to Fi.

"Let's find Maggie."

Vallon motioned for Fi to get the file box and ran into the kitchen to pull Maggie's soft-sided carry case out of a cupboard. She went to the back door and Fi followed, carrying the box. The door opened onto the rain.

"Maggie!" Softly, so she wouldn't disturb the neighbors.

No sign of her, and Vallon's stomach turned. "She couldn't have been changed. I wouldn't let that happen to her."

But the doubt was there. She'd never been good at holding onto anybody. What made her think she'd be able to save her cat?

She reclaimed her shoes and jacket from the front door and Fi donned her camo jacket and the two stepped out into the back yard.

"Maggie! Maggie!" Hopefully loud enough the cat would hear.

"Vallon, there!"

Vallon turned around to where Fi stood in the rain near a splash of light from the kitchen window. Rain beat a tattoo on the branches of the cedar and juniper that grew under the kitchen window. A small white snout protruded from under a black mask and two glowing eyes.

"Maggie." Vallon knelt down and held her hand out to coax her cat. "Come on, puss, puss, puss."

Maggie backed further under the brush.

"Come on, girl. Kitty, kitty, kitty."

Bright little eyes stared out at her in clear satisfaction that she was nigh-on unreachable, backed in as far as she was among the cedar boughs. Vallon sat back on her heels. Her knees were soaked from kneeling on the sodden grass. Her hair hung in lank lengths around her face. She was going to have to get down on her belly to get the cat, and she was going to have to do it soon. The scent of licorice was growing in the air, almost overpowering the cedar scent.

"Vallon?" The stage-whispered male voice brought Vallon up off the ground in one smooth movement to face Jason where he came through the rear gate.

"I thought I told you to leave?"

"Shh." He held his finger to his lips. Crossed the grass to her. "Xavier and I were on our way to our cars when we spotted a black van parking a few blocks down. Eight men climbed out and they're heading this way. I recognized one of them. Saw him heading into the AGS while I was working up the courage to go in."

Vallon set aside her need to comment that the men could set aside their differences when the mood suited them, and whirled toward the front of the house and -reached-. Up the block came the flare of power that could only be Xavier.

Then she swept her awareness downhill, wondering why Gleason would be sending men after her now. But there was no flare of Gifted power.

Which meant it wasn't the AGS coming for her. "Dammit. We have to get out of here."

"Isn't that what I was saying?" He went to grab her hand.

"Get Fi out of here. I have to get Maggie."

Jason shook his head. "You take Fi. I'll get Maggie. Don't try for your car; they've marked it. Xavier's at his suburban up the hill and around the corner. I'll meet you all at Denny's."

It wasn't how she wanted it, but there wasn't much she could do. "If you see—feel—anything, anything out of the ordinary happening with the house, you get the heck out of here, understand?"

He nodded and she leaned up and planted a kiss on his cheek. "Thanks Detective Bryson. Your wife was a lucky woman."

And then she was running across the sodden yard, Fi's hand in hers. She stopped to check the lane and heard Jason swearing at the cat. When she looked back he was belly-down under the bush.

Then she slipped out of the yard, dragging Fi with her from shadow to shadow, up the hill past garbage cans and locked garage doors, praying they wouldn't be seen.

Chapter 19-Bells Rung Underwater

Swearing none too softly at the cat, at the rain running down his neck, at the cold mud soaking into his shirt, and at his own stupidity for getting himself involved in the whole damn thing, Jason stretched a hand under the cedar and touched damp fur. Just get the darn cat and blow this pop stand to catch up with Vallon and the others.

He caught a fistful of cat scruff and found himself holding a struggling, yowling, scratching bit of fury as he dragged Maggie out into the rain. Just get her in the cage.

But a hand caught his shoulders and dragged him to his feet. In the process he dropped Maggie and the little vixen caught him a good one with her claws on the back of his hand. Then she was gone in a flash of black and white, and he was being manhandled around and shoved up against the house next to the stairs, his arm twisted expertly behind his back.

Overhead the darkness was lightening toward dawn.

"I think you're making a mistake, friend," he tried, hoping he could bluff his way through this thing.

"Shut up." Boots shoved his feet apart. Hard hands expertly patted him down, removing his Sig 226 pistol and wallet with care. "Well, well. What we got here?"

Hard hands yanked him away from the wall and herded him up the stairs and into the house.

"Boss! I found something out back."

Jason blinked in the brilliance of the kitchen lights, then looked at the man who held him. Big, broad, brawny, and dressed in black with a black skullcap and shoeblack on his face. One of the muscle he'd seen piling out of the van.

"You looking for a war or something?" Jason asked.

"I said shut up." Hard hands dragged him to the living room door. "Boss! You might want to see this."

A cold wind from the living room said the front door was open, probably down. Another man, the one Jason recognized, came to the doorway and they shoved Jason back into the kitchen. The new man looked Jason up and down, then checked the ID held out to him.

A slow smile rolled across the familiar man's face, his entire demeanor changed, and Jason didn't trust him for a New York minute. Xavier de Varga was easier to trust.

"Detective Bryson. Always a pleasure to meet one of Seattle's finest."

The man crossed the room and offered his hand in too much bonhomie. Jason hesitated and then allowed the other man's overly powerful handshake to crush his. Let boss-man think he was in control.

"And you are?" Jason asked.

"Pardon me. Very poor on my part. Wolf Amundson, Homeland Security, Seattle Station Chief." Amundson's smile broadened showing smooth white teeth that reminded Jason of the man's namesake. Ready to rip out his throat.

"And what brings a Station Chief to Vallon Drake's house in the middle of the night?"

Amundson's brows rose. "A good enough question. I will ask you the same."

The man spoke oddly, as if he'd spent his life schooling an accent out of his voice, but hadn't quite accomplished it.

"I was catching her cat. Had caught her—until your man interrupted." Jason sucked the blood beading on the back of his hand.

"Unfortunate. And tell me, do you come to catch cats at four a.m. for all the denizens of your fair city?"

Jason shifted uneasily, because the fact that Homeland Security was here said whatever was coming down was a heck of a lot bigger than he'd thought, and Vallon was in deep shit. So was he, for that matter, because there was no acceptable excuse for him being here. He shrugged.

"She called me. She told me she was going out of town and asked me to get her cat right away. She was afraid of the cat running off and getting hurt or something." Jason looked around. He hadn't noticed the house having this licorice scent before.

"An odd arrangement, when I believe you are investigating her for murder."

"I guess she doesn't have many friends." Jason stiffened at Amundson's measuring look. "Don't tell me: you're the guy my partner called."

A small nod, and the man circled Jason as he studied him. "Tell me, how well do you know Agent Drake?"

The stink of licorice had increased. Jason searched around him for the source and wondered if it was on Amundson's breath. "Well enough to think she may not be responsible for the murder. I suppose that's why she called me."

No surprise as Amundson stopped in front of Jason. "Your partner suggested you thought as much. So how do you explain it?"

Let the evidence speak for itself. "If you look in my wallet you'll find two photocopies."

Amundson opened the wallet he held and found the papers.

"One is of a drawing Agent Drake agrees she drew. The other is of the wall at the scene of the crime. See any similarity?"

Amundson eyed the two copies. But then his face stiffened briefly, the reaction quickly smoothed away. "They are the same scene— except for the body. What do you suggest?"

The man's increased accent suggested an emotional reaction to what he saw.

"It suggests perhaps that archway existed. My partner suggested perhaps Homeland Security has, or had, something going on at that location. Perhaps it points to other motivations for the murder." The licorice stink made him want to gag, and yet neither Amundson nor hard hands seemed to have noticed.

"Absurd." Amundson let the papers flutter to the floor and ground them under his heel.

"Is that your official response, because I can pass that along to my partner?"

"Where is Agent Drake, Detective? There's a great deal she needs to answer for, not the least of which is what happened to Agent Lamrey."

"You're saying she killed him?"

"I'm confirming no such thing."

The air had gone electric in the room, and it wasn't from Amundson's pithy conversation. Something was happening. Something like what he vaguely remembered had happened with Vallon. A sense of falling. A sense of terror and being eroded by a wind so great it stole his soul, his mind. In that wind, only Vallon had been solid.

"Where is she, Detective? She's unstable and dangerous. You'll make the city a safer place if she's picked up and held."

"Really? Can she be held?"

He saw Amundson stiffen. Beyond him, a haze seemed to bleed from the kitchen wall like a morning mist, which certainly seemed to meet Vallon's criteria of something weird happening with the house. Jason knew he had to act now or never.

He leapt back from the danger. Slammed an elbow into hard hands' gut and grabbed for the door.

It melted under his hands, was putty he could-not-hold. Slammed his shoulder into it and –

Fell through. Amundson—quicker to react than Jason had expected—dove after and grabbed his legs so they both tumbled down the back stairs and slammed into the small pad of pavement in the backyard.

Jason struggled up, kicked Amundson in the chest before he could stand, and sprinted across the sodden grass. Amundson was after him, grabbed his coat, swung him abround so Jason caught sight of the house, the grounds.

Everything was silent, eye-sick, Escher angles and melting walls that couldn't be. That just couldn't be. He froze.

Long enough that Amundson's fist slammed into his chin. He stumbled back into the brush by the gate. His head connected with the wood. Lights flashed in his head and bells rang. He wanted to be sick. When he opened his eyes, more so.

Vallon's house wasn't there. A modern monstrosity, all too much pink stucco and too little glass took up most of what had been the yard. Lights glimmered in the kitchen window and Jason wondered who lived there.

Amundson stood over him panting, fists still ready, but then his expression flickered. The anger faded and he looked down at his hands, unfolding from their clench.

"Don't you ever talk Homeland Security down again, Detective. And don't let me catch you trespassing on the site of one of our investigations again. Vallon Drake might not be home now, but we'll get her. We will."

He turned back to the house. Stomped across the miniscule yard and slammed inside.

Jason's stomach rebelled then and he crawled to his knees and retched. What he'd seen. He could have been in there. He had been in there.

When he was done being sick he staggered up and fumbled at the rear gate. A chubby, black and white cat came up and rubbed along his sodden pant-leg, mewing pathetically.

Jason leaned down and picked up the little animal. She snuggled into his arms, purring.

"Now why didn't you just do that before? You could have saved me an awful lot of grief."

A contented chirrup was his answer, and a head-butt with a pink nose.

§

"So she's after me now," Vallon said, but the huge SUV's engine roar almost smothered her words as Xavier guided it down the on-ramp onto I-5 North. He drove silently, skillfully, as Vallon suspected he did everything. There was something about the way the man moved that suggested he'd made a study of every motion he made so he did it *perfectly* each time. The thought made her hot all over.

Even with Fi in the backseat, it was as though Xavier filled the whole SUV. Vallon couldn't get away from him and his cedar and incense scent, so he seemed to fill her pores, she breathed him in. And yet his entire focus was the road and the vehicle. His face, illuminated by the dashboard lights, showed total concentration.

Northgate shopping center slipped behind them as the highway hummed under their tires.

"Why are we heading North? We're meeting Jason at the Broadway Denny's aren't we?"

Still he was silent.

"Xavier?"

Still nothing as the SUV sped through the first light of dawn.

A little pissed, now, she took a chance and grabbed his arm. "Would you talk to me? We should be headed south."

"Do you really think this Jason is your friend? That he will not betray you to those who came for you?"

"He was the one who came back and warned me. Why shouldn't I trust him?"

Xavier cast a black glance at her that suggested he reassessed her again and found her wanting. He looked back at the road. "He is not one of us."

Okay, she was pissed now. "One of us? Of *Us*? What *Us*? Jason helped me—a couple of times. And *he* wasn't following me!"

"So I have been no help." That taunting grin was enough to make her grind her teeth.

"What the heck was it that we did back there, anyway?"

"Used the power than runs in the blood. Our blood." Another amused curve formed on his lips as he focused on the road.

Their blood. Literally? Something to consider, but she shook her head. Outside the treed verge of the highway rushed by. Overhead the sky was lightening, the too-long night ending.

"Come on, Xavier, be straight with me. Where are you taking us—or I'm—we're—getting out now."

"At 120 kilometers an hour? Not very wise, Agent Drake. You and your friend would be killed."

Her fists curled at his almost sarcasm. She grabbed the car door handle. "So what? Are you kidnapping us? Taking us to your secret lair? And for your information, in America we talk in miles, not kilometers. It sort of shows you're not from here."

A forbearing sigh, and finally he took his eyes off the road long enough to look at her. "This was definitely not in my plans, Agent Drake. I had not intended to take you into my care, only to speak with you. Unfortunately you seemed determined not to talk, and then events interceded and so you are here."

It was the most direct answer she'd gotten from him. "So you were trying to talk to me down by the harbor?"

A nod as he drove.

"Not abduct me."

Another nod and a glimmer of a smile in her direction. "Not that having you around would be so bad, no?"

"So what did you want to talk to me about?"

Xavier glanced over the seat back to a wide-eyed Fi. "That is a conversation for another place and time."

"So where are you taking us, then?"

"Somewhere safe, where the others cannot find you."

"Can't find…." She started to protest, then thought better of it. Not being found by whoever had attacked her house was likely better for her health. "Then I need to call Jason."

She hauled out her phone and was about to flip it on, when Xavier reached over and plucked it from her fingers. "Not a good idea. In fact, you will remove the battery and card from the phone. It is too easy to track your whereabouts. GPS."

Her protest died on her lips. He was, unfortunately, right.

It was her turn to sigh as she took the phone back and pried out the offending bits of electronics, then slipped the pieces into her pocket. "Jason's going to be pissed."

"Your Detective Bryson should not be involved at all. As I said, he is not one of us—not Gifted as you call us. He cannot know about us."

"He already knows." She felt Xavier's hot glance again, and his scent increased as if he was angry. Her afterburn simmered and boiled, but she fought it back. "I didn't want to believe it either, but at the house—when I went upstairs to get Fi some dry clothes—," She looked over her shoulder again. Fi looked very small and vulnerable, strapped into the backseat next to the file box. Vallon smiled. "When I went into my bedroom he told me he remembered."

"Impossible."

"You think I don't know that? But he did. He described what had happened and feeling all stretched." She rubbed the pounding spot between her eyes and wished like hell she wasn't trapped in *his* car, going someplace only *he* knew of. "My god, my head feels too full. None of this should be happening."

"Perhaps you misheard? Your words sound like the defense of a lover."

That stopped her for a moment. "Is that what you think?" she said quietly into the silence. "I don't love Jason." Which suddenly became very important for him to understand.

Silence in the car as she sat back in her seat, arms crossed protectively. Xavier took the exit onto I-405 and headed south again. So they were staying in the Seattle area and not running for the border as she'd begun to suspect.

"I'll ask again, where are you taking us?"

"Not to the AGS, if that is your fear."

Vallon relaxed, because that was probably the first place Homeland Security would look; even if it made more sense to go there for the safety in the number of Gifted on site.

"I take it you don't care for my organization."

"What I care for is my business." He glanced at her, but then his gaze softened as thin grey light filled the vehicle. Dawn. "Again I must apologize. The AGS does not understand what they dabble in."

"And you do?"

That mysterious smile was all he gave her.

She held her tongue to show him she could be just as reticent, and wondered what had possessed her to even consider climbing into this man's car.

Finally, as the light in the sky increased, he cut west at the Bothell exit and then wended his way through treed suburban subdivisions down along the shores of Lake Washington. As the first weak sunlight pierced the clouds, she recognized the dark spruce of St. Edwards State Park on the west side of the road. Mist clung to the treetops and the sun's rays glittered on the rain-slicked branches.

Just south of the park they turned off the main road, but Vallon held her questions to herself. She'd know soon enough where they were going. The trouble was, she couldn't be sure if she *could* trust Xavier. He played the game too close to his chest and revealed nothing of himself. Guardian, my ass.

Except he had helped her save Jason and her house and had apparently gotten her and Fi to safety. Why he'd done that, she had no idea. He hadn't helped the other agents.

Her wrists still ached from his grip and the raw use of so much power. And she was too aware of every nuance of his movement, the position of his jaw, the lick of his gaze towards her. Not to mention the scent of cedar and incense that was acting like a frigging aphrodisiac on her.

A symptom of the afterburn, she was sure, and not wholly unpleasant. In fact, not unpleasant at all.

She found herself looking at him.

Aquiline features with a patina of long toil and fatigue. His black five-o'clock shadow just enhanced his dangerous appeal. No man any right-minded woman would ever be interested in.

But then when had she ever been right-minded where men were concerned?

She yanked her gaze away and looked out the window at the treed streets. He followed the confusing net of narrow roads down toward the water, then drove into a property swathed in mist from the lake, parked in a lot that was masked from the road, and turned off the car.

He said nothing, but climbed out. Vallon stayed where she was.

"I'm just supposed to trust you and follow you into those woods?"

"Yes."

As simple as that. No insistence. Nothing. Just a fact he expected her to accept, and she could either get mad at it or take it as a sign that he had nothing to hide. She climbed out, helped Fi out of the car, and hefted the file box under one arm. Sighed.

"Where—where are we?" Fi's gaze seemed to lock on the mist swathing the trees. She stepped closer to Vallon and Vallon placed her free arm around Fi's shoulders, even though the afterburn made any touch almost painful.

"Damned if I know, sweetie, but he tells me it's safe."

Fi gazed at the dark-clad figure that was already heading into the trees. "I don't know. I don't know. Maybe I should go."

Vallon squeezed her shoulders. "Don't be silly. You want to be safe, don't you? We have to hide out."

Fi's pale gaze returned to searching the air among the treetops, the mist under their branches, then wide-eyed she locked on Vallon and suddenly clutched her arm.

"Hide. Must hide. She's looking." Terrified wide eyes and a low moan as she spun away to look back the way they'd come. "Nowhere. Nowhere. Nowhere to hide."

"She who, Fi? Who is she?"

But Fi was only shaking her head, shaking in her boots, and losing it. Vallon grabbed Fi's hand. "Come on. Let's see how safe Mr. I'm-your-guardian can make things."

She followed Xavier where he had disappeared under the trees. A well-laid path of cedar tanbark perfumed the air and cushioned their footsteps. Ahead, the misted water glinted leadenly through the trees except where errant sunbeams laid gold leaf on the lake. The path forked—one path leading toward a small, darkened cabin masked by the trees and the other winding down the slope to the lake. With all of Saint Edwards Park backing the property it was truly a secluded spot.

A low whistle led her toward the lake and she came out at a T-shaped dock over motionless dark water. She stepped out onto the wood planking and her stomach lurched as the water's dampening effects hit.

Nestled against the end of the dock floated a two-story, cedar-and-glass-sided houseboat. Xavier stood on the small deck that made up the porch, the door opened behind him and the soft hum of a generator coming from somewhere on board.

"Come inside, please. You will be safe here." He ducked through the door and a light flicked on, spilling golden light onto the dock.

"This is safe?" Boats were never safe. She hadn't liked them since her first bout of seasickness as a kid. "Stay behind me, Fi."

She made it down the dock and stopped. With trepidation she set the file box down, then stepped down onto the porch and felt the slight give of the water. Bile filled her throat, but she swallowed it back, scowling at the boat even though it was charming with its convex portal-style window beside the door and the nautical doorknocker. She cautiously checked inside.

Spacious, with good sightlines. Good clear light and a good view across the lake to Lake City and Briercrest, with their thickly treed subdivisions.

A set of wrought-iron stairs spiraled to the second floor and Xavier worked in a cupboard beside the small kitchen, until finally another low hum started and a burst of heat blew through air vents.

"Come in and close the door and soon the place will be pleasant." He must have seen her hesitation for his lips curved, but on him it was more like a predatory scowl. "What? You do not trust my hospitality?"

"I'm not sure whether I should trust you at all."

"*Que vergonha.* Pardon—what a shame. The brave Agent does not trust the one who saved her life."

"I didn't need saving."

His dark look said what he thought of that foolishness and she felt herself color. She sighed and straightened and went to bring Fi and the box inside.

But Fi shook her head. "I don't like it. Don't like it at all." She started backing along the dock, until Vallon pulled her to a halt.

"This is safe, Fi. She can't get you or me here. You'll be okay."

Fi looked at her in disbelief as Xavier joined them on the dock. He looked haggard in the shimmering light—as if he had expended more energy for a longer period than any Gifted should. Watching out for her?

"It's true. It's the water, Fi," he said gently. "It blocks the power. Surely you feel it."

Fi eyed the dark liquid beneath the dock.

"Remember, Fi? Remember school? It's just like how moisture in the air diffuses laser readings and makes them less accurate." She caught Fi's hands and tried to coax her forward.

"You are unused to being cut off from the earth. She is part of you," Xavier said.

"The earth is a she?"

"The ancients named her Pangea."

Vallon rolled her eyes. "So I'll just run right out and believe in the lessons of the ancients. Maybe I'll believe in vampires, too."

"Do as you wish, but in this there is truth. Over water you are most difficult to locate."

Vallon turned to him. "And I'll be sicker than a dog if that water starts to move—at all. I've always been prone to seasickness."

"Then you are in luck. The forecast does not include wind."

He waited as she turned back to Fi, who strained for the shore. "See, Fi? Nothing to worry about. It's only the water."

But Fi was still shaking her head. When Vallon tried to tug her to the boat, Fi freaked and plowed a fist into Vallon's stomach.

She nearly dropped the box as she doubled over.

Fi leapt for shore, sprinting into the trees as if all manner of demons were on her trail.

Xavier was after her before Vallon could catch her breath. She abandoned the file box on the dock and went after, catching up to Xavier as he fought with banshee-screeching Fi.

"Stop it! Stop it!"

But Fi didn't stop. She swung her fist wildly, bit and kicked and clawed at Xavier so he swore all manner of foreign epithets and a bloody welt ran down his face.

Vallon waded in and wrapped her arms around Fi. Hugged her until Fi suddenly went limp and collapsed, sobbing pathetically, in Vallon's arms.

"Please. Please, please." She lifted tear-reddened eyes to Vallon. "It hurts." She knuckled her forehead.

"I know it doesn't feel right, Fi, but you have to believe me. Trust me. It's safe." She cast a glare at Xavier because he damn well better be trustworthy after all this. He was examining the blood from his cheek as if he had never seen it before.

"I don't feel good on the boat, either, but we have to go there to be safe. Remember?" She stroked Fi's thin face. "Remember how you warned me? Well, here we'll be safe. She can't get you."

Suspicion and disbelief. "On wwwater?"

"On water."

Fi's gaze slipped towards the lake and then to Xavier. "Will he be there?"

"Yes. He will. But you don't have to have anything to do with him. I'll deal with Mr. de Varga."

Fi regarded him again, cocked her head. "He—feels different."

Xavier looked at her with interest. "And how would that be, Fi?" Her name came out more rounded than normal in his accented voice.

"I'm Fi, not *Fi*." She tried to imitate his deep voice. "You feel—." Another considering gaze. "You feel really big—and different."

"Just what everyone wants to hear, sweetie. The word is 'tall', Fi. Mr. de Varga is tall, like I'm tall. Call me big and you'll piss me off."

Fi went all serious. "I *don't* mean tall." Then she grinned. "I called you big in the academy."

"Yeah, and I whupped your butt because of it." Fi was back. Vallon hugged her friend, thankful that the immediate crisis seemed to be over. At least momentarily. "So can we go onto the boat? It's going to feel strange, but you'll be okay."

When Fi nodded, Vallon led them back to the dock. Xavier brought up the rear, leaving Vallon with the feeling he didn't want to chance either of them getting away.

The small house was already warm when they entered, but a tremor ran through Fi and increased into a steady shiver while she muttered under her breath. Vallon sat her down on the couch that faced out to the lake and found a blanket to wrap around her. Then she turned to the file box Xavier had brought in and set on the floor. It seemed like weeks since Landon had given it to her, and she still hadn't cracked the lid.

"Maybe you can make us some tea while I get started on this?"

Xavier nodded. "I will do better than that. How about scrambled eggs?" He didn't wait for agreement, but doffed his black coat, revealing a slim build and strong shoulders. He rolled up shirtsleeves, showing ripcord muscle the afterburn targeted on as he hauled out a mixing bowl and eggs and whipped them in quick, measured strokes. Soon the room filled with the comforting scent of cooked eggs and toast, and Vallon had to admit she was beginning to like this man.

She clamped down on the lust and forced herself to look away. Across the lake, the far shore was bathed in detail-swallowing mist. A single sail coasted silently southward.

In an experiment, she -reached- and her power reverberated in her head like underwater bells with the scent of roses—and was that licorice?

She coughed, spluttered up, and found Xavier's gaze on her. "Not a good idea, Agent Drake. There is a reason you are here. Your perceptions are clouded, but so are those of your enemy."

"So no one can find us here?"

"Not by any means familiar to the AGS."

"But there are other means?" She met his steady gaze, but it gave away nothing. Just darkness and a sense of difference she just couldn't put her finger on. Finally she shook her head. "You and your damn secrets. You're not going to tell me anything about what happened at the house, either, are you?"

"It was not my intention."

Every muscle in her body tensed in frustration. She plumped down on the couch and dragged the file box to her, flipped the lid as Xavier brought her a plate and a mug full of tea fragrant with mint and chamomile. "It will relax you—and Fi." He glanced in Fi's direction and took her food and drink. "She has the addict's look. I am afraid for her."

"Addict?" Vallon studied Fi with a new eye. She sat huddled with the blanket around her like some dime-store Indian, her blonde dreads falling around her face like vines. Her shivers had only increased, and so had her mutterings. "Fi would never do drugs."

"Not drugs. She appears as one who has become dependent on the use of the Gift."

That took Vallon's attention from the food and the box. She chewed a moment.

"Thank you. This is good. I hadn't realized I was hungry." Another look at Fi. "She never really liked using the Gift. She did in school, but she wasn't like me—always getting into trouble for using it off school grounds."

Xavier crouched in front of Fi, gently caught her chin and brought her glazed gaze up to his. She'd already bolted down the food like a ravenous animal. "It is the Gift, isn't it little one?"

Her pale gaze flickered away like a distant point caught in sun-glare, and Xavier sighed and took the empty plate from her. "There is no reason to feel shame, Fi. It is something tempting to us all. You are very brave to be here." He nodded encouragement.

Then he stood up and went back to the kitchen for his own plate of food. Ate it thoughtfully. "It will be harder on her, but in a few days it will be better."

The jumble of questions in Vallon all came welling up. "A few days? I—we can't stay here a few days. I have an investigation to run and limited time to do it."

She looked at her watch and swore. Ten hours left and she hadn't even begun the process of sorting out who from the AGS was trying to kill her and had killed the other Agents.

"I can't stay here. The person doing this is out there—and everyone at the AGS is in danger."

"As you are in danger."

She waved that fact away. "Listen, you obviously know stuff. Is there anything—anything at all you can tell me that might help me in this?"

His gaze met hers, and even in the muddied environment of the houseboat she felt his power, like magnetic north. She swallowed and saw him stop himself as he started to shake his head.

"First tell me who those men were last night."

The question surprised her. "I can't be sure. But my best guess is Homeland Security. Oh, shit."

She sank back on the couch beside Fi, and felt suddenly weak. If those men were HS, then everything had sped up. Her sixteen hours was down to none.

Chapter 20-Magnetic North

The little gift Wolf had planned to present to Fitzsimmons had not worked out, and he dug his fingers into his thigh, the pain holding his rage in check. It should not have happened like that. That big empty house.

How had she known to leave, unless someone told her she was at risk?

He ground his teeth and stared into the fading darkness through the van windshield as the vehicle pulled away from the curb. They cruised past the big stucco house that showed only darkened windows to the street. Empty house. Nothing of use inside except for the evidence he'd planted.

With him were his three silent men, their scent of sweat and gun oil a balm to his senses. Once they'd worked together overseas. Now they backed him up here on the darker side of Homeland Security's work.

They knew better than to talk when a mission had gone sour. They knew him too well.

"Page, any update on tracking the Drake 'twenty' through her phone?" As part of his responsibility as Liaison to the AGS, he'd tapped all of the AGS phones and had tracers on all of the Agent cells. Fortuitous, now, it seemed.

Page, a big, ham-fisted man who'd done three tours of duty in Iraq with a multinational security company before signing with HS, grunted his assent and stabbed a button on his phone. He muttered into it and had a quiet conversation, and then hung up.

"Our girl's gone black, boss. Phone's not on line."

Wolf went a little colder. "Then she knows we are on her trail. Damn woman. Damn all these Gifted."

The plan was to make his career on this—gain control of the AGS and deal with his other problem—not have it all blow up in his face. But from the rumors he heard from Washington, nothing really worked the way it was planned when it came to the Gifted and the AGS. Though at first no one had believed in the Gift, once they were acknowledged, whatever they did always led to little 'problems'.

"I figure someone warned her, boss." Page again.

"An inestimable deduction. The question is, who?"

"Someone at her shop?"

"The AGS?" Wolf thought a moment. "That white cretin certainly. He is the one who let her leave."

"Boss? There's something else. The technician tracked back. He said that her phone showed she was at the house at the time we were pulling up. Then she left and traveled north until the GPS suddenly went dead."

"Are you saying someone warned her at the house?" Wolf half-turned in his seat. Page shrugged his mountain of shoulder.

"Might have."

And that made too much sense. Wolf smiled as he swung forward again. "Call them back and tell them to get a fix on an SPD Detective named Jason Bryson. It might be a personal or a Seattle PD phone, or both, but get it—them—trace any call and track it. When you're done, call Seattle Police and have them patch me through to a Homicide Detective named Blacklock. I have the information he requested."

"It's pretty early, boss. Detectives don't usually take calls this early unless it's an emergency."

"It is an emergency."

Because he needed all the help he could get pulling this one out of the fire.

§

Jason sipped his third cup of coffee and checked his watch for the twentieth, or was it the fortieth?, time. Damn it, Vallon and de Varga should be here by now. Hell, they should have beaten him here.

If they were coming.

Around him the quiet porcelain clink and the voices of people getting off graveyard shifts were white noise in the Denny's. You didn't get the tourists at this time of day, nor the truckers in this location. It was more of a neighborhood restaurant than most Denny's.

If they were coming. Or it had all been a plan to ditch him because he knew too much, had seen too much. His fist squeezed the coffee cup until it groaned in his hand. He set it down and sat back. Just what had he been part of? Was it really possible to change things in the world with your mind?

"Can I warm that up for you?" The middle-aged waitress with a thousand-watt smile held a pot up for him, to explain why she was here. She glanced around at the three other places at the table. "You still think they're coming?"

"God only knows."

She hefted the pot at him again, but he waved her off. His nerves already jangled enough.

As if in answer to her question, the cell phone chose that moment to buzz. He scooped it off the table from beside the gawd-awful cup of coffee and managed a smile at her as she turned away. He picked up the phone.

"Bryson."

"Where the hell are you? I've been calling your place the past twenty minutes." Clint Blacklock's voice held the edge of excitement that always came when a case was about to blow wide open. Jason straightened and tried to pull himself away from the ruminations about change and possibilities.

"Sitting in a Denny's drinking coffee."

"And you'd do this, why?"

"Thought I might meet interesting people."

Silence, and then, "Anyone in particular you're hoping for, Slick?"

"Nah. Just fishing."

"Never figured you for a Denny's kinda guy."

"And I never figured you for a partner who'd call me at this ungodly hour. Are you in the office?" He checked his watch. As he thought, barely coming to five a.m.

Blacklock was silent again. "Can we can the crap?"

Jason sighed. Blacklock was in the office and that meant things were breaking. "I will if you will."

"You with the Drake woman?"

That made Jason sit up straighter. "Nooo. Why?"

"Because I just got a call back from my contact in Homeland Security. The AGS has had another death, and apparently Vallon Drake is linked to this one as well. Trouble is, when they went to pick her up, she'd bolted. They're looking for our help to bring her in."

Jason sat rigid in his chair. Had there been another incident? Had Vallon done what Homeland Security said? Hard to think that was the case, given what had happened tonight. But to dispute what Blacklock told him would be proof positive Jason had been where he shouldn't be for the second time in as many days.

"Interesting. Any idea where she's headed?" He had to find her. Something not kosher was going on here, and it obviously had something to do with Homeland Security. Which meant that, with Blacklock's leanings toward that agency, Jason was pretty much working solo.

"Not really. Apparently they lost her heading north on I-5."

So she had exactly no intention of meeting him. But that made no sense. She'd been pretty adamant about getting her cat, and that didn't suggest she wasn't going to show. Which meant de Varga was at the heart of this. Kidnap?

"So she bolted." This was the dangerous part—for Vallon and for him. "I wonder if she had help. Someone must have tipped her off."

"My sentiments exactly." Silence over the phone. "Slick, you haven't gone and done something you shouldn't have, have you?"

Only everything in the world.

"What d'you think?" A beat. "Hold on a minute—don't answer that—because I know I screwed up. But I didn't help Vallon Drake disappear, if that's what you're asking."

Nope. He was looking for her, too.

The sigh of relief was audible over the phone. "I'm sorry I had to ask, but, well—you get this look in your eyes when you talk about her."

"That was before I got my head on straight." He waved his hand at the waitress for the bill. "Look, I'll be in there in a few. In the meantime, could you do some checking for me? Remember that guy I told you seemed to be following Vallon Drake? De Varga? Well what if he's in on this? Could you do some digging? Also check whether any information has come in on that company he works for."

"I'm on it, partner."

Jason signed off and left a two-dollar tip for the waitress, then headed for the door, not looking forward to the squalling cat in his car. But at least he'd find Vallon. Even if it meant he also betrayed her.

§

"What are you talking about, Vallon?"

Xavier stood in front of her, crouched down as he had with Fi in the houseboat living room, concern on his face, and dammit, she wasn't like Fi.

She was strong and didn't need anyone. If she had a problem, she dealt with it. But right now she felt numb and it must have shown.

She forced herself up, feeling as if the entire houseboat shifted beneath her feet.

"Frigging Homeland Security. From what I know, they've been gunning for the AGS for a long time. If I can't find out who's doing this, they're going to use me as the scapegoat. They'll say I went rogue, and use the fact the AGS can't control its own to take the agency apart."

She grabbed the box, pulled it to her, and began pulling out files. "I need paper and pens." He watched her silently. "For notes."

He crossed to a desk near the door and retrieved what she needed. "They will not be helped if you fall apart, Vallon. Take a breath. Be calm."

"Easy for you to say."

"Vallon?" Fi's quavering voice; and dealing with Fi was about the last thing Vallon needed, but she couldn't not help her friend.

"What is it, sweetie?" She set the files down and went to Fi.

"I'm so cold, Vallon. So cold, and I miss her so much."

"Miss who, Fi?" Fi's shivers had increased to horrible, wrenching shudders. Vallon stroked Fi's hair, sat next to her, and wrapped arms around her.

"My Mama." Fi said like such a small child it broke Vallon's heart and stabbed her right through with old memories. She wondered how Fi had lost her mother. Had it hurt as much as the loss of her Dad?

"Let's pretend I'm like your Mama for right now, okay? How about we get you to bed so you can have nice warm blankets on you. How does that sound?" She raised her gaze to Xavier and he nodded.

At Fi's acquiescence Vallon helped Fi stand and led her up the spiral staircase and into a neat little guestroom, with pristine white walls with garden photographs and a bed covered in a white bedspread with ornately embroidered red and yellow and blue flowers around the hem and on the pillow covers. "Reminds me of Villas in—oh—maybe southern Europe. Spain?"

Xavier considered the room and then shrugged noncommittally as he drew drapes across the view onto the lake and Vallon pulled back the covers and helped Fi bed down. The girl shuddered so badly Vallon didn't know what to do. "She's so cold."

"Wait a moment."

Xavier disappeared out the door for a few minutes and came back with a hot water bottle wrapped in a plush towel that he presented to Fi. "This should help warm you up."

She wrapped it in her arms and smiled. Vallon stood to go, the need to get the file box like a pulse in her head.

"Vallon, please stay."

She closed her eyes. "Fi, honey, I have work to do now, but I'll be just downstairs."

Fear bloomed in Fi's face. She shook her head, until Xavier intervened between them and sat down on the edge of the bed. "Fi, I swear an oath that in this place you are safe. I will ensure it."

So formal, so serious, but then again, he was a serious kind of guy. Almost nice. In a most infuriating way.

The seriousness worked for him this time. Fi took a breath, and looked back at Vallon.

"You'll be just downstairs. Okay." She closed her eyes again and Vallon led Xavier out of the room and closed the door.

She swung back to Xavier and found him close enough she was forced back a pace. Damn him for always making her do it. Especially now when he seemed almost like a decent guy.

"That was nicely done."

A raise of brow was all he gave her.

"You were kind to her."

"As were you. She is so sad, like a half-empty shell. I do not like to see that." He eased past her and down the stairs, leaving her to grind her teeth and stare after him. She -reached- for Fi, wanting to understand what he meant.

Fi's Gifted flame was there, but the gold was stippled with black. When Vallon reached to touch it, it seemed as if her perspective were all wrong. She couldn't triangulate or get a firm reading. It was like trying to use a magnet on non-magnetic stone. She pulled back and looked at the closed door to the room wondering if what was going on in the flophouse could leave you like that?

Considering the possibility and what it might mean, she followed Xavier down the stairs. "It's almost like part of her is gone."

Xavier glanced at her from where he sprawled in a chair sipping his tea. "Yes."

"What could do that?"

"Loss."

That she understood. After her father died it was how she felt. "But I'm still here and I'm not like that."

Xavier's intense regard said she wasn't making perfect sense. "I lost my father. He's in that box. But I don't think I feel like that."

A slight smile and shake of his shaggy head that made her want to push that dark tangle back from his eyes.

"No. You do not." His voice was a low purr that brought her body to attention.

She tore her focus back to the file box waiting where she'd left it, open and too full. She sipped the now-tepid tea, looking at Xavier as she unloaded the files onto the table.

"The AGS figures whoever is doing this has to be from within the AGS. No one else has the power. Do you think their assessment is correct?"

He sipped his tea and gave that same sardonic smile of his that could make her either want to strangle him or jump his bones. She just opened the top file and started to read.

Simon Lamrey's file included notations on every case he'd ever worked. His career spanned much farther back than she'd known, and she realized he had been closer to her father's age than her own. Weird she hadn't noticed. He was that well preserved. He'd actually served with Janet Hunt and her father and Rebecca Murdoch, Fi's mom.

A little queasy feeling settled in her stomach. Was she that poor a judge? Was she doing what more than one school counselor had told her, and trying to find a new father?

"There are more than your AGS who would know how to do this, but I believe your killer is AGS-based."

"Pardon me?" her thoughts were blown right out of her head as she looked up at him. "*You* are going to answer *my* questions?"

"Where it does not compromise other things, yes, I think I may."

"Now that's an understatement of equivocation if I've ever heard one." She crossed her arms. "So? Who else could be doing this? What do you think's going on?"

He shook his head, his hair rustling like feathers around his shoulders, but he would not meet her gaze. "I do not know much more than you. I truly am here as a guardian, a watcher only."

She wasn't going to let him off the hook, because he knew things—things that might obviate her having to read every one of these files. "I notice you aren't telling me about any others, but let's hold that thought for a moment. Why are you here?"

"Very simple. Because here is where you are—the AGS, all the others, all based here in Seattle and—I—knew of it."

The way he'd caught himself said there were others like him out there, but she'd let that go as well. For now. "So you're here to guard us from something?"

Another one of those too-intense smiles. "Yourselves, mostly. Guard you from yourselves."

"You sound like some sort of parent—or a government oversight committee, or those friendly aliens we see in Sci-Fi movies. And you certainly did more than watch when you broke down the door to my house." She raised her chin at him, daring him to answer.

"That was—unfortunate, but necessary." His gaze was locked on her now, taking her measure—probably to decide what he could say.

"Hmm. I wonder what that makes me." She looked down at the file containing all Simon's testing at Landon's behest. Psychological, emotional, physical. A perfectly healthy specimen until he woke up inside a concrete wall. "Did you have anything to do with the change at the parking garage?"

"No. Though I was there."

"Why didn't you save Simon?"

At that he looked away to the water for a long time. Finally he looked back at her. "Perhaps I am not a guardian. Perhaps I am an observer. I am not supposed to intervene."

"But...."

"I broke—you would say, protocol—when I assisted you, yes."

Vallon wanted to ask why, but looked back at the file, anger heating the afterburn. Simon could have been alive—heck, all of these people could have been alive, if someone like Xavier had intervened.

"You mean my father could have been saved, but no one bothered."

It came out as almost a soft growl, but Xavier didn't even seem to notice the danger he was in.

"Your father. That was long ago. He was the first. No one knew or was prepared. It was the changes that took him and a few others that drew—my attention to Seattle. It is why I am here."

It would explain his presence if he represented some more powerful group of Gifted. So she had to accept his story—at least for now. "I saw you at the garage."

"Yes. And I would have spoken to you that night, but you were followed and I did not wish to be seen."

That set her aback. "Followed?"

"By your detective. Don't worry. He saw nothing."

"Except you disappear!" She stood up. "And a fine surprise that was. Damn it Xavier, what are you? Who are you, and who do you represent? How do you just disappear? For that matter, how did you save my house? I know what you had me do, but no one can access that kind of earth power and live to tell the tale. I've tried."

That got a rise of his brows, but he didn't respond. Refusal, or picking his words?

She began to pace the room, kneading her forehead. The Janet Hunt file was on top of the stack and she picked it up and began to read as she walked. And walked. And walked, hoping to release her anger and released some of the built up energy of the afterburn.

All Janet's cases lay here. Addressing Mount St. Helen's eruption. Ameliorating the great drought of 1988. She'd been part of the panel who had discussed whether to use the Gift to 'fix' the Alfred P. Murray Building blown up by Timothy McVeigh, and thus remove the damage to the American psyche. She'd been part of the AGS senior agents who had warned the government to prepare to defend against other acts of terrorism—like 9/11. Janet Hunt had been, along with Vallon's father, one of the legendary founding agents of the AGS as it was today. Another point Vallon hadn't known.

"You can access the power if you know how to protect yourself. I believe someone has either learned the method or developed a new one. Perhaps the latter, because these changes feel different to me."

Xavier leaned back in his chair, the window with its view of the lake at his back so his head and shoulders were silhouetted against the blue. He cocked his head at her.

"I think I tell you more than I should."

Shock that he'd actually answered and the force of his regard seemed to tug her across the floor. Or perhaps it was the afterburn. At the last moment she turned away and rounded the sofa to stand at the window.

"And yet it doesn't help me at all."

"Perhaps there is another way."

Vallon nearly leapt out of her skin. He was right behind her, and how the heck had he moved so quietly? But now his aura of incense and cedar sent the afterburn roaring. She turned around, barely kept her hands to herself to ease past him. When she had enough distance that her mind worked again, she turned back and caught a strange look in his eyes—desire?—quickly masked.

He crossed the room and pulled her stack of files across the table, sorting them into two separate piles. Then he shoved one of the piles across the table to her.

"Here. We both sense the person we are after is a woman. These are the files of the female agents."

Vallon considered the stack of files and looked at him. "Now why didn't I think of that? Oh, I know. Maybe it's because these are the victims?!"

"Perhaps. So perhaps you read the men's files and I will read the women's and we will point out the interesting points to each other."

It was as good a plan as any. She dug into the files. Simon Lamrey. Rafe Goodman. Jasper Brook, Ethan Silverman. Others. She kept burrowing back and back into the early years of the AGS, making her notes, so she felt like she could almost see and feel the excitement of the AGS as it shifted from being an almost-forgotten experiment in the US Geological Survey, looking at the ability of a few Agents to influence the landscape, to suddenly being troubleshooters for natural disasters and all the changes that can undermine a nation of people who do not understand the power they hold.

"Heady days, those."

She met Xavier's gaze. "Yes. They were. My father told me about them many times. How they thought they could change the world, given enough time."

"How do you say? Idealists?"

She looked down at the last file in her stack. "I suppose you could say that. I think my father was one, although sometimes I think he was starting to lose faith."

"Perhaps it was only his generation finally growing up."

"Maybe." She thought back to her father, his smiles becoming less and less. Fewer hours to spend with his daughter. "Or maybe the job was more than he expected."

"Or less."

She met his gaze. "I'm not sure what you're talking about."

He shrugged. "It is like most of our lives. As I read these files there are many similarities among the agents. Most were there close to the beginning. Many worked the same files. All seemed to be as you say, idealists. They had a great purpose. But as I look at the files, I see the cases they worked on become more—how do you say it? Mundane? When you lose your joy in your work, perhaps you lose your edge as well. You become easier to kill."

"Mundane? But the AGS has a purpose to protect. There *are* terrorists out there and there *are* attacks on our soil. That's why Homeland Security is there, why we're there. How can that be mundane?"

Xavier cocked his head at her. "Perhaps there is another way. Perhaps someone saw what was happening in this country and chose to take action to keep their edge. They would take the battle to the threats."

"Learn to kill?" To hide her shock, Vallon picked up the last file, her father's, hesitating before paging through it. But the pattern Xavier mentioned was there as well. Great purpose to the mundane. Could it drive someone to the viciousness to do what was happening?

She knew how her father felt. She'd had such excitement when she graduated and joined the AGS. Now it wasn't much more than being a beat cop. It was why she'd established her little workroom in the basement. Why she tried new things: to keep advancing.

Had her father felt the same way before he died? But to kill others to make yourself feel alive. Or perhaps the killer was helping dissatisfied agents escape.

At that thought she shivered and looked at Xavier, suddenly sure she knew why he was here.

"You were assigned to see what we did with our Gift. I don't know who sent you, but someone did, and you were watching me because it was happening to me, but I fought it. I was looking for new outlets for it and you couldn't be sure what I'd do."

It was as if a mask dropped over his face. Gone were the signs of any partnership. He was a mysterious foreign force studying an enemy. A scientist with a subject, just as she'd always been. At least she understood that type of relationship, but for some reason it renewed an old ache she'd thought she long ago destroyed.

"So. I have it right." She smiled. "Oops, underestimated me again, did you?" She kept it light, and plucked the file he held from his fingers, liking the fact she had him on the run. Rebecca Murdoch, she read, and a knot formed in her belly. She flipped through it: the investigation into her disappearance at three forty-five on December fifth, ten years ago. Someone had taken out the entire road she was driving. She'd barely had a chance to call the AGS as she died. Something like what had happened to Janet Hunt, Vallon supposed. She stopped. Something wasn't jiving.

She sank down onto the couch and looked at her notes.

"There's something. There was a spate of deaths ten years ago. Then the number reduced to a trickle, but they picked up in frequency two years ago."

She looked back at Rebecca Murdoch's file and started reading more closely. Fi's mother had also been there when the AGS was young. Psychometric testing showed significant Gift, as well as high scores on ethics and innovation and attention to detail. All important to work in the AGS, especially under its revised mandate to monitor for and block all Gifted activities and potential foreign incursions. As with all these files, the key aspect seemed to be that she was an agent important to the AGS.

Experienced. Long service. Whoever it was, was taking out the AGS's best. Which meant they had a grudge against the agency, or else they were trying to cut it off at the knees. So this wasn't about the specific agents. This was about the agency as a whole.

Vallon flipped through the last form and stopped at the physical health records. Three children. Girls. No names, but numbers cross-referenced.

All her focus on the investigation fell away at the notation.

Cross references:

#67 S. Lamrey

#35 G. Gleason

#23 F. Drake.

Chapter 21-Precursors

The day Fi Murdoch left the Redmond Academy just northeast of Seattle was a date Vallon preferred not to remember. Now it all came stabbing back. The air heavy with the scent of wet pine and spruce from the forestland surrounding the school. Light rain. Vallon standing on the wet cobbled pavement before the ivy-covered, east stone tower of the Academy, clutching Fi's hand for dear life because it was impossible she could be leaving.

She needed Fi. Needed her as she had needed her father. Fi was the sister Vallon had never had, without all the battles. Fi was the other half of her brain. Fi was the only person Vallon had left to love.

"Come on, Fiona. Get in the car. We're leaving." Beside the open car door, the imposing, business-suit-clad figure that was Rebecca Murdoch turned back to her daughter. Impatience filled her face.

She'd caught thirteen-year-old Fi and Vallon as they were returning from one of their adventures out to the creek that ran behind the school. 'Science projects' they called them, but really they were just meeting boys. But Mrs. Murdoch's Mercedes had been idling in the parking lot farthest from the Academy's main buildings, along the path Vallon and Fi used so they weren't seen returning with those self-same boys.

Fiona had scanned the stone building behind them.

"But all my stuff's still inside."

"We'll get you new stuff."

"Mom, come on. I like it here."

A shake of Rebecca's long, blonde hair. "Well, they don't like you. They're holding you back."

That sent a shiver through Fi, and Vallon squeezed her hand. Fi always said she couldn't stand up to her mother. Now she understood why.

"Mrs. Murdoch, they do like Fi here. We all do. And she's doing great. She helps me with my English homework all the time."

Rebecca Murdoch's cold blue eyes met Vallon's. "Isn't that nice for you, Vallon. I'm sure your father appreciates that my daughter helps you. There's a certain irony in that."

Vallon frowned. Her father was dead. He didn't appreciate anything anymore, she wanted to say, but instead she focused on not letting Fi go.

"You don't understand. Fi doesn't want to go, do you Fi?" She looked at her friend. All the tendons stood out on Fi's neck as if it took all her strength to give her one little head-shake.

"Well, it doesn't matter what Fiona wants at the moment. Get in the car, darling girl, we have to go. Now. We'll talk about this later. Besides, I've a better school for you to go to that's not in Seattle."

Fi's gaze wavered. She sighed and slipped her fingers from Vallon's hand.

"Fi?"

She wouldn't meet Vallon's gaze. "I'm sorry, Vallon. I have to go."

"But you don't have to go. This is stupid. We're half way through term and you're top of the class."

"She's not top of the class, you are. She needs a chance to shine."

The hate in the woman's voice spun Vallon around. No one hated her. There was no reason to hate her, because she was just sort of average in school, except for—.

"I'm only good at one thing, Mrs. Murdoch. Fi and I—we help each other with schoolwork. That's why we're so good together. Mrs. Johnson calls us formidable. Please don't take Fi away."

"So she can be your crutch before you stomp on her?"

Grabbing Fi's hand, she dragged her towards the car. Vallon leapt to help her friend, and Mrs. Murdoch shoved her so hard she stumbled and fell. She scrambled up and grabbed for Fi, just as Mrs. Murdoch slammed the car door behind her daughter.

She swung to Vallon, her tall, blonde visage filled with anger. "You are just like Francis. Always just thinking of yourself. Well I'm not like that. I'll not leave Fiona behind."

Then she had swept around the car, climbed in, and burned rubber leaving the school grounds. Vallon had stood frozen, the misty rain matting her hair on her forehead, her light jacket soaking through.

"But my Dad couldn't take me. He died," she said, as behind her the tower clock had tolled four.

Vallon shuddered and raised her gaze to Xavier's.

"You were far away. Where did you go?"

"Not where. When. I was remembering Rebecca Murdoch." She tapped her finger on the file and tried not to look at the cross references on the medical listing. Rebecca Murdoch had had three children with different partners, one of whom had been Vallon's father.

The man Rebecca Murdoch hated. And there was the small thing of the time of Rebecca's disappearance. She flipped back to the report to double check.

"Something's wrong with this file. Or at least either it's wrong or there's something here. It says she disappeared on the road at three forty-five, but I remember that day really well, because it's the day she came and removed Fi from school. It was the last time I saw Fi until the other night. When she left it was four o'clock."

She stood up, knowing she was on to something. "We need to know everything about Rebecca Murdoch. Everything. I'll bet she set it up. She took off with Fi and then started killing the other agents."

"But she was not the first, Vallon."

She shook her head. "I don't care. There's something here. I know it." She drummed her fingers on the file. "I need a phone."

"Why?" He was on his feet, too, facing her across the box of files. Her father's file was still in her hand. Who was it cross-referenced to?

"I need to have someone check whether Rebecca Murdoch is still in Seattle."

"I thought she was supposed to be dead?"

"So did I. So did everyone. But I'm betting she's not. She might be the person behind this."

"But what would be her motive? It does not make sense."

"What if something happened to her? What if it got her angry? She knew all those agents."

"But I repeat. She was not the first to disappear."

She wracked her brain, came up with something that almost made her sick to think of.

"What if none of the early disappearances were? What if, as you said, the agents saw what was happening to their work? It was becoming mundane, not living up to the expectations they had so they—they left and went somewhere in secret.

"But now Fi's back and she keeps talking about 'she'. We both know whoever is taking out those agents is a 'she'."

She saw him consider. "There is a certain logic to it."

"Then I need to check something. I want to ask Jason to check something for us."

His face stiffened and he turned back to the window. Finally a great shudder seemed to run through him. "There is something else you need to know. Yes, there have been the successful attacks on agents, but there is something larger happening here. Something I have been tracking. Deep in the earth there are changes taking place. We—I—am not certain, but it appears that someone heats the earth's crust more than the earthquake subduction zone usually does. There is concern that a large earthquake or eruption may occur."

Fathoming the power that would take almost left Vallon breathless.

"You're saying someone's trying to cause the 'big one'?" She stopped. "Ohmygawd. All those temblors we've been having—precursor quakes." There was a great deal of evidence that large quakes were foreshadowed by a series of smaller quakes that transferred energy to a specific fault, causing it to let go. For years, California geophysicists had been tracing swarms of quakes that led to more major ones along the San Andreas.

"I have to make that call. Now!"

Xavier went to the desk again, pulled a cell phone out of a drawer and brought it to her. "It is clean. Call, but make it short. We do not want to chance them having your detective's phone under observation."

§

Wolf straightened his suit jacket over his shoulders before knocking on the hotel suite door. The last hour had been busy, setting things in motion.

He knocked and waited for Fitzsimmons to answer. The man had chosen the best suite in the Hotel 1000 luxury hotel. The glass and steel building positively reeked money which seemed odd, given Fitzsimmons was on government pay. But it was possible that heading up Homeland Security brought a whole lot of perks beyond the power. Wolf shifted his suit jacket again and knew he looked smart. He'd fit right in.

A click, and the door opened into an empty foyer that gave onto a parlor of marble counters and fireplace and luxury furniture, set before a breathtaking view of Elliott Bay and the harbor. Far different than the old brick buildings of the Pioneer district just to the south. Wolf glanced back at the door. Closed circuit camera and automatic door release. Nice.

Fitzsimmons stepped out of the double doors that led to a tousled bed with silk sheets and duvet. "About time you got here."

The man settled his pristine tie under his prehistoric visage and Wolf pulled his gaze away. "It took more time than expected to forge the letters. We had to make it realistic that Vallon Drake was obsessed with Lamrey. I wanted to check them personally."

Fitzsimmons' gaze was cool as he gathered his briefcase and headed for the door.

"As long as it turns up the Seattle PD heat. We need them looking for her, and looking hard."

"The courier should be delivering then to Clint Blacklock as we speak. It should light a fire, I think."

"And you've got that detective's phone under surveillance?"

"Of course." It was the best Wolf could do after the disaster at the Drake house last night. How had the woman managed to slip out of his hands was beyond him. Warned by the damned cop, he was coming to believe, though how the cop had known eluded him.

"Good. Then I believe we have enough to pay Gleason and company another visit. Best we get there before they destroy anything of use."

"Sir?"

"Apparently there's been a decision to purge the files. Unfortunately for them, power outages are making the task somewhat difficult." His thin lips curved into a vulture smile. "Shall we?"

Wolf swallowed back his sense of destiny as he followed Fitzsimmons out the suite door and down the silent elevator. It was coming. Everything was coming. Power would be at his fingertips. He'd be in charge of the AGS soon enough.

As soon as they lopped off the head of the snake.

§

Jason peered at his office computer screen, but still read nothing. Beside him, the cat mewed plaintively in the cage he'd borrowed from animal control.

"Shh," he muttered, tapping the top of the box and feeling particularly unsympathetic to the cat at the moment. His scratched hand hurt like a sonofabitch.

And then there was the fact that the cat's owner still hadn't called, and something could have happened to her.

"Like Xavier de Varga," he murmured, scanning yet another screen of information on the man and the multinational company he worked for.

"You want to mutter that a little louder, Slick, or was that just for your own ears?"

Jason looked across the two desks to his partner. Blacklock was the epitome of the buddy-partner this morning. He'd been chatty and helpful and generally trying to humor Jason out of his funk.

"My ears," he grumbled.

"Then maybe you should remember to use your inside voice."

Jason tossed him the finger.

Trouble was, he didn't feel like being happy. Vallon Drake had skipped out on him—to be with someone else, he suspected. And just when he really needed to understand what the heck was going on.

Because there had been changes.

Because the frigging guy from Homeland Security hadn't even noticed. And if people were changed—well then, there were a heck of a lot of possibilities out there.

He put a stop to the little swell of excitement his ruminations caused. Focus on the computer's report, or all his speculations were worth absolutely nothing.

Xavier de Varga. Portuguese National. Frequent entry into and egress from the country. Often by direct flight into SeaTac. Other times entering the country via car from Canada. The last time he'd arrived had been six months ago. His visa was current.

So de Varga had been in the area long enough to have set things in motion, and now Vallon was missing. A wave of worry washed through him and he stabbed the scroll button on the computer.

De Varga's passport described him as a geological consultant. Further checks had shown he had Doctorate degrees in geophysics and—archeology. Weird combination, but then the guy was weird, with talents like Vallon apparently. Well traveled, but mostly through southern Europe—Spain, Italy—long stay there—Turkey and North Africa—Algeria, Tunisia and—Libya.

Jason straightened in his chair, ignoring the scent of wet cat and her soft mew of request.

Terrorist country. He'd bet any money Vallon didn't know that fact about her new playmate. And she'd given him, a perfectly red-blooded, American fella, the kiss-off for the guy.

So just what would take Senhor de Varga to points unpopular. He touched the mouse and brought up the company documentation. *CartosNationele* was a Venice-based company with major offices in Istanbul, Lisbon, Singapore, Vancouver, and Hong Kong. So that could explain de Varga's extensive travel, but it didn't explain the links to North Africa. The company could just be a front.

He looked up the company profile and read: CartosNationele *is devoted to the geophysical sciences and works with governments and independent organizations across the globe on matters of earth tectonics, mineral exploration, oil and gas exploration. Along with our extensive geophysical resources, we give back to the communities we serve through anthropological and archeological exploration and restoration.*

Jason sat back and shook his head. "Weirdest company profile I ever read."

"Knowing you, bet it's about the only one you've ever read." Blacklock came around the desk. "You should try investing in the stock market for a while. That'd teach you a thing or two." He leaned over Jason's shoulder to read. Pursed his lips.

"You know, it is kind of an odd combination. Oil exploration and archeology. But then, oil exploration can take you into some pretty out-of-the-way places and archeologists probably always need patrons. Who the heck knows what you'd find."

He reached over Jason's shoulder and scrolled down to financial statements. Whistled. "Whatever they're doing, they're doing pretty good. Look at those year-over-year figures."

He pointed and Jason tried to follow along. As Blacklock kept going, Jason got the sense this was a pretty well-run organization.

Blacklock poked another key and the screen changed. Instead of facts and figures, photos of various worksites came up: oilfield in sand; pit mine somewhere in a vast plain; a deep hole in a ridge that showed ruins under careful excavation.

"Any of those Libya?"

"Libya?"

"De Varga's passport shows he's visited there a few times."

Blacklock shifted the cursor to a search engine and typed in Libya. A news release came up announcing the partnership with Exxon to do exploration in the Libyan desert.

"I guess that explains it. Guy has the skills to work on that type of project?"

"Yeah." Jason shook his head. "So what's tall, dark and mysterious doing here? Not too many deserts or mines hereabouts. I just don't get it."

He was about to return to de Varga's information when his cell phone vibrated across the desk. Jason almost leapt for it. Stopped himself when he saw Blacklock's interest and forced himself to be casual. He flipped open the phone.

"Bryson."

"Jason? Can you talk?"

He bolted upright in his chair. "What the hell's going on? Why the heck'd you ditch me like that?" He cast a glance at Blacklock and stood up, walking his cell phone into the coffee area. "I thought we trusted each other. We were working this murder together," he said quietly.

Through the open door he caught Blacklock's look of disapproval, but waved him away, all his focus on Vallon. He needed her more than he'd ever needed anyone before. Except Cheryl, and if Vallon were able to change landscapes and people like whoever had changed her house, then just maybe Vallon Drake could bring Cheryl back.

"We are. We have been. Xavier was just concerned about going someplace we couldn't be traced."

"So you're safe?" Blacklock was on the phone.

"Yes."

"Thank god." And he meant it. He had to keep Vallon safe.

"Jason, I hate to ask, but I need you to do something for me. Will you help?"

"Of course." Blacklock was still on the phone, and the disapproval rating on his face was going way up. He kept trying to catch Jason's eye, tell him something.

"Terrific. And thanks. I owe you."

Jason nodded.

"I have a lead on a woman I think might be involved in the killings and I was hoping you could help me track her down."

Blacklock ad settled the phone in its cradle. He shook his head. "Your funeral," he mouthed.

"What do you need?"

"I'm going to e-mail you a photo. I'd like you to run it through the face-recognition software attached to the city's street cameras."

"What the hell are you talking about, Vallon. There's no such thing...."

"Cut the crap. You forget: I work for part of Homeland Security. Seattle hosted the World Trade Organization and in preparation for the event there were cameras installed at a lot of gathering places in the city. I want you to check footage for the last three months against the photo."

"Shit, Vallon, that'll take days. Months."

"We don't have days or weeks or months. Something's coming down, Jason. Something bigger than either you or I imagined, and if we don't stop it, Seattle might just get written off the map. You get my meaning?"

"You mean…." He couldn't say it with Blacklock looking at him.

"I mean the clock's ticking and I don't know how much time we've got, but given what happened last night, I figure it's going to be sooner rather than later. Now can you do it?"

"I'll try."

"Thanks. I'll call."

The phone went dead. Jason walked back to his desk in time to hear the soft ding of mail on the computer. A photo downloaded of a handsome blonde woman.

"So what's going down, Slick?"

"Would you fuckin' quit calling me that?" He met Blacklock's patient pig-eyes and knew he really didn't have any choice. There was no way he could meet Vallon's request in the timeframe she'd set.

"Sorry." He sighed. "Listen, it was Vallon asking for help. She's tracking whoever took out that Agent and she wants to access some face-recognition software tied into Seattle street cameras that Homeland Security put in place. Got any idea how we might do that?" Because as far as he knew, no such system existed.

"Interesting. Can't say I'm familiar with such a system, but I sure as hell know who will be."

"Don't tell me. Your connection."

"He's like a brother."

Jason looked down at the pad and thought about the risk he was taking. "You think you can put in a request without saying it came from Vallon or me?"

The hesitation in Blacklock's response spoke volumes, but finally he nodded. "Let me see what I can do, but Slick, you gotta know I don't like it when you compromise my principles."

Jason grinned. "I know it, and just let me say I didn't think you even had principles."

"Thanks a bunch."

"Let's just keep this between the two of us and see what we find. Okay?"

"Fine."

Jason stood up and hefted Maggie's cage. "About time I saw a lady about a cat." He grabbed his coat and headed for the door.

"Think twice before you do something stupid."

"Right," he tossed over his shoulder as he left the squad. "Like that's going to happen."

Chapter 22-Rainbow Flesh

Vallon clicked the phone shut and handed it back to Xavier. She still held the two files of her father and Rebecca Murdoch. At least the call was done. Jason was on the job. She inhaled the room's scent of incense and cedar and wished she hadn't. Her afterburn ached low down and sexy, like an incessant itch she desperately wanted to scratch. "Short enough for you?"

"We will hope. It will depend on whether they were monitoring Detective Bryson's phone closely."

"He was pretty pissed off."

"He should not have been. He knew you were with me. Safe."

"Sure. You'd expect him to think that." She shook her head when he didn't pick up on the sarcasm. "We better get this photo to him asap."

He accepted it and led the way to the stairs, Vallon following in his wake, still holding the files. She should just look and get it over with. See who her possible mothers were. Was she Rebecca Murdoch's child? Fi's sister?

Upstairs Xavier unlocked a door across from the bedroom Fi occupied. More than a complete office. A bank of computers filled one wall; fax machine, scanner, and a few machines she wasn't sure of against another. File cabinets built into the wall.

Xavier slapped the photo face down on the scanner and did what needed to be done while Vallon went to the window.

Sun finally found its way through the patchy clouds and placed pearlized highlights on the lake. The sunlight was hot through the window, and hot on her hands, still clutching the files.

"Something has you bothered."

Again Xavier had done his move-too-quietly-for-words thing again and his nearness made the whole world seem to tumble into a somersault. Unfortunately when she turned she was trapped in the corner of the room, with sunlight flooding his face with a warm gold glow. Yesterday's beard darkened his jaw and the nascent afterburn wanted to rub her hand over that sandpaper line.

She forced her gaze away and back to the files. Sighed.

"These. Memories. Both. I don't know." She shook her head and tried to ease past him, but he wasn't about to give way.

"This is not the time to be running away, Vallon. There is too much we must face in our future."

That brought her gaze up to his and she steeled herself. "You want to know? You really think you want to know just how pathetic I am?"

She clenched her eyes shut for a moment, then forced them open, forced herself to breathe slowly.

"Oh hell, what does it matter? The thing is, all this reading the files made me remember the last time I saw Rebecca Murdoch. She was really pissed at something. At the time I thought it was me. Maybe it was—partially—but I think she was really mad at my Dad. She said *she* was taking Fi away. At the time I thought it was just a mean taunt because my Dad was dead, but what if he wasn't? The way she said it makes me think she was saying my Dad could have taken me, too. If he'd wanted."

Dammit, her voice had faded until she was almost whispering, but it was the only way she could seem to get the words around the huge stone caught in her chest.

Xavier's gaze was too hot on her face. She tried to turn from him, but he caught her biceps. "You think your father left you behind by choice?"

She fought the rush of afterburn. Jerked herself away. "What am I supposed to think?" she snarled. "We both came to the same conclusion that no one was killing off those early agents. They left on their own for points unknown. My Dad left me by his own choice, because he didn't need all the problems I entailed."

Shit. Two tears had cut loose in long lazy lines down her cheeks. She backhanded them away and glared up at Xavier.

"Is that enough? You got everything you need to feel better than me?"

"Vallon." He raised a hand towards her.

She lifted her chin. "Because it doesn't matter to me what you think."

"Vallon, listen."

"I don't need anyone. Anything."

"Vallon, if you please."

He caught the files from her hands. Set them down and studied her, then gently touched her face to wipe away new tears with his thumbs, and dammit, "I don't need your pity."

But his touch made her shiver.

"Is that what this is?" he leaned into her, his fingers trailing down to lift her chin so his lips could find hers.

So exquisite she thought she could die. Soft and hard, his incense and cedar scent so thick she might drown, and the afterburn raged so loud she couldn't think, forgot her name and, "Holy hell, I want you."

His mouth found her neck, her ear. "It is mutual, *meu caro.* Almost since the first time I saw you." He bit her earlobe and she moaned as she ran her hands down his hard back, narrow waist and found his ass. Hard as well. He pressed into her and the urgency of the afterburn had her fingers making quick work of his shirt. She yanked it from his jeans, nuzzling his chest's olive flesh lightly covered in fur. Bit his nipple and heard him gasp.

"*Bela Menina,* you go too fast. This is something to be made to last." He pulled her hands from where they worked at his jeans' button and brought them to his mouth and kissed them. "You—we will do the most beautiful of dances together, but anything truly worth doing must be done slowly, and well, to be savored. Otherwise you lose the nuance of the dance, no?"

Holy hell, he was a sweet talker.

He kissed her lips, her neck, under her hair, all the time holding her hands in his hard ones until she was ready to scream for the need to DO THIS.

Then he pulled back, still holding one of her hands. "If you wish this, come."

"Anywhere you lead, pardner." Her voice sounded hoarse and coarse to her ears, but Xavier only smiled, truly lighting his almost-black eyes as if he actually liked her weak attempt at humor. Liked her?

Out of the office, and down the hall to a door that guarded the front of the houseboat. The room beyond was encased in rainbows—or at least that was how it looked until she realized there were small imperfections in the wide windows that acted like prisms. She preferred to focus on the rainbows and the sheets of light on the wide white bed, the single crimson pillow at its head. The bedding, the floor seemed to spark and glow almost as golden as the flow of earth power.

A sanctuary, it looked like. His hidden place. A place he could recover from the darkness he usually dwelt in. Her darkness.

She turned to him, fighting the throbbing demands of the afterburn.

"You don't have to do this. I'm not a risk like this, if that's what you're worried about; I can manage myself."

A low chuckle as he pulled her into his chest. "Of course you can. I have seen."

For some reason that made her blush and he chuckled again, lowered his lips to her ear.

"I have watched you not only for duty, but for my own pleasure, *Bela*."

His hands skimmed her back, caught the back of her shirt, and yanked it over her head. "Better, yes? Skin to skin."

For an answer she lifted her head, caught him in a kiss so fiery she almost forgot to breathe as his hands stroked her back and sides. If she was a cat, she would purr.

He led her to the bed, helped her discard her jeans and did the same, then laid them both down on the pristine bed. "You are so fair."

He held out his arm to compare it to the pale skin of her belly, placed his palm there, hard and heated across her skin, and she arched into his touch. He ran a single finger down her breastbone to the edge of her panties, but no further, then leaned down to kiss her breasts.

Vallon slammed his chest with her palm, rose to her knees and pushed him down, straddled him. Her hair fell around her face and she closed her eyes inhaling his clean cedar and incense, and let the afterburn take her.

"Let's get this over with, shall we?" She rubbed herself along him. Cupped him in her hand.

But he rolled her off of him, stroking her sides as if he would woo her into submission.

"It will not be best like that, *Bela*. It will not." Then he breathed into her ear and he tasted her neck, her shoulder. His tongue trailed down to her breast and she arched into him as he stayed there. As his hands gently heated her flesh.

Finally, finally he slid her panties down her legs, almost making a ceremony of it, kissing each inch of flesh, before tossing the flimsy silk aside. Then he sat back and looked down at her.

"Você e muito linda e nao o sabe."

"What is that?"

"You are lovely."

She rolled her eyes. "Bet you say that to all the girls."

"Aah. Do I?" He shed his underwear and laid himself beside her, slid down and opened her like slow petals, refusing her urgency, slowing her down until she was ready to rage at him, scream. Then he raised himself above her. Stroked her face as he entered.

"Oh Criador, ha quanto tempo eu queria isto."

She wanted to scream with the pleasure, the building. The room went silent except for their breath. Except for the creaking of the bed, their low moans, the sound of giving flesh. Scent: cedar and anise, incense and roses. So potent they would never leave her.

She was caught in his scent, caught by his flesh and his hands that knew with laser accuracy just what to do, and something more. In the midst of the rainbows that colored their flesh he opened his Gift, too.

Heat flooded her, golden, huge, so they lay entwined and floating on the earth's power. He thrust into her and she fought a stab of fear.

He thrust into her and she caught her breath in pleasure.

He thrust into her and carried her so far of herself all the earth stretched around her and she spread, floated, sank in, became part of.

Something greater, as he thrust into her and she arched her back, wrapped her legs, and—"Xavier, take me!"

The world exploded as he pulsed inside her, as he threw his head back and yelled. *"Criador, a você eu dou-lhe este amor."*

Then he collapsed still inside her, their breaths, their scents mingling as he smiled at her and stroked her. As she floated, still connected to—something.

It could not be true.

She waited for him to be gone. That was how it usually went, now that the afterburn had been replaced by afterglow. Simon had always showered and left her. The others had as well.

She touched his face, felt where his five o'clock shadow had burned her skin, and studied those dark, dark eyes. Secrets lurked there, that was obvious. But something more swam in his gaze. Honest caring?

Right, Vallon.

No one was that honest or that obvious. She shoved back the swell of emotions that rose when she looked at him. Stupid-first-blush-infatuation, girl.

"What was that?" she asked. Keep it fact-based, analytical. That was always safest. "It was like you actually took me somewhere. Beyond compromising positions and all that."

She screwed up her face to keep things light and humorous and met his too-serious gaze.

"You have not felt it before?"

"Mister, I've felt a lot of things, but not like my body just exploded and I'd become part of the earth."

"Mãe do Deus. Your pardon." He shook his head and smiled as he lifted himself on one elbow and trailed a finger down her side. It was a good smile but still held hints of mystery. "It is just I cannot believe you do not know."

"Soooo?"

"You *are* part of the earth, *Bela Menina,* and this is the giving back. Pangea provides the Gift for you to use, so you make offering to her; and that is the act of procreation, just as you used her power to create, no? A balance, a gift in return."

She considered. It made some sense but sounded perilously close to a religious belief.

"I never thought of it that way. The afterburn just makes me feel sexy." She sat up to face him.

"Not that simple, *Bela Menina*."

"What is?" She rolled off the bed, but he grabbed her, pulled her back to cradle her against him, demanding she relax in his arms, when every bit of evidence in her life said it was wrong.

"You don't need to do this. It's done, okay? You don't need to stay."

He kissed her head and his warm hand came up to cup her breast. "Perhaps I like this. This moment with you. There are too few in life." He kissed her again. "Perhaps we do it again, simply for our pleasure?"

Was that a sigh? She looked over her shoulder at him and caught an unfamiliar look that painted an unusual gentleness in his face. Somehow, it eased the tension she felt. But she would not believe.

She stood up, but he put his arms around her. "There's strength in being together, Vallon."

"Yes. It relieves the afterburn."

His arms loosened and he turned her around, her still-sensitized breasts mashed against the breadth of his chest. But she wouldn't meet his gaze. There was too much vulnerability that way.

"You fool yourself, and you are not a fool. What has happened here, Vallon?"

That brought her gaze up. "We relieved ourselves. Fucked." She pulled away hoping he'd leave her. Or not.

"Is that all?" His arms came around her again, trapping her and yet she couldn't bring herself to pull away.

"I have wanted to do this a very long time." He kissed her hair. "The anticipation has been most—agonizing."

Believe him? The prospect frightened her. She didn't know if she'd ever be free of his scent of incense and cedar, but she wasn't made for quiet times in front of a fireplace, even if for the first time in her life she felt totally quiet inside. The afterburn more than just satiated.

A low, terrified, moan cut through the quiet. Vallon jerked away.

"Fi!" She scrambled for her underwear and jeans and sweater. "Dammit, dammit, dammit. I'm fucking around when Fi needs me."

She glanced at Xavier—handsome, troubling, powerful, Xavier—and felt like a fool as she hopped around on one foot pulling on a sock, a shoe. A pity fuck. That was all it had been.

He swiftly dressed and beat her to the door. A bang came from downstairs.

The guest room door was open. So was the office door, and the contents of the two files and the photo of Rebecca Murdoch lay scattered on the floor. Fi had seen them.

They swarmed down the stairs but the damage was done. The houseboat door swung open in the morning breeze, the wharf empty.

"She's gone."

"We must find her. If it is her mother, she will notice her away from the water's protection. Stay here. It is safer."

"No way, José." She grabbed her jacket off the couch, feeling safer having the tools of her trade handy. She wasn't going to get caught without them again. She stepped onto the dock just as a loud buzzer sounded on the boat.

Xavier froze on the wharf. He scanned the shore. "Damnation."

"What is it?"

"An alarm. Someone comes."

Chapter 23-Secret History

When Wolf opened the Town Car door, the brisk spring wind carried the mushroom scent of the forest that surrounded the AGS. Rhododendron bushes jostled the sides of the low, rain-stained building, the first blossoms sodden pink in the watery morning sunlight. Overhead the clouds still clung to the hilltop, but southward the trees gave way to allow a distant view of Mt. Rainier.

All the signs of a good day, a bright future. He filled his lungs with the fresh scent and turned back to Fitzsimmons, who climbed out of the car as if he were an old man. Even power didn't stop the advance of age. Which meant it was high time the man stepped aside in place of younger leadership.

"Did it ever occur to you that Gleason and his agency could wipe you off the face of the earth without even drawing a sweat?"

A cloud crossed the sun and left Wolf in shadows as he turned back to Fitzsimmons. The big man looked at him intently, waiting. Almost as if he knew Wolf's thoughts. Wolf kept his face smooth. He smiled.

"It has, actually. I have never trusted them, regardless of Gleason's assurances of their defense of the natural order. No one with that much power can be trusted."

"My sentiments exactly," Fitzsimmons said, and looked at the bunker of a building with its lack of windows.

Leaving Wolf wondering whether the power comment was pointed at him. But there was no way Fitzsimmons could know what he planned.

Quelling the ill-ease, he followed Fitzsimmons toward the bunker. The place seemed intent in sinking into the earth instead of enjoying the view the hilltop afforded.

He used his ID card to open the door and suspected that somewhere an alarm would be sounding to alert to their presence. They strode in and sure enough, Gleason's familiar appeared as they reached the T intersection of the halls.

"Director Fitzsimmons. Chief Amundson." The woman, Moore, inclined her head in a vaguely oriental motion. "Chief Gleason is waiting for you. Please follow me."

She was a cool thing. Inscrutable slit eyes. Skin of ivory. She turned them away from the operational center of the AGS toward a bank of doors at the other end of the building.

"Where are we going?" Fitzsimmons barked.

"Chief Gleason thought perhaps you would prefer a quieter venue. The war room is under reconstruction."

"So quickly?" Doubt in his voice.

"Chief Gleason has many contacts he can draw on."

"How fortunate for him." Still the doubt.

"He has tremendous—foresight."

The way she met Fitzsimmons' gaze told Wolf all he needed to know, and there was no way he wasn't visiting the war room.

"Perhaps we should take a look. As Liaison to the AGS, I will have to approve the expenditures."

"Very well. Come this way." Her heels clipped down the hallway, but another door opened. The white gnome poked his head out, and then stepped back.

"Director Fitzsimmons. Chief Amundson. What brings you here so unexpectedly?" His voice was its usual uncomfortably high-pitched tone, but there was a jittery tension in there too. He was Gleason's creature, so it was not unexpected.

"Not unexpected, Snow. Not at all." Fitzsimmons kept walking. Wolf passed the man by and felt him shift into the corridor to watch them go. Felt the little man's fear.

What was the vernacular? Let him stew in those juices. Yes, let Landon Snow stew in his fear.

Moore opened the war room door and stood to one side to allow them to precede her.

A flurry of activity suddenly stopped. Agents at their desks looked up at their entry, then looked away. Fingers flew across keys. But no workmen worked at the devastated map pit. There were no workmen anywhere Wolf could see.

"Everyone stop what they're doing, please." Fitzsimmons' voice boomed across the room.

Hands stopped on keys. A few hesitant key strokes.

"I said stop."

Agents jerked under the lash of his voice.

"Amundson, Moore, get everyone out of here. Now. Find someplace everyone can wait."

Fitzsimmons strode through the desks to Gleason's door. It opened before he got there and Gleason stepped out.

"What the hell's going on here?" Gleason stood toe-to-toe, glaring down at the Director.

"Come, Gleason, let's go inside. You don't want to do this in front of your Agents."

Gleason scanned the waiting faces. "Like hell I don't. Moore— everyone—stay where you are. You have jobs to do." He turned back to Fitzsimmons, and Wolf had to admire the man's balls to face down the Director. "Now what's on your mind?"

"What's on my mind is the fact your Agent Drake has apparently disappeared. Chief Amundson went to question her last night and she had left her home. Not quite as exhausted as you claimed, I'm afraid."

Gleason looked like a thundercloud. His glare caught Wolf like a blow. "If you knew half as much as you thought you did, you wouldn't be here acting like fools. We believe Agent Drake was killed last night. Her presence disappeared off our maps. The only way that can happen is if she dies."

"Interesting." Fitzsimmons cocked his head. "Explain that to me."

"You know we track change phenomena through our maps?

Well, we also track our Agents. Each one of the Gifted has a—I suppose you could say a signature—that other trained Gifted can track."

"Why wasn't I told of this before?" A low rumble of anger filled Fitzsimmons' voice. It was one thing Wolf had learned about the man. He wanted to know everything and had a mind like a huge filing cabinet that kept everything categorized, everything readily accessible.

"I didn't think you needed to know."

Wrong thing to say. Wolf barely held back the smile as the explosion mounted. The room had gone deathly still, like the eye of a storm.

His cell phone buzzed too loud.

"Would you get that damned phone?" Fitzsimmons growled.

Wolf scrambled to respond. Did *not* want to be the focus of the Director's wrath, but was sorry to miss the confrontation. He shifted across the room and juggled the phone to his ear. "Amundson."

"Chief, Agent Cornwall here. I knew you'd want to be apprised immediately."

"What's happened? The cop?"

"Exactly. He got a call from a previously unflagged number. It was the Drake woman. The call wasn't long, but it was enough we were able to unblock it and pinpoint the GPS coordinates. The northeast shore of Lake Washington. I've got men standing by."

Wolf glanced back at Gleason. He had the bastard now. Right in the palm of his hand.

"Get them out there. Send me the coordinates and I'll meet them there."

"Sir, there's one more thing. Your Seattle PD source, Detective Blacklock? He's been leaving messages that he needs you to call him."

Shit, he wanted to be there when the Drake woman was caught. He checked his watch. "What's his number?"

He got it and signed off, then punched Blacklock's number in and held his hand up for quiet. This was more important, even if he was making himself a target for Fitzsimmons' wrath.

When the phone clicked he didn't bother to wait for Blacklock to say who it was. "It's me. You called. Make it quick."

"She called."

"I know."

"She asked for a facial recognition scan of Seattle street cameras for a face she's sent us."

"That is a tall order."

"How about for the last three months?"

Amundson laughed. "Better and better. But send the file. I'll see what I can do."

"She seemed to think this was life or death."

"Fine. Send me the face."

"Done."

Amundson signed off and the email pinged on the phone. He checked the face and groaned. Everything was coming apart. No, everything was coming together. He knew where the face would be seen. It had already been picked up numerous times because they'd been tracking it themselves. He'd give Blacklock the info later, but now was the time to step back into Fitzsimmons' good graces and to watch Gleason begin his dramatic fall. Aah, this would be good.

"Director Fitzsimmons, may I interject?" He crossed to the two men now immersed in tense conversation.

"What is it? Why aren't these people out of the room?"

Wolf managed to keep the triumph off his face. "Sir, I think you need to hear this." He leaned into Fitzsimmons' ear. Whispered, and saw the other man's face clear. Yes, this was the way to Fitzsimmons' heart. Leave him the armament to go in for the kill.

When he was finished, Fitzsimmons waved him away, and turned to Gleason. "I believe you said you can track all AGS Agents. Is that correct?"

"I said it." The AGS chief had a rod of steel up his back. Too proud, and Fitzsimmons would see him taken down a notch. Wolf held his breath, waiting for the trap to close.

"Then tell me, Chief Gleason. Why did my men just trace a call that had Vallon Drake very much alive?"

"What the hell are you talking about?" But Gleason's face had gone pale.

"I mean she just telephoned the good Detective Bryson. How do you explain that? How do you explain that your supposedly failsafe means of tracking Agents has failed?"

Fitzsimmons' voice was soft and as intent as a wolf pack surrounding its prey. He stepped closer to Gleason, looked up at the man, his large nose for all the world like a beak that would gut the AGS Chief. "Well?"

Wolf took pleasure in the way Gleason's throat worked. Finally he shook his head and stepped past Fitzsimmons.

"Clark, Chavez, run a check on Drake. See if you can find her anywhere."

The two agents scurried back to their desks. Soon screens flickered to life with maps, and Wolf shifted closer to see: topographic representation of Seattle. The screen seemed to pan across color-coded landscape. Nothing unusual. Nothing to even hint at the power of what these creatures, these 'people' could do.

The woman pushed herself back from her desk. "I'm not finding anything, Sir."

"Try near Lake Washington," Wolf ordered.

The woman glanced at Gleason, who nodded.

"Just do it," Fitzsimmons roared.

"Yes, Sir." She turned back to her computer, hunched over the keys, and the screen swooped away and honed in on the lake's shoreline. She seemed to study—nothing that Wolf could see. Were they making a sham of this whole thing for his and Fitzsimmons' benefit? He turned back to Fitzsimmons.

"Sir, I'd like to suggest that Chief Gleason be relieved of duty. It seems he's held back information and frankly, as long as Gleason is in charge, I don't think we can ever be sure that the AGS is aboveboard."

Wolf caught Gleason's glare, but didn't acknowledge it. Let him be shamed in front of his people. Let him know what it felt like to be brought down to the realm of mortals.

Fitzsimmons' predatory scowl was all Wolf needed to see. He'd fed his boss the required lines, now it was time to see Gleason brought low.

"A fair assessment, wouldn't you say, Gleason? You've kept things from me, and you'll continue to do so. Am I right?"

For such a big man, the nod he gave was incredibly small. "There are things about this operation you can't possibly manage. Hell, ask Amundson. He can't even see the Gifted on the maps. How the hell do you expect to oversee something you can't even tell exists?"

"A challenge to be sure." Fitzsimmons nodded and Wolf held his breath, because he could do this. He'd found ways to deal with recalcitrant Agents before. It would only take Fitzsimmons giving him carte blanche.

The Homeland Security Head glanced at Wolf and smiled so that Wolf's skin crawled.

"I believe I have the solution. Amundson, as my right-hand man, you're the new Chief of the AGS, responsible for bringing it in line with my expectations. Gleason, you're his second in command, responsible for ensuring a smooth transition. Do you both understand?"

Not what Wolf wanted. He barely managed to breathe as he found the fortitude to nod.

§

Landon sat in the debris of his office and tried to steady his breath. Panic was not what he needed right now, even if they were here. Even if they were about eight hours earlier than he'd expected. He had to make a decision.

The illumination from his desk lamp revealed the abomination of his orderly workspace. The table tops filled with cardboard boxes that were stuffed with carefully wrapped glass beakers and tubing. Bare spaces on the walls, empty spots in the bookshelves.

The air still stank from all the precious herbs and decoctions he'd been forced to pour down the sink.

Months of careful work destroyed, just when he'd thought he was on to something. His gut twisted in frustration. Gleason's attitude towards Vallon. Homeland Security, and then Vallon's disappearance.

He couldn't think of much more that could go wrong—except this.

He raised his gaze to the small figures on the computer screen. Fitzsimmons and Amundson in the war room, the state of the room clearly revealing what Gleason had ordered. Agents purging computer files. In Gleason's office, Landon knew a shredder hungrily ate the most confidential of documents.

Another of the beasts idled beside Landon's desk. He looked down at what he held.

Page upon page upon page of genealogical printouts, some of them modern day, but many of them not. Gleason knew he had the modern files; it had been Landon's idea to begin with, ever since the AGS formed and Gleason had tasked him with trying to increase the Gift. After all, you could train a dwarf to dance, but that didn't make them appropriate for the Metropolitan Ballet.

And what they were getting from recruiting were the dwarves. Landon was sure of it. There had to be others out there who had a greater Gift. It fit the bell curve model. He—the others of the AGS—might sit somewhere on the Gifted range of humanity, but there had to be those outliers at the upper end of the curve. They had to exist, so he'd taken two initiatives.

The records of the AGS breeding program weighed heavy in his hands.

He stroked the papers, then fed them to the shredder, the whine and grind hurting his ears. He knew the genealogy of the AGS's Agents so well that he could see them printed on the darkness when he closed his eyes, like the recipe for a golden future. The world could be beautiful, wonders saved, wrongs righted, if only the AGS Agents had more power and the will to use it rightly.

Another glance at the computer screen. Not what the Homeland Security would do, he was sure of it. They'd love the knowledge he had, but with the only source in his head, he could hide it from them. They would never know what he'd done, the careful arrangements he'd made with hand-picked pairs of agents. Most of the time.

The records of his work became crosscut packing material, impossible to restore. He ran his hand over the larger stack of paper still on his knees.

In addition to the breeding program he'd instituted a genealogical program that had started researching the family histories of those with the Gift. He'd hoped to locate common ancestors of his agents, perhaps identify other branches of their family trees to find more Gifted. So far it had borne limited fruit, but he was convinced it would. Vallon Drake's existence convinced him. His special little girl.

He fed the precious sheets of paper into the machine, let them become confetti, because one day he would use this paper as exactly that. He—Gleason, the AGS — would find a way to avoid the depredations of Homeland Security. They would.

But he couldn't be sure.

He glanced again at the computer screen. Amundson was on the phone. The man's whole body seemed to twitch with excitement—he probably didn't realize how easy his broad-boned face was to read.

Landon minimized the screen and brought up his genealogical program and read. He'd already erased all the breeding records he kept on an external drive and smashed the drive with a hammer to ensure the records couldn't be recovered.

That left this program, this file. His hope of exposing a group of more Gifted beings. In the hands of Homeland Security it would create an unprecedented paranoia. He couldn't let that happen, but he couldn't lose what he'd found so far, what still waited to be gleaned from the records.

"Damnation, this shouldn't be happening."

He hit save-as and waited impatiently as the material was copied to a specially built flash drive that had far beyond the normal capacity. When it was done, he placed the cord of the drive around his neck and stuck the smooth metal under his pajama top, just as the door to his office opened.

Gleason, framed by Amundson and Fitzsimmons.

Landon swallowed. Damnation, he should have noticed them leaving the war room. He casually shifted his hand to the delete button on the computer.

"I wouldn't do that."

The harsh clip of Fitzsimmons' voice stopped his finger from the stroke.

"What's going on here?" The big man stepped into the room, his head bobbing as if he searched the scents with that over-large nose of his. "What is this place?"

Gleason tried to intervene, but Fitzsimmons wasn't having any, he pushed past to the tables, touched the packed boxes and unwrapped a single glass beaker. "Well?"

"It doubles as a library and a lab." Landon said, standing and crossing to the Homeland Security head in the hopes he wouldn't see what was on the computer. The small metal pendulum on his chest seemed to burn him. Surely they would see it, demand it.

He rubbed his throat, tried to shift the pajama collar closer to his neck.

"I've been researching a variety of avenues to improve the Gift in our agents."

"Drugs?"

Landon nodded. It was as good a story as any, when his actual research had been a little farther into fringe science.

"Why is everything packed up?"

Landon glanced at Gleason, but there was no help there. "I'd been working on a series of experiments, but the whole thing was contaminated with a mold. I tried sterilizing the equipment, but finally had to give up. I'm going to replace the whole batch and see if it might go better that way."

He held his breath as Fitzsimmons' hooded gaze held his. Finally: "I see. And the shredder is for?"

"Old records. Chief Gleason decided it was time for some Spring cleaning."

Silence, and Landon decided to take the initiative. "Is there anything else? I really do need to get back to this."

He made a motion towards his desk and its single haloed light.

"I have to hand it to you, Snow, you are one smooth bastard." Amundson moved around the room. "There're books removed. You can see the dust around where they stood. They get moldy, too, Snow?"

Landon shook his head and held his place because all he could hope was that Amundson wouldn't know what he was looking at on the computer. Genealogy. Fine and dandy. The file didn't contain any of his observations or notes. Those had all been shredded.

Amundson stopped at the computer, considered the complex display of family histories.

"What is it?" Fitzsimmons asked.

"Looks like genealogical charts or something."

Landon looked at the floor, assumed an expression of guilt and sent what he hoped was a pained expression to Gleason. "I'm sorry boss, I didn't delete it like you asked."

Fitzsimmons' and Amundson's gazes locked on him, so he made a show of sighing and shook his head. "It's a hobby of mine. I get bored; I play around doing family histories. Gleason told me to stop about six months back. I didn't."

He casually retreated to Amundson's side. Landon went to hit the delete button again, but Amundson caught his wrist and smiled like the wolf he was. "Why don't we just leave that? Your ex-boss thought you should come with me on an urgent little venture."

Landon looked back at Gleason. Amundson's hand squeezed his wrist tight enough he thought he felt the bones crack.

Gleason nodded. "I've been demoted, it seems. Amundson here has been placed in charge and now, apparently there's been a development. Vallon Drake's not dead. You're going with him on a recovery mission."

Landon wrestled with his horror at the AGS's fate and the joy he felt for Vallon. He knew it showed. "Recovery mission? I'm no field agent."

"Obvious," Amundson muttered, his distaste for the situation clear.

"She's gone rogue, Landon. She's running. I told these two gentlemen you're the best hope we've got of talking her in without devastating consequences."

Chapter 24-Moving Mountains

The wind sighed in the tall cedars as Xavier led Vallon in a crouch along the path that led from the lakeshore into the woods. The forest earth was springy underfoot, the groundcover low bayberry and scaled coils of new ferns. Overhead a large black bird coasted between the trees and croaked. A raven, no less.

She -reached- seeking Gifted. A low glitter of flame off to her right. -Reached- farther and, "Landon?"

She started to straighten to peer through the new growth of huckleberry leaves. Xavier grabbed her and yanked her down and away.

"But…."

"He is not alone." He waved her to silence and led her away.

Vallon -reached- again and realized he was right. Not just Landon. The dark figures of unGifted moving stealthily ahead of Landon's bright little flame into the brush, and with that recognition came the questions. There was no way Landon Snow would be out here of his own volition. He hated leaving his little world of the AGS and his work.

Which meant something was seriously wrong.

She paused.

"Do you wish to find Fi or no?" Xavier whispered harshly.

A nod. Of course. And the two of them ducked off the trail, and low and fast after the bright glow of Fi's flame leading them northward into the park. But Vallon couldn't shake the feeling something was wrong. The world closed in on her. Everything was ending. Her chest couldn't get enough air.

A shout from behind said they'd been seen, and everything went from bad to worse.

"Vallon!"

Landon's voice almost turned her around.

Xavier's hand caught her as they leapt across a stream. He steadied her, and for a moment she was swept in his power, the unique sense of being together. She clamped down on it, because such things couldn't be trusted. But then, she couldn't trust Landon either. There was no one but herself in this world. And Fi, who she had to help. That was how it had been in school.

She focused on Fi's familiar anise and mint feel, warmth and ice, and led out in pursuit.

Xavier and she had gained ground on Fi. She was running scared and they were running strategically, cutting across ravines and hillsides to catch her. Behind came the others—not Landon. He was left behind.

"What are we going to do?" she puffed.

"Let us see." He suddenly stopped. Turned, and his eyes went black. She felt the flare of power and wondered if he were going to wink out as he had when she first saw him.

Instead the slope below them misted and ran. The land folded. Folded again, toughening the landscape their pursuers had to cross. Then the flow of power winked out leaving behind the acrid stench of ozone and ether.

He staggered a little, but grinned. "Now we outrun them." Sardonic smile.

She nodded and -reached-. The Homeland Security force charged across the first fold of land.

"It won't slow them for long."

"Long enough." He grabbed her arm and herded her uphill.

Fi's flame flared northeast where the land lifted in a steep climb.

"There are many paths. They all lead toward the parking lot or towards the old seminary."

She had already seen. But the AGS must know that, too. When she sent her senses behind, the group of unGifted had split in two, with one group retreating to Landon and back towards the lake.

"They'll try to cut us off."

The mists still hung between the tall trunks of the second or third-growth forest as they charged up the hill. The air smelled of ripe sap and tan bark and the ferns they crushed when they stepped off the trail. Up. Her thighs strained as they took the second steep slope up from the creek that bisected the southern half of the park.

Vallon's breath tore in her lungs. Xavier came behind, his steady footfall like a metronome, his hand there to steady her when she slid on wet loam. They climbed towards the red brick tower of St. Edwards Seminary that rose beyond the yew, hemlock, and Douglas fir that filled the park.

"We're not going to catch her like this. She's got fear on her side," she puffed.

"And an addict's need." Xavier came up beside her as the trail widened and gave onto open land.

"It makes sense. I found…." Ahead the trees parted onto a broad open field, a lone figure sprinting away on the far side. They started to run.

How could she explain the weird things she'd found near Pioneer Square and at the shelter?

"You found rifts in the earth's crust where the power runs close to the surface."

She glanced at him, nodded, but didn't speak. She needed all her breath for the race they were in. Behind, the Homeland Security force topped the hill. They'd be out of the trees soon. Ahead, Fi ducked into the avenue that led toward Juanita Drive, the main road away from the park. If someone picked her up, it would be tougher to find her.

"Vallon Drake, stop. By order of Homeland Security, give yourself up."

She spun around and backed a step. Six men had exited the trees. All of them had guns drawn. They'd been faster than she'd expected.

Xavier grabbed her arm, dragging her back.

"But…"

"We must go if we are to stop this thing."

Hesitating, she turned back to her pursuers once more. A bullet traced past her head.

"Hold your fire," someone yelled. "They want her alive."

She ran, following Xavier in a mad dash across the lawn toward the Seminary. Behind came the pounding of feet. There was no way they could escape on foot, and Landon and the others would be coming by vehicle any moment.

But she wasn't giving up.

They reached the old stone building and ducked around its corner. Beyond lay the gymnasium and a small parking lot reserved for park vehicles. Two vehicles sat there. A green State Park pickup and a low-slung black coupe pointed nose-out to the road.

Xavier grabbed her arm and dragged her to the black car. "Get in."

"How the hell…?"

Voices beyond the seminary said the Homeland Security team was almost here. She got.

Xavier pulled a key form the visor and turned the ignition. The engine revved and they took off in a squeal of tires just as their pursuers rounded the stone building. Vallon turned in her seat. Muzzle fire flashed and the rear window of the vehicle exploded in a shower of glass, but then they were speeding out of the open area, toward Juanita Drive. If they could just get there before Landon and the others. If they could just catch Fi.

Vallon -reached-. Landon and company were still winding their way up through the streets that led down to the lake, but coming on fast. Fi—she was closer.

"Slow down. She's just around the next curve."

"I know."

Vallon turned to him. "How the heck did you arrange for this car? Did you just will it into existence or something?"

A wicked grin. "Perhaps. Or perhaps I simply rented a parking space from the caretaker. I make sure I have backup options, Vallon. It is critical to my work."

"What is your work, again?" Maybe he'd answer this time. "And how the heck do you do what you do without vellum and ink?"

"At this moment?" Another grin. "My work is keeping Vallon Drake safe."

Of course he ignored her technical question and she was going to pursue it when, in a squeal of tires he yanked the car to the curb and leapt out. He dove into the edge of the woods to return with a kicking, scratching, screaming Fi.

Vallon scrambled out after him and grabbed Fi's hands.

"Fi! Fi! Fi, honey." She released one hand to stroke Fi's face and got a fist in the temple to show for it. Landon's vehicle turned onto Juanita Drive and they were just about out of time. "Just bring her."

She ran back to the car, hauled open her door and scrambled into the glass-filled rear seat. "Hand her to me."

Vallon grabbed Fi's hands and Xavier shoved heroically, finally managing to slam the door behind her flailing legs.

Vallon wrapped her arms around her struggling friend as Xavier scrambled inside, and the car shot forward. The back seat became a wind tunnel from the shattered window. It whipped her face with the lashes of Fi's dreadlocked hair.

"Fi. Fi, you have to listen."

Fi head-butted her in the face and Vallon's vision went red. It was a few minutes before she could start again.. "Yes, that photo was your mother. So was the file. The other was my Dad, Fi. Remember my Dad?"

The change of subject seemed to settle Fi slightly. Her struggle lessened. "Where did you get them? How did you know?"

"Know what, Fi?" Vallon released Fi's hands, stroked her hair, and pulled her back so she leaned into Vallon's chest. She wrapped her arms around her shivering friend.

"Know about her." It came out sad and sweet as a small child. And all the pieces fell into place. Fi stolen away from the Academy. Fi returning with warning. Fi linked to the strange lights that drew the gifted. And Rebecca Murdoch's hate of Vallon and her father. She decided to take a chance.

"It's her, isn't it, Fi. It's your mother you were warning me about."

A small sob and a nod.

"I said she shouldn't do it." Another sob. "She doesn't listen anymore."

Fi struggled to turn and sit up on her own and for a moment Vallon thought she was going to go on the attack again, but she only faced Vallon.

"She scares me."

"Where is she, Fi?"

Fi shook her head and brought up a handful of shattered safety glass. She studied it as if it was the most important thing in the world, and Vallon knew she couldn't push. It was up to her to find out what she needed another way.

"You got a phone in this car?"

A nod from Xavier and he reached for the glove box. It opened and he tossed a cell back to her. She keyed in Jason's number.

It picked up on the first ring.

"Vallon?"

"How'd you know?"

"I'm a good guesser. And I've been waiting for your call. I got the results of the facial recognition."

"That was fast."

A pause and then, "If I were paranoid, I'd say almost too fast." Another pause. "Vallon are you okay? I've got really bad feelings about this."

"I'm fine. I'll be fine."

"Where are you?"

"You know I can't tell you that. Someone might be listening."

"Now who's being paranoid?"

"For good reason. Now what have you got for me?"

"Rebecca Murdoch has been caught on camera in the Pioneer Square area near the Smith Tower at least five times in the past three months."

It made sense. Too much sense. "Thanks, Jason. That's what I needed to know."

"Hold on a minute. Where should I meet you?"

"I'm not involving you in this, Jason. You've felt her power. It's too dangerous."

"Like hell."

Vallon clenched the phone to her ear. "Now you listen. Really listen. You've got to watch out for you. Get out while you can."

Stony silence on the phone, was followed by a grunt that she hoped was acquiescence. "Jason?"

"Yeah."

"Thanks." She hung up and slid the phone into her pocket. "Pioneer Square."

Xavier nodded and the black coupe picked up speed and swept onto I-522, heading for the original heart of Seattle. Vallon checked over her shoulder. No sign of pursuit, but when she -reached- she felt them, like a dark swarm with Landon as a glowing heart. They weren't coming after. She thumped back against the seat, Fi against her side in the cramped space and thought about what she knew. Damn it, just what the hell had her father been involved in that had turned Rebecca Murdoch into a serial killer?

"Xavier, you mentioned concern that -," she looked at Fi, and reconsidered her words. "- that you thought her plan is to release the power of the subduction plate here in the Northwest."

"The earth's plates move, Vallon. And here, where the Pacific Plate dives under the continent, there is a problem. The Pacific Plate sticks as if it had Velcro holding it in place."

"I know. The continent's edge buckles and bulges as a result. If the Velcro came unstuck all at once it would cause a massive quake that'd destroy everything. It's happened before—the evidence suggests every five or six hundred years. The many small quakes the area has had could be precursors.

"And Seattle is long due for a quake, even if it's not the great one," She added.

But something didn't fit.

"If large quake occurs, it could cause a chain reaction through all the faults down the coast. The destructive force is horrible to even think on, but all her efforts have been focused on Seattle. If she wanted to cause major damage down the coast, she could have, easily enough. The San Andreas is a fuse waiting to be lit," Xavier said as he guided the car expertly around a curve.

"Those fissures in the soil that allow the web of power to flow close to the surface—those are unique to the Northwest, aren't they?"

Xavier glanced at her in the rearview mirror as the car entered Lake City, headed toward I-5. "It is a unique facet of the Pacific Coast. It exists in California, too. But Washington and Oregon most of all."

She thought about it. "That's why there are so many Gifted here."

It made sense. The geology of the area with its volcanoes and seismic activity. That might draw her kind, and AGS counts of Gifted showed there were more Gifted per capita in the Northwest than in other parts of the country. Certainly she'd known she had to have her house *because of* the cracks in the foundation.

"And that brought the AGS."

Because the Pacific Northwest was a good place to recruit people into the agency. Likely a good place to find people for a breeding program, too. Or else all those people were the result of a breeding program.

She felt sick to her stomach. That was why Agents were encouraged to sleep around in the AIDS era. They were frigging looking for genetic diversity. "A frigging cattle farm."

"Pardon?"

Her gaze met Xavier's. "Nothing. Nothing at all." Her father had just been a stud put to breeding. He never loved her, wanted her. She was just a biological specimen, a potential weapon, just as lasers were weapons.

"Vallon, tell me." His voice held a velvet command, and she didn't do commands.

"Why the hell should I? What I think is my business, just as your business is yours."

"My business does not cause me to look as if I might be sick."

"Tell you what. You tell me why you're in Seattle and I'll tell you what I'm upset about." She pulled Fi in to her side. Fi who was no doubt also a product of the program. Fi who was quite possibly her half sister.

"I've already told you as much as I can."

Vallon could have screamed. He was bossy and dismissive and far too superior. The trouble was, his mystique was also fascinating. She wanted to understand what led to the tenderness she'd felt and seen. And the power.

"Then let me tell you what I think. You're one of them—the ones who know more than the AGS—who look down on us like primitives."

A quirk of brow and he focused on the road. "A paranoid notion. Who would say this?"

"I wouldn't describe Landon Snow as paranoid."

"The albino who was with the men from Homeland Security?"

Vallon sighed and -reached-. Landon was still there, but his path had split off from the black coupe's. They were no longer pursuing.

"He's my friend." If only she truly believed it now. He had to have known about her and her dad. Hell, he probably planned it. She'd talk to him. Force him to tell.

If she had the chance. The fact that Landon was with Homeland Security said the worst had happened. Either Homeland Security had taken over the AGS, or Landon was working with them. She couldn't imagine the latter happening, so that meant the worst had happened to the AGS. She was in this alone.

The car swept down onto I-5 and south towards the grey glass towers that dwarfed the space needle. A stray beam of sunlight lasered off the windows of the tallest tower as the car took the Mercer Street exit.

"I don't think she's planning to cause a quake, even if there have been a lot of them lately."

As if on cue the road lurched, and Xavier had to wrestle the car to keep it on the road. Lurched again, and the car in front of them slammed into a parked car. Vallon grabbed Fi and braced for impact, but Xavier managed to wrench the coupe sideways and around the crash.

Was that how it had been for Janet Hunt? Quakes shook her off the road?

But this road steadied. Xavier accelerated through the traffic toward Elliott Bay and Alaska Way.

"Xavier, I think I know what she is doing. She's been messing with Mount Rainier. What if—what if she were trying to localize her destruction? What if she were trying to localize it here, to take out the AGS? It would be consistent with her psychological and ethics profiles."

Another glance in the rearview as the car sped south following the shore. This time there was an edge to his gaze and closer consideration.

"A volcano would be easier to localize for damage except for the ash cloud and gases. But Mount Rainier is miles from Seattle."

And that was what she was afraid of, for she'd already seen Mount Rainier grow a long tentacle towards the city.

"But what if she's shifting it closer?"

Chapter 25-Compression and Control

The big man rounded on Landon with such a look of hate that he fell back a step, but not before Wolf Amundson could grab him by the collar and—lift. Landon was left on tiptoe feeling even more ridiculous and helpless as his feet came half-out of his moccasin slippers and his pajamas rode up to expose his ankles to the wind. Around him the lake breeze soughed in the tall cedars and spruce edging the parking area.

"What did you do?" Amundson growled, his breath as hot and as coffee-stained as his teeth.

"I—I don't know what you mean." Landon steadied his voice and met Amundson's glare. "And I don't appreciate being dragged out into the woods in my house-clothes and made to look like Public Enemy Number One in front of your men."

"How did you warn her?"

"Warn her?" He couldn't hide his shock and Amundson must have seen it for his grip eased, allowing Landon to sink back into his shoes.

"How else did she know we were here?"

Landon pulled loose and shifted his Gore-tex jacket over his shoulders. The big man peered down at him as if he were a child, and it would be a rainy day in hell before he'd let this big oaf ridicule or blame him.

"Perhaps it was the noise your men made? They weren't exactly silent. All those *orders* before entering the woods. And I can still hear your men even now."

Actually he couldn't. After the initial shock that they'd been spotted and his glimpse of Vallon, the six men had pursued Vallon and her companions with a silent ferocity that had been most unnerving. Still, he held Amundson's eye and watched his face color and darken at the clear reference to Amundson's need to take command of the operation.

But perhaps making Amundson an enemy wasn't such a good idea. He swung to look at the scene. The Homeland Security black van and Amundson's car blocked the exit from the small, private parking area. "Of course it could be something more mundane. Pressure plates in the drive. Motion detectors in the trees."

Amundson nodded at the leader of the strike force and two men trotted off to check. Three men suddenly materialized out of the trees.

"Report," Amundson barked before the strike team leader could open his mouth.

"They're headed towards the old Seminary."

"Then we'll cut them off." Amundson swung to the team leader. "Get the men loaded! She's not getting away."

Amundson grabbed Landon's arm and half dragged him to the car. He shoved Landon at the passenger seat and he climbed in the car, arranging his coat, his pajama bottoms, his feet neatly on the floor. Then he glanced at Amundson.

"She'll know you're coming for her. She'll know I'm here, too."

"And that should worry me? My men will catch her before she reaches the seminary."

Landon shifted in his seat, considering what he'd seen. A glimpse of Vallon's blonde hair and pale face. But beside her had been someone who had left him so breathless it had taken everything he had to hide his reaction.

He glanced at Amundson. "Let's hope you do."

The two vehicles careened up the winding roads towards Juanita Drive, Amundson swearing at each curve, each corner where they had to slow.

Landon clutched the door handle and braced himself against the sway. "Accelerate into the corners, damn you. Centripetal force will hold us to the road and we'll make up time that way."

Amundson cast a glare his way. "You want me to catch her, do you?"

What could he say?

"Yes." But if she were caught she couldn't finish her investigation. A small price to pay for the chance to examine the stranger.

They reached Holmes Point Drive and sped up as the road widened and aimed through the last few curves to Juanita. Amundson's cell buzzed. He fumbled for it as he swept the car into a sideways drift onto Juanita and slammed his foot on the floor northward.

"Amundson."

His face clenched in anger, but then relaxed. He glanced at Landon and smiled so wide it made Landon feel like prey even as Amundson eased back on the gas.

"We missed them. They have gotten away."

Landon waited because he knew there was more.

"But we know where they are going. She just talked to her friend the Detective. We monitored the call. They're heading to Pioneer Square, and we're going to beat them there."

He eased the car in to the curb, did a U turn, then dug a police cherry out from under the seat and placed it on the dash. When he flicked it on the car filled with red strobe as he tromped on the gas. The black Town Car swept down the road, the van trailing in its wake.

"You have all our calls monitored."

"Not all, but those in this case, yes."

"Do the police know?"

A low chuckle that was answer enough.

"It's not admissible as evidence, then."

Amundson shrugged. "It is not evidence we want."

And that was true, but Landon figured they weren't quite talking about the same thing.

Because Landon Snow might not be able to cause change. He might not even be able to read landscapes or feel the pulse of the earth's power, but he could read Gifted; and the dark man with Vallon possessed more Gift than he'd ever seen before—except in Vallon herself. But the man's power was compressed and controlled beyond anything AGS Agents were capable of. So this wasn't a savant with wild talents. This was a man with training and control.

Everything he'd theorized about. Everything he'd sought. And by his read of Vallon and the man who must be Xavier de Varga, there was a connection there. It had been there in the flicker of flame that seemed to connect them at the navel.

And that meant there was a chance to get close to him.

And control.

§

Along the water the numerous flags flapped in the brisk breeze off the bay. Container ships sat off shore and a huge, white cruise ship stood docked at the cruise ship center like a white magnet for all the tourist shavings that crowded the sidewalks, excited to be here in Seattle.

Vallon stared out the window. If they only knew the risk they'd placed themselves in, they'd run screaming.

But instead everything looked normal, even though her muscles were so taut with tension she could scream. Restaurants. Tourist gift shops. The elevated 99 viaduct. Then the ferry terminals to Bremerton and Bainbridge Island.

Back from the water's edge the cityscape changed. No longer the glistening modern towers. South of the city center the buildings reduced to red brick and narrower walking streets.

Xavier found a place to park under the raised viaduct. He helped Fi out of the car and leaned a hand in to Vallon. Fi stood, head up, sniffing the salt air and diesel. She turned, faced uphill towards Pioneer Square.

"It's darn tight in here." Vallon accepted Xavier's hand and started to uncramp her legs just as another tremor hit.

The ground heaved. The parking lot pavement groaned and cracked. Car alarms sounded along the line of cars, and Vallon grabbed Xavier's arm as he staggered. But Fi squealed and took off like a bat outta hell.

"Fi, no!"

No use. The woman raced up the sidewalk and threw herself into traffic in disarray from the quake. Vallon took off after her and knew Xavier followed in her wake.

Up the hill, past Western and Post streets, toward Pioneer Square proper. Another earth shudder tossed Vallon against the brick wall next to the Best Western Hotel. Brick crashed down around her. Xavier threw himself against her, shielding her from the worst of it.

She shoved him back, leapt out of the way of more falling brick. People flooded the sidewalk from out of the building. Where was Fi? Vallon stood on tiptoes, craned for her.

"Can you see her?" she asked, aware Xavier's gaze was on her.

"Are you all right?"

She tossed him a cool glance even though her nose, her whole body seemed full of his cedar and incense scent. "I didn't know you cared."

She shoved through the excited tourists and scoured the crowd. "There!"

Wasn't that Fi, plowing into the people filling Yesler Street between First and Second Avenue? She couldn't sure, but had to take the chance. She elbowed her way through the people, Xavier at her back.

The earth lurched. It lurched again so hard people fell to their knees. The excited conversations changed to screams.

"We have to find her. She's our best chance of locating Rebecca."

"If she is the one we want."

She glanced over her shoulder. "Who else could it be?"

"Vallon."

A hand fell on her shoulder and she spun around, but not before she saw the displeasure on Xavier's face.

"Jason. What the hell...."

Another shudder, and the rumble of brick fall filled the air. From Pioneer Square came screams and a roar, and a surge of people slammed Vallon against a wall, Xavier on one side of her, Jason on the other. From where she was, it looked like one of the buildings had come down.

"This is about the least safe place to be in a quake." Jason grabbed her arm.

She jerked back. "Not just a quake." She drove into the surging crowd, using her height and her elbows to gain headway against the wall of people.

"Vallon, are you telling me this is…."

"Change. And you should get the hell away while you can." She kept on up the hill and into Pioneer Square proper.

"Like hell, I will."

She ignored him and pressed on. Xavier caught her hand, and awareness of him over-filled her. She yanked away and yet missed him when she did.

Yesler Street was filled with Gore-tex-clad tourists unsure where to go. Around them the heritage building walls swayed and broke. Once this had been the skid road for logs heading down the hill to mills along Elliott Bay. Then it had been the skid road for Seattle's down-and-outs. Now it was the home to trendy carpet and clothing stores and a Mecca for bookstore lovers.

Where? Where had Fi gone? The warehouse where Vallon had found her before? She started uphill.

Pioneer Square proper was filled with debris from the collapse of the face of the building on the west side of First Avenue. The street was filled with bricks and mortar, crushing parked cars, and a line of traffic that had been in the street. Screams came from people crushed and caught underneath. More debris had crushed the famous glass pergola.

And still the ground lurched and groaned.

The crowd parted around Vallon and she found herself in the open.

Had Fi been caught? Fear clutched at her. She had to know. She plunged toward the wreck of metal and glass.

"Hold it right there, Drake."

The voice stopped her cold. She started to turn.

"Don't move. You, too, Bryson. And you."

Someone stepped up to Jason and yanked his arms behind him. Wolf Amundson stepped around the others to face her, a drawn pistol in his hand. Beside him, unbelievably, came Landon.

"I'm arresting you on suspicion of activities undermining United States security."

"What the hell are you talking about?" Her glare shifted to her mentor. "Landon, what the hell is he talking about, and why are you here?"

Landon only shrugged, his gaze shifting to Xavier; and that made her skin go cold. "Landon? I'm trying to do what you asked me to. All hell's going to break loose if you don't let me—us—go."

The little man looked even more gnomish today, still clad incongruously in pajamas and moccasins and huddled in his jacket against the brisk wind. His body seemed almost to convulse at each lurch underfoot.

"Landon?" Through clenched teeth.

Something must have shaken loose in him, because suddenly he grabbed Amundson's arm. The gun went off into the pavement, but on top of the earth quaking, it sent the crowd nearest them screaming and surging. Landon was lost in it. Amundson went down.

Xavier threw a suddenly free fist at their captors. He grabbed Jason, and suddenly the metal cuffs on Jason's wrists fell free.

Vallon bolted through the crowd, Jason and Xavier at her heels. They went straight up Yesler, but Jason grabbed her arm.

"This way."

He dragged her left to where James Street joined Yesler, towards a storefront.

"Where the hell are you taking us?"

He threw a wicked grin in her direction. "I held out on you. The cameras always caught Rebecca Murdoch near the Seattle Underground."

Xavier surged past her, Jason and Vallon at his heels, but something grabbed her jacket and hauled her back. Amundson. She tried to turn and punch him. His grip on the back of her jacket made it impossible. He grabbed for her arm and she blocked him, then. wrenched free of the jacket and dove after Jason.

Chapter 26-Pillar of Fire

The window of the glass-fronted tourist shop had already exploded into the street. Jason shouldered the door open, Vallon right behind and Xavier bringing up the rear. No staff; they'd already abandoned their posts.

"Here."

Jason bolted past them and around the counter to a set of wooden stairs that led past brick walls covered with photos of Seattle Underground attractions and antique scenes of Seattle before the great fire.

"The underground." Vallon hesitated, not liking the idea of being underground in the midst of the quakes.

"It makes sense, does it not? And it explains how we have not been able to sense her."

Vallon caught his meaning. "The tides. The same tidal water that used to flood Seattle's streets acts as a block, just like your -." She glanced at Jason and let her thought die away. "All right. Down it is."

She took the stairs two at a time as the building shuddered under another tremor. Pictures crashed off the walls. Clouds of dust rose up from the underground walkways that were what remained of what had once been the first floors of the Pioneer area of Seattle.

The ancient heart of Seattle, the city's first amenities had had no end of trouble with toilets and sewage backing up due to tidal flooding.

After the great fire, city fathers had planned to fix the problem, but Pioneer Square businessmen had rebuilt before the problem was solved.

When the city had built up the streets high enough to stop street flooding, it had left the first story of buildings beneath street level. As people tired of climbing ladders to street level, the original first floor of buildings had been abandoned—or had become saloons and card clubs. Eventually the underground street level had been forgotten, and would have been lost except for efforts to preserve the city's heritage.

A string of bare electric bulbs flickered and turned amber in the dust-filled air.

"Wait here." Xavier plunged forward to check out the tunnel ahead.

Another rumble and a loud groan grew above them. The earth wrenched again and the wall along the stairs split. One section slid right, while the other stayed where it was. Brick pulverized and fell. Glass shattered off paintings.

The sound increased as the shaking continued. It grew to a shrieking that had Jason covering his ears.

The structure was coming down. Nothing could sustain the torque the wall was experiencing.

Nothing.

Vallon grabbed Jason's hand, dragged him into the tunnel. She forced him into a run, just as the world exploded.

The blast force threw them forward and sent the tunnel shuddering into blackness as the string of lights went out. Debris pelted Vallon's back, her head, her legs. Wooden panels collapsed on her and the dust filled her lungs.

A pause in the earth's protests and she shoved the panels off.

"Jason?" She coughed. No answer. "Jason?"

"Yeah. I'm here. Sort of. Wherever the hell 'here' is."

She heard him stumbling to his feet. "You all right?"

"Yes. You?" The sound of his voice said he was closer. She reached out and touched a pant leg. A hand caught hers and hauled her to her feet, whether she needed help or not. "Christ, that was close."

Vallon took back her hand and peered through the dust. It sent her coughing again. Every muscle in her body seemed to ache. "Shit.

Amundson got my tools when he got my jacket. Without them we're not going to be getting out that way by my doing anytime soon."

She turned back the way they were going, waiting for her eyes to accustom to any light that might still be in the tunnels.

"The good news is Amundson can't get us. So I guess we go on."

She headed down the tunnel, picking her way over and around fallen timbers as the earth rolled and moaned around her. More dust filled the air and coated her skin, her tongue, with the taste of old clay.

"Xavier?"

"Here."

His welcome voice was closer than she'd expected.

"Vallon, you are well?"

"God, would everyone just quit worrying about me and take care of themselves? I may not have testicles, but I'm quite capable of taking care of myself."

A snort; she couldn't quite tell who it came from.

"The way back is blocked so I sure hope you've found the way forward." She turned in the direction she thought Xavier had gone, fighting to stay upright against the wrenching motion of the earth.

"I believe I have. Surprising in its simplicity, really. Link hands so we stay together."

Vallon hesitated, not liking it, but disliked the thought of being lost in the darkness more.

Xavier's warm hand covered hers. Jason's solid grip caught her other palm, so she suddenly felt as confined as a child.

Xavier led them farther into the darkness. With the dust particles in the air it felt as if they were walking through heavy velvet. Sound seemed to die almost before it began. A layer of grit lay on her skin, and the darkness seeped into her pores. The continued tremors through the soles of her feet only left her cut loose from all vantage points. The closest thing to triangulating her position was the contact of Jason's and Xavier's hands.

She -reached- to steady herself, but the feel of water almost doubled her over. Only Xavier's squeeze of her hand and a slight flow of power, stopped her from staggering.

She almost pulled loose, but not before she realized he was somehow using the Gift to guide them.

"How can you stand it?"

She felt the shrug through his hand. "It must be done. And here we are."

He pressed her hand against the wall and she jerked back in surprise. It wasn't a tunnel wall at all, simply a façade, an illusion.

"How?"

"She uses the Gift to hold the earth upright. Here."

He placed his palm over her hand and ran power through her so she could see how it was done. Nothing as powerful as what he'd used to save her house. A simple golden thread from the soil. It pulsed into the wall, and the earth under her palm fell like water to the ground.

Air moved across her skin and a faint glimmer of light came from down the tunnel they'd exposed. She looked at Xavier and Jason.

"I suppose she knows we're here now."

"She is consumed with other things, I think."

"Let's hope," Jason said, and entered the tunnel. Xavier stopped him.

"You should reconsider, Detective. This is no battle for someone like you."

"And I say I'm not that unlike you. Ask Vallon. I seem to be able to change things, too. Ask Vallon. I managed to change my wife's gravesite. Besides, I'm not leaving Vallon to face this alone."

At this Xavier grinned. "And I would."

"You never know, do you? I do know that *I'm* dependable."

A snort, and Xavier ducked into the new tunnel. It sloped down gradually at first. The glimmer of light proved to be a string of electric lights hung from the ceiling. The grey concrete walls held what looked like government markings.

"I think this is an old cold war bunker. Someone got power to it."

"You're probably right. There's even air circulation. I remember reading somewhere about the old tunnels, but I think everyone just assumes they're the Underground."

Vallon looked up at the ceiling, feeling the weight of Seattle above her. All her secret delving into the earth hadn't prepared her for how it felt to be under the earth herself. At least the shaking didn't seem to have done the same level of damage here, even though the air carried a thin haze.

When the tunnels branched off, Vallon stopped, even though Xavier headed unerringly towards the tunnel that led down.

"Wait. There are people here. Gifted." She motioned to a level tunnel headed away from Xavier's destination. -Reached- and scented Fi's anise and mint.

Xavier looked past her. "You may go there if you choose, but my path lies downward."

"But Fi."

He must have felt her need, for he sighed. "I fear the damage she'll do if we delay. Power builds under the city. Even the water can't disguise it."

Through the nauseating flow of the tidal flats she sensed what Xavier described. Golden rage, too large to measure and destructive beyond belief.

She jerked back, and swayed. "Whoa. That's a punch in the gut. But Fi's that way. I can't leave her."

"She chose to come here."

"And you said it was an addiction. So what? We just abandon her because of it? Do as most cities do to druggies and alcoholics? Is that it?"

"I do not blame the victim, Vallon. But many will die if we do not stop Rebecca Murdoch. You know this."

"But...." She scrubbed at her eyes, unsure what to do; because he was right, dammit. But it was Fi....

"Vallon, listen." Jason caught her shoulders. "He says I'm not going to be much good to you in this. Why don't I get Fi, and you and Xavier go do whatever it is you have to do?"

Vallon thought about it and finally nodded. "Fi's there—maybe a thousand feet farther down the tunnel, but there are others there two. Maybe two dozen people. Get them, too, if you can."

Jason nodded and turned, but Vallon caught his arm and leaned up to kiss his check.

"Thank you. Thank you so much."

He gave her a pained look, a shrug, and he was gone.

"I owe him a lot." She turned back to Xavier as the earth rattled around them. The concrete groaned and a huge crack ran down the center of the ceiling. "Let's get this over with."

Xavier led on as the tremors increased again. The tunnel heaved. The concrete began to hail down on them, leaving bare earthen tunnels.

"How the heck was she planning on getting away if she destroys her way to the surface?"

"I do not think she plans to get away."

That gave her pause. If Rebecca Murdoch didn't care if she lived or died, it was going to make dealing with her that much more difficult.

They rounded a corner and the lit tunnels ended. One moment the concrete was there, light bulbs pulsing with the quakes, and the next the tunnel was rough earth drilling steeply downward. A gust of sulfurous heat blasted up at them.

Xavier paused. "Perhaps you should leave this to me."

"Like hell. She killed Simon and Janet and she tried to kill me."

She pushed past him to lead into the tunnel. The slope, the crumbling soil underneath, made it hard to walk. She balanced by running her palms down the walls, and felt as if she were traversing a snake's gullet.

Rough soil and stone. The weight of the city above and around her now. Heat gusted in her face. Down and down, Xavier close at her back.

They finally came out at a high-ceilinged cavern that was about 50 feet across. Sulfurous heat blasted her back from the entrance. When she started forward, Xavier grabbed the back of her jeans. "Wait," he mouthed.

His pupils dilated as his face reflecting the cavern's ruddy glow. Vallon didn't wait for his verdict. She -reached- and the power almost knocked her off her feet. She staggered back against his chest and his broad hands steadied her, but not before she felt what had been done. She went to speak but his fingers stopped her.

"Please," he whispered, and looked back the way they'd come; pushed her lightly in that direction.

"Vallon Drake and company. Welcome to the end."

The remembered, taunting voice stopped Vallon from leaving even if she had wanted to go. She shoved away from Xavier, stepped into the cavern, and realized it stretched into the distance, north and south to either side. Only a laser could cut the darkness that filled its length, but here a pillar of light subdued the darkness.

"Hello, Rebecca. It's been a long time."

"Long enough for you to find someone else to feed off, I see. Just like your father."

Clad in white, Rebecca Murdoch stood proud and fair fifteen feet away. She still had the regal bearing Vallon remembered. She still had the full mouth, but her eyes had transformed into huge black pupils that had lost all but the faintest ring of blue.

The heated air whipped her golden hair around her face. Beyond her, the pillar of golden light shimmered floor to ceiling at the far side of the cavern. It was a Hollywood scene that left Vallon feeling dim and dark and unable to triangulate on her side of the cavern.

Beyond Rebecca ran a narrow crack in the cavern floor that emitted the ruddy light and the sulfur-and-iron stench. Over it ran a narrow stone bridge. The 'cracks of doom' came to mind from a favorite childhood novel. Or the pits of Moria. But even the ruddy light couldn't lessen the glow of that golden pillar beyond Rebecca.

"I'll take that as a compliment." Vallon stepped further into the cavern.

"Vallon, do not move." Xavier's voice. "She tries to lure you within her reach."

"You think she can't get me here?" She scanned the cavern, -reached- again, and knew. "She's shifted Rainier's whole magma chamber. She's used fissures in the earth's crust to channel the magma. You think she can't get me wherever I am in these tunnels?"

"You should go while you can. I will deal with her."

"So sweet. A man to help poor Vallon. Vallon, dear, I think he cares for you." She swung her gaze to Xavier. "Don't you know she uses men up and throws them away? Her father used me like that—a broodmare for his get."

Vallon shivered. Was that what the notations on the files meant? No way in hell was she Rebecca's daughter.

Rebecca lifted her chin at them. "But then, that's what makes this whole escapade of mine so delicious."

The woman was insane, but that didn't negate the fact that she had power. How she came to have this much power was the question. Vallon's gaze was drawn back to the glowing pillar.

Perhaps....

Vallon -reached- for it, trying to understand: Power. Pulsing power channeled through the earth—warm, welcoming, and tuned to—Rebecca. Licorice, but there was a caste to it of Fi's anise and mint.

She dove deeper into the flood of power that flowed up from the floor, but seemed to cycle in a pattern so beautiful she could not look away.

"Vallon watch out!"

The yank on her arm also wrenched her awareness out of the pillar. She stood swaying as the floor trembled, as a crack appeared directly under where she'd stood.

"So you're determined to kill me."

"Darling, Vallon. I prayed you would come. My greatest fear was that you had actually left the city after my little attack." Rebecca showed her white teeth. "But here you are, ready and waiting. Shall we get this over with?"

"Why are you doing this? What have you got against me? Seattle? The AGS?"

Rebecca's lovely face hardened, and if anything, the last blue disappeared from her gaze. "You think you know what the AGS is? You think you know?"

Her voice rose piercing and echoed in the room. The walls seemed to reverberate with it, sound crashing down the lengths of the cavern and back again until Vallon had to cover her ears.

"Tell me," she said.

"All those years I believed. But your father—he grew discontented and led a number of us away in the belief there were greater things we could do."

Xavier took another step forward and her head turreted towards him. "Stop right there." She panned back to Vallon. "So what were those greater things, you ask?" Conversational. "Weapons."

It came out in a hiss, a spit. Rebecca glared. "'Gild the Lily,' Vallon. That was what they called it. They wanted us to be weapons, and even then I still believed and gave my aid—until something went horribly wrong. An earthquake. A tsunami and entire islands gone."

The woman's face had gone haunted.

"Southeast Asia," Vallon breathed, almost immobilized at the memory of the horror of Christmas 2004.

"My two daughters were vacationing on the Phi Phi Islands when it happened. They were lost. I'll not see something happen again. The AGS is a threat because they breed us. Every Gifted is a threat because they have the potential for power. Seattle draws those with the greatest power. So Seattle must die."

A rumbling vibrated up through Vallon's feet and broke through her shock. The ground shook.

"Vallon, you have to leave."

Rebecca turned and ran lightly across the stone bridge, just as the floor cracked and the bridge collapsed into the heated pit in the floor. There was no way across to where she took up position beside the pillar.

"No way," Vallon said. "This is my battle. You heard her. My father helped cause this." She planted her feet, reached for her vellum and swore.

Cracks lasered across the floor towards them.

"I'll back you up. Amundson got my kit."

Xavier caught her hand. She shivered, then opened herself to him, as his awareness slammed deep into the ground dragging her with him. Down.

Down into the earth, through the heat and thunder of knotted power gathered under the city. Vallon struggled to hold to him, to stop herself from burning up in the heat.

Xavier's presence was a brighter torch in the brilliance, as if he not only used the power, but became a flame of cedar and incense He pulled the power to him, spread brilliant hands wide, and sent forth blinding sheets of power into the darker depths of more-stable earth.

The pulsing knot of power seemed to flicker and dim. The magma cooled as he dispersed the power broadly.

The earth wrenched. Wrenched again, and threw Vallon's awareness deeper. Into the deep places of the shifting plates of the earth.

Never had she been so deep. Never had she been aware of the way the continent folded and warped like stoney cloth as the Pacific Plate dove below. She wanted to scream. Wanted to run, but something stopped her. She -reached-. To where so much energy was pent up in fault upon fault, upon fault, where the two plates had temporarily locked together. All along the Pacific coast. And what Xavier was doing:

"Xavier, no!" she slammed into him and back into her body and collapsed to her knees. Xavier staggered beside her.

"What?" His gaze was unfocussed.

"You're going to unlock the big one. The power—it's going to unlock the faults like a zipper all along the coast. You'll kill everyone."

With a crash the floor of the cavern fell away, leaving a heaving lake of magma. Sulfur burned her lungs and the heat seared her hair, yet across the cavern still stood Rebecca.

"Go, Vallon, help the others and be safe. I'll deal with her directly."

She hesitated.

"Please, Bela Menina."

His black eyes burned as he grabbed her for a kiss, but then the earth shook and the magma bubbled. He looked from her to face across the cavern, and the floor began to crumble towards Rebecca. His doing, no doubt.

Vallon touched her mouth. She didn't know how to do what he did. There was nothing she could do without her pens and vellum. She turned to go. Stopped.

"I'm sorry," she said, because she didn't want to hurt like this.

"Sorry?" For a moment his gaze focused on her.

"I might love you, I think. And most anyone I care about dies."

§

Amundson slammed through the doors of the Seattle Underground, his men at his heels. Where was the woman? Stairs ran down one side of the room, partially clogged with fallen brick. Otherwise the place was empty.

He started down, picking his way into darkness. Another wrench of the earth, and brick hailed down on him. He kept going and the walls groaned. He looked up. The red brick that yawned over the stairs ran like a wave, dust filling the air. Then they caved towards him.

Down or up?

Down was the place of graves.

He leapt up, shoving his men before him, as whole bricks slammed the arms he used to shield his head. He staggered and the shattered doors were—there—through the blinding dust. He slammed through into the street as the world seemed to explode. Bricks pummeled his back, the force tossed him forward and hurled him to the ground next to the woman's abandoned leather jacket.

Dust made it hard to see as he lay there. He'd bet a month's salary Drake was responsible for bringing the building down around him. In the street, people screamed. Someone stepped on his hand. If he didn't move he was going to be trampled.

He struggled up and wiped blood off his face, and checked to make sure all his men had made it. Everyone accounted for, but the entire storefront was gone, and one side wall.

"Where's Vallon?"

He turned to glare at the white gnome who'd appeared beside him, but Landon Snow didn't look like much of an adversary anymore. His white hair stood in wild disarray. Dirt smeared his face and hiss pajama bottoms were covered in filth as if he'd fallen and crawled somewhere. In the process he'd lost one of the ridiculous moccasins he'd affected.

The earth lurched again and Amundson looked back at the building. Another wall crashed down, sending another wave of dust and debris into the street.

"Nowhere she's coming back from."

§

Vallon ran up through the steepest of tunnels, Gild the Lily pulsing in her head. Her blood. She was the product of her father's breeding. Bred as a weapon. Her thoughts kept returning to the thousands who died in the tsunami that took out much of the Thai coastal resorts, not to mention other areas around the Indian Ocean.

Her kind had done that.

Maybe her father had done that.

She staggered out of the steepest tunnels into the concrete bunker and stopped. Her breath tore at her lungs and rang in her ears. She used her hand against the wall for balance and fought to keep from getting sick. Her father had done that.

There must have been a reason. There had to have been. But just thinking about it left her weak and she couldn't afford that. She -reached- for Fi and Jason and the others.

Anise and mint lay ahead and to her left.

The tunnels shuddered around her and she fell, but scrambled up and kept going. Up and to her left. A maze of tunnels, and she no longer knew exactly where she was, but there was no time to attune herself to magnetic north. Besides, the magma, the wrenched folds of the earth, all torqued the earth's magnetic field around her. Up was the only direction.

She came around a curve scenting Fi's mint and licorice and stumbled over a body.

No one she knew. The woman lay clad in office attire a few seasons out of date, and filthy. Her limbs were thin, as if she'd been starved for a long time.

But it wasn't Fi, and a tangle of bodies further up the tunnel drew her gaze. Beyond them, a pillar of light filled the corridor, its brilliance brighter than any she'd seen in flophouse above.

A trap for Gifted, like light to moths, but she needed to understand what it was.

She stepped forward cautiously, picking her way through the fallen crowd. What had happened to them didn't matter.

Only the light mattered. Only understanding it, feeling its warmth, its comfort. She stepped up to it and outstretched her hand.

"Vallon?"

The croak pulled her back before she went too far, but it took a moment before the man pinned to the wall swam into focus. Jason, lay there between two fallen Gifted. One of them was Fi. He looked up at her and his face was pale as the palest milk tea, his lips almost blue.

"Jason, my god. What's happened?"

She went to her knees, hauled Fi off of him, and ignored her protests and groans. Her glassy gaze was locked on the pillar.

"Seems I'm not much of a cop." He gave a weak smile. "One of these idiots stabbed me with a piece of rebar when I dragged him from his bed. Trust a vic to be the one who takes me down. Not even a decent firefight."

Vallon pulled back the blood-drenched left side of his trench to reveal a gaping round tear in his shirt and a ragged red wound in his chest.

"Oh god." She yanked his shirt out of his trousers and ripped a length from the hem. Then she wadded it up and handed it to him. "Press down to stop the bleeding."

"I don't think that's going to do it, sweetheart."

"Save your feeble Bogart impressions for later. Just hold it. I've got to do something about this." She nodded at the scene around them, figuring he probably couldn't see the pillar.

Jason leaned back against the wall, his eyes closed.

"Damdest thing I ever saw. I got them away from their beds—rooms of them, all laid out like flowers or stars. Didn't want to come though. Asshole stabbed me, but Fi gave me a hand. We got 'em going and then we get this far and they just collapse. Fi took me down with her." He coughed, deep and fluid. Probably a good thing he was upright, otherwise he'd have drowned in his own blood.

"Jason, you have to stay awake."

His eyes flickered under the lids. "Mmm awake."

"Jason, you have to stay with me, hear?"

His eyes opened. "I'm here."

"Good. Now I'm going to try something using that so-called power, but—something might happen." She didn't have time to go into the dangers of a pillar he couldn't even see. "If I don't wake in five minutes, do something to bring me back. Okay?"

A slow nod. "This is about that light, isn't it?"

Surprise stopped her from proceeding. "You can see it?"

He closed his eyes again. "Not sure what I see. I'd say a ghost if I didn't know better. Flickering light." He went silent a moment. "Go on with ya. I'm here."

He wasn't exactly a likely candidate for backup, but she didn't have much choice. Vallon hunkered down and cautiously turned her gaze toward the pillar and -reached-.

Warm like a bath.

Welcome, like home should be. Welcome and warm like open arms, and it drew her in from her cold place with her transit on a mountain peak, and she was [Within. One-of. Together.]

She could give up her struggle and triangulate and sink into the shimmering warmth, the sheets of color that produced the golden light.

Vallon flowed out.

Vallon flowed down. Down. Down.

The brilliant earth flow rushed around her, seared into her, ate through her and she was—who was Vallon? Vallon didn't matter anymore.

No! It came out as a roar, and the golden power obliged, lifting her, lifting her up through the dark soil and she was:

Part of a pillar, flowing with the others. Cherry and chocolate. Mowed grass and wet soil. Mint and licorice. Lily and myrrh. A cornucopia of scent.

All flowed up through her-their-our body. Down deep to the ground, the earth, the molten power, then up again.

Brief awareness that her body sagged over a dying man, and then she-they-we were gone again, down. Down to comfort and warmth and no tasks to do.

No! She was Vallon. There was no task *too difficult* to do. She was a fighter, dammit.

With a snarl she pulled partially free, and let the cycling power haul a part of her down again. What made this happen? Where was Rebecca?

She flowed up through the earth, seeking. There.

Power, one with the pillar. Power, drawn from the pillar; all one and the same. Rebecca's hands moved over vellum and the cavern was flame and heat and the magma boiling in a cauldron too deep and wide for anyone to stop it now.

But someone tried.

Through the waterfall of the pillar's colors she -reached- and saw Xavier fight, the ruddy light painted his leather trench crimson. He stood with arms outstretched, and she could imagine his eyes—black as night, his scent of cedar and incense.

Almost at his feet a huge chunk of floor fell into the seething cauldron. It was clear he couldn't hold much longer against whatever Rebecca had become.

Vallon had to do something.

Up through to her body again and down. She clawed her way towards Rebecca; saw Rebecca's pen stab at the map she had drawn of the cavern.

A roar and more floor fell away. Xavier teetered and fell back.

Vallon plunged through the pillar—just as Rebecca drew from its power.

Vallon followed the power and rammed through into rage and hate and fear so great it riveted her in place. Worse than the fears her father had left her with. Worse than the fear of always being alone.

Rebecca's fear of what could—would—come as surely as the night followed day and the morning mists blocked laser instrument readings--if the AGS turned the Gift to weaponry.

Vallon shuddered at the thought and almost let go. Power stripped her back to the pillar. Back up to her body. She clung to the link she'd formed—more terrifying than any bond with a man.

Rebecca/Vallon triangulated on Xavier and Vallon seethed with Fi's mother's hatred. Raged, because this powerful stranger blocked *her* purpose. Feared, as Rebecca feared, because he might defeat her.

[He will defeat you,] Vallon managed to send.

Rebecca staggered, and almost knocked Vallon loose from her tenuous link. The pillar's cycling started to lift her away, cycle her back to her body and away—down into the earth.

No! She grabbed for the rancid hatred, and Rebecca's power wavered. Xavier reformed the footing under his feet. The floor grew towards her, magma cooling. Heat dissipating through the walls. Stone dripped to stalagmites, forming stone pillars across the floor.

Rebecca stabbed her pen at the vellum she held. Pillars cracked. Floor trembled.

Xavier steadied them.

Rebecca -reached- for the power in the golden pillar. Reached for the strength that flooded in from the earth through the comatose Gifted above.

With them acting as unwitting channels to the unending earth's power, there was no way Xavier could defeat her. Vallon had to stop her.

She stabbed through Rebecca's concentration and flooded through the other woman. Change, Vallon willed, just as she would change a landscape. Change!

Rebecca screamed. She clutched at her head and staggered to her knees. The pillar wavered as Vallon tried to control what Rebecca did with her pen.

Fi's mother struck: A bolt of power rammed into Vallon's head. Her body screamed. The pillar wrenched her back. Her last sight was Rebecca—stabbing her pen through the vellum.

Vallon slammed into her body. The pillar's power shuddered like a broken gear, the power cycle broken. The pillar broken.

She fell over and lay shaking on the floor. Afterburn burned through her and so did the terror. It filled her nose with a sour, coppery smell.

She bolted upright. Not her shaking. It was the tunnel. Concrete walls flaked and faded. She scrambled to her knees and heard a groan. At least the pillar was gone.

Jason. Xavier.

She -reached- and the power pulsed. Her connection to the earth almost flickered out, she was that tired. The afterburn throbbed like a migraine. Whatever the pillar did for Rebecca, those it fed on—those that fed Rebecca—were left naked and hollowed out as an old tree.

[Xavier?] She managed to reach through the earth, her body trembling.

There. His bright form flickered at the edges, but still his core burned bright as he worked. Blending, mending. His essence a barrier to the maelstrom around him, as across the cavern Rebecca Murdoch shredded her map.

Fissures formed in the floors and walls. Still Xavier held. Somehow he felt Vallon's presence. A whiff of cedar and incense. [Go. Get free. I'll hold as long as I can.]

[But you can't do it alone.]

[Creation above. Would you do as you are told just this once?]

Then he was gone. His brilliance holding against the insanity Rebecca set loose.

Vallon opened her eyes and vertigo swung the tunnel around her. She managed to find Jason.

His espresso gaze flickered until he closed his eyes. "I was worried there a moment," he sighed.

His words were barely audible above a growing rumble in the earth. Beside him Fi stirred and opened blue, blue eyes.

"Vallon? Where did you come from?"

"We have to get out of here." Vallon staggered up. The fallen Gifted stirred around her. "We have to get out of here," she yelled, and grabbed the man closest to her. "Get the others up and heading up the tunnel. This whole place is going to blow."

He looked at her uncertainly.

"Just do it, dammit."

He did, and she turned back to Jason. With Fi's help they managed to get him up, even though the tunnel's trembling worsened. Xavier's barriers weren't holding. The tunnels provided the perfect channels for the magma to get to the surface. If she and the others, were to have a chance, they had to move fast.

She and Fi half-carried Jason in a staggering run up the tunnels following after the others. The lights flickered and dimmed. Dimmed again, and the floor wrenched and shuddered. The whine of metal torquing grew as the tunnels contorted around her.

"We have to go faster."

"Leave me. Behind."

She snorted. "Like that's going to happen. I need you to clear me."

Jason hung silently in her arms.

"I better do that, huh?"

"Damn straight," She agreed, but his pallor made it hard to believe he was going to make it anywhere.

The other Gifted, unburdened, disappeared up the tunnels.

"Just like old times, huh Vallon."

She glanced across Jason. Fi's gaze held a clarity Vallon hadn't seen in a long while.

"Trouble and Trouble ride again. Are these frigging tunnels ever going to end?"

The tunnel wrenched so hard it threw them down. Wrenched again, and somewhere not far behind them a huge crash and a cloud of dust said the ceiling had come down. The lights went out. Vallon struggled up from covering Jason.

[Vallon! To safety!] A string of love-hate-caring that caught her breath and then it was gone.

She swayed and tried to re-establish contact. [Xavier?]

Nothing.

[Xavier?]

No sign of his bright flame, but a maelstrom of power rose twisting and burning through the tunnels. "We have to move!" She fought to her feet, trying not to cry, and hauled Jason's almost dead weight up. Fi helped as much as she could.

Her chest was so tight it was hard to breathe. She shouldn't feel this. She's trained herself not to feel.

"I don't care," she muttered, careening them through the darkness, choosing the tunnels that seemed to lead most steeply upwards.

But the clean air she followed steadily deadened. Heat chased them upwards. A blast of iron brought a little moan from Fi. The darkened tunnels seemed to go on forever.

A hint of must through the growing heat brought Vallon's head around. "Stop."

"Fi, can you hold him?"

"I'll try."

"I can hold myself up. Just prop me against a wall."

The sound of Jason's voice was a relief. "I didn't know you were still with us."

"I'm what you call, conserving my strength. Let the ladies do the work for a change."

"Nice." Fi's voice, surprisingly dry, but there was no time to rejoice that her friend seemed almost normal.

Vallon followed the scent. Concrete dust showered down. The horrible writhing of the tunnels seemed to have slowed, but the walls vibrated around her with a humming sound she knew wasn't good. Pressure could cause such a vibration. So could something moving through the tunnels.

They had to get out of here—fast.

She ran her hands over the tunnel wall, following the scent. In the darkness her palms found a break in the concrete that gave onto damp earth and stone. When she felt along it, there seemed to be a fissure that led upwards. It might be wide enough for her if it didn't cave in. A slight movement of air suggested cool breezes above. She took a chance and climbed up until she caught a glimpse of dim light above.

The way looked broad enough they could get through.

She scrambled back down to Fi and Jason. The humming sound was so loud it hurt her ears. She helped Jason up and led them to the fissure.

"There's light up above," she yelled. "Fi, you go first and help Jason. Jason, I'm afraid you're going to have to climb. I'll push from the rear."

A blast of heat came from down the tunnel with a sound like a train. A distant red glow brightened moment to moment. They didn't have long now. Any moment the magma would come.

She shoved Jason into the fissure. Fi was already climbing, reaching down to help. Vallon shoved form behind.

He was so weak she almost had to carry him, and her own strength waned. Up and, slow, laborious, up.

"I'm up," Fi yelled. Then she burst into laughter as she reached down for Jason's arms. Vallon helped shove him the last few feet, then scrambled up and understood Fi's reaction.

An old toilet—the kind that had frequently flooded during the days when the underground had still been above ground—lay on its side on a wooden platform that had split in two. They'd climbed up through the privy.

"Figures," was all she had energy to say.

She shoved to her feet and almost fell, but kept hold of the wall and stood. Grey light came through the door to their left.

She went to help Jason up. "We're almost there."

He shook his head. "I'm done. Leave me."

"Like hell." Vallon blew her hair back from her face. "Not after I've carried you this far?"

She grabbed his arm and heaved him up. Afterburn ate through her veins like acid and from the privy came a blast of heat and sulfur that set all three of them coughing. They were almost out of time.

"Just a little farther." Who was she kidding?

Half-dragging Jason, they staggered through the door and found themselves in a corridor, with a ceiling of a long line of glass bricks that let in daylight.

That explained the light, but it didn't explain the fresh breeze that blew in their faces. There had to be a way out.

The earth shuddered and sent them stumbling. They careened around a corner into a stretch of collapsed tunnel.

A pile of debris blocked the tunnel and their path, but above it hung blue sky and the silhouetted form of what could only be Smith tower.

Pioneer Square. And freedom.

Behind came a hiss and the scent of wood burning. The toilet platform most probably. The magma was here. Vallon -reached-.

The magma core was almost to bursting.

Chapter 27-Almost Hero

Stay or go?

Landon staggered as the earth wrenched again and again, but he didn't reach for Amundson to steady him. If anything, Landon hoped a falling building or change would wipe Amundson out, but so far the big man seemed ridiculously blessed. He stood in the shadow of the swaying Smith Tower as if he knew nothing dared touch him.

If they got through this, either Landon was going to have to deal with Amundson—or there was the alternative: leave. There was no way he could work under the man. Certainly no way Landon could continue *his* work while Homeland Security remained in control.

Already Amundson's eyes said he was getting ideas watching Gleason and the other Agents who'd won through to the area. Too much calculation, like a theodolite taking multiple readings to determine a point even though he couldn't see any better than Landon what the Agents accomplished.

Yesler Street was mostly abandoned except for the AGS crew and a fire crew working the saltwater taffy factory that had caught flame. Most of the civilians were gone—down to the waterfront and into the open areas near the Mariner's stadium southward, leaving the air empty of screams and too full of the groan and roar of concrete and brick collapsing under strain. The dust-filled air stank of ozone and burnt sugar—and hopelessness.

Fear came off the AGS Agents in waves. Overwhelming sea change in so many ways. There was no way Gleason and the others were going to hold back what came.

"I might be blind to Change, but I can feel power, and there's more here than this motley crew can contain."

He realized he said it too loudly when both Amundson and Gleason glanced at him.

"We have to try." Gleason said, trying to be the rock he usually was, but today there was actually fear in his eyes.

Landon caught Gleason's arm and pulled him aside. "We were stupid. We shouldn't be here. We should have left when we knew they'd targeted Vallon."

"We didn't know they'd try for her so soon. We were trying to fix things."

Landon couldn't deny it. "We still should have left and set up shop somewhere else. Or sent others to do so. We still should—could. There's enough confusion."

"Like Fitzsimmons would let any agents go."

Landon leaned in closer. "Some of us would make it."

"Too many would die."

"So you'd rather be a servant, a virtual prisoner in your work?"

"I'll be an employee—like 95% of the population. At least this way we'll have a chance to mitigate what happens. You said it yourself: they can't see what we do."

"You're a fool if you think that."

In disgust Landon left to hobble down the hill feeling foolish for his attack on Gleason's attempt to save them. Foolish with his one bare foot, his soft, white sole complaining at the rough ground. The other foot not much better in the beaded moccasin.

A groan and the heap of brick that had been the face of Bill Speidel's Underground Tour wasn't there. He refocused his gaze, straining to see the change. Long enough for a breath of sulfur and ozone, and then the building stood before him. He glanced back at Gleason. His doing.

Landon shoved his hands into his pockets and frowned. Having part of the Gift was an injustice, a twisted taunt of life.

The ground undulated and jerked and the road split at his feet. The Underground building-front swayed and teetered out over the street. Then the upper story slid, brick by brick, before giving way to an avalanche that collapsed into the hole that had enlarged in the street. A miasma of dust and heat and sulfur, he recognized from his transmutation efforts.

If he were going to do the pragmatic thing and get the hell out of town, now would be the time to do it. There was no way Gleason and the others were going to unmake what came from beneath.

But that was Gleason, wasn't it? A devotion to duty that wasn't exactly logical to a man of science, but that evoked that loyalty in others. In him, too, damn it.

Landon looked down at his feet, and for once in his life allowed himself to acknowledge how ridiculous he was. Cotton pajama bottoms in a red plaid. He was hopeless. The whole situation was hopeless, and had been hopeless since the agents started dying, if they'd only known it. It was destined that the whole house of cards would come to this.

Well, since when had he taken the safe path, the logical path? Hell, he was an *alchemist* for god's sake, and just how out of fashion was that?

He glanced uphill. A couple of the Agents had collapsed from their efforts. The afterburn would take them down one by one. But Gleason got them on their feet and encouraged them. For all Vallon's reservations, he was a good man.

He looked back at the hole in the street and sighed, then turned to trudge back to Gleason

Stay and take what came. Go out with a bang. Be an Almost Hero for once in his life.

Not that anyone would remember.

§

"Almost there, Jason. Almost there." Vallon lugged him to the pile of debris. "If you can climb we can get free."

Already Fi had clambered part way up the unsteady pile, and had turned back to help with the almost comatose detective. But the way her hands trembled, the pallor of her face said she was almost done in. Vallon knew how it felt.

"Just go, Fi. I've got him."

"You can't manage him on your own."

"Watch me." She shrugged him further onto her shoulder in a quasi-fireman's carry. "Jason, gotta go."

A hissing sound, and the sulfur stench took her breath away. A dark creeping cloud flowed from the corridor they'd just traversed.

"Acid," she coughed. "Get, Fi."

With the sulfur fumes meeting the wet soil and air, sulfuric acid was the result. It would kill her and Jason if she didn't get him out and away.

She tried to help Jason up the debris pile, but his legs didn't work. Deadweight.

"Dammit, Jason, I'm not leaving you."

She let him slide to the bottom of the pile just as a blast of heat came from the corridor. A red glow filled the gloom back where the corridor turned and sent a long finger towards her. More magma joined it.

"Shit." She grabbed Jason by the shoulders and hauled.

His body up onto the pile. She clambered a few more feet and felt the instability of the pile. The whole thing could come down if she stepped the wrong way. She reached down for Jason and struggled to pull him farther up the pile. What the heck she was going to do when she got him to street level, she didn't know, but she wasn't going to leave him to die here so horribly.

She'd already lost one lover to the lava.

A small choked sob as she clambered farther up, and she almost fell. The sulfuric acid burned when she inhaled. It strangled her and made her bare skin peel.

The red fingers of magma had flowed into the room, and up against the debris pile. Bricks softened and began to dissolve.

"Not like this. Not like this. Jason, wake up."

But he was dead weight in her arms as she continued up. Fi looked down.

"Vallon?"

"Just go. The air's too bad here. Get help if you can."

The magma filled the floor and began to undercut the debris pile. It shifted and began to rattle and roll into the deadly pool. Bricks moved under her as she grabbed Jason and hauled his arm over her shoulder. Up. One step at a time, for all the good it was going to do.

"Help. Help!" Fi's voice came from overhead. She must have made it to safety. That, at least, was good.

But the pile was sinking from street level. If she didn't get there soon, there'd be no way.

A groan and Jason's eyes flicked open.

"Vallon?" His voice was barely audible over the squeal of steam and the brick cracking in heat.

"I'm a little busy at the moment, but if you could possibly move those limbs of yours it might help."

He glanced down the pile of debris. "Fine kettle of fish you got me into."

"I told you to stay home, but oh, no, the big man has to come along." She was panting but couldn't seem to get air.

"Who else was going to protect you?" A cough, and blood spattered both of them.

"Jesus, Jason." The fumes sent her into another paroxysm of coughing. Her throat was raw.

With his feeble help she hauled him up another foot, and then suddenly people were around her. A fireman threw Jason over his shoulder and another half-carried her up out of the pit, and she collapsed on crushed brick and battered pavement.

"Vallon?"

She looked up at Landon's voice and there he was, squinting against the daylight. She nodded because she couldn't breathe. Tears ran from her eyes, but there was no time for that. At least Jason was getting proper first aid.

"I thought you were dead." Typical Landon.

"Not yet," she wheezed. "I need Vellum." It came out as a croak and another coughing fit took her.

"You need a hospital."

She shook her head. "A hospital won't stop that." She lifted her chin at the pit. "Vellum and a pen. Please."

It took everything she had to speak past the blood in her throat. She climbed to her feet. Gleason and the interloper, Amundson, were there, but she'd only trust Landon. She had to save them both because there were damn well questions he had to answer.

When he still didn't act, she staggered across the trembling street and grabbed the tools she needed from Margorita Chavez's exhausted hands. Then she returned to the pit, where magma now filled the room. The last of the debris pile melted into it, so no one else was getting out this way. At the pit's edge Fi still crouched, Landon waited, and the firemen worked over Jason. She knelt down beside Fi and -reached-.

Power. There was no sign of Rebecca or Xavier, either. Earth power alone fed the huge magma chamber that Rebecca had brought under the city. The chamber swelled and strained, and the earth domed from the building pressure. The cause of the quakes and the utter destruction to come.

Already the city had raised about ten feet. If she didn't stop it, there would be another volcanic peak where the Emerald City once stood.

"Tell them to heal the street. I have other things…." Her voice gave out, but Landon listened this time and scurried uphill.

How do you stop a volcano's eruption? Dissipate the power? That was what Xavier tried to do; but Xavier's efforts had threatened the entire west coast.

Vallon plunged deeper than she'd ever thought she could.

Down, past the underground, the volcano's heat having dried the ground. Down past the emergency bunker. Down past the chamber where Xavier was lost, where she'd last seen Rebecca screaming as the pillar disappeared.

Down. Molten magma seared her skin, but she sought something else. Golden channels of power, the web beneath the city that funneled the power to the nexus of the magma core.

There. Veins glittered in the earth, brighter than gold, hotter than blood, scented of frankincense, the power humming in them like an angelic chorus.

Her pen poised above the paper, but what should she draw? The power building under her feet was not something she could simply wipe away. She couldn't just send into the earth, either, or the entire tectonic plate edge could give way.

There was only one other way.

Her pen quill touched and ink sank into the paper as she sank into the soil and her vision doubled. Golden web of power. White vellum as she drew it down, stretching herself along the web. Stretching herself farther than she ever had, down, down to the true veins of the earth.

She sent the dangerous power coursing through them and the earth groaned. Still not enough to stop the danger. Whatever Rebecca had done, now the earth itself fed the building storm. There was no way her simple effort could send enough power away.

But Xavier had thought he could do it. He had been more than a guide to the power.

More than a guide to her, too.

She shut that thought down, because what had he been to her?

Part of the power. That was what she'd seen. Part of the power as she'd been part of the pillar. She shivered, and pulled back until she hung above the Vellum as if she soared above the City.

If she stretched thin as a wraith along the skein of power lines, would that be enough to feed the power away?

The city wrenched again, more violently than before. The Smith Tower swayed, from central Seattle came the sound of shattering glass and the scent of fire. She dropped her pen and it skittered away until Landon caught it. He returned it to her and their hands met. His Gift.

Fi there beside her.

No way could she do what she was considering on her own, but she'd never asked anyone for help before. She met Landon's gaze with a question.

"Do whatever you have to, Vallon, but do it soon. I'll do whatever I can to help you."

He must have seen the desperation in her eyes, or felt it in her grip. Fi scrambled closer.

"I'll help, too."

Vallon kept one had free and Landon held the other. Fi placed a hand on her both of theirs as Vallon -reached- deep once more.

This time two presences rode with her—deeper than she had gone before. She stretched herself out along the veins of power. Stretched herself further with Landon and Fi's gifted power. She stretched so thin she thought she might disappear, but Landon was there, whispering encouragements in her ear.

It wasn't enough.

She sobbed over her vellum. Grief bubbled through the earth. The magma chamber bubbled and grew—larger. Larger. Larger.

It blew in a terrifying wave of power, blasting up through the tunnels, destroying the soil, forcing earth upward, upward toward the sky.

The rumbling was a cacophonic stereo of outer and inner ears and she could not allow this to happen. Could not let her city be destroyed. Or Fi. Or Landon. Or any of the others.

Vallon arrowed through the soil to the heart of the magma. She reached out and gathered the immense power. Drank it in and fed it out to Landon and Fi, let it circle and cool through their veins and return to her where she stretched, stretched further and sent the power out to the world again. And more. And more again.

Like a single, long circular breath of a saxophonist. Like Rebecca Murdoch's pillar.

The explosion faltered. But she could not stop her inhalation of power. She drew more to her, and her fingers flew over the vellum.

The power to reinvent the city. The power to destroy Seattle and more. The power to send the entire west coast into the ocean, and she had to find something she could do with it.

She drew the magma core under a mountain. A familiar mountain: Rainier, with its peak in the clouds and its feet in the mountains. Its heart far underground.

The magma shimmered and glowed as the power found it. As she drew power from its heart, and then bound it through Fi and Landon to herself.

Her flesh burned as the power fed into her. As she grew to immensity, as she grew until she felt the shift of the tectonic plates on her skin. The roughness of mountains like calluses on her heels. The whole of the northwest, the whole of the U.S.- the continent - and—she--it—they were one.

The world stopped as she considered the wonder. So completely united, there was no longer any Vallon to protect or surrender. There was no rejection or acceptance. There was just 'be', the power coursing through her veins as she fed it out through the soil.

[Vallon?] Fi's voice. Yes, Fi was with her here in this strange place of warmth and being.

[Not Vallon. We.]

She used her pen and sketched, and, like a person moving a swollen limb, using all her power she shifted and the world shifted, too. Landon fed her untapped silver power. Fi fed her the long-time love of friends.

Vallon screamed as the magma core's power tore like a foreign body through her-its-their flesh. She fell as the core came to rest at its rightful place.

She lay, double vision looking up at the blue sky above the shattered towers, and at the cedars and spruce swaying on the flanks of the smoking mountain.

Then her consciousness snapped her back to her body and she was small again. So small and alone. Fi and Landon collapsed beside her, such precious friends.

"We did it," she whispered to Landon's smile.

She waited for the pain of the afterburn.

This time it didn't come.

Epilogue-Incense and Cedar

The afterburn never came, and neither did Xavier.

The swaying cedars and the scent of Lake Washington water greeted Vallon as she parked her Subaru beside Landon's practical little white Nissan and climbed out in the parking lot by the wharf that had moored Xavier's houseboat. She swayed with the double vision of the place—as if she both saw it and *was* it—a feeling she still hadn't quite been able to shake even now, two weeks after the quake hit the City. Not that she was sure she wanted to.

Landon waited at the edge of the trees.

"How's the AGS?" she asked.

"As well as can be expected under the new management." He wore an uncharacteristic grey suit, and with his diminutive frame he could have been a child dressed up for a wedding, or the last elf in the world.

She shook her head. "And you?"

"Finding my way. I must say that little episode in the city really threw me for a loop."

Trust Landon to use understatement.

"There's speculation they're going to evict me from the apartment," he said.

"That sucks. You'll have a tough time replacing that kitchen." She crossed to him, gravel crunching under her new Doc Martins, her chest a little tight.

"How's Fi?"

"Doing okay. A little freaked by everything that happened, and she still isn't quite the girl I remember." Vallon shook her head. "It's sad. Fi's going to be dealing with her addiction for the rest of her life. But she seems to be settling in to the house. Thanks again for advocating for it to be changed back."

"The least they could do."

"I doubt it."

"And Jason?"

"He got out of hospital today. He's staying at his partner's for a while. How's Gleason doing?"

"So far, good. Managing to keep Amundson busy changing the visuals but away from the heart of the AGS."

"I appreciate whatever he did to get me my freedom."

"It cost him. He gave up his office."

She couldn't quite bring herself to feel sorry for him, but, "Tell him thanks."

Seattle's underpinnings had mostly been repaired, the Gift's damage undone, though the earthquake damage would take a lot longer to repair. So everyone was alive and well and dealing with the change.

Everyone but Xavier. She turned toward the trees and inhaled the cedar scent, remembering how she had come here with him. And what had happened. She sighed, and then pulled herself away.

"You okay?"Landon looked up at her, a concerned gnome.

"Fine."

"It's okay to still be finding your feet after the hospital, Pigeon. I am."

"I'm fine, Landon. No worse than you, except I won't be running any races in the near future." The sulfuric acid had scarred her lungs. Doctors were still hoping they'd heal.

"You've got that look in your eyes, Pigeon. What are you thinking?"

That made her smile. "Just how different things are. I wasn't sure I wanted to be here last time."

"And you are now?"

She looked away because she hadn't been back since her escape with Xavier, though she'd wanted to. "It's the right thing to do. If anyone can make heads or tails of Xavier's stuff, it's you."

"You're sure?"

She nodded.

"Then let's get this over with."

Regardless of his words, he couldn't hide his excitement from her. After the bond they'd formed to deal with the magma core, she didn't think she'd ever be able to fully break the connection to Landon or Fi. She'd never feel fully alone again, and she hadn't had time to decide if she liked it.

She led him into the trees and down to the water where she and Xavier had left the houseboat tethered, a pang of grief settling next to her heart. It should have been Xavier she was with.

In some ways she'd rather keep this place away from prying eyes, but Homeland Security already knew of it, and the information in the computers she'd seen would be invaluable to Landon's research. By their very existence they answered his questions about the presence of other Gifted.

"Landon, I asked you something before, but you never gave me an answer." She paused for effect. "What do you know about 'Gild the Lily'?"

She heard his step falter, but she didn't turn. In some ways the question was a test, to see if he'd come clean and if she really should trust him, regardless of their bond.

He cleared his throat. "A long time ago, Pigeon, your father and a group of agents, including myself, postulated that it wasn't enough for the AGS to just be a protective arm of government. We hypothesized that there was a place within the AGS for Gifted to assume a—shall we say—a more proactive role."

"As weapons."

More silence and then, "Yes."

"That's the one thing I didn't tell Gleason in debriefing." Well maybe not the *only* thing. "That's why Rebecca did what she did. She said Gifted caused the Indian Ocean tsunami, that killed two of her daughters. She wanted revenge for something the AGS never did." She turned to him. "Unless you know something I don't."

He met her eye to eye and shook his head.

If he were lying he was very, very good. If it were the truth, she suspected they had bigger problems.

"Good. Then I don't have to kill you."

She could see he wasn't sure if she meant it, and she wasn't going to clarify it for him.

A beat and then, "So why do you think she said that?"

"She was crazy, Vallon. Anyone who would try what she did is totally, utterly, crazy."

But the words didn't quite ring true. There was something he wasn't telling her, but when had Landon Snow ever revealed all his secrets? She would have to look into it.

The air smelled of cedar and rain and the new growth of huckleberry growing under the eaves of the trees as she led him down to the shore. She stopped.

The clear water of Lake Washington reflected the clouds and blue sky. It gurgled under the empty dock that pointed towards Briercrest and the afternoon sun. No houseboat.

"What the hell." She stepped down to the dock, her tread echoing through the water and turned back to the shore and Landon. "I don't understand."

He gave her a rueful smile. "Well, either Homeland Security is better at their business than I want to think, or someone else is. I'm betting on the someone else."

They spent fifteen minutes exploring the shore, but there was no sign of anyone who might have moved the houseboat. Landon left her in the parking lot and she folded herself behind the wheel, taking comfort in the old denim and leather she wore, regardless of Homeland Security's dress code.

That the houseboat was gone she should have foreseen, but she hadn't expected the confusing hope and despair it gave her.

She turned the key and spun out of the parking lot, heading for the city and the obsessive last job that would triangulate her map.

Broadway looked different in sunshine. The AGS had worked overtime to heal Seattle's towers, and along Broadway the usual suspects of University and college students and 'artistes' filled the sidewalks, sipping their lattes at outside coffee houses. The mélange of delicatessens, drycleaners, and import shops sent their various odors into the air as Vallon pulled to the curb and climbed out of her car, determined to do what she always did and bring the heritage house back.

But it was there.

Unbelievably, it was there, and she hadn't done it. No parking lot; the blue heritage house stood at 1525 Broadway, its white fence overhung by the willows and cedar hedging that shaded that part of the sidewalk, the entire scene still with the shiny look of new skin. She didn't live here, but this spot would always be where it all began.

The fact it was here at all suggested the garage, Simon's death, and Xavier had all been a dream, but the tightness in her chest belied it.

Vallon stopped at the gate, wondering who at the AGS had done the job for her. Gleason, possibly. She'd come to realize he was an ally.

A whiff of ozone and incense and cedar caught her nose.

Not Gleason.

Not anyone at the AGS.

She scanned the streets, -reached-, but there was no figure in black watching her. But it was definitely incense and cedar of Lebanon and the pain around her heart eased.

Hope could do that. So could wanting someone in your life. Xavier's final gift?

No way.

It was the determination to find him.

About The Author

Karen L. Abrahamson wrote her first poem at age six. Since then she has written and published poetry, short fiction and novels. Her non-fiction has appeared in newspapers and magazines. In her words, "a bad day of writing is still better than the best moments of working for a living".

After a wandering youth that took her across North America countless times, she currently lives in the Metro Vancouver area of Canada with two Bengal cats who inherited James Dean's rebellious attitude. When she isn't writing she makes her living as a consultant for non-profit and government agencies.

To read more of Vallon Drake's adventures in the American Geological Survey turn the page for a sneak preview of Aftershock, Book 2 in the series.

Aftershock

Chapter 1 – The Dragonfly Desk

The dragonfly desk hung in the ozone-scented air of the main American Geological Survey map room, its elongated movable stanchion joining the bulbous desk to the floor like the seat in a carnival Octopus ride. Unlike the Octopus ride there was no carnival atmosphere, no lights, no families, no laughter, only silence that hummed in Vallon Drake's ears. The desk's motor, however, hummed up through the metal seat she sat in directly into her spine as if the damned chair vibrated her bones apart at the cellular level. As if she was falling apart when she had just put herself back together enough to come back to work. She'd thought she'd be coming home to family.

Instead it was like entering an enemy camp.

And that was enough of that kind of thinking. Even if being on the desk was the most thankless, difficult job at American Geological Survey headquarters. The desk only emphasized the empty hollow feeling that seemed to grow like a cancer in her chest. She toggled the controls and the desk swooped low, out over the infernal map pit in the center of the room. Heated metal tinged the air and she pulled her cardigan a little tighter around her neck, because apparently she'd forgotten just how cool it could get up close to the ceiling, with the incessant air con blowing down past the fluorescent lights. It might be August outside, but in here she needed a parka. Or a turtleneck, at least. Damned engineers who'd designed the map hadn't thought about the people who had to work with it. Instead they used the air con to manage the heat buildup of the map that could quickly turn the map room into a sauna.

The map room was an empty cavernous affair, now that the AGS agents' peripheral desks had been relocated into a separate room in the AGS building. The floor around the map pit seemed perilously empty and the high ceiling seemed to echo with the lost voices of AGS agents.

Or their ghosts. With all the deaths there had to be ghosts floating around. Of course, if she was a ghost, hanging around the AGS map room was about the last thing she'd do. Unless she'd decided to come back and terrorize the AGS's new management.

Actually, that might be fun, given they already saw her as a problem child, even after she'd almost died saving their asses during her last little adventure.

The map lay below her, a blue-green-brown marvel of modern technology. Its surface was a fine membrane of cells that had the tensile strength to hold up a person and the delicacy to form whatever landscape the desk might happen to be looking at. It also was sensitive enough to the living landscape that the desk agent could see imminent Change as it simmered beneath the surface. Right now it held a Pacific-Northwest-from-space kind of view that included Washington, Oregon, Idaho and half of British Columbia, too.

She sat back in her chair. Strange. Usually the desk kept its observations south of the 49th parallel. Her fingers flicked to the computer keys to bring the map back to American coordinates, but a flicker on the Canadian part of the map stopped her. Something was happening along the coast line of British Columbia. The map features trembled as they always did when under the influence of significant Change. She stopped. It wasn't really her business, but darn it, Change shouldn't be happening anywhere, and this massive a Change couldn't just be an accident that came out of someone's dreams.

In fact it would take more Gift than most AGS agents possessed. That size of change and maybe it could be....

A low warm flush ran through her body. Xavier? Was it him? Was he here? The records of Xavier de Varga said he had often entered the US from Canada. Could it be the mysterious stranger who had terrified her at first, but who had proved to be her more-than-friend had actually returned? Damn man hadn't shown his face since the Murdoch thing was over and she'd been left hanging the last four months waiting.

Well, I see you, Mister. And I'm coming for you.

She stabbed the coordinates and the map readjusted, the fine membrane shivering in a series of small waves and that stilled into a view of a long Canadian fiord and a harbor—or the harbor it was becoming. She -reached- and her awareness slipped over the intervening landscape and the ozone and ether stink of Change soured her nose. The map landscape shimmered as if the nanites that worked in the map couldn't decide whether to be the trees that still stood there, or the metal tanks and pipelines that flickered into existence along the waterfront. The essence of the trees flowed out of the pine and spruce and became the metal pipes that cut back through trees that wisped away like smoke, and around the town eastward, the landscape reshaped. The Change had a metallic undertaste of copper, not the scent of incense she knew as Xavier.

So it wasn't him.

She almost pulled back, but something about the place was familiar. It had been in the news. The town had to be Kitimat and the pipeline that crawled across the shifting landscape had to be the Northern Gateway project that planned to have oil supertankers ply the western Canadian coastline on their way to China. The Canadian government must have gotten tired of all the protests and have decided to simply place the pipeline and harbor in place. There's been talk of doing something similar in the Midwest with the Keystone XL pipeline, but Gleason had refused, citing the AGS mandate and the secret US legislation to maintain the landscape. But once the Canadian changes were in place long enough, the population would simply accept they had always been there and the change would be fixed. Until then, though, there were going to be some pretty tired Canadian Gifted holding this change in place.

She sat back shaking her head. The Gift wasn't meant to be used like that, otherwise there'd be no solid world to hold onto. The AGS's total mandate was to hold America secure against just such attempts to Change the landscape to one party's advantage. Heck, if terrorists ever got hold of the Gift, they could wreak havoc without an agency like the AGS to intervene.

She touched the computer console to bring the view back to Washington and Oregon. The new map wavered in the eastern sector as if it couldn't quite find its form. Odd.

She -reached- into the map to steady it, but something interfered like waves of different wavelength's meeting.

That made no sense. The map was a closed environment except for its sensory connections to the landscape.

She -reached- further, her hands flying over the computer console. There were no plans for large Gifted activities in Washington that she'd been briefed on. A whiff of ozone and lightning tanged the air and that shouldn't be there either. Something was happening. Her finger hovered above the radio call-button that would send an alert to all field agents.

Which was where she should be, instead of cooped up in this damned desk.

Where was the change? Nothing in Seattle, though small ripples ran through the map like water over ice. Nothing in Yakima or Wannatchee. She touched a button and the map expanded her viewpoint. Not the neck of Idaho, either or Montana, though the ripples in the landscape were worse. They became more intense the farther east she went and the map shimmied dizzyingly below her.

What the hell was going on?

Vallon yanked her gaze back from the map and felt the earth's slight tremor like a deeper shiver up her spine. Whatever it was, it was hellishingly big to be outside Washington and Oregon and still so clearly felt. Change on a large scale and—

The room jerked. Jerked again and then settled into a steady shudder that set Vallon's teeth rattling. Not huge, probably most people wouldn't even feel it, but here on the desk and above the map, the vibrations cut through her concentration.

Quake, and a big one. *Where*?

Her fingers flew over the keyboard as she broadened her search. Yellowstone wasn't coming alive, thank God. The San Andreas hadn't unzipped—the California Station would have been all over that. She

-reached- out through the earth past where the Yellowstone doomsday volcano still slumbered.

[Where?] she sent to the desk agents in LA and New York, the two main stations to Seattle's headquarters. Instant awareness flooded into her, one chalky mint and the other salted like seaweed. Halston and Yamamoto. In both those locations were maps similar to hers, except they lacked the capacity to go farther afield than the continental US.

[There.] Halston and Yamamoto fed her readings and she triangulated through the growing vibrations.

She followed the Station lines toward their point of intersection, seeking, reaching. What was the source? What was happening?

Suddenly, the landscape churned around her. The map became a seething mass of tormented earth, of landscape rising and falling in waves, of earth exploding upwards. Steam and geysers blew up houses and cities. The force threw her back in her chair. An attack. It had to be.

Her hand slammed down on the large red emergency button on the left of the desk and she -reached- for the earth, for the tormented soil, for the houses, the towns, the cities that were wisping away. She would not let it happen. This was American soil and she and the AGS were here to make sure shit like this didn't happen.

She grabbed for the change but it was impossible to grasp. Too large, too powerful and from too many directions at once. *That didn't make sense—*

Hold the cities and towns. Form a barrier. She screamed at the LA and New York desk agents and felt them add their strength to the fight, but something dark rose out of the east. She stopped, trying to comprehend what she saw. A wave of Change. It grew as it neared.

Large, so large her brain could not comprehend it. It made her want to cover her head and run. Instead she reached out for it, would break it apart.

It slammed into her like a tsunami into a sandcastle. Seared cinnamon and burned almond and pomegranate assaulted her nose and suddenly she was drowned in caustic Change. She floundering for purchase, fought for her feet, but the Change lifted her up and tossed her.

She slammed into her body and into the back of the desk's chair. The desk wavered above the map and the air stank of ozone so thick it hurt to breathe as she hauled herself forward and over her console. The entire map vibrated with shock waves. Her head filled with agent voices demanding to know what was going on.

"Shut up. Just shut up. I'm working on it."

No blasted Change was going to stop Vallon Drake from what needed to be done. She -reached- back into the earth and sped eastward again prepared to do battle.

The Coastal Range and the Rockies wisped away one moment and thrust up taller the next. Denver fell and grew larger than it had ever been. She sped across the great plains, now an inland ocean, now not, the stink of ozone so powerful she could barely breathe. There! There another wave crashed outwards toward her and she drew on the earth's rose-scented ley lines to feed into the landcape and hold it against Change. The new wave came on, eating away the landscape, wiping away everything and leaving disaster in its wake. She held where she was as the wave grew. As it devoured everything and seemed to reach to the heavens as it met her. But she was not allowing it to go any further. The western landscape would hold with her. It would. She linked with the ley lines that ran like veins through the earth, but here, in the plains, they ran deep so they pulsed like a lost lover's remembered heartbeat. Much harder to feed her strength from something so difficult to access.

The wave crashed down like a mountain. Power and Change crisped her innards. A churning sea drowned her in overpowering fermented pomegranate, almond and cinnamon. Who? Who would do such a thing? The power ripped her loose from the ley lines. She tumbled across the landscape. The Change seared like acid and then— was gone—disappeared as if it had never been except for a faint whiff of almonds.

Vallon gasped and slumped back into her body, the reek of cinnamon and anise filling a huge burned out place inside her. The map undulated as if some leviathan moved under the surface. But the ripples ceased and the map returned to normal. The room was normal, but so cold she might never be warm again and the stink of ozone and ether so thick her stomach churned. She fought to steady her breath and the hollow, empty feeling.

"What the hell was that, Drake?"

"What's going on?"

"The whole flipping city winked out for a moment."

"Vallon?"

"Vallon?"

"Vallon?"

Voices clamored in her headset.

"Just be quiet a moment. I'm trying to think," she muttered and tried to slow her heart's thunderous racing. What had just happened? So hard to think with the fluorescent light stabbing her eyes and she wanted to stuff her hands in her ears to stop the noise. She yanked the headset off her head and dropped it on the seat beside her, her body throbbing with all the sensitivities that came with afterburn.

"Drake! Drake, get the damned desk down here, right now!"

The deep voice thundered into her poor injured brain. Chief Gleason never did have much sympathy for agents even when they were suffering from afterburn. Correction, Deputy Chief, since the new management stepped in, though it didn't seem to have affected his attitude.

"Drake? Do you hear me?"

She stirred in the desk and managed a nod, though movement sent fierce red bolts of pain right into her brain. She slid her hand across the curved console because she didn't think she could lift it, and touched the down button, then sagged back in her chair and kept her eyes shut against the vertigo that came as the desk swooped across the map and settled against its floor mooring. She didn't move. It felt like her innards might just fall out of her eyes, or what was left of her could just disappear into the chasm of emptiness inside her. Shadows shifted around her--probably agents who had responded to her hitting the emergency button, but she couldn't be sure.

A hand fell on her arm and she almost cried out at the surge of heat and awareness that came from the Gifted touch.

"Damn it all to hell, Drake! Warn a man when you've got afterburn. Gloves! I need gloves here." And then someone had her by the shoulders and half-lifted her out of the desk console and stood her on unsteady feet. "Here. Drink this."

A cold, mint-scented bottle was thrust into her hand. She stood there wavering, trying to understand how this had happened when *she hadn't done anything. She hadn't had a chance.*

"Would you drink the inhibitor before you fall down?" The growl of Gleason's voice cut through her questions. She brought the bottle to her mouth and let the cool, cool liquid pour down her throat. It would help for a short time. Hopefully give her enough time to give her report before she collapsed.

Cool poured into the raging heat in her limbs. It filled her up like water, slowly working towards her head. She staggered back a step as the cold completed washing over her and opened her eyes just a slit.

Wrinkled blue suit, white shirt and striped tie that hung too loose on a bony frame in front of her. Not like the usually neat and tidy Gleason at all. She followed the tie upwards to its neat oxford knot, and then higher past the wrinkled neck to the cadaverous face that peered down at her through intense dark eyes over a roman nose that seemed to inhabit most of his face. His bald head reflected the fluorescent lights and his body radiated the scent of squeaky clean. Of course all that intensity meant she probably wasn't going to be able to find a corner and curl up and either die or sleep.

"Report, Drake."

Oh, yeah. So much for concern for her. That was Gleason.

"Something happened, Sir. Change. Eastward. I had to triangulate using LA and New York." She felt everyone around her still. "That's not the worst of it, Sir. It was huge. Massive."

"We felt it."

Of course they would have. Anyone with the Gift would. She paused to gather her thoughts but the clack of crisp footfalls on the map room's tile floors made her want to curl up with her hands over her head. Her sensitivity to light and sound had never been this bad before. What the heck was wrong with her?

"Gleason. What is going on here? Report."

Her heart sank. Just what she didn't need. It was bad enough having to deal with Gleason, but he at least understood what it meant to be Gifted and the horrible debilitation of afterburn. But this was the new Chief, Amundson, and his oh-so-perfect white-blonde hair and pale eyes and his school-perfect diction. He was the new boy in town and he was all about pissing contests to see who had the biggest one. He also didn't give sweet 'f'-all about the Gift or how it worked, given he didn't have a lick of Gifted blood in his Teutonic body. The sick taste of bile rose up her throat. She turned away, back to the desk to steady herself and keep her head down. Let Gleason deal with him. Just let her go home. Better still, let her find Xavier and deal with the afterburn in the most pleasurable of ways.

"Well?" Amundson demanded.

She felt his gaze on her and how he stiffened when he recognized her. Yup, there was no love lost between her and the new Chief, ever since she'd eluded him during the Murdoch affair.

"It seems our Agent Drake had to deal with an earthquake. As you can tell, it has hit her quite hard.

What the…? No simple earthquake would do this to her. Not to *her.* What was Gleason thinking?

She opened her eyes in time to see Gleason's bony six-foot-four frame step between her and Wolf Amundson and then ease the new AGS Chief away.

Gleason lowered his head down to Amundson's slightly shorter blonde one. "This is her *first* day back to work. If I'd known she was still so weak I would not have allowed her back and I certainly wouldn't have put her on the desk."

"*You* would not have allowed it?"

Gleason seemed to freeze. There was a hole in the murmurs of the agents in the room and then Gleason inhaled and looked at the other man. "I know you wanted all agents back to work, but I am still in charge of administrative matters such as illness leaves."

It was like watching two tectonic plates grind against each other, or the posturing of sumo wrestlers. For a moment Vallon's mind played with placing sumo wrestling attire on the two men. She stifled a giggle—damned inhibitor actually did exactly the opposite and loosened the bonds she placed on her tongue.

"For now," Amundson allowed. "I want a full report on my desk before the day's out." His solid frame almost vibrated with the need to knock down his adversary. His pale blue gaze locked on Vallon and she had to look away from the hate. "Immediately. Before she goes home."

"Of course." Gleason nodded, his bald head looking almost too big for his shoulders. He stood there until Amundson stalked to the lone office that gave onto the map room and closed the door behind him.

The door clicked shut and Vallon's knees gave.

Fantasy, Mystery and Romance
from Twisted Root Publishing

If you enjoyed this book, you might enjoy other titles available from Twisted Root Publishing in your local bookstore or wherever e-books are sold.

www.karenlabrahamson.com